Bereft of Me

Bereft of Me

Emma Tibbett

Tivshe
Publishing

Library of Congress Control Number 2021910548

Paperback ISBN 978-1-954175-06-8

Distributed by Tivshe Publishing
Printed in the United States of America

Cover design by Dark Queen Designs

Visit www.tivshepublishing.com

To my parents

Drafts

To: aluzh@fbi.gov
Subject: Banshee Murderer

Agent Luzhkov,

Things were fine before the reckoning. They always are. Something of a black death crawled its way through the halls at Bridgewood High, contaminating the essences of several people with whom I was close, then some with whom I wasn't. The only questions were who and how. Was I the cold-hearted criminal offing people at Bridgewood? Was it the principal Dr. Oakhurst? Or maybe it was that daytime custodian resurrected from the Stone Age. Or was it you?

As I'm sure you've experienced before, many criminal cases start off eerily simple. A family man with years ahead of him commits murder-suicide. A bunch of bored, neglected teens convene to rob a bank. This time, a high school was purged of its attendees. Nobody deserved to go out the way those fourteen people did during my senior year. *Nobody*. Especially not perfect ice hockey players such as Leo Capodi. He's the most haunting aspect of all this. If there ever existed a man so magnificent he could out-renaissance Leo himself, I'd like to meet him. But not during school hours because simply by being in his presence I'd be forced to fear for his life—on *everyone's* behalf.

My name is Jamie Hessen, and the accounts that follow constitute my official confidential retelling of the incidents at Bridgewood High. I apologize for not contacting you in person, but this would only complicate my healing process. The only reason I am providing my name is that you already know me.

I would like to surrender in this war I've waged against myself by regarding as water under the bridge both the lack of a motive and the fact that I could have been the fifteenth victim, had it not been for my narcolepsy with cataplexy, a condition that has plagued me since childhood.

I have yet to learn the reason behind these homicides—if there is one. Closure may never be found, and if it is, it will never be enough to rid me of this trauma, so I need to do as much as I can to see that justice is served.

Preface

I WAS CLOSING my locker between classes when Leo
tapped my right shoulder, giving me a little jolt. He smiled
apologetically.

He and I only talked every so often—not because he didn't
like me or because we were too busy for each other, but because
I was generally too quiet to look approachable. In a school like
Bridgewood, it isn't very common not to talk to each other,
but I was known as the narcoleptic girl who would pass out at
any sudden movement, and that was a pretty redoubtable title
according to everyone with whom I went to school. Even the
teachers usually left me alone. It was like a God-given "get out
of jail free" card.

Bearing his sweat-stained hockey jersey and rolled skinny
jeans, Leo almost didn't seem real to me. Like a hologram—or
better, an oil portrait from the sixteenth century, automatically
holding it in high esteem. Sashes of shiny brown hair fell over

the high points of his cheekbones as he stood before me, and his body mass absorbed all of the fluorescent hall light, dimming my periphery almost completely. There was a spotlight on him.

He must have said something, but I didn't hear it over the sound of my own heartbeat.

"So ... no? You ain't heard nothin'?" he pressed, drawing his hickory eyebrows together with concern, the crease in his forehead probably meaning that I was of no help to him.

"I'm sorry?"

"I asked if you knew anythin' about Nichole." His voice was viscous, like his tongue had been washed with molasses, and the way he spoke, he sounded like a New Yorker. As he repeated himself, his shoulders bobbed up and down impatiently. I'm sure my own body language indicated that I was confused, so he shook his head in lieu of hearing a dissenting reply from me. "She and Teach've been gone for 'bout a week now, and I know you got history with 'em."

Only one teacher in this school was unanimously referred to as Teach, and that would be Mrs. Tomlin, the hot ex-Rutgers professor who was flying through her fifties. It didn't surprise me one bit that she clung to her Roman Catholic values in a place like Bridgewood, where detention rates were higher than the students themselves. Frankly, the only reason she was so widely cherished was that she had a tight little facelift and a flirtatious nature with the male upperclassmen. Word traveled fast when she'd been transferred from Biology to Physics for teaching creationism. But when she suddenly became truant, seemingly as a result of her transfer, it shocked the student body. Everybody, including my best friend Tommy Hicks and I, just assumed she was too ashamed of her demotion to flaunt her Botox around school property, but soon after, the second domino fell: Leo started to seek me out on a regular basis. Well, the domino fell for me at least, but no one else cowered before this red flag.

The girl in question, Nichole, was Mrs. Tomlin's daughter. Equally blonde, equally plastic, inside and out. And yes, Leo was right, we had quite a history between us. At one time we'd been friends, before what was now known as the infamous Oregon Trail incident when she'd turned my life upside down. She, Tommy's sister Reba, and Leo's cousin Sistine were the Mean Girls of our generation. On Wednesdays, they wore black.

"Sorry, I don't know anything." I shrugged helplessly. Leo just nodded, visibly disappointed, but lingered by my locker for a moment and hung onto his backpack by the one strap that wasn't completely threadbare. He obviously wasn't ready to walk away, so I figured I should talk some more. "Why, what for?" I asked.

It was odd that he asked me of all people, but I quickly gathered that it might have been because Cousin Sistine and her two friends were absent that day, too. Had he asked her instead, she would have lied to him anyway, that psychopath.

"Well, I was supposed to do somethin' with 'em and they're M.I.A. is all," he said, bouncing on his feet. No wonder all his Vans were creased at the toe.

Because I admired him so much, I ignored the suspicious thing he had just said to me and told him I would be late for Calc if I didn't get going. Mrs. Pitt wouldn't appreciate that.

It pained me to walk away from Leo. I mean, I could practically see the rays of heavenly light radiating off of him, blowing his feathered mane back like a stallion with slightly questionable grammar—but I did it anyway for the good of everyone. That's what people like me do: we avoid attention even when we want it. Besides, I kind of *had* to stay in the shadows because if I didn't, my consciousness would officially be considered a flight risk. That's cataplexy for you.

"Yo, Jamie?" he called as soon as I turned my back. I kept

going, thinking I may have imagined it, but then he came to walk beside me. He had his hazel eyes pinned expectantly on mine as if I were supposed to hook our arms and say something in a Transatlantic accent, but I did the normal thing and hummed in response. The beaded chain he had tucked carelessly into his pants pocket caught the light and glinted.

"No one knows we talked, capisce?" He nodded at me, clapping me on the shoulder nearest to him before sauntering off like he were walking on water. Or ice if you want to get technical.

Either way, he was divine to me.

I spent the rest of my day wondering where the hell Nichole and Mrs. Tomlin had run off to and if Leo was secretly involved with their whereabouts.

I must have had a pretty radical sleep attack that day because the whole encounter with Leo dissolved from my memory over time like a dream after waking up. It's *still* vague in my mind. I bet there was some more drooling on my end, and some more uncomfortable stares on his.

Teach

WHEN I WAS six years old, which is about as far back as I can remember, my sidekick was a twiggy girl named Reba—yes, like McEntire. She and I had first met in kindergarten and were inseparable for a couple of years after that. We spent most of our time beating up her twin brother Tommy with pillows, watching PG-13 movies like *Titanic* because that was oh-so scandalous, and practicing drugstore makeup on each other. Those were good times I'll never get back for many reasons.

I loved this girl a lot until I realized she must have been born under Saturn. She had developed such a loaded God complex by the third grade—an enigma, I know—when she learned her namesake was a celebrity, that she abandoned everyone she felt close to and started to consider us her "subjects." Rightly so, we abandoned her right back in a matter of weeks.

Because she was so engrossed in her newfound confidence, Reba went down in infamy two grades later, dragging her only friend Sistine and eventually Nichole along with her. Reba was the epitome of supercilious, which is hard to accomplish as a fifth-grader. You wouldn't believe the kinds of drama that mutated into when she hit puberty—thankfully, not all of it involved me.

Reba's descent into mediocrity, brought about by psycho-social ramifications, gave rise to Tommy. At the time, he was an unpopular, scrawny little wimp with a boring name (sorry, Tommy), but he gave her hell when she tried removing him from her life, too. Tommy's rock-bottom status soon skyrocketed, and he replaced his sister on the rungs of society.

Long story short, Tommy and Reba were at war due to their polar policies, until alas, Reba's sovereignty crashed under Tommy's victorious front. He was never picked on again, especially after Reba realized she was indeed a commoner like everyone else. The result of the Hicks feud is second on the list of miracles I've ever witnessed; there are only two, by the way.

Fast forward to senior year and stop on the day Leo asked me about the missing Tomlins. I remembered Sistine and Reba were missing from school as well, but sadly I wasn't wise enough to mention that to him when it was still relevant. Looking back, I know speaking up would have made a difference in someone's fate, and I deeply regret not doing that.

Seven school days after we spoke, the administration officially began to worry about Teach, and maybe even the Three Musketeers as well. I couldn't tell you who was deemed more important: the students or the teacher, both having unexcused absences because God forbid, we don't tell the school why we're gone. To avoid glorifying the ominous situation, though, the principal went to extreme measures just to pretend there *weren't* federal investigators closing down the school one wing at a time, even though we'd all spotted the black SUVs parading into town. No, we were just having renovations done, Dr. Oakhurst claimed. Then there was the black mold hearsay. Then the weather-related cancellation—in March. Simultaneously, Laurie Tomlin's picture was splattered on Channel 8 News as a missing person's report.

Like we didn't have enough stress just trying to graduate in time. As a cataplectic narcoleptic, I can assure you stress was *not* my cup of tea.

One benevolent Friday afternoon, I said something regrettable to Tommy while we were hanging out: "There are two people in this world I find *heavenly* attractive." Immediately, he started shaking his head and laughing, so I knew I was doomed for a roasting.

Not that we wouldn't have been out mingling together under different circumstances, but this was the third day we didn't have school, so we took advantage of the day off—ten school days after Leo had spoken to me if that clarifies your timeline. Tommy and I were sitting on my front porch because it was nice and crisp outside, not a rain cloud in sight. I had a smile tattooed on my olive-toned face, loving the weather, and Tommy's umber skin looked radiant under the sun despite the contortion of his face after hearing my remark.

"Uh-huh. We just gonna forget your whole K-Pop phase, or what?"

"Thanks for that." I glared. "But in case you were wondering, they're Leo and Anton Capodi. Ugh, if Anton weren't betrothed, God knows what I'd do to him ...."

"Besides jump his fossils?" Tommy snorted. I didn't reply with words right away but nudged him in the arm and bared my teeth at him.

"You say geriatric, I say silver fox." We left it at that.

A moment of sweet silence passed before I asked him, "By the way, what do you think is going on at school?" It had occurred to me that the situation was indeed very abnormal. We'd never had a spontaneous closure before—not since the Coronavirus, but even then, Dr. Oakhurst was very transparent with the student body. Something was different this time around.

Tommy shrugged. "Wouldn't worry about it. The school board is so hypersensitive these days. It's probably, like, drug-related."

By default, I believed Tommy, but only momentarily because then it registered in my mind that a woman was missing and there had been no news of another drug ring, which the media would see before the police. So, my qualms began then and there—even before I bothered to check Reba's, Sistine's, and Nichole's social media accounts for activity.

Tommy must have seen it in my wary eyes and spoke up again, "Yo, you need to relax, J. Lemme buy you some Starbucks or something. All this worrying ain't good for you."

"Since when were you such a gentleman?" I teased.

"Chivalry ain't dead, Your Majesty," he said, scoffing at me immediately afterwards as though I'd underestimated him. "Your meds gettin' to you or something?" He stood up off the steps and held his hand out for me to hoist myself up.

I rolled my eyes. "Lemonade, please."

We got into his Honda and rode off in a radio-filled four-minute drive. I recall feeling a bit tired as I slouched in the passenger seat, so Tommy took me through the drive-thru as opposed to going inside, and I called on Saint Vitus to make my new medication start working better. I wasn't asleep completely, but as I tried rolling the window down, I experienced what is known as automatic behaviors, where I doze off in the middle of doing something. I was out until we arrived back at my house, where Tommy had to carry me out of his car. Unfortunately, narcolepsy strikes more than I'd like to admit, in front of more people than I'd like to admit, after I've taken more pills than I'd like to admit. Tommy understood my struggle as if it were his own.

I dreaded the day I would collapse in front of Leo, but

Tommy seemed convinced that that wouldn't happen because I'd taken a ballet class once. In boy speak, that meant I was agile. You get it.

"Speaking of Leo," I said all of a sudden. Tommy aired me an annoyed look, hooding his eyes the way he does when I've said something ridiculous. I know that look of his all too well.

"We weren't."

"Humor me," I whined, so he threw his head back and groaned in resignation, slurping loudly from his Pink Drink just to get to me. I tend to pull my narcolepsy card on him much too often. "So, he told me not to tell anyone, but whatever: apparently Leo had to 'do something' with Teach and Nichole that no one is supposed to know about, and now they're missing."

"Shit, J," Tommy gawked, "is he involved? Maybe he was arrested for causin' school to close. Think we'll have to go on Monday? God, I hope not. I like havin' snow days in the middle of March." Tommy had a tendency to ramble sometimes—I think it started when Reba's downfall gave him a voice. I found it endearing.

"No, nothing like that," I said. "I can't remember why he asked or why it was important. It just ... felt out of the ordinary."

True, it did feel out of the ordinary, but that was because I was half-convinced he came to me in a sweet dream. I'll say it again: it was weird enough that he chose to tell me of all people, knowing my rich past with the Tomlins. The mutual hatred between those women and me was like St. Elmo's Fire: naturally-occurring and as conspicuous as a beacon in the night.

Later that evening, my mother received an automated message from the principal that said school would be back in business the following week, and that they were sorry for the scare.

Everything would return to normal, Dr. Oakhurst told us. But it definitely wasn't normal when we went back.

I was supposed to have Teach for Physics now. Over the five-day weekend, they'd generated new schedules to accommodate her leave from biology—only she *still* wasn't there. Neither was Nichole, for that matter, so the problem had yet to be solved. Administration had just *given up*. But the main reason I was frustrated was that Physics was my least favorite course, and I couldn't imagine why the rearrangement of classes meant I had to leave my current teacher, Mr. Handy; I just knew Teach would fail me on purpose. (Needless to say, that didn't end up happening.)

I present to you: reasons I hate Bridgewood.

So, for class that day, I was forced to deal with an incompetent substitute and a bunch of rowdy juniors because technically Physics was an eleventh-grade course.

And when I stormed off to English afterwards, hoping I'd find some solace in my favorite teacher, I was struck by even more disappointment. It came to me in the form of a wad of notebook paper, thrown by Tommy from the back of the room, informing me that Ms. Stratford wasn't there that day either. Leo told people later on that she was out for a "personal loss," and I still don't know how he heard that. I resolved to buy her some fine dark sympathy chocolate upon her return, but in the meantime, I was officially upset. Plus, the sub had tampered with the lighting, and it was giving me a bad headache.

"Like I couldn't have used my eyes to figure this one out," I complained to Tommy, thrashing the crumpled paper in his face as soon as I found my stool. Sometimes, he needed a reminder that he was being obnoxious—but so did everyone else, which is why I let it slide with him most of the time. Other people wore me out.

"I wasn't sure if they worked right, else you'd be *allll* over this," Tommy joked, running his hands up and down his front invitingly, then over his cornrows. Ignoring his comment, I sat down, pulled to my seat by the weight of my chest after having had such a rough morning.

Maybe it was said rough morning that caused me to doze off during English that day—something that rarely happens, despite my episodes being sporadic—only to be rudely awoken by a textbook slamming onto the table in front of my face. It felt as though I'd been unconscious for hours (for with narcolepsy, I fall into deep sleep within seconds), so I had difficulty lifting my head at the noise. I resolved to just stay put; I was so dreary.

"Excuse me," said the substitute. I didn't answer, knowing the class would do its thing for me; usually, I'd be more polite, but that day had been exceptionally rash.

"Yo, Ms. Ross?" Tommy said, and silence ensued for a couple of seconds. I could hear Leo and others whispering to their seat partners. Also, some awkward chuckling arose from the group of girls off to my right, including Aleida Brown and Caroline Empfert, and then finally, a deep voice across the room bellowed out the syllables of *narcolepsy* like it was a pregame chant. That must have been Bryan Lukin, the renowned quarterback doofus who somehow made it into the Honors classes. His input—the stuff I paid attention to, anyways—was merely fuel for academic debate, and I was almost positive he'd been trying to piss off the sub from the minute he saw her at Ms. Stratford's desk.

"You have narcolepsy?" the sub asked, softening her voice. Finally, I raised my head from the nest I'd made out of my forearms and used my heavy eyes as an affirmative to her question. Time was crawling.

Just as I began to think the period couldn't become any more interesting, Ms. Ross opened her mouth to speak, but the class telephone started ringing. As she waddled over to it,

Bryan called attention to himself once again by shouting in a guttural voice, "Shit!"

"Sorry, Dr. Oakhurst—that was a student. *Mind your language, young man!*" Ms. Ross said through her bleached teeth.

"Teach was just found dead," he explained, holding up his phone for citation.

Teach was just found dead.

Teach was just found dead.

It never left my memory, the way Bryan's naturally warm skin paled under the LEDs as he lowered his phone. The way Ms. Ross froze in place as she heard the same words being fed through the landline by the principal. The way my jaw slackened, my heart labored, and my eyelids succumbed to gravity, like I was under anesthesia. Goddamn cataplexy.

Teach was just found dead. It had been a gunshot wound.

Ice Hockey

SCHOOL CARRIED ON normally in the days to follow, although it became increasingly hard to walk through the halls without bumping into slouched shoulders and saying "sorry" like it was the new "hello." No one was capable of feeling joy—or anything else, really. I wasn't Mrs. Tomlin's number one supporter, obviously, but every second my mind wasn't on schoolwork, it was overtaken by thoughts of Teach being liquidated at the whim of a finger. Every time I sat down, it was a million times harder to stand back up.

And poor Nichole. Despite everything, my heart sank for her.

Again, she, Reba, and Sistine missed school after the news of Teach's demise spread. Leo was out as well, and Tommy was contemplating taking a mental health day like everyone else. While he did share my opinion of that foul woman, he also kept her in his "spank bank," so of course I couldn't blame him for being rattled up. Murder just doesn't happen around here. It *can't* happen here. It's Banshee.

Friday, he asked, "How you feeling?"

I looked at Tommy and melted. In his eyes lay a deep, russet sorrow, an ember not yet stifled. Yet there he was, asking how *I* felt. Clearly, he was the empathetic half of this ensemble.

Without having verbally answered him, I shook my head a couple of times, blinking away what could have been tears. "You?"

"It's a loss," he dismissed. "It happens." But by the way he looked down after speaking, I could instantly tell he was sheltering himself for me. I imagined he was afraid I'd have a cataplexy attack incurred by his true feelings.

"Mourn, Tommy." I sounded exhausted, probably because I was, but not at all due to him or his selflessness. My telling him to think of himself was like telling an infant to walk; it wasn't possible, not in the moment.

Naturally, it took some time for the rest of the student body to recover from its major misfortune. Nichole and friends showed their faces again, as well as Leo. It seemed like nothing had happened, but the shockwaves were just getting started.

One month after the incident, after media coverage had finally diminished into nothing, I went to one of Leo's hockey games. He didn't play for the school, of course, because we were way too underfunded for any sport besides football, but I liked hockey, so to say. Or maybe I just liked boys in gear who knew how to ice skate. Basically, I just needed to go out, and this was my golden opportunity.

Tommy dropped me off at the rink, but he couldn't stay; I thought it'd be better for me if I were alone anyway. That changed when a surge of anxiety from being housebound for so long started to make me regret my decision. To my luck, a familiar face was sitting in the near-empty risers: Caroline Empfert, one of my former best friends and current acquaintances. She had played a major role in the Oregon Trail incident. I dared myself to go sit beside her, but that fell through; instead, I resolved to plop myself directly in front of her and hope for a conversation to start itself.

Leo played offense, and he made too many moves for me to track without the help of screaming parents. He looked so … in his element, I guess, even though he was either attacking somebody or causing a massive spill his entire time in the rink. Leo was the selling point of the team: no Leo, no Banshee Messiers. I don't recall seeing anyone else score at the game anyway.

Nothing notable happened until the very end. The players congratulated one another and left the rink, and people started either filing out or putting on their own ice skates. Caroline and I were some of the only stragglers remaining, and as soon as she stepped down the risers to get past, she recognized me.

"Hey, Jamie!" She grinned, plucking her knit cap off of her curly mane. She looked svelte even under several layers of clothing.

"Hey!" I exclaimed, extending my arms for a hug as though I hadn't seen her in years. "I didn't realize that was you behind me, or else I would've sat by you." A blatant lie.

"Oh, that's okay." She shrugged, jabbing her thumb in the direction of the floor a few levels below us. "Wanna go say hi to the team with me?" I gave her a puzzled look. "You know, 'cause Pete and I went out last weekend?" I wasn't certain if he was the goalie or one of the forwards because there were two Peters from Bridgewood on the team, and both of them talked exclusively about hockey.

"Oh! O'Quinn or Windward?"

"O'Quinn." Goalie.

Caroline gestured for me to follow her, so I had no choice but to hop down those bleachers and tag behind her. I really didn't have a problem with the idea, but I was afraid I'd feel out of place in the midst of a bunch of six-foot-cherubs plus Caroline. At least I'd get to see Leo in full gear up close.

Upon seeing Caroline and I approach the team room, Peter O'Quinn cheered out in celebration. The rest of the guys were leaning their sticks against the walls or unlacing their skates, Leo included. I sat down on a flimsy wooden bench and pretended not to see him while Caroline and her beau caught up.

"That you, Hessen?" Leo said to me, installing himself down on the bench a few feet away from me. Mission: accomplished. "Didn't know you liked hockey."

"I love it," I hoaxed.

"Oh, yeah?" He slid closer to me as he filled a duffel bag to the brim with various articles from his uniform. "You watch NHL or anythin', J?" *He called me J.*

"Uhh ... I watch you guys," I offered nervously. He shook his head lightheartedly, refocusing on his duffel, and some wet pieces of hair cascaded down his forehead.

"Gotta say, I didn't think you'd be here."

I had to strain to keep my lips from smiling too wide. I bet my heart was the size of a lung after he said that, so I made it a point to say more things up his alley. To listen to that subtle Queens intonation and watch his eyes light up like candles when I got something right. We only chatted for about three minutes before Caroline interrupted and said she and Peter were heading out.

"What, you ain't comin' to my place?" Leo asked Peter on his way to the exit.

The goalie turned around and shrugged. "Next time, bud." Then he was gone.

"God dammit," Leo cursed, and then he made a face like he regretted using the Lord's name in vain. "Well, guess I got an empty slot now. You wanna come hang with us?"

"And do what?" I wondered, narrowing my eyes skeptically.

He leaned in for effect and gestured at the rest of the boys in the room. In a low voice, he explained, "Us guys, we do pissin' contests, drink, and post it all on Snap. It ain't rocket science." Then he winked at me and added, "Nah, it's movie night. *Fantastic Beats* or whatever. It'a be chill."

"You mean *Beasts?*" I said, and he laughed, pointing affirmatively. "Yeah, sounds good." *Ohmygodohmygodohmygod.* Even today, it's got the same first-time effect on me, just thinking about what was happening: me and Leo … and the Banshee Messiers.

"You need a ride? I was *gonna* take Pete with me, but now he's goin' somewhere with Empfert."

"Sure!"

I didn't believe it was happening. It was so dreamy, being in that room permeated with athlete's foot and damaged pucks, perspiring under the brightest, most unflattering fluorescents I'd ever seen. We got into his stuffy muscle car after Leo told the team to meet him at his house ASAP, and upon turning the ignition, his phone buzzed erratically. He had it set on "dark mode," but I could still make out several charcoal-colored paragraphs in the chat room. Looked like Leo was involved in some drama.

"Sorry, it's Nichole. I gotta answer." He sounded disappointed, which I understood. I waited as he typed rapidly in response. "Oh, she's comin' too, by the way."

My face fell. Jaw on my lap. I didn't say anything but stared dead at him instead, knowing something wicked was bound to happen if I still agreed to go to his house. When his thumbs slowed down from typing, he glanced at me and asked if that'd be an issue, though I'm sure he already knew it would. What a dick move.

That was where it all fell apart.

Maybe this moment sparked my idea of the Renaissance Man. You see, in a perfect world, he and Leo would have been one in the same, but this world is not perfect. Far from it. So now he's Leo's alter ego, the one I have rewritten countless times in my mind to cater to my hopeless romantic wallflower needs, whereas the real Leo Capodi was just a boy with a stark face, glossy hair, and a strange affiliation with my three biggest nemeses.

"What?" I eventually whispered, the pain audible in my voice. He hadn't even pulled out of the parking space yet when I lost control: my legs uncrossed themselves, my neck muscles went limp, and my fingers could not finish buckling my seatbelt. I was almost completely weakened, but my affection for Leo—who, I must emphasize, was practically the love of my life—softened the blow a bit, keeping me able to move *some* parts of my body. His face contorted and he waved his hand in front of me.

"I'm not asleep, you ass." It was the last sentence I could say with ease, and then my mouth felt numb. I was gone.

"Fuck's the problem then, huh?" he asked, obviously getting defensive, but for what, I didn't know. I didn't budge; I didn't argue. Couldn't, rather. His temper only made me feel worse. Heavier. Like I was sinking into that fancy leather seat, joining it in all its glory. Soon his face relaxed as he realized what was going on with me. I guess he'd never witnessed it up close like this before. "Jamie?"

If I'd known Morse Code, I would have told him to call Tommy. I expected to be mobile by now, but I wasn't. That's the funny thing about cataplexy—sometimes the attacks last thirty seconds, sometimes thirty minutes.

"Shit," he cursed to himself, freezing up in panic. "You good?" Finally, he called Tommy on the phone, knowing he'd know what to do, but I don't remember their conversation at all. I was more focused on my racing heart, as it was the only part of me I could feel, and the embarrassment that I'd just suffered. Leo's insensitivity to my condition was anathema—the *one* thing I couldn't let slide.

I fell asleep halfway through the drive, though that was un-related to the cataplexy attack from moments prior. When I came to, I was propped up on the porch steps at Tommy's house, with Leo squinting and mumbling into his quartz rosary at a slight distance and Tommy himself supporting my head from behind. They weren't speaking. I noticed Leo had still not showered from his game, so not a lot of time had gone by. Or maybe he felt guilty and was obligated to stay with me while I cat-napped.

I was looking at a fraud. A beautiful human being falsified by his foul temperament.

"Hey," Tommy said softly when I stirred. He'd put on a silky red do-rag since the last time I'd seen him. I sat up as soon as I knew I was capable, stretching my muscles out, but I didn't say anything. I didn't need a second glance to see the tension around me. "Might wanna lay back down, J."

Leo nodded in agreement and tucked his rosary in between clasped palms, hiding his mouth behind his fists.

"I'm fine," I said.

"It ain't about you," Leo insisted. He exchanged a glance with Tommy, then raised his fingers in apology for his curt tone. "It's Stratford."

I genuinely cannot remember any of the events that took place after they told me of her brutal, replicated death.

Peanut Gallery

BELIEVE IT OR not, Tommy caught me crying in the hallway in between Physics and English the week after Ms. Stratford passed away. That doesn't happen very often, and not because I think I'm tough—it's just that I usually collapse every time I'm moved to tears. My emotional numbness kept me mobilized, though, and those tears flowed as loosely as oxygen into my lungs.

Truth is, I had asked Mr. Handy if I could leave Physics early to "use the bathroom," but I really just dumped all my belongings into my locker and sunk into the floor. When the bell rang, people oozed out of their classes, kicking past me while I tried to recompose myself. As soon as I stood up, Tommy bumped into me—I hadn't even seen him coming, despite his flashy choice of shoes.

"Yo, you good?" he asked me. "Why you crying?" (He wasn't used to seeing me like that, all things considered.)

"Don't worry about it," I assured him, wiping my cheeks with the heels of my palms. I regretted it immediately afterwards because they had been pressed into the linoleum floor just seconds before, and I felt disgusting.

"Why ain't you ... you know?" he added, lowering his gaze as though that made the question more sensitive.

"No clue."

"Wanna fix your makeup or somethin'?" I just shook my head—I had stopped wearing makeup after I'd fallen asleep while doing mascara and stabbed myself in the eye with the wand one too many times. Besides, I had a decent complexion and naturally dark lashes, so I wasn't missing out on much.

"It's just that English is next," I explained, hoping that that would be enough, and fortunately it was. He put his arm around my back and didn't say anything else, which I appreciated.

"If it makes you feel any better," he said, "we don't got Ms. Ross as a sub today. There's a new temp."

I laughed. "I guess that's nice."

"Yeah. Let's go."

He released me from his grip and spun me around by my shoulders so I was facing the English wing. I say wing, but only one classroom in the school was designated for English, and it was located between the nurse's office and a chemistry lab, which is why the desk Tommy and I shared was actually a lab station.

Fewer people were in the hall with us now, but to my luck, the three that remained consisted of Reba, Sistine, and Nichole. Seminal.

"Looks like someone's been crying." Nichole giggled when she saw me. Tommy and I both paused, already fed up.

"No, actually I fell eyeball-first into the floor. Shit hurts," I said, though looking back, I don't know why. That walking Barbie just fired me up, and I had no filter around her.

Nichole and her toxic little gaggle snickered at me, causing me to roll my eyes and shift my weight while she went on. "Whatever. I just came to recognize you for your amazing talents in the art of cockblocking, but there's no award for it. Oh— but you can kiss my ass instead if you'd like!" Automatically, I knew what incident she was referring to. She whipped around and bent over, and Sistine slapped her hand down on Nichole's rear end. Tommy made a face at their distastefulness, appearing thankful that his sister didn't participate in the vulgarity.

I sneered. "That's hysterical." It wasn't my fault Leo had missed his own *"Fantastic Beats"* party and Nichole didn't get to bear witness to his hockey team's repartee. Well, maybe it was partly my fault, but I didn't care.

"Thank you, thank you!" Nichole curtsied, facing us once again. Seeing her face made me sick. She wasn't ugly, but I still preferred to look at her backside over her front.

"Seriously, Reebs?" Tommy grimaced as he and his sister exchanged eye contact.

She stepped forward and put her hand on Tommy's forearm, trying to mimic sincerity. "Cry about it, Thomas."

"*Thomas?* C'mon, that's cold."

"It's *your* name."

"Quit it out!" Sistine exploded. "I'm so glad I don't got siblings."

Once upon a time, while God was putting the final touches on the Capodi family tree, he decided he had already created enough heirs to his suppositious throne, and so he added a speck of dirt to the otherwise perfect gene pool. That dirt particle would later be born in the year 2003 as a female named Sistine. Thankfully, Sistine was only cousins with the angel himself, Leo, and did not befoul his image aside from their avuncular relations.

"Yeah, it shows." I huffed. Tommy laughed, and the other girls just rolled their eyes in disgust like we were vermin. "Why don't you just walk away already? No one invited you here."

"'Cause this is public domain, and we won't get in trouble if we're *all* late to the same place."

Nichole had a point there. I slumped my shoulders in defeat and leaned my back against a locker when, out of the corner of my eye, I saw a group of four coming from the other end of the hallway. They were going to be late, too.

"Hey, Tommy," Bryan Lukin's sophomore sister, Jade, called out. Quite infamously, she'd had a big crush on my best friend before someone else piqued her interest.

She was strolling hand-in-hand with Peter Windward, the forward, while Bryan himself and Aleida Brown third-and-fourth-wheeled. Bryan acknowledged us, too, assessing the situation and quickly finding that we *weren't* hanging out for funsies.

"Oh look, the peanut gallery!" Reba exclaimed as they grew nearer. Her beaded braids were practically uncoiling from her hair the longer she looked upon all of these peasants. I could see in her eyes how much she wanted to leave, but since she couldn't under Nichole's jurisdiction, she became especially hostile. I didn't blame her.

Bryan, despite his devil-may-care antics, seemed especially offended by what she'd said and nudged Jade in the arm, telling his three companions to "take a walk" in his abnormally gruff voice. (Seriously, I'm still not sure whether the elderly can hear the octave in which he speaks.)

"Chill out, Pearl Jam," Reba scoffed at him after his brotherly gesture. "The show just started."

I hadn't known him to be so invested in this kind of drama before then. His face lit up with amusement, and honestly, I was excited to see what would happen next. A fight between two honest idiots is just a facet of true entertainment. To my surprise, he rattled off a series of questions that made me reconsider my opinion of him then and forever onward: "Oh, you think this is a show? Is that why we're the peanut gallery?

Are *you* the one getting pelted with tomatoes, then?"

All right, so maybe one idiot and one often-concussed football player.

"Yeah, you needa take your bullshit someplace else, sis," Tommy tacked on, fist-bumping Bryan. It was a weird interaction that, frankly, carved itself behind my eyelids. I never would have looked at those two as friends until then because Tommy was equally as critical of people as I was, if not more.

"Only Reebs and Nicky can call me that," Sistine butted in. Another idiot in the mix really takes the cake.

"I ain't talkin' to you," Tommy snapped at her. "This is none of y'all's business anyway. Move along."

While I genuinely appreciated Tommy and Bryan's efforts against the Bad, the Worse, and the Worst, something was still clawing inside me, begging to be said. To put it simply, word vomit. Heat that inherently rises. I probably seemed more tempestuous and childish than ever when I finally blurted out, "For your information, Nichole, I don't even *like* Leo. Have as much of him as you want."

His name hadn't even come up in the conversation, but we all knew it was about him.

Tommy looked taken aback. Yes, he was there when my opinion of Leo initially went haywire, but I still hadn't told him that I was officially crush-less. Hell, I hadn't even told myself; it really just flew out of me like some kind of Freudian slip. But facing Nichole right then and there, despite the horrible loss she was having to deal with, I knew she was still a sadistic degenerate at heart—her friends, too—and they were much too close to Leo for me to still want anything to do with him. I think even Bryan was a little surprised to hear that from me, despite his impartiality.

I should've known Leo was out of reach from the moment I found out he and Sistine were cousins, and that was all the way back in fourth grade.

"That's *right*, she can have him," Sistine restated, pointing her finger supportively at Nichole. I just rolled my eyes, and Bryan even laughed a little. It was like watching a parrot talk.

"Bro, he ain't yours to sell," Tommy reminded her. Us, rather. He reminded *us*.

Reba spat at him. "Well, ain't you mouthy for a reject."

"How ironic!"

I brought my hands to my face and sighed, regretting having spoken at all; if I had just stayed in Physics like I was supposed to, this whole ordeal could have been avoided. At long last, the late bell rang, so Nichole dragged Sistine and Reba away from the scene; Tommy patted me on the shoulder in farewell and walked with Bryan to English because I still needed to gather my things from my locker. And I would have done that, had I not fallen asleep as soon as everybody was gone.

I was roused by the hand of an older man whose name I'd briefly forgotten. Clearly not a lot of time had passed because the halls were still barren, and Tommy hadn't sent a search team out for me yet. But standing immediately to my right was a cart of cleaning supplies and the concerned-looking man holding a push broom whose fathom was wide like the wings of an albatross.

Mr. Edwards.

"You okay, kid?"

I blinked until I was fully awake as the scent of sweet coffee and a hint of bleach infiltrated my nostrils. The janitor hovering over my face was eccentric-looking yet altogether too familiar, and not just because I saw him every day—his crazy gray hair appeared to be electrically charged in the way it stood up from his head, and his narrow eyes were upside-down smiles welcoming me to the conscious world. What a sight for sore eyes.

"Ya dead weight. I can't pick you up, hon."

"Cataplexy," I uttered out. I don't remember what triggered it that time—maybe an acrid dream from my sleep attack—but

I was recovering rather quickly. Mr. Edwards drew his neck back slightly as he considered what that weird word meant.

"You're Miss Hessen then, aren't cha?" he realized, pointing down at me in what looked like wonder as he tucked the broomstick under his arm. It made me uncomfortable, knowing the staff talked about my condition behind my back. He began to smile as he spoke: "Yeah, us daytime staff members had special training about students like ya. Sit tight while I go fetch the nurse."

"Don't," I said hurriedly, and he recoiled at my tone. The way the word flowed legato from my stiff lips made it sound like I had recently suffered a stroke; in fact, it probably sounded more like "dun." I would have tried sounding more polite had I not panicked, but Mr. Edwards was already facing the direction of the nurse's office, which was incidentally just outside of the hallway.

My lips twitched as I regained full power over them. Finally, I said, "She can't do anything. I just need a minute." Then, I stood up on my own and raised my palm at him to assure him I was fine. "I already took my meds and everything. It just happens."

"How long does it last, ya cata ... cata ..." He rolled his wrist over and over, trying to search for the suffix.

"Plexy," I finished for him. "Less than two minutes on average."

"You know ya stuff." He nodded at me, impressed. "Though it's good thatcha do."

I just smiled and nodded back, unsure of what to say. I was grateful that he'd been there to keep me company while I was paralyzed, but now I needed to get to English. Not that I was afraid of being marked tardy—teachers weren't allowed to ask me why I was late to class, should that be the case.

It was weirdly enlightening, speaking to a custodian for the first time in my life. Especially one so unruly-looking, who, now that I thought about it, was obviously just a grandfather who enjoyed having creamer in his coffee and wanted to get out during the day. Everyone just assumes they're mean old grinches who don't have lives of their own, and that they're the kind of senior citizens who yell "Scram!" to children on their property, or young felons who hate interacting because they're afraid of breaking probation. But they're not. They're humans with families and passion and *com*passion. They only isolate themselves because they aren't respected, and whether this was the reason behind all the janitorial deaths here at Bridgewood, I can't be certain.

Bryan Lukin

BY SOME MAGIC coincidence, Bryan asked me if I wanted to go to a Messiers game with him after school the day Nichole and friends had approached me in the hallway. I had trouble saying yes because one, Leo would obviously be there and two, I had many a reason not to like Bryan, but he looked and sounded quite hopeful, so I folded. I told myself we wouldn't have to show our faces to the team afterwards—that had been a one-time event, and I had only done it because of Caroline. Right? Bryan wasn't close with anyone on the team, was he?

Well, there was his friend Peter Windward ... and Chris Arden, who was a forward, too. Besides these two, Leo, and Peter O'Quinn, all the other teammates came from the school district in the next town over—so basically Bryan was close with everyone on the team that he could be, within reason. Lucky me.

"You need a ride or anything? I can pick you up," Bryan said to me during my walk to Tommy's car in the school parking lot. I didn't like riding the bus because the commotion messed with my nerves. And since everyone knew where everyone else lived, we didn't exchange addresses—just a consequence of living in a town small enough to count as a village.

I nodded at him. "That'd be great. I'm not legally allowed to drive because of my narcolepsy." Many narcoleptics can, but I was not blessed with reactivity to medicine, so I can't; also, I didn't want Bryan to wonder. Admittedly, I was acting a bit fake toward him for a number of reasons: he had that reputation I referenced earlier, and I was nervous that being myself around him would awaken his inner gnat. On top of that, I sensed legions of too-polite I-feel-awkward-but-I'll-deal-with-it conversations coming up in the near future.

"Oh, I didn't know that."

Now, this might come as a shock, but right off the bat, I liked that he didn't make things awkward when I mentioned my driving disability. I take back everything I said two paragraphs ago.

I looked up at him and found that his eyes were trained on the ground. He had at least half a foot on me, but all of a sudden, he seemed gentle up close, and respectful, too. Not a gnat anymore—more like a yellow lab, humankind's favorite dog. Maybe it was all those sports-related concussions that made him so annoying everywhere else. Or maybe he was just putting on a front that he was mature so he could get with me—we'd see about that.

"Hey, why'd you come join that argument in the hall today?" I asked out of the blue. I wasn't sure whether it was to test him or just because I was curious, but either way, I was pleasantly surprised with his response:

"Everybody knows Nichole's a bitch to you," he said, finally looking me in the eye. His were soft and bronze, though I always imagined they'd be blue. I could never tell because I usually kept my distance from him, and from said distance, his curly hair was his most charming attribute. Now, though … I could cry over the right pair of browns.

"Oh, yeah?"

"No doubt. I was there in—what, fifth grade?—when shit hit the fan with her," he affirmed. "Remember? We had that Oregon Trail project together, and she, like, stole your ideas? I mean, isn't that how this whole thing started?"

I balked in between two parking spaces as a sense of surprise washed over me, and I put my hand on his arm to stop him from advancing. He, too, put his hand on my shoulder, seemingly by a protective instinct. His eyes alone asked me if I was okay in a hundred different ways. I thought that was sweet, even edging parental.

"I forgot you knew about that," I said to him, afterwards feeling embarrassed for assuming he cared as much as I thought, but he sort of blushed and smiled at me.

"It's obvious she's jealous of you." He laughed. That comment had gone completely over my head because it was pure nonsense and because I was preoccupied by his sharp change in demeanor. I'd never seen him act this way with his friends. He continued, "Anyone can see it, and I'm not even that bright." He knocked on his temple with one large fist, confirming my concussion theory. I chuckled at his meekness.

"You know," I said as I began walking again, "the kinds of things you say in English … how do you just blurt them out?" I figured this was my opportunity to erase my prejudice against him, and it was too good not to take.

"Makes class more interesting." He shrugged. "You're not in many of my classes, are you? I think you'd hate me if you were."

"I believe you." He nudged me in the arm playfully, and I nudged him right back though Tommy's car came right into view after that. "What time's the game start tonight?"

"Six. Dress warm," he advised, waving me goodbye. My heart was beating fast. The butterflies in my stomach were unlike any butterflies I'd ever felt before—non-Capodian butterflies for once.

When I looked back at the car, Tommy, standing outside the driver's side and leaning through the open window slot, tutted and shook his head at me. He started to climb in, but his eyes remained on mine, unimpressed. As soon as I was within earshot, he complained, "Man, you fall in love *so* easy these days."

Caroline was at the game that night, too, but this time we made eye contact right away and waved to one another. I considered sitting next to her for real this time, but I figured that that might translate as a slap in the face to Bryan. This was a *date*. So, I played it safe and let him pick our seats.

"Did you know Caroline and Peter are going out?" I asked him once we passed her, trying a little too hard to make conversation. He was naturally a talker—we all knew it—but I didn't want him to feel like his efforts were one-sided because that had happened too many times to me in the past, and I didn't have a rich dating history to begin with.

After all, I had newfound hope of Bryan being the one for me. Sometimes, perfect people just don't make the cut.

"What? He was dating my sister a minute ago," he claimed while feigning shock.

"I meant Peter O'Quinn."

"No kidding. Who else is dating who? I'm never in the loop." Another surprise to me.

I sighed in consideration, leaning backwards a little ways even though there was no back to the risers we were sitting on. The only relationships I knew about were ones he knew about, too. "I know Jade had her eye on Tommy for quite some time before she moved on and got with Peter Windward."

"That's right," Bryan confirmed, swiping his tongue across his teeth as he thought about it. "But she told me Tommy rejected her."

"I heard no such thing!" I gasped emphatically, bringing my palm to my mouth. "You know, don't tell him I said this, but Tommy always seems so distracted these days anyway. He doesn't ever tell me who his crushes are."

"That's too bad." Bryan sighed. "No hard feelings about Jade though. She can be a bit of a hopeless romantic, but she's got someone now."

I smiled at him. "I hear that."

I grew hot in the face after uttering such an embarrassing thing. I was afraid it'd been the wrong thing to say because it sounded presumptuous, and his reaction had been to raise his eyebrows at me and turn to face the rink, seeming uncomfortable for a split second. But then he rested one of his catcher's-mitt hands on the bleachers behind us and everything was fine again because I could just tell the next time he shifted, that arm would be cleverly placed around me. And I didn't hate that idea; I just let it happen.

Bryan seemed very into hockey for the remainder of the game, which I never anticipated about him. Rumor had it that he was getting a scholarship to some university in the city for his football skills, but I personally liked hockey more than football, so his sudden regard for the sport was nothing for me to look too far into. I had to remind myself, *It's a sport, Jamie. Guys like sports.* Except when the game was over, my stomach dropped ten feet because Bryan told me he wanted to personally congratulate the team for its win. I couldn't even protest on account of how ridiculous and egocentric I'd sound.

"I just wanna say hey to the guys and then we can get going. Sound good?"

We went into the team room, entering a few feet behind Caroline. She went straight to her sweaty boyfriend, but Bryan shepherded me to the wall where Leo, Chris Arden, and Peter Windward were all chatting and toweling off. I say shepherded because I would have been perfectly content waiting in the hall by myself, but Bryan wasn't having that.

"Yo, Bry!" Leo shouted upon noticing us, his catlike face glowing with perspiration. He waved us over, though his focus was on Bryan for the time being. "You see me knock that bitchboy down?"

"Which one?" Bryan teased, causing a riot amongst the boys. I stayed quiet.

After they settled down, Leo put his hand on my shoulder in greeting and pulled me into him for a quick side-hug. It felt forced after what had happened between us. "Hey, Hessen. Thanks for comin'."

"Thank Bryan, not me," I told him. He gave me a humored look and laughed a little, gesturing from me to my date.

"Is this happenin'?" he scorned. I nudged his armored arm off of me, and that was a clear enough message. I could've sworn I sensed disappointment in his eyes, but that was probably just my old self daydreaming. "Must say, I *am* surprised. Good for you, Bry."

Bryan just flicked his wrist dismissively, saying, "All right, all right. Next subject." The guys proceeded to laugh like they were proud of him. Here we are, Agent, learning new things about the humility of Bryan Lukin every day!

"You guys did really well out there," I contributed, looking at Chris specifically. I had never spoken to him seeing as he was a junior, but I rarely saw him walking with any other juniors in the hall—only with the guys in the very circle we were standing in, and even then, I didn't see much of him. But he seemed to be pretty close with them.

"Thank you so much!" he beamed, extending his hand to high-five me. His voice was high-pitched and airy. Boyish. Kind. It comforted me to know he was a Banshee Messier,

forcing his gentleness into a room full of avid ice hockey players. In lieu of saying "you're welcome," I nodded at him and
smiled; God, he was so admirable.

Bryan's company had actually been overall satisfying for
the duration of the game, and I think I may have exaggerated
Leo's insensitivity in my head because he was pretty decent
himself; it was just one foul incident that had turned him into
the monster I'd placed in Nichole's hands. I felt bad for thinking all these things while on a date with someone else, though.

Incidentally, I saw Caroline and Peter walk out of the room
together, and it reminded me of how uncomfortable I was because I wanted to walk right out with them. Bryan and Leo
standing within a three-foot radius of each other, with me in
between, practically cowering under them because of their
heights … it was overwhelming, and noticeably so. They were
both so likable, but I could tell right then and there that I had
to make a choice, whether they knew that or not. And it would
be fair game because I had good and bad things to say about
both. I just wanted to leave so I didn't feel like I was drowning
in my own pee and indecision anymore.

Having a male best friend and all, you'd think I would be
more boy-savvy.

"I'm getting hungry," I whispered to Bryan, clinging onto
his sinewy arm for effect. Technically, I wasn't supposed to eat
so late but that was the least of my concerns. He peered down
at me with an encouraged ferocity in his eye—it was that inner
puppy again, enticed by the thought of a meal.

"I thought you'd never say that," he admitted lightly, cocking his head toward the exit. Then in a normal volume, he said,
"We gotta bounce. Great game, guys." And then we were off.

After a couple minutes' worth of deciding where to eat,
we finally landed on Subway—I believe the conversation went,
"You can't go wrong with Subway!" and "No, no, you can't"—
which was coincidentally within walking distance of the skating

rink. The sky had gone black since we had last seen it over two hours prior, but it was still warm like a fever outside. We ate our subs at a small round table just outside the restaurant in appreciation of the breezy evening; I even started to sweat in the humidity, but that could have been because I was so over-dressed. Skating rinks are cold as hell.

Pretty soon, the only light left on was the Subway sign and occasionally my phone screen whenever I had a new text from Tommy. The notifications were useless in illuminating our con-versation, but we didn't need much light to enjoy ourselves. Half an hour after we finished eating, Bryan and I were still talking. He was a lot deeper than I (or anyone at Bridgewood, probably) realized.

"So, what's your take on the murders?" he asked me, bal-ancing his metal chair on its hind legs. "I can't tell if I'm scared or … or scared, really." He chuckled at himself while awaiting my answer.

"My take?" I started, exhaling through my teeth. Obviously, it was a difficult subject. "I was just as shocked as everybody else if that's what you mean. But sometimes I think I'm the only one who was upset about Ms. Stratford."

"You're not," he practically hummed, his voice recogniz-ably lower and gravellier after having eaten. He was still leaning backwards, but his eyes were narrow as though something I said had piqued his interest, and a smirk started up on his lips the longer we sat in silence. "I gave that woman so much shit, but I loved her."

I smiled gently. "Is that why you always argued with her?"

"Duh." He chuckled. There was a certain sadness in his smile that truly spoke to me. "She was like my mom."

"Mine too." I sighed. "People showed no respect for her when she was alive. They don't realize it's not too late."

"And you know what's so twisted?" he asked me with an air of passion, sitting forward at last. I took a sip from my soda.

"Dr. Oakhurst is doing jack shit about it. Not even a memorial service."

"I know!" I exclaimed, nodding furiously. "It's not like their deaths are in *any* way acclaimed by us saying one last goodbye. It's not that hard to say a eulogy, at least to the senior class."

"Yeah. It's not right." Bryan shook his head, then relaxed a bit. "Do you ever … think about who's next?"

"I generally try not to."

I looked down at my lap and fiddled my thumbs, afraid that if I spoke any more on the matter, I'd lose control over myself and ruin our night. Bryan picked up on my apprehension, silently offering me his hand to hold. I obliged and couldn't help but smile at him for that small gesture.

Psycho

"YO, HESSEN!"

Leo's voice boomed through the hallway, seemingly bending around people and hitting me directly in the eardrums. Lately, I'd been thinking about him—nothing new—but in a different light this time. He was faulty under pressure, unlike Bryan, for instance, and that was dangerous for me. Dangerous to think about, dangerous to associate with, all around dangerous.

So, maybe I'd pondered who I would choose between the two of them given a scenario in which I had to pick. A part of me still feels bad about it today, but I had my heart set on Bryan. (You could say I'm swayed easily—it's no secret.)

"Leo," I said in greeting, not turning my head or even my eyes when he materialized beside me. *He thinks we're all buddy-buddy now that I've had the pleasure of seizing up in his car.*

Looking back, I can't believe how hostile I acted toward him that day. Let this serve as a disclaimer to you; my excuse for acting so brash is that still being in school after two teachers died was like a bruise to the soul, and also, I was PMSing.

"How you doin'?"

"Fine, Tribbiani. You?"

"Come on now," he said, fanning his arms out pleadingly. "You ain't shook up? Not even a little bit? You were the only one who liked Stratford." *Explains why you're so chipper.*

"Well, I'd really rather not dwell on it," I snapped, "lest I falleth comatose."

"Capisce, compadre." He held his hands up in defense and then stuck them in his pockets as we strolled past Mr. Edwards. Suddenly, he grew serious and started sputtering like a lawn mower: "I, uh ... I-I just hope all's good. Shit's been tough is all."

"Thanks," I mumbled, and he flashed me a tight-lipped grin.

"You comin' to my game tonight, J?"

"I went to the last one."

"Pretty please? Maybe Lukin'll escort you."

"I gotta go to English."

Just saying it hurt my heart; it felt like a boa constrictor was scaling my throat. I stopped walking, still staring forward, but my vision blurred as my eyes unfocused; I was probably on the brink of a cataplexy attack, but I took a calming breath to ground my feelings. Leo paused a foot or two ahead of me when he realized I'd fallen behind and gestured for me to join him against the wall for a more private conversation. Although that was the last thing I wanted, I had no choice. You know, for decency's sake.

"You okay? For real?" he whispered.

I just huffed; my defenses were up. "Look, I don't know why you care."

"I dunno either, but I do. Talk to me."

How charming. I did my best unimpressed look for him as other students passed us by. "Sorry," I said in utter refusal.

"Don't you trust me?" he asked, chuckling ineptly and nudging my arm. "What'd I do?"

"No offense, but you weren't exactly my knight in shining armor when I passed out in your car."

He shrugged. "I got my own shit to deal with. Sistine, Nichole …."

"Oh, right—all your prior engagements have to do with *other* girls." I couldn't believe I had said that.

"Hey!" he exclaimed. "You're outta line. Sistine is my *cousin*. And Nichole's in mournin', too, and not to mention she's real tight with Sistine, a'ight? Don't get mad at me for feelin' bad for you. I mean, who are you to me except some psycho investment I got myself into, huh?"

I gasped. "Psycho?!"

His face was turning pinker by the second. "Why do you gotta be so fuckin' selfish? I'm just bein' friendly."

"You are *not* being friendly."

"Whatever." He stormed off and left me in a quiet haze, alone in that hallway except for Mr. Edwards, whose push broom nearly dusted my shoe over. He raised his wispy eyebrows at me as he passed, probably keeping an eye out for me "lest I falleth comatose," as I had once said.

So, needless to say, after a brief cataplexy attack, I felt much worse about going to English than I would have if I had just trusted Leo and let him comfort me. Something about the fact that he wasn't Bryan (and the fact that he wasn't bowing down to the narcoleptic girl like everybody else) rubbed me the wrong way.

I know it's bad. I know. But even the janitor was on my side now, and I relished that.

Leo Capodi

FINALLY, DR. OAKHURST decided to hold an assembly regarding our safety. It hadn't really bothered anyone that there was an active killer on the loose in Banshee, specifically Bridgewood High, and that alone repulsed me.

The call to action of his speech went something like this:

"If you or any of your friends see suspicious behavior, do not hesitate to scan the QR code the Student Council has been pasting all over the walls. Fill out the Google form it leads you to, and in the meantime, we will see about instating a task force as soon as possible to handle any security issues.

"The best thing for all of us is to try not to panic. We're safe and sound as long as we don't bring any more special attention to the incidents that have already occurred, and rest assured, the police are confident no one in this room is a target. Their advice to you is to walk in groups of three or more and stay inside at night to ensure your safety. What other concerns do you have?"

To me, every equivocal thing Dr. Oakhurst had said only meant the police were equally as stumped as we were. Only about three hundred students attended Bridgewood given Banshee's minute population, but everyone's hands shot up like cattails from a bog, and we suddenly looked enormous in count.

Tommy and I looked at each other briefly, he grabbing my wrist instinctively and me searching the rest of the auditorium for Nichole and her black-hearted squad to see if they were making light of the situation for any sick reason at all. What can I say? Their minds functioned differently than most, and I wanted to observe.

Police officers lined the exit, occasionally pulling students from their seats to ask protocol questions. "What if I'm the next victim?" Tommy whispered to me in a panic, waggling my hand as we watched the cops. "Or you?"

"We won't be next. Didn't you hear Dr. Oakhurst just now?" I reasoned, to which he only rolled his eyes. "Have you seen Nichole?"

"She's out there being interrogated," he told me. "Wonder what the questions are. Probably like super sugar-coated 'cause her mom's dead and all. Yo, what if they want to ask *me* something, and I blurt out a secret or accidentally take the blame for everything? Did *I* kill all the teachers, J?"

"Shut up!" I said, holding a finger up to his naive lips. "You can't say things like that. People can hear you."

"You're right, you're right, my bad," he realized, composing himself. "Look. McDreamy's gettin' the third degree, too." He pointed at the exit off to the left of the stage, and there Leo was, his wavy, topaz hair jouncing as he moved, his chin pointed at the carpet due to nervousness. "You think he'll crack under pressure like me?"

"Definitely," I snorted. "He's an asshole, so he has it

coming."

"Whoa, what's all this now? Mr. Perfect ain't so perfect anymore, is that what I'm hearing? I mean, I knew you stopped *crushin'* on him—"

"I didn't tell you why, did I?" I sighed, abashed at the memory that came rushing in. "He invited me to his house knowing Nichole would be there. You were there to see the aftermath. Remember, when you guys told me about Ms. Stratford? But it doesn't matter, there's somebody else now anyway." I didn't want to elaborate any more.

"Serves him right." Tommy shook his head in disgust. "And you can tell me all about this 'somebody else' soon as this all blows over. You know Reba's been spending nights over at Nichole's house for the past couple weeks. Ain't that weird?"

"Not really—I mean, they're best friends," I said. "Do you think Reba would've been at Leo's place too, then?"

He shrugged. "It's a possibility. Just glad he warned you."

"If you call that a warning," I grumbled. "He's so … he's so …" I struggled to find the word, so Tommy offered a couple of offensive ones for me, but they didn't quite click.

Don't get me wrong—I was thankful that Leo apologized to me, but he'd been too arrogant lately for it to hold any lasting significance. What he said to me in the hall, calling me "psycho" and everything? I didn't appreciate it.

He was just like Reba. I bet they had rubbed off on each other over the years, being around Sistine and Nichole all the time. I could draw so many connections between their lives.

Wait. Connections. *Connections.* The word broke a dam in my mind that would never, under any circumstances, be repaired.

"Criminal," I whispered in horror, finding my word at last. I leaned way forward in my seat when it dawned on me. "Tommy, oh my God. He's the killer. He—"

"Sit yo' ass down, man."

"I'm serious!" I exclaimed. "Think about it. Remember how

I told you he came up and talked to me a few weeks ago asking if I'd 'heard anything' about Nichole? Back when everyone still thought Teach was alive? They're *connected!*" I laced my fingers for effect.

"I ain't following."

"Suppose she *was* alive when that happened. Leo told me he had to 'do something' with them later that night, and it was like a week after that when we found out she was shot. It doesn't make *perfect* sense ..."

"Then how do you explain Stratford?"

"Everyone hates her guts, including Leo, so that's why it took so long for them to realize she was missing! Leo's the one who told us why she was absent in the first place—something like she was *suffering* a *personal loss!* Hello? The loss was her life!"

I knew I was getting ahead of myself, but the intensity of my emotions just kept multiplying and multiplying, and before I knew it, I was trembling all over. Tommy narrowed his eyes at me.

"Be straight for a second, J," he said cautiously, but the dread in his eyes made it look like he agreed with my conspiracy. "You ain't just saying all this to get him in trouble, right? I know you mad and all, but is this for real?"

I just nodded, nearly bursting into tears. My grip weakened, so I placed my hands on the armrests for stability.

Realizing I'd been trapped in a car with him, that he had a temper, that he was going to lure me into his house where my three biggest enemies were probably hiding out to jump me, that he had asked me personally to go to his hockey games *knowing* I'd wind up in the team room with him ... I looked at the ceiling and said a few rare words in a praying position. *Thank you, narcolepsy!*

My condition had saved me from imminent death.

After all, Leo had seemed reluctant to call anyone for help that day and looked like he was praying when I regained consciousness. Praying for another chance to get me alone, that is. Everything was falling into place.

"Look!" Tommy cried out when a pandemonium formed among the students. People in front of and beside us were pointing their trembling fingers at the exit to the left of the stage while Dr. Oakhurst tried speaking into the microphone to calm us down.

His efforts to shush us were futile. He, too, looked at the open doors and saw what we were clamoring on about: Leo Capodi, struggling against a pair of handcuffs, was being escorted out of Bridgewood High's auditorium. Dr. Oakhurst fell silent.

I'm sure you vividly remember the moment the whole case was thrown off balance. It was the second to last week of April, and Leo had already been bagged during the student safety assembly. The dust was beginning to settle.

I was a mix of emotions. I felt sad for him and his family, ashamed of myself for being damn near in love with a murderer, and relieved that the threat was finally gone.

My relief was short-lived, however. A day later, Bridgewood was shocked to learn that a third teacher had been killed. Suddenly, things weren't as clear; they no longer added up. Leo was still at the police station being questioned at the time of the murder, likely still wearing the metal bracelets in which he'd been led away. My mind couldn't grasp it, and when he was released from custody the same day, it definitely did not sit well with me. The first question to pass through my hazy skull: who is he working with?

This time it had been Mrs. Blane, the most favored, and only, geometry teacher. No one in my grade associated with her anymore because most of the seniors had suffered their three years of math and were done with it alas, but God, did we still love that sprightly woman. And by we, I mean the whole student body *except* for me because my opinions are oh-so popular. I was still recovering from the previous death anyways. The only valuable woman in society, I swear, had been Ms. Stratford.

Here's the main reason I was hurt, though, contrary to everyone else: no one, save for Bryan and me, saw the goodness in Ms. Stratford. She was an outcast, a habitual instigator, a frightening woman, but most of all, she was the best English teacher I'd ever had. She saw people for who they really were and didn't let risible curriculum requirements occlude her myriad philosophies. No, everyone was too distracted by Teach's assassination to care that Ms. Stratford was gone, too, and when they took Blane right from under our noses, the entire school was in hysterics. Ms. Stratford was just another casualty, no strings attached. It was like she had never even taught there. Surely you can discern by now that Teach and Blane were the "hot" teachers whose obvious patterns of favoritism didn't seem to faze the rest of the students. I, however, value candor in a person; Ms. Stratford wasn't just the only teacher to have that trait but, apparently, she was the only *person* to have it, too.

I didn't know whether to feel justified or unsatisfied that Leo was an official suspect, knowing the danger was still out there. I was tired of being afraid. Exposure to three murders seemed to numb me from any more shock, though my sense of alertness would be on point for the rest of my life. At this point, my biggest concern was that Leo had people doing the dirty work for him while he was cooking up lies with a lawyer, and now he was out casing the streets of Banshee, preparing to strike again. Everyone else, on the other hand, was crying relentlessly because they were *officially* terrified for their lives. Dr. Oakhurst even appointed police officers to guard us during school hours.

Not long after Mrs. Blane had bitten the dust, it was time

for Tommy and me to be questioned by the guards, but I'll delve into that later.

In the meantime, I'm sorry my email has gotten so long. I'm finding that the more I share, the more I remember, and while remembering is something I explicitly *don't* want to do, I promise I'm trying my best for you. Besides, this is the only way I can disclose everything without feeling like I need to leave out the uncomfortable details for dignity's sake. By telling you this in story form, I'm really just loopholing perjury. Please take great care in reading this email; I don't speak tangentially.

Cemetery Drive

IT WAS A beautiful, pristine night contrary to the rest of my day.

There were *actual* stars in the sky. I thought I'd be pushing up daisies the next time stars were visible at night in the twenty-first century, but I suppose it could have just been a while since I was outside this late.

I wasn't supposed to be out. I was very cold, but not because the weather was subpar—it was the kind of cold where you know your body is simply calibrating itself with nature, where you start to wish humans were cold-blooded so you could avoid that feeling and just absorb the night without interruption. The kind of cold where it's pleasant out, but the breeze runs through your veins before long, and you're left shivering under a football player's oversized hoodie.

His body beside mine was like a radiator; I noticed that night that I had poor circulation.

Bryan and I weren't actually doing anything, and we hadn't been for hours. He picked me up from my house for an impromptu tryst, and while we were breaking my doctor-issued curfew, I didn't mind the risk one bit. I'd never had the chance or perhaps the courage to be adventurous.

He had parked his car on a long, narrow, one-way road widely referred to as Cemetery Drive because it divides a shallow cliff and an age-old cemetery. The cliff, and what lay beyond it, made for an astonishing sight at nighttime, so we sat on the ground next to each other and took it in while our eyes adjusted to the dark. The Delaware River was somewhere off in the distance; I could hear the water rushing very faintly, though in my ears it sounded like static from some breadth away.

"Are you tired?" Bryan asked me at last, breaking our silence. As my father would say when I was being noisy on a road trip back in my childhood, he "broke the sugar bowl."

"No," I hummed. "I tend to have trouble sleeping at reasonable hours." He chuckled.

In time, his arm found its way around me—he must have been feeling braver than he had during the hockey game, but it was safe to assume that we both really liked each other now, so there was no reason to be *too* cautious. I rested my head on his shoulder and shut my eyes for a moment; he had a subtle woodsy scent, like when you pull a tea bag out of piping water and catch a whiff. Intrinsically relaxing.

"Our lives will never be the same after this," I realized, staring blankly ahead of me. The sugar bowl lay in shards.

He nodded in agreement, and more silence followed. It was a silence that somehow warned me he was going to ask or tell me something serious—something up-to-speed with my own pessimistic comment. Look at me, already memorizing his speech patterns and body lingo, like the perfect future wife.

My gut was right. He spread his fingers out over my shoulder blade and mumbled, "What happened to Leo yesterday really freaked me out."

"It's a shame," I agreed, keeping my voice quiet out of respect. "I wonder what he said that got him in cuffs."

"The wrong thing," Bryan suggested, releasing an exasperated sigh out in front of us. "It was hard to watch. He's always been my friend."

I turned to look at him, his face just an inch or two away from mine. "I think he deserved it, to be honest."

"Bold of you," he said defensively, his brows arched in surprise. But I knew my reasoning would sway him.

"Leo's been acting out for the last two months," I told him, giving him something to think about. I shifted a little so that I was facing him and not the drop off the precipice. "He and I never used to talk, but now he thinks we're close enough to argue."

"What do you mean? Like old married couples or like best friends?"

"There's no difference," I said. Bryan tilted his head sideways, nodding a little in consideration. "You just don't say certain things to acquaintances unless you want something to do with them. He called me selfish, said I was psycho, and … so on. He's obviously having some criminal regrets."

He sucked in a breath, shaking his head in disgust. "Aw, that's—that's really insensitive." He cringed. "I have trouble believing he could say that to someone like you."

"I'm telling you, he has a temper!" I nodded along. "Ergo, he deserved it."

"Well, let the record show that I don't think you're either of those things." I smiled up at him and mouthed a "thank you," looking away out of modesty. A shiver ran through my frame and probably transferred to Bryan too, given the magnitude of it. He caressed my arm and shoulder, shifting closer to me all the while. "We can go back to my car if you want. Crank up the heat?"

"No, this is fine," I assured him. I wanted to live in the moment for as long as I could.

"What time do you have to be back?"

"Stop worrying," I said, elbowing him gently in the side. "This is just fine."

He smiled a bit but didn't look completely convinced. "Parents have good reason to be worried about their daughters being out at a time like this. I'd just hate to get you in trouble."

"Oh, you won't."

My mother was reasonably lax with me, the exception being my health, but I could provide her with a steady argument that being out past ten o'clock on a school night was in no way compromising my well-being. Besides, if she knew Bryan, she would decide for herself that he had a protective quality about him.

I let out a breath, content with how the evening had played out. The moon and stars were twinkling still, although now most of them were hiding behind clouds. It was a twinge darker out because of that but no less chilly. I recoiled when I felt a droplet of rain on my forehead.

"All right, maybe we should go now." I laughed, holding my palms out for the rain as it picked up. Bryan grabbed my right hand, the one that was closest to him, and hoisted me up with him, inclined to guide me to the passenger side of the car.

When he came into the vehicle through the other door, his gray T-shirt was dotted with raindrops. It was bright in the car, but the lights timed out soon.

"I hope I'm not keeping you away from anything," I said slowly to match the pensive, moonlit aura.

"Now *you're* worrying too much," he teased. Just by the look in his eyes, I knew he was planning to make a move on me, and that made my heart thump frantically—but I was more afraid of having a cataplexy attack. It would ruin everything.

Maybe this double-sided anxiety seems normal to you, or

maybe it's confusing, but let me put it this way: my nerves and hormones were carbonated, and if anyone, including myself, were to shake me, I'd explode. There has always been a kind of inner turmoil in me; dormant or not, it's there. And it's not always narcolepsy or cataplexy that detonates when I'm disturbed.

Whatever this unnamed third party was must have woken up when Bryan brought his hand to my face, sweeping away the remnants of raindrops. His skin was warm and callous. I waited patiently, afraid that if I put forth any unnecessary effort, I would blow it. *Don't shake yourself, J.*

Up close, his bergamot scent was somehow quieter than before, and very effective in calming me down. When I was younger and still able to watch movies, I'd seen in *Hitch* that men are supposed to lean in ninety percent and women only ten, and that's precisely how it happened in reality, but it felt like time had become obsolete because it took *forever*.

And when that moment did come at last, I was feeble all over—delightfully. He weakened my core just by sinking his fingers into my cheek, but his lips were a whole other story. They were soft like suede and they moved by a force only as natural as the wind. My heartbeat was sprinting, but the rest of me felt like it was in a pool of cream, moving slow and steady, yielding to the energy around me.

Unfortunately, my nerves got the best of me and I jerked my head back not even two seconds after our lips touched. My hands and thighs were tingling, and I knew I wouldn't be able to exit the car on my own if I tried—not that I wanted to.

"You okay?" Bryan asked, leaning his forearm on the center console. I nodded and squeezed my eyes shut, fighting the sensation with every fiber in me. Then, slowly, my legs regained feeling, and the animation that now characterized them floated up through my core, my chest, all the way to my fingertips. "We should probably head back, but I want to see you again.

Tomorrow?"

"I have plans with Tommy," I frowned, "but Saturday is my do-nothing day, so ..."

"What a coincidence!"

On the way home, I remembered our houses were pretty close, so that gave me hope of spending more time with him in the future. Little did I know what I was in for.

Tommy Hicks

FRIDAY AFTERNOON, TOMMY and I went to get ice cream.

The week had been rough, and I figured I'd say something about Bryan to him then to get everything truly off my chest. Tommy was already a part of my Capodi conspiracy, so I didn't have to plan much else to say, but when we got to the ice cream parlor, it was already a bust because half of Banshee was there, and Tommy had just barely convinced me to stick it out. It was going to be hard telling him about Bryan after all.

"Just grab us some seats, and I'll order," he insisted, gesturing toward the sea of tables. "I'ma get you cotton candy." My favorite.

It was chilly inside, understandably, but too muggy to eat outside. Many of the students from Bridgewood—people I didn't necessarily want to start my weekend with—were hovering in line or crowding around tables. Only a few two-seaters remained vacant, so I sat at the one closest to the door, facing the gigantic TV in the corner of the dining area. I was growing impatient with Tommy the longer he stood in that never-ending line, but again that was beyond my control.

"Look!" cried an awfully familiar voice, riddled with giggles, from a table somewhere off to my right. It took some neck craning for me to see through the potted plant leaves blocking them, but alas: Sistine and Nichole.

The former was pointing at the flatscreen, a grin plastered across her skinny face. When I followed her finger, I saw that the news was reporting on Bridgewood School District's unfortunate tragedies; there were photographs of the three late women, as well as Leo Capodi, in what appeared to be a mugshot. He looked exhausted to say the least. I tried to reserve the rest of my judgments for when the facts were released, but I still had a flaming phobia of him, and nothing would fix that.

"Whatcha lookin' at?" Tommy asked me after returning about a minute later. I nodded at the TV, unsure of how to say it any better than Max Figuerra, the anchor. Tommy's face went blank as he handed me my dish of ice cream. "Shit ... this mean he's incarcerated now, or what?"

"He was released Wednesday due to insufficient evidence," I enlightened him, planting my shovel of a spoon into the bottom of the dish. "Thing One and Thing Two are laughing their asses off about it, though."

"Who?" he asked. I cocked my head to the right, and he, still standing up, scoffed loudly enough that they noticed.

"Nicky, look who it is," Sistine whispered loudly to Nichole, ogling Tommy and me. I rolled my eyes. "Need somethin', bucko?"

"Yeah," I snapped. "Why are you so happy? That's your cousin up there. Family should mean something to you."

Sistine cackled, her teeth exposed in a hideous, snarly smile. "That's all you give a shit about, girly? My 'family' hates me."

Cue the dramatic air quotes.

"Is it because you have half a brain?"

"No, asshat. It's 'cause my mama's a fuckin' Capodi, and my daddy ain't. Family ain't nothin' but a bunch of names." Even Nichole widened her eyes at that.

"I hope you rot," I spat. "Let's go, Tommy."

It wasn't long before my pink and blue ice cream had melted into lavender and we were sitting outside on my front porch, like the good old days, only this time we were suffering in the untimely humidity. Tommy kept complaining about his car getting damaged in the weather, and I kept complaining about Tommy complaining. It was just a Honda. Besides, Sistine had had the biggest influence on my mood out of all the other aspects of that day.

"Why don't we talk about something else?" I finally suggested. Tommy sighed, holding his head in his hands and chuckling at himself as beads of sweat collected in his fresh, shaped-up hairline. The vapors in the air were making our hair frizz up, mine where my ends were split and his at the crown of his head, as he had a month-old fade. I laughed, too. "Wanna go inside?"

"Nah, it's actually kind of nice," he decided. "I just got my shit in a twist 'cause of you-know-who."

"Yeah." I nodded. "Where was Reba during all that?"

"You think I know?"

I chuckled at his blindness, wondering if he also believed in Sistine's "family ain't nothin'" clause. Eventually, I decided he probably didn't because he still had two loving parents and a thousand local cousins, so I changed the subject. "Well, I have something to tell you. Finally."

"No shit," he said. "Does it got anything to do with your whereabouts last night, missy?"

"It does," I confirmed. So, I proceeded to jog his memory regarding the time Bryan walked me to the car after school, and how I'd gone to a hockey game "by myself" earlier in the week despite my recently established animosity for Leo. Tommy didn't look so pleased that I had lied to him, but he listened, nonetheless. That was when I told him Bryan was more philosophical than I had imagined and that he was a good kisser too, at which Tommy rolled his eyes. Saying it out loud made me feel as though it had happened too soon, and Tommy's response didn't boost my confidence at all. The feelings for Bryan that I thought I'd cemented were now starting to quake.

"No good date ever took place at a cemetery, sicko," Tommy said after receiving all of this new information. The way he had reacted reminded me of a funnel being filled with too much water: it needed lots of time to empty out completely, but there were still droplets clinging onto the plastic cone at the end, refusing to go down.

"That may be true, but we weren't *at* the cemetery," I argued, pointing my finger at the sky to uphold my statement. "It was actually really nice. I'm seeing him again tomorrow."

"You know he's a schmuck, right?" He laughed. He was obviously in disbelief. "He plays football *and* club basketball. He ain't got time for you. Plus, he gets hurt, like, every weekend. Watch out tomorrow!"

"Funny," I said, starting to feel *and* sound hostile. "He only puts up a front at school to get class to be more interesting. Bet you didn't know that."

"If you call O.D.D. a front," he scoffed. I back-handed his arm, but he just shook his head. "Who you gonna have all those deep conversations with? 'Side from me?"

"Your conception of 'deep' is severely flawed, Spank Bank," I pointed out. "If you'd been there on that date with us—which, thank God you weren't—you'd think otherwise. I mean, what if you went out on a date, and I was suddenly all up in your business, saying how … how … how bad she is at makeup?"

"Hypotheticals are invalid," he said, "*always*. And I know you're full of shit 'cause I see Bryan more than you, and he ain't right for you." *Disagree, disagree.*

"Except he is. He *gets* me!" I tried, following Tommy as he began walking across my front yard. I couldn't comprehend why he was so worked up, or why all of these cheesy excuses were pouring out of my mouth.

He clicked his tongue at me, slapping his hands down in frustration. "Man, this ain't *High School Musical!* I said he ain't right for you, J."

"So, who's right for me? Personally, I don't think that's your choice," I objected. He finally stopped pacing, though I was confused about the look that formed on his face. His eyebrows were pushed together like he was angry at me, but his eyes were focused on the grass. He parted his lips as though he *wanted* to answer me, but he didn't.

"Look, Tommy—I don't know, and I don't *care* why this bothers you so much. I really, really like him."

I whirled around to go sit on the porch steps again in resignation, shaking my head at nothing in particular. But Tommy's silence made me feel empty, so right before I reached the steps, I glanced behind me. He looked so helpless with his shoulders slouched and drops of sweat building on his dark forehead.

"*I'm* right for you," he said.

Selfish

COME MONDAY, I avoided Tommy at all costs. Bryan didn't know about the situation because I didn't tell him about it when we got together on Saturday, and I didn't plan on telling him in general. Besides, now that the weekend was over, I had to focus on not panicking around the guards in school twenty-four-seven; I could tell by the way they were looking at me whenever I passed by that I was due to answer some questions for them pretty soon, and I was right.

Leo was back in school for the time being, though now he was under round-the-clock surveillance by Officers Petty and Hart. Honestly, it only made me feel more tense, and I don't think I'm the only one who responded negatively to their presence.

Leo's eyes had these mauve rings around them, and his hair was greasy, and his cheeks were especially sallow. He only wore the previous week's clothes, and everyone could tell because they were either dirty from hockey practice or were standout fashion choices that no one else in all of Bridgewood could pull off. I imagined he was too self-conscious to practice personal hygiene with two cops breathing down his neck, and that gave me all the more reason to blatantly disregard him.

During English class, I was slouching on my stool when a third officer entered the room.

"Jesus, we got Banshee's entire police force in here," Bryan noted. He looked at me over his shoulder and winked, and I smiled back at him. Poetry in motion.

"Officers," the bulky old man said, saluting upon entering. "Pardon the interruption. I'm looking for Thomas Hicks."

Leo made a show out of turning around to stare at Tommy, who stood up slower than ever, eyes locked on the quasi-criminal. It was painful to watch, but he was out of the room in no time, and the class returned to rereading *Catcher in the Rye* for analysis.

"Lukin, you're up," said the gratis temp who obviously didn't want to sub for a school that was currently going down in infamy. She droned, "Pick up from Chapter Twenty-Two."

Bryan sighed in submission, flipping his flimsy, timeworn paperback open and beginning to read aloud. He was interrupted when Temp raised her chubby palm and said, "Hold it. What's your take, Lukin?"

"It's pretty self-explanatory." He shrugged, pausing to observe Temp's irked reaction, before flashing a cheeky smile. "Oh, you wanted me to elaborate? Well, Holden's pretty naive, and by taking us through this fantasy of his, he proves that his worldview lacks reality." *God, if only Tommy had been here to hear that.*

I balled my hand up into a fist and placed it onto the tabletop as gently as I could manage, though I was frustrated. It killed me knowing Tommy was choosing ignorance over reality in terms of Bryan's intelligence, and there was virtually nothing

I could do to change his mind because he was so stubborn.

Swimming in my angry dive-pool of thoughts, I lost touch of my surroundings the farther I descended. All I could see was a clear image of Tommy's face when he told me how he felt about me. The water clogged my ears, and before long, the pressure above me pushed me to find oxygen again. When I broke the surface and rejoined reality a minute or two later, the class was exactly as it had been: Bryan and Temp conversing cordially while other students hid their phones between the pages of their novels.

The police officer who was questioning Tommy returned and called my name loud and clear, and Leo gave me the same dramatic glare, telling me through telepathy not to say anything against his favor. I shuddered as I walked out of that dead silent classroom, switching places with a suddenly pale Tommy. A new kind of pressure was crashing down on me. Just outside the door, I found a blonde woman sitting at a folding table with a tape recorder perched on top of it and a Styrofoam cup of coffee that was the color of sand.

"This'll be easy," said the officer. "I just need you to answer a few on-the-record questions for me about the murders, and we'll send you on your merry way."

"Okay." I gulped. The woman clicked a button that turned on the recorder light. "I should warn you I have narcolepsy, and—"

"Don't worry about it," said the officer. "Your pal, Thomas, told me all about it. You're in the clear."

"Oh." Considering our little friend skirmish, that had been very considerate of him. Though I wonder why I came up.

"Speaking is Officer Michael Jahr, currently at Bridgewood High School, Banshee, New Jersey to interview Jamie Hessen, senior student, on the triple teacher homicide. So, Banshee is just about the smallest place I've ever been to. Those guys in there are transfers from Morristown, and I just moved out of

Camden 'cause this case is really turning into something. It should be a lot easier for you to point out suspicious behavior because this town's so tiny, relatively, shouldn't it? Okay." In a way, he spoke to me like he was Lady Tremaine and I was poor little Cinderella, except in a much more modern, I'm-just-tired-so-please-cooperate kind of way. He hummed out, "Let's start with that. Has there been any specific unusual activity lately? It may not seem relevant to the murders, but anything helps."

"Uh ..."

I had to think about it. I leaned against the wall and pressed my hands in between my back and the white blocks, though that didn't stabilize the tremor in them. The stigma around police officers justifies my anxiety during this questioning, and I assure you, there was no other reason for me to be so skittish. I was just feeling a bit pressured to not forget any details, on top of everything else I was dealing with at the time.

I started speaking before my thoughts were complete: "Friday I was at this ice cream place with Tommy, and the news was on, and Leo's cousin and her friend were there—" I began, though I had to pause to breathe because I forget to do that when I'm nervous. It was like doing a slideshow presentation that, if I failed, would have legal repercussions. "His cousin Sistine and her best friend Nichole were laughing at the news report because Leo's face was on it, and they have a strange relationship with him, to put it nicely."

Jahr just nodded and wrote into a notepad that I hadn't noticed earlier. It must have been stored away right next to his gun or his baton, both of which I refused to look at.

"And before Teach died—Mrs. Tomlin, I mean—Leo told me he had some business with her and Nichole that was supposed to be on the down-low." Now that I had said it out loud, I wasn't sure how important the detail actually was, but there was *something* about it that nagged at me.

"Why did he tell you if it was a secret?"

"Probably because he knows I have beef with Nichole and her mom, so we keep tabs on each other." He raised his hoary Jack Nicholson eyebrows at me, held his palm up like a stop sign, and asked me to explain myself. I admitted, "She and I have been butting heads since fifth grade. It doesn't have anything to do with her mom or Leo."

"We *are* talking about Nichole Tomlin, correct?" he clarified. The confusion probably originated in the fact that everybody else who'd been interviewed probably seemed indifferent to her. I just nodded at the officer, but then I muttered a verbal affirmative because the only record of this interrogation was that of the outdated tape recorder. "Anything else you have to say about Sistine? You're the first person to name her, but her interview answers checked out." *Great. He already doubts me.*

"She gets detention a lot," I said, almost like a warning. "She was absent when Mrs. Tomlin died, probably because she's so close with Nichole, and, um … she was also gone when Ms. Stratford passed away. But I don't know anything about where she or Leo were when Mrs. Blane died, so that's all I can say for certain."

"Very well," sighed the officer. "Their whereabouts, on the other hand—that's what this conversation is trying to establish. Leo's if not Sistine's. I have yet to learn of an alibi or hear a confession. As you know, Leo was released on the evening of Debra Blane's death, though his probation officers reported no abnormalities regarding his behavior. Unfortunately, though, the evidence labs take a lot of time to evaluate the DNA samples we collected, so answers remain unclear. It's not like we have any of you kids' prints on file."

Something was very comforting about how colloquial this man was with me. But it clearly wasn't enough to appease my pressing anxiety because just then, I was ambushed by the beginnings of a sleep attack. I convinced myself I could breathe through it for the sake of clearing my name, which had been a mistake.

"You all right, kid? You look a little green," said Officer Jahr, glancing at the woman operating the tape recorder as if she held the answer. Then he flicked his wrist at her and said, "Amy, let her sit for a minute."

"I'm fine," I slurred before flaking out at last. I vaguely remember him catching me before I hit the floor, but I could have hallucinated that part.

Apparently, I had been out for a half hour. Jahr and Amy were too uninformed about narcolepsy to know what to do with me once I'd lost consciousness, so they must have had someone wheel me into the nurse's office to let me crash there. That had never happened at school before—at least not for thirty minutes it hadn't, and I was normally just stuck snoozing upright in a desk chair as opposed to the literal gurney Nurse Hardest owned. I was relieved to find that I wasn't strapped to it when I awoke.

Nurse Hardest had sent for Tommy to come and escort me back to class after the thirty minutes were up, even though I was stable enough to walk on my own by that point. It felt uncomfortable being alone with him in my curtained-off room, staring down at his neon Nikes instead of me.

"Guessin' your interview didn't go too good," he finally mumbled. I shook my head. "No?"

"*Au contraire*," I told him, trying to ease the tension. "The cop said you talked about me."

"Yeah." He sighed, edging closer to me by a hair. "I had to make sure you wasn't a suspect."

"Thanks." I took a deep breath and stared sorrowfully at my best friend. "I just ... I hope you didn't feel like you had to do that because of what happened."

"You can say it, you know."

"Well, I don't want to."

"You're gonna have to deal with this," he reminded me, a little louder this time. "You gotta learn to stop bein' like this, J. Ignoring problems? Actin' like how I feel don't matter? *Selfish*."

I recoiled with surprise at his sudden confidence. "Why does everybody keep saying that about me?" I asked, dropping my hands helplessly as I flashed back to my argument with Leo. "I'm not selfish."

"If it's that popular of an opinion, I think maybe you *are*. Just somethin' to work on."

Nurse Hardest stepped into the room for a moment and held her finger up to her lips to silence us, so I stood up and left, Tommy following close behind.

"I can walk by myself," I muttered to him once we were out of the nurse's earshot. I was irked for an understandable reason, I think. How could he call me selfish? I'd never asked anything of him. In fact, the one thing I wanted was to be left alone.

We entered the hall where my locker was. When Tommy caught up with me, he put his arm out in front of my chest to stop me from moving. Caustically, I exclaimed, "Watch out, Tommy! I might start to think about *myself* if you're here too long."

"A'ight, that's enough," he snapped. "You wanna know why so many people think that?"

"Hit me. I'd love to know."

He started counting on his fingers. "You can't take a damn compliment. Yeah, that don't make you modest—shocker. And your whole world revolves around Leo and Nichole, no matter if you want it to or not. When I'm talkin' to you, you change the subject, askin' all 'Was the Bitch Squad with Reba last night?' and 'Why's Leo such a jerk?' Would you have realized any of that if I didn't just call you on it?"

"That's bullshit and you know it." I scowled. "I don't even

like him anymore."

"Nah, but he set the bar for you! That's another thing—your standards are *waaaay* too low for your own good," he said, "and your self-respect is like … AWOL. Pfft, Bryan Lukin? For real, man?"

"Say one more thing about him," I challenged him, pushing him backwards by the shoulder so I could shuffle past him. I was finally shaken, and after my cap had been unscrewed, the carbonation within me hissed. "I can't believe you're saying all this." My voice broke, seemingly indicating to Tommy that he'd won, but that was the last thing I wanted him to think after the barrage of character flaws he'd just thrown at me.

"Right, 'cause I can't say what I wanna say around you, or you'll be paralyzed—but look at you standin' all tall even though you're pissed at me. You're full of it, you know that?"

"I can't help the fact that I have cataplexy," I said accusingly. "Why would you even mention that? That's like threatening to cut me out because I've fallen asleep four times today."

He groaned, clicking his tongue. "Quit beatin' around the bush. You prioritize yourself, even when I been standing behind you for seven years. You let your condition stand as a reason to make me censor myself around you when you *know* you can handle anything I gotta say. You would've realized I was in love with you if you *tried* to look."

"How was I supposed to *know* to look?"

"My point exactly! Not like I been shyin' away from you."

I had to laugh at that statement. "Do you think this is affection? The second I say something you don't like, you bite my head off and call me selfish. And you're just going to have to get used to the fact that *we're* …," I paused to gesture at the space between us, using vigorous hand motions, "never going to be a thing. If anything, you should've known that if I wasn't picking up on your 'hints,' they weren't strong enough. You're blaming me for your own faults."

I turned around and walked the other way, surmising that both of us had won the argument in our own ways. That wasn't satisfying enough for me, but there wasn't much else I could do. My blood was boiling under my skin, and with each step I took, my feet pounded indignantly against the vinyl floor. One more routine waxing, and I would've been able to see myself in the reflection of those tiles, and how florid I must have become. I started to quicken my pace because the dismissal bell rang, and I was going to be late for my next study hall if I didn't hurry. And, I figured, the faster I walked, the less likely I'd be to fall asleep mid-movement. The people in that hallway were packed like sardines, and they only slowed me down. My adrenaline was what kept me from crashing to my knees.

A high-pitched gasp escaped me when I ran face-first into a random student's backpack. He turned around promptly, revealing the face of Chris Arden, one of the guys who played for the Messiers. He was standing in an unmoving little pentagon consisting of Bryan, a boy named Willam McGuire, the two Peters, and him.

"Oh, hey!" Chris smiled at me. "Jessie, right?"

I just stared, wide-eyed and silent. I'm sure I looked horrified from their perspective.

"Hey," Bryan said once he looked up from his phone and realized it was me. He touched Chris' shoulder as if to ask him to move aside and then guided me to the other side of the hall, where less traffic flowed. "You're upset."

"It's Tommy," I practically squeaked. He bent down and made that universal I-couldn't-hear-you face, but I just shook my head as tears threatened to invade my lash line. The humiliation of collapsing right then and there would have been too much. "I'm gonna be late."

"C'mon, what's the matter?" he persisted. Clearly unaffected by the prospect of tardiness, he sat down on the edge of the radiator built into the wall to level his gaze with mine. "You can trust me," he promised, his voice becoming easier to hear as the hallway congestion lessened. Those eyes of his were pleading.

I looked off to the side in anxious ponderation. What was so abnormal about fighting with my best friend? Tommy and I had met before he was "cool," as some would say, but we had become close after Reba, Sistine, and Nichole officially joined forces. Still being a somewhat popular loner at that time, he saw me as the bold girl who'd been abandoned, and I saw him as the friend I'd always hoped to have in Reba; their personalities were quite similar, but their quirks distinguished them entirely. Something just clicked between Tommy and me, I guess, so I found it weird that someone who was *destined* to be my friend was angry at me—though I suppose he had found it equally strange that I didn't reciprocate his feelings of adoration.

After a while, I shook my head at Bryan. "I really shouldn't say anything."

"You don't have to," he said and pulled me close to him, determining that I was not going to open up. He smelled like foresty autumn spices. "What do you say we go out tonight? I know today hasn't been too fun."

"It really hasn't," I mumbled in confirmation, shutting my eyes as he embraced me. "What do you have in mind?"

"We could see a movie," he offered. "Anything you want. And dinner, too. My treat."

"Okay," I agreed, though I hadn't seen a movie in years. Too risky—but I was suddenly feeling up for it. "Do you think I'm selfish?"

"Everyone's a *little* selfish."

"But am I a lot selfish?"

"Why do you ask?"

"Why don't you answer?"

Bryan sighed. He put his hands on either of my shoulders and moved me about a foot away from him so he could look me in the eye, establishing that his next words were a promise. "People say things they don't really mean. I get called stupid, hyperactive, you name it—but that doesn't mean it's true. I, for one, *know* it isn't. You're not selfish, Jamie."

I was swooning. His words, combined with the richness of his eyes, made my heart swell, and at each passing second, I felt a little bit better.

"You just have enemies," he added, "and the people who call you selfish are enemies, even if they're close to you." I'll be the first to admit how much that stung. But it was definitely the truth—at least for the time being.

"I don't like thinking of Tommy as an enemy," I frowned, and then the corners of Bryan's mouth turned upward, and he shut his eyes momentarily.

"*Tommy's* the one who called you selfish?" he clarified. I had expected Bryan to make a backhanded remark about him, but he didn't. Instead, he proceeded to point out that best friends have meaningless arguments every day and that they aren't permanent affronts. This one certainly hadn't been meaningless to me, but I understood the message he was encoding: that I was only hurting because someone I trusted with my life had spoken negatively about me, suggesting that I didn't merit his trust in return. But I knew I did, especially because Tommy had talked about me in his interview with Officer Jahr. We were both just ... disillusioned.

"You could be a therapist," I mentioned, gazing into Bryan like he was Prince Charming. He laughed at me, one eyebrow arched upward while the other remained linear. I lowered my chin. "Seriously, how'd you do that?"

"Do what?"

"Cheer me up." I smiled faintly, squeezing his arm. "I thought I was gonna pass out, but I didn't. That's really something."

"Let me fill you in on a little secret," he said, beckoning me closer so he could whisper through my hair. "It's because I'm

Batman."

When I drew my head back, my jaw fell open melodramat-ically. "Nerd." He scoffed at my response, stood up off the radiator's edge, and stuck his arm out for me to grab onto. All of a sudden, I was Kate Winslet in *Titanic*, being escorted by Leonardo DiCaprio next to that iconic staircase.

Our moment was cut short by two things: first the late bell rang, and so my point of making it to class on time was instant-ly ruined; and second, Mr. Edwards came whistling down the hallway with his back turned to us, his push broom conquering the floor and a pair of blue earbuds dangling around his neck.

"What are we seeing tonight?" Bryan asked as we started walking. "I hear the new *John Wick* movie is in theaters now."

"I'm down! Though I must warn you, I am squeamish."

I wound up falling asleep before anything on screen could trigger my cataplexy.

It's important to take note of these happy moments I en-countered every so often, brief as they were, because they kept me from taking off my rose-colored glasses.

Thrift Shop

I RECEIVED AN intriguing text message on Tuesday afternoon after I woke up from a spontaneous nap. I was reclining in the passenger seat of Bryan's car—I had started riding home from school with him instead of Tommy for obvious reasons—when the vibrations of my phone startled me awake. The message turned out to be from Caroline. Something about her reaching out bothered me, perhaps because I didn't remember ever receiving her contact information.

"Rise and shine," Bryan said to me when I finally stirred. We were already in our neighborhood. "Who's texting?"

"It's Caroline. She …" I paused, my eyes adjusting, "… wants to go shopping?"

"You make it sound like you don't shop," he said, rhythmically tapping his fingers on the steering wheel to an imaginary beat. "Am I correct?"

"You are," I mumbled, still staring at the message in

confusion. "She and I don't really hang out to begin with." Caroline and I had been close once, back when my group consisted of Tommy, Caroline, and Nichole. At the time, Tommy, who'd been a shy outcast before, was gaining friends, and Caroline was always inviting me horseback riding with her. My dad had worked with hers—both were pediatric neurologists. You can imagine the kind of image Caroline and I had because of that. This was in fifth grade, when Nichole ripped her away from me during the Oregon Trail incident and left my inner circle consisting of only Tommy. Caroline and I had since made up, but we'd never been close like we were back then.

"Well, you know, she had kind of a personal Renaissance, if you will, after Reba and Nichole dropped her."

It was almost concerning how caught up Bryan was with my drama circle, like he had tapped into my mind when I was asleep and all the sticky thoughts in there were in his domain now.

As I contemplated the ways I could politely decline Caroline's offer, Bryan continued on, "I wouldn't be surprised if she were out walking homeless dogs right now. Girl's too nice for her own good."

"So, she's asking to hang out with me because she's *nice?*" I summed up, skeptical. "Bryan, I don't think you understand how girls work. This is obviously a setup."

"That is such a harsh prejudice!" he said laughingly. "I think you should go with her and find out what her evil plan is, you cynic."

My guilt would eventually outweigh my hesitance, so the following weekend, when Bryan was busy having a banquet for club basketball, I sacrificed my do-nothing day to go with Caroline to the strip mall riddled with antique stores, plus a severely outdated Forever 21. It was actually a cute area to shop or just to browse and take pictures, so I wasn't too worried about not having a good time. Caroline was very colloquial—just how I remember—which made things easier for me. During the car ride alone, she told me she had quit horseback riding a few years ago and that she was more focused on tennis now. So far, I had picked up zero traces of an evil plan in action.

We walked into this hipster part-cafe-part-gift-shop. (For you city-goers in the FBI, that means bootleg Cracker Barrel.) It was rustic and not very well lit on the inside, and the gift shop sold candy and resin figures almost exclusively. Caroline and I took a cute selfie against a wall decorated like a half-timbered house, then walked the perimeter for ten or fifteen minutes. She bought her little brother a bag of organic jelly beans.

"Anywhere you want to stop?" Caroline asked me once we left. It was like exiting a movie theater: too bright for my poor, unadjusted eyes. "Jordan asked me to get him a souvenir, so I'm all set for the day." She raised the beet-colored candy for effect.

"How about that thrift store across the street?" I suggested, pointing my finger at the baby blue building jammed between a yarn vendor and the Forever 21. "I always like looking through old stuff. I'm still waiting for the day they sell vinyls here."

She didn't even have to accept my suggestion before dragging me across the cobbled street by my wrist. On the way, she excitedly asked, "Vinyls, huh? Do you have a record player?"

"No, but there's something so primal about them." I chuckled. "The frayed edges, the fact that it's not in a jewel case ... you get it." I gestured at her distressed Beatles shirt.

"I do," she nodded, "and I like the eyewear section too 'cause sometimes I just *need* a new pair of Ozzy glasses. Do you ever have that need?"

"I can't say I do, but I respect it."

We giggled at each other and entered the classroom-sized store. A bell jingled when we opened the door, and a couple of old lady customers looked up at us before returning to their own thrifting. Stepping inside was like hitting a wall of dense, humid air—decades-old air that tasted funny. It was eerily quiet despite the bluegrass music playing somewhere overhead.

Looking around at the items organized by year, I hummed out, "God, I feel just like a hippie in here." As if agreeing with my statement, Caroline held up a denim jacket with pink and orange flowers painted all over it. It had been in the display window.

We went to work right away. I ended up finding not one, but *two* pairs of "Ozzy glasses," as Caroline had called them, so she and I each collected a pair to buy. Some trendy Jackie O. glasses were perched on the adjacent shelf but nearly fifty cents more expensive. I wasn't going to wear more than one pair of sunglasses, and I wanted to spend the rest of my money on more practical or sentimental items. I guess I'm stingy.

"Over here, Jamie," Caroline called to me. She was standing in the corner of the store by a metal railing that was shedding off-white paint flakes onto the purplish carpet. A large "ONE WAY" street sign was poised against the wall behind the railing, pointed oddly at a downward angle; voilà, we discovered a descending staircase lay beyond it. I couldn't believe I'd missed it all the other times I'd been there, but in my defense, it blended with the carpet. It was almost invisible.

"So, this must be the furniture section," I realized once we were down there. Upstairs, the merchandise consisted of various articles of clothing and other garb, but down in that mildewy dungeon, I finally laid my eyes on crate upon crate of records from years ago. There was a CD rack as well, which was cleverly installed into an old TV stand for sale, but I decided I'd visit that after flipping through those faded cardboard vinyl sleeves. My priorities were set in stone.

Caroline shared my interest in the records and pointed out a few that I'd seemingly missed because there were so many. I resolved to buy several of them since they were dirt cheap, and that way I could either push myself to invest in a record player or just hold onto them for their nostalgic value. So far, the latter is what I've done.

"So, how are things with Bryan going?" she asked me, setting her shoulder bag in between us on the floor while we rummaged through the ground-level crates.

"Really well!" I smiled. "I might be seeing him later tonight."

"It seems like you two jumped right in." She chuckled, evidently intimidated, but I didn't understand why at first. "Pete and I haven't even gotten to second base yet."

"Wait, what?" I whispered as the gears in my head stopped rotating. I sheltered my O-shaped mouth behind an open palm. "I've only kissed Bryan once, and even that was *way* sooner than I expected. You have nothing to be worried about."

She furrowed her dark eyebrows at me and leaned backwards a little from her kneeling position, palms resting mid-thigh. "But Tommy said—"

"Tommy talks about me and Bryan?" I interrupted.

She nodded, grimacing. I slumped, dropping my records down on the floor in frustration. Caroline continued, "And apparently he's been exaggerating ... sorry, Jamie, I shouldn't have brought it up."

"No, you didn't know," I said in her defense. "Thanks for telling me that, actually. I doubt he would've been the one to fess up." She just nodded, bringing her focus back to the vinyls in front of us. My shins were starting to ache from crouching for so long.

"Well, I'm glad you two are taking it easy," she complimented. "You deserve that."

It was clear as day why people liked her so much, and I wished we hadn't grown apart over the years. Her ability to smooth over tough conversations impressed me, coming mostly from my antisocial tendencies. And who knows? Maybe we'd still be riding ponies and having sleepovers in big lake houses together if I'd realized back in the day that Nichole was the problem, not Caroline. But if there was still time to get close to her, especially then, when I most needed a female friend, I was determined to do it. Plus, her parents liked me.

No. You can't just use her as a rebound, J. It was Tommy's voice in my head this time—you know you're too close with someone when their subconscious becomes *your* subconscious. I can't say that has happened with anyone other than Tommy, so maybe that's why I wanted to use Caroline as a crutch. To hear someone else's voice in my head. Someone who I *couldn't* fight with, even if I tried.

Ugh, my problems are so cyclical.

I stood up so I could fork through the crate that was eye-level with me at my full height when, across the dank room, the most horrendous eyes I think I've ever seen were waiting for me to glare back. I whispered, "Jesus Christ."

"What's that?" Caroline asked, pressing her lips together in curiosity. When I didn't answer her, as I was transfixed by the she-devils standing across the room, she rose to her feet and gave me a weird look.

"I swear to God, every time I go out, I run into those bitches," I muttered, irate. She tilted her head—she must have been surprised by my language.

"What bitches?"

I pointed discreetly over the top of the crate, where Sistine and Nichole were trying out different threadbare armchairs, stealing a glance over my way every few seconds. That's how I knew they were just there to torment me—girls don't go thrifting for *armchairs*.

"*Them.*"

"Well Banshee's a pretty social town if you ask me," Caroline explained, "especially Bridgewood girls. Also, I'm kinda friends with them … I mean, I wouldn't ask them to hang out over you, but we say hello to each other in the halls and stuff. Plus, Pete says Reba's actually pretty chill, though he *is* afraid of

Sistine." Her verbiage reminded me of Tommy. Perhaps in his incessant storytelling, he'd rubbed off on her.

I snorted. "If I tried saying hello to any one of them, they'd think I was having a seizure."

"Oh, don't be ridiculous. Look, here they come. Hey, guys!"

I shook my head at no one in particular as Sistine and Nichole produced exclamatory remarks from their ape mouths.

"You look so cute today, Caroline!" Nichole beamed, touching my companion on the shoulder. "Where'd you get that bag?"

"Amazon—for half the designer price." She grinned. "Free shipping, too!"

"Look at youuuu!"

Sistine had her ginger hair tied back in two Dutch braids. She didn't say anything, but instead sneered at me from a short distance with her chin pointed down, almost like she was *trying* to look menacing. Her shadowy, stone cold eyes bit into me the longer I reciprocated that glare of hers. I wanted to be civil for Caroline's sake, but the wretch standing in Nichole's shadow was taunting me, so I couldn't help but speak up.

"How's it feel?" I asked Nichole, knowing anything I said to her would hit Sistine just as hard. "With your Casanova being on probation and all."

The blonde flicked her eyes at me, her big, painted smile morphing into disgust. Caroline looked down.

"Nothing I haven't dealt with before," Nichole replied with a huff. Then she and Sistine disappeared, though the stench of their supremacy lingered. Caroline glanced at me, her coffee-bean eyes having widened to the size of asteroids.

"I stand corrected." She chuckled to herself. "I may be too mellow to stand up to people, but I do recognize passive aggression when I see it. That's not directed at you, by the way."

"I got it." I sighed. Things were tense after that, so I suggested we check out and call it a day. She agreed that it was probably best but ensured me she'd had a good time. It was, by definition, Awkward City.

Back at home, my mother was making lunch in the kitchen and was in an unusually sprightly mood. She hadn't been expecting me for another hour or so. The TV, a room away, was blaring an album by the Bee Gees—a possible explanation as to her joy—and it wasn't until she pivoted away from the microwave that she noticed I was even present.

"Oh! God, Jamie, you startled me." She placed one hand on her heart and grinned at me. "Whatcha got there? Some records?"

"Bee Gees," I said, singling out the *Saturday Night Fever* album that I'd only really bought because of her. I set them on the table along with my new shades while my mother searched the countertop for a remote control to turn the volume down. She was hopping around still, smiling at nothing. "You look like you're about to roller-disco your way to better thighs."

"I'm just having one of those days." She shrugged as the music grew quieter. "Makin' lunch."

"For two?" I asked, gesturing at the two Tupperware dishes she pulled from the microwave. "Who's your friend?"

She paused for a moment, her penciled eyebrows raised. I folded my arms as she spoke: "Sam."

"Is Sam a woman?" I pushed.

"No, he's ... he's divorced." And then the kitchen door burst open, and a bearded man in a flannel shirt walked in, almost like we'd cued him with the word "divorced."

"Hey, Fran," he said, his happy brown eyes losing their panache as soon as he acknowledged me standing in between him and my mother. He lifted a finger at me, but I didn't let him squeeze an introduction in. It seemed like he and Mom had specifically planned for this type of catastrophe but were unprepared, nonetheless.

"You go by *Fran* now? What happened to Frankie?" I

snapped. That had been my father's nickname for her. Mom set the Tupperware down on the counter and looked this Sam person in the eye over my shoulder.

"I've been seeing Sam for about two months now," she said slowly, "and I didn't tell you because ..." She made a slight gesture at me, but then Sam came to stand beside her and put his arm around her. I felt ambushed.

How could anyone keep a secret that big for that long? It would be like me hiding my narcolepsy from people.

"Look, I'm not here to replace your dad," he promised me, extending his hands out very carefully. "We're just trying something new together, and I think you'll appreciate how happy your mother's been."

Appreciate my ass, I thought, for my knees buckled under me and my shoulders grew as heavy as the angry pit in my stomach. I didn't even get to tell him he would never amount to what Larry G. Hessen was because by then I was lying on the floor, unconscious with a minor contusion.

"Aaaaand there she is. Yo, Mrs. Hessen, she's awake now."

I felt a hand on my knee, and I was looking at the crown molding in the ceiling when I woke up. The lumpy cushions under me were those of the ugly couch my mom had picked up from a random curb a few years earlier, so I had to assume she wasn't the one who relocated me after I fell. She would have brought me to my room, or at least left me in the kitchen with a pillow under my head. My mind was cloudy. I could barely emote when I met eyes with Tommy and then Sam, neither of whom I wanted to look at. Mom was nowhere to be seen, though I could hear her voice faintly in the background.

"I have a bone to pick with you," I muttered, pushing Tommy's palm off of my knee and attempting to sit up. He gestured urgently for me to stay horizontal.

"She ain't always this annoyed," Tommy joked to Sam, who shook his head with a closed smile on his face before he turned toward me and sat on the armrest next to my feet. Tommy continued, "Your mom's on the phone with the doctor. You almost cracked your head open, that's why you passed out."

"I what?" I gasped, slapping myself in the forehead to find out where exactly the injury was, though I was a bit too eager and felt the pain rush in all at once. I discovered a cold towel lying under my head and reached for it.

"I wouldn't move that," Sam suggested; he winced as he looked down at me. His body was blocking the sunlight from entering my line of sight. "Your mother says this has happened before, and we probably don't have to go to the ER."

"You just told me I cracked my head open. Of course, I have to go to the ER." Both of them sighed at my adamance and emphasized the "almost" Tommy had used. For the record, there was no blood, but I still had reason to be worried because I'd had a few narcolepsy-related injuries in the past, and none of them were pretty. I looked at Tommy for a long moment before saying, "Go home."

"I ain't here 'cause I wanna be," he snapped at me. "Your mom needed a hand."

"What, this pansy couldn't carry me himself?" I scoffed, gesturing at Sam. He gave me an offended look and glanced at Tommy for help, who just shrugged.

"No. She knows *I* know how to deal with you," he explained. "Y'know what? Leave Sam outta this. He's chill, and pretty funny, too."

"Oh, he's funny? Now I don't miss my dad anymore!" I screwed my eyes shut as the bruise throbbed. At that point, I tried my best to focus on the rest of my body. I had also hurt my shoulder on the way down, and laying there with a cushion spring jabbing me in the back felt like it was going to turn my whole backside black and blue. I breathed out, "Just go home and let me deal with this myself."

"Look, J, you probably have a concussion. I ain't leavin' you."

"You're not my fucking nurse, for God's sake! If you're not leaving, then tell Bryan to come over."

"You two exes or something?" Sam whispered to Tommy, who rolled his eyes. "Didn't mean to assume."

"This is what happens when your best friend's a female. Ain't no way out." He left the room, texting and shaking his head to himself, but was soon replaced by my mom. She knelt beside me and petted my hair with a sympathetic glow in her blackish eyes. It had been a while since we last spent this much time around each other.

"Dr. Beaufort says you'll be fine," she whispered soothingly. "You don't need any stitches, but you'll need to take it easy from now on. If you feel dizzy or faint, I want you to text me so I can bring you the right meds. Oh! I have to test you for a concussion. Stand up, hon."

I did as she told, groaning as the blood rushed out of my head. My hair felt heavy, and the pain made it hard for me to keep my neck straight. She asked me, "What song was I playing when you fell?"

"'Jive Talkin.'"

"Can you walk toward me with your arms out like this? Pretend you're on a tightrope." She was standing in a T-pose about three yards away from me. I didn't have any trouble. "Great. Kneel down on the floor for a sec ... aaaand stand back up. Sam, sweetie, could you move over a bit?"

Sam stepped to the side as we continued the homemade concussion test. The light that flooded the room after he moved made me flinch, but my mom used it to look into my eyes and make sure they looked normal. She'd had a world of experience conducting this test on me.

"This seems really sketch, Mom." I groaned. She touched

me on the shoulder and assured me that I didn't have a concussion, even though the pain was sharp enough to qualify. Then she and Sam went into the kitchen. I knew they were just going in there to talk about me in private. My anger, my fall. I sat back down on that horrible couch, waiting in silence for a few minutes.

In no time, the front door opened, and in came Tommy and Bryan together. Time was passing so fast yet so slowly around me.

"I heard what happened," Bryan said, frowning before sitting next to me. He had an air of caution about him, as though he were afraid to touch me, to stir my thoughts too hard. I shut my eyes, holding the towel against my head; it didn't take me long to realize there was a melted ice pack hiding inside that mound of fabric. It was too tepid to numb me, causing me to question how long I'd been out. Bryan lowered his voice, "I'm sorry about your dad."

I rested my cheek on his shoulder, grimacing with pain, and he proceeded to hold the ice pack against my head for me. "He died in surgery when I was fifteen. There was a whole lawsuit."

"I had no idea," he whispered. "My mom died when I was six, but I have a pretty close aunt to make up for it."

"Aren't you lucky? I just have a Sam."

He snickered lightly enough that I could just barely feel his breath on the crown of my head, but not so light that I couldn't picture his closed-lipped smile. When I tilted my chin up to see his face, he looked back at me, and it was that simple: I didn't try and look happy for him so long as he didn't try to pity or match my chagrin.

I noticed his eyes were the color of his hair and equally as lustrous, though in the sunlight emanating through the blinds, they had this orange tone that made his skin all the warmer. I could sleep next to a person like him and never have to move a muscle, even with my condition.

"See y'all later," Tommy announced from somewhere behind the couch. He sounded annoyed that I had chosen to focus on Bryan instead of him. He shouted a goodbye to my mother as well before finally leaving the house, dragging his feet as he exited. His volume had interrupted my moment with Bryan and worsened my headache.

"What'd you do today?" Bryan lulled, his voice deep and curious.

I took a big, dramatic breath. "I went shopping with Caroline like you suggested, got Nichole to be even madder at me, found out my mom's dating again, aaaand almost concussed myself for the third time."

"Rewind," he said, keeping his voice soft. "What's this about Nichole?"

"Well, *magically*, she was at the thrift store Caroline and I went into, and I *had* to say something," I complained. He made a confused face. "To feed my massive ego, of course."

"How'd that go?"

"Oddly well," I summed up. "But Sistine was giving me this horrible look. It was like she'd put a 'kick me' sign on my ass or something and was waiting for the first volunteer."

"Oh, well you know how she is. She looks at everyone like they have a 'kick me' sign—but then she does the honors herself 'cause she's a psychotic bitch." I laughed at that one and grabbed his hand to press our palms together; I found it amusing that my fingers ended where his started.

"They haven't been hanging around Reba as much lately," I observed, remembering the ice cream parlor and the thrift store. "I wonder if she did them dirty."

"Of course, she did them dirty," he snorted. "It's Reba."

That's valid, I thought.

I reached across Bryan's lap for one of the TV remotes, which I had apparently been lying on top of while I was unconscious and searched through the channels for something interesting. Bryan suggested we put Channel 8 News on because he had seen one of their vans on his way to my house, and I didn't feel any need to object. At that moment, my mom and Sam shuffled into the room and stood behind the couch, watching the report with us in silence.

For Whom the Bell Tolls

"*BREAKING: SEVENTEEN-YEAR-OLD CAROLINE Empfert was found shot in her own vehicle today, the afternoon of Saturday, May first,*" Max Figuerra recited from a sheet of paper lying flat on his desk—the heaviest paper in the world, perhaps, for it bore the darkest news Banshee had heard in a long time. And that wouldn't be the last of it either.

I drew in a sharp breath and stood, my unsteady fingers fumbling across the buttons on the remote. I sloppily rewound it and listened to that sentence three more times until my lungs compressed in my chest, and my teeth chattered as I registered the news. In my head, it sounded like china crashing onto the floor and splintering into a million shards. My eyes brimmed with tears and clouded over as I stared at the television screen, though I was too shocked to say anything for a while. I find it weird that I was still conscious. Alive, even. But my bottom half wobbled under me at last, and a low sound escaped me until it escalated into a scream.

"I just saw her!" I shrieked.

I was truly hysterical. I had *just* seen the victim—what would have happened if we'd stayed at the thrift store? What *wouldn't* have happened?

Every other hand in the room was touching me in a matter of seconds, whether for cushioning or comfort I couldn't tell you. But seemingly in slow motion, I toppled over and landed on the floor between the couch and the coffee table. Every appendage of mine suddenly went limp like a ragdoll—but there was such a heavy sorrow disillusioning me on the inside, and it felt like my whole body was stiff like a plank. I couldn't perceive anything except that tension. I was frozen in place, but still I writhed and squalled involuntarily. It was a totally different kind of pain: heartache.

My mother cried out my name. Someone switched the TV off in the meantime, though I don't know who it was. Everyone hovering over me was suddenly darker because of my adverse vantage point; however, I could still see them clearly. Bryan's skin had turned an ash gray color, but he maintained a straight face. His lack of frenzy helped calm me down. Mom was crying just like me, though probably for a different reason, and Sam looked only slightly defeated, if not completely indifferent to the news report. His bushy brown eyebrows were drawn together with concern for my well-being, which was decent of him. But for as long as I stared at their faces, I wished desperately that my narcolepsy would kick in and pull me under; it never did. It doesn't work that way. I was forced to experience that tragedy in the moment, second by second, regardless of my soaring stress levels. The floor was colder than my ice pack had been and sent shivers down my spine once I regained the ability to feel. I wondered if I was having a seizure.

The news wouldn't leave my mind. *I just saw her.*

Mom gave instruction for Bryan to carry me into my

bedroom so that if I were to fall asleep or have another cataplexy attack, I'd be in an appropriate, non-dangerous setting.
She and Sam hovered in the doorway only for a second after
Bryan put me down on the wrong side of my mattress. There
was a little divot in the side I normally slept in, and Bryan sat
in it, staring sadly at me. I couldn't stop my tears from stream-
ing. I remained silent for a little longer until at last, my fingers
twitched.

"I understand if you want to leave," I murmured, gazing
blankly at the ceiling. I turned my face slightly to the right to
read his countenance, still partially numb.

"Why would I leave now?" he countered equally softly.

"We're in this too deep," I proposed. I don't know what had
gotten into me. I reflected on my conversation with Caroline
that day and how she had assumed my relationship with Bryan
was maturing abnormally fast ... and how I was starting to
agree with her. I hated how close I felt to him; everything
about it just seemed forced and impure. "You don't even know
me, yet here you are, knee-deep in my problems."

I felt a tingling sensation all over. That meant I could move
everything again, only very slowly for the time being, given my
general fragility. I'd become so used to the tingling over time
that I normally didn't notice it.

I sat up, noticing the hurt look on Bryan's face. "What do
you mean, I don't even know you?" he asked.

"I mean we *just* started dating, and I'm uncomfortable," I
explained, slumping against the headboard as my face twisted
up even more. Tears, tears, tears. They were so hot. I normally
didn't cry this much, and I was amazed that my body let me
do it freely. It wasn't exactly a "strong" emotion I was feeling,
rather a muted one I'd been keeping under wraps for far too
long. "And I wouldn't be surprised if you were uncomfortable,
too."

"Why'd you call me over here if you felt that way?" he asked, lips parted. "I—I guess I'm just not following because I feel the exact *opposite* about you."

"God, help me," I whimpered, looking to the ceiling as if there were a deity up there who had planned this moment. I continued to weep quietly, so afraid to watch his expression change that I shut my eyes entirely. "Caroline said ... Caroline said ..."

"What?"

"She told me people think we're already making it," I bleated, "because Tommy is spreading rumors about us. Tommy, for God's sake!"

"All right." He sighed, and I felt his hand on my knee after that. I finally opened my eyes and glimpsed into his; he looked about as upset as I was feeling. "I'll talk to him and take care of this. Promise. But you need to keep me informed about how you're feeling, like if you want out."

"I don't know what I want," I said. "Today's been so fucking awful—"

"I know. I know." He drew his hand away from me and gazed at the floor next to my bed, probably to avoid making more eye contact with me. I knew at that moment that I had hurt his feelings. He looked back at his lap, but I could still see the exasperation in his face. "I think I should go."

"Okay." I frowned. He leaned forward and kissed my forehead, but instead of letting him leave, I slung my arms around his neck and reminded him, "I never stopped liking you."

This time he didn't say anything at all, though his honey eyes did wander across my face in a way that suggested he wanted to speak. What would he even say though? When I released him from my grip, he left me alone, no goodbyes, no questions asked. Through the window, I even saw him linger in his car before driving off way above the speed limit.

Now that I was alone, I had nothing to distract me from my relentless troubles. I burst into tears yet again, staring at the shelf on which I planned to keep those records I'd bought. Caroline had picked one by The Cure for me, thinking I'd like it, though I'd never heard anything of theirs—I would have to play it sometime in tribute to her. Or else I'd be restless forever. The conversation we'd had had ended on such an abrupt note, just like her life.

I can't talk about her anymore, Agent. I'm sorry.

Visiting Hours

I SLEPT THROUGH almost all of Sunday and stayed home from school on Monday. Bryan blew up my phone, but I only answered him a couple of times—not because I was too "uncomfortable" to even communicate, but because I was feeling woozy the whole day and couldn't afford to have any more emotions coursing through me.

Mom and Sam checked on me at different intervals. I pestered Sam every time he came into my bedroom because I thought he should be at work supporting my poor mother, but my furious words fell on deaf ears. Mom brought me takeout for lunch and dinner; I could see she was torn up about the news, likely because Caroline's father had been a colleague of *my* father and so they were mutual friends.

"Sweetie, you've got company," she said to me sometime after seven o'clock. "Come on out to the living room before he leaves." She nodded at me encouragingly while I heaved myself out of bed, eyes puffy and hands shaky.

"If it's Tommy, I'm gonna sue you. I know how."

"Save your energy, hon."

She led the way to the living room but split off to resume her business in the kitchen while I was supposed to talk to my guest, who definitely wasn't Tommy. Or Bryan, for that matter. His long, wavy hair covered his eyes as he sat hunched over himself, but I could tell who it was right away.

I let out a panicked gasp and took two steps back, but he stood up and inched toward me, holding his hands up in surrender. His deep-set face was covered in lines, just like mine— that meant he'd been crying, too. Out of guilt, I assumed.

"Jamie, please," Leo uttered out, still approaching me. "I didn't kill her."

"Like hell you didn't," I whispered, my chest heaving. He would not stop coming toward me, but I had no place to go now that I had literally backed myself into the wall. I could feel my hands trembling still, and my knees wobbled beneath me as my fear intensified. "What about the ... the teachers?"

"Teach? We had bible study after school!" he burst out, finally planting his feet. "You gotta be the first to believe me. Please, I got cops up my ass at all times. I ain't a killer. I-I *can't* live like this, J."

"Ha!" I snorted, though I wasn't amused at all. "Bible study? What's next?"

In the meantime, my mind had questions. *Why would my mother let a convicted murderer into the house? How did he get here by himself? Why is he still free?*

If I hadn't been leaning all my weight against the wall, I would have definitely sunken to the floor.

"Sit down," I demanded, my tremor worsening. He looked over his shoulder at the couch and nodded, slowly backing into the middle cushion. That made things easier for me physically.

His eyes weren't nearly as beautiful as I'd always found

them; now they were red, foggy, and raw along the rims, like blood rain pouring down from an already dark sky. It was like he'd tried getting high beforehand but felt no buzz. The irises were murky because they were full of remorse and fear and everything bad; some of the badness in his eyes was forgivable, but I couldn't bring myself to trust the rest of it.

"Why are you really here?"

"I know you like me," he started, resting his elbows on his knees. "Or ... used to. I thought maybe you could help me out. I really need somebody right now."

"But Bryan," I reminded him.

"I know, I heard ... I just figured old habits die hard," he bargained in reference to my crush on him, which I'm fairly certain Nichole told him about. His conceit was not helping. "I ... I thought you might think I ain't the bad guy. 'Cause I'm *not*. I thought you'd figure out the truth before anybody else. You just seem like you would." He was right. I had figured out the truth before anyone else.

"You had me in your car," I said through clenched teeth. "You were going to kill me. ... You're lucky I passed out. *I'm* lucky I passed out!" All the panic in me that had subsided before suddenly returned and was thrashing around like liquid on a bumpy drive. I felt my strength slipping away.

"And I'm sorry for what happened," he agreed, "but I was never gonna *kill* you. It was movie night, like I said. Whole team was waitin' at my house after that."

"Why should I believe you?!"

"You—" he started, but he stopped himself in resignation, clearly frustrated. "I dunno, J. This was fuckin' useless. I thought you could keep me company."

"And why would I do that?"

"For Empfert," he said slowly, standing up. He looked beyond hurt. *It's for show. It's for show. It's for show.* "She didn't deserve to die."

I took a minute to correct my erratic breathing and finally stepped an inch or so away from the wall, seeing as he was still standing by the couch, and it didn't seem like he was going to come near me anytime soon. He did look pretty desperate, though, now that I had taken time to analyze his mannerisms.

"Please, J," he whispered. "I can't shower. Sistine won't get outta my house. I ain't gettin' through this without your help. I, I ain't even sleepin' at night."

I shifted my weight, given that he clearly hadn't come here seeking actual amity—he just wanted the things I had to offer. "Why me? What do you expect me to do, teach you my narcoleptic ways?"

"See that? You're already makin' me laugh," he said, gesturing at the couch space beside him as if to invite me. But he wasn't even smiling.

"No," I said, voice wavering. "I'm sorry. You can't be here."

This is precisely why I have no faith left in humanity. The Renaissance Man—if you forget, this is the name of Leo's utopian alter ego, which I fabricated when I still had a crush on him—*he* wouldn't test me like the real Leo had. *He* wouldn't kill innocent women. *He* wouldn't try to isolate me or charm my mother into letting him inside the house. No, he would advocate against gun violence. He wouldn't be on probation, for God's sake. I supported this version of Leo for way too long and suddenly, the reality of who he was became crystal clear to me.

Monster.

After I ordered him out, Leo stared at me, his face numbing to my ice-cold words. He lowered his chin and saw himself out of my house, no adieu. I couldn't blame him for choosing the silent fork in his walk of shame. Though I couldn't help but empathize; the degree of helplessness he had been feeling was all too familiar. But he was a transgressor, and I was not going to let my guard down.

Get it together, J.

"Why'd he leave?" Mom asked, poking her head into the living room. I sputtered in disbelief for a moment before finding any actual words.

"Are you kidding me? You let Leo Capodi into the house!" I shouted. She crossed her arms, shaking her head in quiet confusion. "Watch the news, Frankie!"

"Oh, God! I'm so sorry!" she exclaimed, realizing instantly what she'd done. She looked embarrassed and started toward me slowly, her face now rosy in a way that I pitied. "Honey, I know I've pushed your limits all weekend. *I know.* Just tell me if I can do anything for you, okay? I'm kinda failing as a mom right now."

I felt bad then.

Sam followed her into the living room. There was a weird dynamic among us now that my mother and her paramour had seen me pass out, scream, cry my eyes out, almost bleed, the whole nine yards—yet I felt as far away from them as I possibly could. My mother didn't know my relationships or my friendships or the details of my drama, but that was honestly pretty fair because she'd kept her boyfriend a secret from me for upwards of two months. At least on her end, it was to protect me, but what was my excuse? Sam ... I didn't even know where to begin. Why was this introverted lumberjack shacking up with my mom? What was his last name, even? Bunyan?

"Actually, I could use some advice," I told my mom, flicking my eyes toward Sam so he'd take the hint and leave. It was sort of an impulse decision on my end, seeking her help—I didn't normally do that.

"Yeah, I think I'm gonna hit the road," he coughed out casually, winking at me even though he *wasn't* slick. "Thanks for supper, Fran." *Ugh. He calls it "supper."*

After he left, Mom sat on the edge of the coffee table. "What can I do you for, honey?" she asked. She still had that woeful look on her face. I glanced down to avoid eye contact and muttered something about Bryan that I don't remember anymore. She was actually helpful.

"He's your first serious boyfriend," she reminded me. "Even though it's only been a few weeks, you're right—you *are* in deep. Ride it out, though, and get over those feelings of discomfort. It's all part of the process. And those rumors Tommy spread? Whatever they may be, he'll come around. He knows you're better than that. *He's* better than that. Get some rest, sweetie. You can invite Bryan over if you want."

So, I did. I invited him over, and he accepted, though he seemed reluctant about it. That I couldn't blame him for— not after the things I'd confessed the other day. Mom let him inside, and he met me in my room, where I was sitting cross-legged on my bed. He pushed the door against the threshold but didn't latch it shut, presumably because my mom was in the other room, and he didn't feel like making things uncomfortable with another Hessen within the span of one weekend.

"Hey," I said.

"Hey," he said back. "Everyone was asking where you were today."

"Really? That's nice." He stood awkwardly beside my bed. "Um, I actually wanted to talk to you about what happened on Saturday."

He nodded. "Me, too. Can I sit?"

"Yeah, of course," I said, pushing my pillows back so he had more room. "Look, about what I said—I'm only uncomfortable because it's been a while since I've dated anyone. Not everyone is okay with the whole narcolepsy thing, and you obviously are. I didn't know how to react to how you treated me and how people *thought* you were treating me."

"Well, I understand the second part, but you didn't like that I cared about you?" he asked, appearing not insulted but puzzled.

"When you put it that way—"

"I just need to know these things before anything else happens," Bryan said. *That's doable.* "I don't wanna do anything that makes you not like *me*. You know, as a person."

"Believe me, you couldn't."

He let out a breath of relief and started to smile at last. "Well, thank you." He chuckled. "I feel better now."

We spent the next ten or fifteen minutes catching up. He told me about his day; I told him about mine. At first, I failed to mention my little visitor, until it dawned on me that it was kind of significant that Leo had come to my house seeking "help." I told Bryan everything I could remember.

"... and my mom didn't even realize," I said at the end, chortling at her naivete, but my face fell immediately afterwards. "That's the second time he's gotten me alone."

"Second time?"

I paused, knowing I probably shouldn't have mentioned my ex-jones for Leo. But it was too late for me to retract any statements, so I had no choice. "After one of his hockey games, he invited me to his place ... but I didn't go 'cause I passed out after he made me mad."

"That why you hate him all of a sudden? Well, aside from the criminal accusations."

"Yeah, exactly." I nodded. "He sounded pretty convincing tonight though, if I'm being honest."

"Don't worry about it. You outsmarted him," he assured me. "Twice."

"I did, didn't I?"

Bryan looked down and bit his bottom lip. It looked like he was searching for the right words to say, and I secretly hoped he wasn't going for a promposal. He looked me in the eye, his warm hands enclosing mine like winter gloves, and asked me, "Just to be clear, I *am* your boyfriend, right?"

I quirked an eyebrow. "I thought so, yes."

He chuckled. "Well great. I felt like we were past the 'just dating' phase." Funny—my mother seemed to think so as well.

"Me, too. Did you happen to talk to Tommy at all?"

"I did, but it didn't go very well. Honestly, I think he'd rather yell at you about it than me."

"That's probably true." We laughed, and I shifted closer to him, using my eyes to urge him to put his arm around me. I liked when he did that, but I think I scared away his affectionate behavior by saying I was discomfited by it at first.

I shut my eyes. "It didn't hit me that people's lives were at stake until Saturday. I was just with her, and then—"

"I know," said Bryan, rubbing my shoulder. "I'm waiting for my breakdown. Any day now."

"Banshee's so small, you'd think the problem would be solved by now," I said. "We know who did it. Take him to a correctional center, for God's sake."

"You into crime shows?" he asked me, drawing his head back a little so he could see me under his bulky shoulder. I laughed at that and told him I had in fact watched a few of the less dramatic ones, and I wasn't surprised he made the connection. He joked, "I wonder if Leo will find a prison boyfriend."

"Maybe they'll stay on the outskirts of a prison riot together and be each other's bitches."

Bryan chuckled. "Before recently, I didn't think he'd be into that kind of thing."

"'Before recently?'"

Bryan raised his eyebrows insinuatingly. "It's a secret, so don't tell anybody."

"'The love that dare not speak its name.'" I gasped. "So, he's gay?" *That would have been helpful to know.*

"Bisexual, to be more precise," Bryan clarified, holding his finger in the air. "I overheard his lunch table talking about it. Ever wonder why he slaps Wes Martin on the ass all the time?"

"No!" I scoffed incredulously. "He must be hoeing around

'cause he was basically coming onto me today." After I said that, my eyes widened a little in embarrassment. The heat in my body congregated in my face, and I clicked my tongue for lack of a better addition to the factoid I'd accidentally revealed.

"Is that so?" Bryan asked, folding his arms. Sassy. "You did *not* mention that earlier."

"Wh … I obviously had bigger things to worry about," I explained nervously.

"Yeah, yeah, whatever." He grinned at me to let me know he was over it. "Will you be at school tomorrow?"

"Oh, I don't know. … I kinda like sleeping in," I joked.

"I wish I could sleep in," he complained. "I get up at five-thirty and work out for an hour every morning. That's why I love my weekends."

"Way to brag," I teased, though I was actually impressed with his dedication. "I should probably work out more before my muscles completely atrophy."

"Is that gonna happen to you?" Bryan asked, his brow pinched with concern. I shrugged humbly. He pieced together the fact that I didn't know.

"I'm pretty sure it won't," I reassured him. "But I *am* supposed to be exercising to help with the insomnia."

"What other things do you need to do?"

"Well, I take Modafinil," I listed. "That helps with the hypocretin deficiency up here." I knocked on the side of my head, though that only reminded me that I had leftover pain from my spill on Saturday. "I'm not allowed to smoke, drink, or eat before bed, and I try not to watch overly sad, funny, or scary movies because cataplexy is where your muscles get weak after you feel strong emotion."

"Do you ever pass out 'cause you're so damn happy, or?"

I didn't want to tell him that I hadn't laughed hard enough for that to happen in years. It mostly stopped happening when my father was diagnosed with coronary heart disease, but to be honest, I can't remember feeling any brighter before that. I take antidepressants along with my Modafinil, although sometimes I think they're placebo. So, just to answer his question, I mumbled, "Only when I'm upset." I really appreciated his curiosity.

"Jamie?" he asked cautiously, noticing that I'd lost concentration for a moment. I blinked at him. "All good?"

"All good." He chuckled in that way where only a puff of air exits the nostrils but still looked at me admiringly with a small smirk blossoming on his lips. "If you wouldn't mind," I started to ask, and he raised his brows in interest, "could you tell me about your mom?" I don't know exactly why I asked. Maybe it was some subconscious apology for how I first reacted to finding out he was motherless.

He smiled bigger and nodded.

Sleep Paralysis

I HAD ZERO oxygen.

My eyes darted open as if I'd been jumpstarted by an adrenaline shot. It was pitch black for a couple of seconds, and then slowly my vision adjusted, only for me to find I was stuck gazing at the ceiling. I could see a person-shaped blob peripherally, holding a long rod up near its shoulder, whispering indistinct words. It had more than one voice and stood in every corner of my room, but it was also sitting on my chest, cracking my sternum like ice. ... I physically could not inhale deeply enough to satisfy. There was too much pressure.

Scrawny limbs crept across the ceiling like roots, shadows of branches. But soon the thin tendrils congealed, taking the form of something much more intimidating: the barrel of a revolver. Twenty, maybe thirty of them appeared and pointed at the silhouette of a little boy, whom I hadn't noticed earlier. Perhaps it was he who was incanting to me, but the voices were androgynous. Perhaps it wasn't a pandemonium at all—it could have been me, struggling to breathe against the invisible ogre perched upon my chest. Jagged breaths caught in my throat as the iron in my blood left a foul taste in my mouth.

Sometimes when I lay awake at night as a naive six-year-old, I would be petrified beyond words and freeze in place under my Tinkerbell covers, studying the ceiling. It was similar to sleep paralysis, only I wasn't suffering from it at that age yet, and I was actually fully awake for it. Those instances turned out to be among my first-ever cataplexy attacks brought on by a fear of the dark.

As it turned out, the scary noises I'd heard in my house each time that happened were from my father, who would be coming home from an emergency call at work. I've told you he was a neurologist, so he was kind of an important figure at every hour of the day. He would stop in my room to say goodnight and find me absolutely still, eyes wide open though, and would complain to my mother that she wasn't putting me to bed early enough. A couple of fights resulted from this complaint, but after he looked into it, my dad took me into his office as a patient and diagnosed me with type one narcolepsy. That was after we'd moved to Banshee, the thought being that living in a small town, as opposed to Newark, would help me sleep, but clearly, we stood corrected.

My diagnosis both eased and stressed my parents. They no longer had to argue about why I was so sleepy or vapid or insomniac, but now came the bombardment of copays and doctor's appointments and ER visits. That was when I first found out my life was going to be strange, and I've never let go of that feeling; it gets me by sometimes. I'm just happy my dad had the job he did, or else my parents might have divorced because of me. I think about these things—the butterfly effect—a lot.

I don't know when exactly the dreadful sensation stopped,

but I woke up in a cold sweat to the blaring of my alarm clock on Tuesday morning, initially forgetful that anything had happened. It came to me in memories throughout the day, like when your friend says something peculiar, and then you realize you dreamed about it the night before. This one certainly fell under the nightmare category.

That morning I was too sluggish to really care about what I looked like, so I wound up wearing thin leggings from my middle school years—I'd been somewhat tall all through sixth grade, but I hadn't gained any healthy amount of weight since then, hence my junior high attire—and a crewneck sweatshirt that had been my dad's. It was burgundy and had some sort of crest sewn into both of the cuffs, though I think my grandmother embroidered them herself. So, it wasn't a bad look after all, just a rather lazy one.

Bryan picked me up for school. He had an unearthly amount of energy every morning, but now I could accredit that to his gym participation. He offered me a granola bar when I got into his car, which I politely declined. I wasn't big on rolled oats.

"Glad you're coming to school today," he said, extending me his hand from across the center console. The interior of his car was extraordinarily large, though that made sense because so was he. I was used to Tommy's Honda, which wasn't spacious at all—in fact, it only had enough room for two doors. "How'd you sleep?"

I took a deep sigh. It would've been weird to say "terribly," though that was the truth. "It was okay."

"Same." He frowned. "My mattress needs flipped."

I wish I could say a flipped mattress would solve all my problems.

First period, I had a study hall, and my assigned seat was next to Tommy. Even though it was technically a free period, the supervisor was way too strict for her own good, so it felt just like a regular class, minus the signed syllabus. I could have stayed home because I'm a senior, but if I did, I'd have no way to get to school. Sucks not being able to drive.

"Yo, you done bein' mad yet? 'Cause I'm over it," Tommy whispered to me. There was one seat in between each student, and he had sat in the one that was supposed to be between us because Mrs. June wasn't looking.

"Now is not the time for ignorance," I scoffed.

"So no." He sighed, drumming his hands on the desk. "Miss you, man."

"I guess I've just been so busy screwing Bryan that I forgot to spend any time with you. Sorry, bud." He narrowed his eyes like he does when I'm smart with him, and I returned my concentration to my cell phone. I had been texting Bryan even though he was in an actual class. I kept telling him how sorry I was in advance in case he was caught with his phone.

"It just came out, J," Tommy said pleadingly, staring at my eyes even though I wasn't looking back at him. "I dunno why I said it. But only a few people know."

"You say that like it's true to begin with," I said bitterly, shaking my head in disbelief. "Go back to your seat already. The witch is looking."

"Does Sam live with y'all now?" he asked, completely disregarding my demand. I threw my head back and groaned. "Just wondering."

"You can wonder in your actual seat," I spat.

"I'm tryna make things right."

Finally, I turned slightly toward him. "Well, it doesn't help that one, you're crowding me; and two, you yelled at my boyfriend when he tried clearing the air with you. I've had a long morning."

"At the time, I didn't really see it as Bryan's business 'cause I only said those things to get *you* riled up," he admitted. "Which I know was my first mistake. Well, second. But apologizing don't seem to work, so what do you want from me?"

I searched his face for any sign of witticism, but he seemed serious enough, and I knew the only way to get him to move to his assigned seat was to ask sincerely. "Please go back to your seat. I don't feel like getting either of us in trouble right now."

"Fine," he said, switching chairs at last. "What else?"

"You can't just take back a rumor." I shrugged. "I guess … you'll need to practice kissing up to me for a couple weeks then."

"*Weeks?* Damn you, Jamie Hessen." He shook his head, but he was beginning to smirk.

"Say sorry to Bryan, too. I don't like that you yelled at him."

"What are you, his mommy?"

"Could be." We both chuckled, but then Mrs. June shushed us from the bottom of the amphitheater. I texted Bryan that I had made amends with Tommy. He sent me a smiley face in return.

My morning had clearly picked up, though I can't say that made me enjoy Calc, Physics, or English any more than I normally would have. I was late to all of my classes that day— no problem—because I walked Bryan to his, seeing as he was busy after school for the rest of the week and couldn't hang out with me until the weekend.

In the parking lot after school, I was well on my way to Bryan's car when I passed Leo's Volvo. A sense of impending doom dropped in my stomach like lead as soon as I saw him. He wasn't sitting down yet and met eyes with me through the windshield. It looked like he had something to say. Three more spaces and I'd be in Bryan's car … but Leo was too quick for me to avoid.

"Wait up, Hessen," he called as I made bigger strides. *Where the hell are those police officers?!* "Hey, I did somethin' for you."

I stopped dead in my tracks, searching frantically for Bryan's attention so he could pick up that I felt unsafe. Undoubtedly, I wore a fearful expression on my face, still frozen as Bryan caught my eye and tried figuring out the problem. I felt like I was looking down from the needle of the Empire State Building as Leo called my name countless more times just to get me to turn my head. It's hard to describe exactly the kind of antipathy I was feeling toward him, but when he touched my shoulder alas, I was done for. My ears were ringing. The last thing I saw before losing total body control was Bryan rushing out of the driver's seat, his jaw set in outrage.

"The fuck is wrong with you?! Fuck off!" he shouted at Leo, crouching to pick me up off the asphalt. There was dirt all over my face, I just knew it, but there wasn't a thing I could do about it, especially once I was suspended in Bryan's grip. I could barely even hear what Leo said to him after that, or what Bryan said in return. I was equally as scared as I had been during my sleep paralysis the night before.

My head flopped backwards due to my limp neck as Bryan carried me to the car. I couldn't see who, but someone opened the passenger side door for him. How kind. I was buckled into the seat in no time.

"Does it hurt?" Bryan asked me, squeezing my hand as he pulled out of the parking lot. "Sorry about that. Leo's an ass."

As soon as I could talk again, I squeezed his hand back. "Thanks," I said. "I might have scraped my hand, but I'm fine." My arm had broken the fall for my head after all, so it stung a little. The sleeve of my dad's sweatshirt was roughed up and covered in pebbles.

"Make sure to clean it up when you get home," he told me. "I feel bad. I think we should walk to my car together from now on."

"I'd like that," I agreed. "Who opened the door for you?"

"Aleida," he said. "She's good friends with Jade, so."

I just nodded at him, shutting my eyes and enjoying the May air that blew through the windows. It was a nice day out. Shame it'd been ruined.

Tommy called me on the phone the minute Bryan parked in my driveway. I knew there was some urgency involved because Tommy never usually called me. I asked if I could stay in the car to take the call, and Bryan said it was fine, but I didn't even get to say hello before Tommy started rambling:

"Come on, J, pick up. Yo, you seen Reba? I asked Sistine and Nichole and Mr. Connery if they saw her 'cause she has Mr. Connery last period, but they didn't see her, and I'm at home, and she's not here, and I'm *not* driving my hood ass Honda to Nichole's house to see if she's there, and—"

"Tommy," I interrupted, side-eyeing Bryan. He had the beginnings of worry strung all through his face. "Is she answering your texts?"

Then I pulled the microphone away from my mouth and asked Bryan if he had seen Reba anywhere that day, though the answer was no. Of course.

"No," Tommy said in response to my question. He was clearly distressed. "Her friends wasn't at school today neither, so I dunno what to think. Tell me she's okay, J. Tell me she ain't dead."

"I'm sure she's perfectly fine," I said slowly to get the message across. "Breathe, Tommy." Bryan lowered his head; even though he could only hear my end of the conversation, he knew exactly why Tommy was upset. It didn't take a bachelor's degree to figure it out.

"I-I just know Leo had a doctor's appointment today, so he left in the middle of the class and came back and that's, like, the perfect opportunity to do some wack shit to an innocent girl, you know? Maybe she's *dead*, J. I can't find her for shit."

"Stop telling yourself that," I commanded him. "Have you talked to your mom or dad yet? Maybe they know where she is."

"They the ones who asked *me*. I'm supposed to be drivin' her home from school now that you got Bryan 'cause they don't trust Nichole, but she didn't come to my car today, and I was gonna hit rush hour traffic if I waited any longer."

"Look, I'm sure you'll figure it out." I sighed. "I know you will. Watch out for the news and ... and check your Snapchat map, see if she's not on 'ghost mode.' I gotta go for now."

"A'ight. I'ma keep you posted."

"Bye." He hung up after that. I looked back at Bryan and bit my bottom lip out of worry. "I don't know about this."

"Why not?" he asked.

"Caroline *just* died," I stressed. "And Leo is still free. ... Why is that?"

"The closest investigation lab or whatever is probably in New York," he reasoned, "so the evidence against Leo isn't being analyzed fast enough. Besides, we're not a priority. That's my guess."

"You know, now that I think about it," I said, "Reba wasn't at the thrift store with Nichole and Sistine. She really has been distancing herself from everyone lately."

"But—"

"And Leo told me he *did* something for me today," I recalled, slapping my hand against my mouth as the pieces of the puzzle clicked into place. "He knows I hate her guts, so what if he *killed* her to make up for being an ass? Do you think he would do that? Is that psychopathic or what?!"

Bryan shook his head, eyes trained down at his lap. "As much as you do hate her, you really came through for Tommy." Clever of him to change the subject. It probably spared me another round of paralysis.

"Well yeah," I said softly. "He's my best friend. She means a lot to him."

"You're a good egg, you know that?"

My mouth sprung into a smile, partly involuntary but also partly to lighten the mood for myself. Bryan leaned across the center console and kissed me, and when we parted, he promised to text me later. He had an important dinner to attend, so I left the car and stood in the driveway to send him off.

Good day, bad day ... they're all the same nowadays.

Woeful

NOW THAT MY mom's relationship with Sam was out of the bag, I felt oddly close to her. We'd never had much of a mother-daughter relationship before, so now there were little to no boundaries set up between us; Frankie was more like my sister than my mother because of it. My much older, preoccupied sister.

I could tell she still felt guilty about letting Leo inside, and after I informed her that he approached me in the parking lot as well, she promised to help me file a restraining order against him. It was going to be an exhausting process, but we took to it anyway, and that brought some relief to Mom, Bryan, and me. In fact, even though she had met him under unfortunate circumstances, Mom really liked Bryan and asked about him frequently.

I was sitting on that uncomfortable couch of ours on Thursday evening, waiting for a text back from him when

Mom switched on the news. Don't worry, there were no more death reports that day, but simply hearing Max Figuerra's voice brought about this panic that ate at me from the inside out. What if getting a restraining order would be the biggest mistake of my life? Leo could still access my mom, or Tommy, or Bryan. After all, Reba was still missing last time I checked, so it was plausible. Two days was a long time to be gone.

"You okay, kid?" Mom asked me upon seeing my saddened face.

"Bryan hasn't texted me back." I frowned.

"Aw, well, don't worry. I'm sure he's just busy."

"But since Leo won't be able to come after *me* anymore," I added frenetically, "what if he goes straight to you or Bryan?" It was strange letting her in on my exact thought process, but it also made for quite a therapeutic change.

She sighed. "Sweetie, he hasn't even been served yet. Besides, we can handle any threats that come to us. I'm pretty much always at home with you, and Bryan's a lot bigger than him."

"That doesn't mean he can dodge bullets *Matrix* style," I pointed out. I couldn't help but shudder at the mere image of him at gunpoint. Suddenly, all I could think about was the twigs reaching across my ceiling for the shadow of the boy. Were all of those twigs really revolvers pointed at Bryan?

Mom patted my shoulder but didn't say anything else. I shut my eyes and put my phone face down on the arm of the couch, hugging my knees up to my chest. Part of me believed in her rational words, but another sliver of my imagination was much too intrusive for my liking and convinced me Bryan was indeed dead—or about to be. I sent him another text just to be sure because there was virtually nothing I could do if he *wasn't* okay, but if he were, well … I could carry on like normal. All I wanted was normalcy. I would have *killed* for it.

Mom put on one of her cooking shows, so I dismissed

myself to go take a shower. The floor of the bathtub was tex-tured like cobblestone so I wouldn't slip, and there were little bars to hold onto, as well as cutouts in two of the three walls so I could sit if I felt my consciousness slipping away. These cautionary measures had been my dad's idea after my parents had to step in on one too many showers upon hearing my body thump against the floor.

That night, I only really needed to wash my hair, so after-wards, I drew myself a bath, and luckily, I didn't have to use any of the safety features. It was quite a pitiful bath, to be hon-est, because I didn't have bubbles or fizzers or flower petals or anything, really, except water that looked greenish against the off-white tub.

With my phone balancing dangerously on the edge of the tub, I checked my notifications every couple of minutes to see if Bryan had texted back, but to no avail. I dared to send him a third text message, and again it went unseen. I started to worry that I was annoying him, which wouldn't have been unheard of; he had previously told me about his meeting with a foot-ball scout that evening, something about the specific terms of his scholarship because it was a major deal. Supposedly this meeting was taking place over dinner, but I *knew* dinner didn't take four hours, even if it was really important food they were eating.

When my phone did buzz at last, it happened to be from Tommy. He said they had found Reba just outside of Banshee, and she was being escorted home by police. How she had got-ten there with no money, the Hicks family still doesn't know—but it sort of relieved me to know she was just out being a teenager and not sacrificing lambs or burning polaroids or lying lifelessly under the interstate. One less thing for me to worry about, right?

Now that I knew Reba was fine, I started to wonder what favor Leo had done for me, but the thought disgusted me.

Instead, I tried focusing on other things, such as my possibly dead boyfriend, the repercussions of this upcoming restraining order, my childhood friend's brutal death ... I was having an incredible night, as you can see.

Finally, when my hair was completely dry from my shower and I was getting ready to sleep, Bryan called me. I couldn't help but wonder if he knew how badly I wanted to hear his voice, safe and sound.

"Hello?"

"Hey." He sounded wide awake and perfectly serene. "Sorry dinner took all night. I would have answered your texts."

"I thought you might've been the first male victim," I admitted sheepishly, sitting upright with my back against the headboard in my pitch-black room. I shut my eyes and left them that way for a few seconds because staring into pure blackness without your eyes adjusting is terrifying; I felt like I was falling in a bottomless pit, surrounded by nothing but my creepiest musings. My fear of the dark had clearly continued into young adulthood. And it certainly didn't help that Bryan hadn't responded to my communications right away.

At length, I stood up and walked around a little bit, groping around the wall for the light switch. Pacing helped because I didn't want to associate my bed with thoughts of Bryan's demise. I'd never sleep again.

"I'm really sorry."

I changed the subject. "They found Reba. She's okay."

"Good, that's good," he said. Awkward.

"Well, now that I know you're alive," I chuckled, "how'd the meeting go?"

"Great!" he exclaimed. "They're giving me a full-ride."

"Oh my God!" I grinned, clenching my fist as I heard the news. "That's amazing! I had no idea you were that good." *Yikes.*

"I wish we'd gone out during football season so you could

see," he said. Every word sounded spirited and happy, so much so that I just knew he was smiling even though I couldn't see his face.

"I do love a man in uniform," I joked.

"Wanna FaceTime?" he asked me after his chuckles dwindled. I accepted the offer, nervous as this was our first video chat, but happy to be able to see his face after such a stressful evening. When we connected, he smiled immediately at me. "Aw, you're beautiful, Jamie."

"Stop it!" I blushed.

"You mind if I change? I'm still wearing my formal clothes," he said. I made a face of indifference, and he proceeded to unbutton his red shirt, slipping it off without replacing it. "Tell me about your day."

"Well, I haven't done much since I saw you last, but my mom and I are working on getting that restraining order," I reminded him. I had vowed to keep him updated on the process because he was still upset by Leo's advent toward me in the parking lot. I resumed, "But I have to admit the thought of it is making me kinda nervous. What if it turns out to be a fatal mistake?"

"How so?"

"Like, what if he goes after my loved ones knowing that'd be worse than actually killing me?"

Bryan shook his head and appeared to sit down on his bed. It didn't have any sheets on it. "I think you're overthinking it."

"Oh, I definitely am," I admitted lightheartedly. "It's hard not to, though."

"I know, I know." He sighed. "Do you wanna come over tomorrow after school? I could show you around my house. I think you could use some distracting."

"Sure."

After we ended the call, I finally drifted off to sleep in the early hours of the morning. I had trouble waking up to my alarm, but I managed to trudge through the day, my sole motivation being my trip to Bryan's house once that final dismissal bell rang. I had promised Tommy I'd hang out with him over the weekend, too, so I had more than one thing to look forward to. Things had started to pick up after all, despite the irregularities that composed my life.

Bryan's house was pretty similar in structure to Tommy's. It was split-level and had lots of elongated space as opposed to square; there was a large dining area connected to the living room, and his bedroom was at the end of a tapered hallway. It was much brighter and happier than my house because the furniture was all either white or birch, and my mom had a penchant for eloquent red walls and walnut-colored cabinets, one that left me squinting indoors due to the darkness. It was quite rejuvenating being in a place that was polar opposite to my home.

We sat down on the white sofa downstairs. Against the right wall, there were glass sliding doors leading out to a deck covered in various Adirondack chairs and a scorched fire pit. The Lukins had a beautiful backyard view—mine was just a forest of bamboo stalks that had swallowed countless frisbees and tennis balls. I complimented the landscape.

"Why, thank you." Bryan smiled. "That was honestly the selling point of the house when we first moved here. It's from, like, the sixties so it needed a lot of work."

"You guys did a great job on it then," I said, impressed. "My mom used the lawsuit money from my dad's surgery to remodel our kitchen, so I know what it's like." That was after she paid the mortgage in full, of course, and so we were stuck claiming curbside furniture for the other rooms of the house.

Bryan nodded. "I never knew about that."

I shrugged. "I don't talk about it much." He rested his arm

along the back of the couch and looked down at his lap for a moment. I could just tell he was going to deepen the conversation, so I brought my knees up to the cushion and turned toward him to get situated.

"Your mom kind of reminds me of mine," he told me. "It's been a while since I've seen her, but there's something so familiar about yours ..."

"Aww," I cooed, bringing my hand to his thigh right above the knee.

"While I was leaving your house last weekend," he added, "she told me she trusted me."

"Is that so?" I asked. He looked proud of himself. "I'm so glad I don't have to formally introduce you two now."

"Oh, me too." He chuckled. "And I don't think I'll have to formally introduce you to my dad or aunt—Jade talks about you a lot."

"What? Really?"

"She thinks it's bizarre that we're dating," he said. "She makes fun of me for having a girlfriend and all, but I get her back for dating Pete Windward. Did you know they've broken up three times?"

"No kidding!" I laughed. "Why's that?"

"He thinks she's still in love with Tommy—which she definitely is—but she's a master manipulator, so he doesn't realize he's being cast aside on her list of priorities."

"That's ... actually kind of sad," I remarked, and Bryan just nodded. "Pete's a good guy."

"Don't get me wrong—she *does* like him," he clarified, "but she has more than one fancy, if you will."

"Tommy's kind of out of bounds anyways," I hummed, not really thinking about what I said. Bryan's neck drew back a little ways at my odd statement, and I cringed at myself. "I shouldn't have said that."

"He saving himself or something?"

"No, nothing like that." I shook my head. "I *really* shouldn't elaborate on this, but remember that big fight he and I had?"

"Course, yeah."

"It happened because he likes me," I admitted. "Well, he said he loves me, to be exact." I felt conceited saying those words aloud, but I knew better than to downplay it for Bryan.

He raised his eyebrows and looked out in front of him, exhaling slowly as he processed this. "You are quite a popular flavor, then. And you're hanging out with him tomorrow?"

"Yeah," I said. "It's not like he's made a move on me or anything. And I always talk about you, so he knows I'm unavailable."

He grimaced. "That doesn't sound like such a good idea. He might think you're leading him on—or the opposite: trying to make him jealous."

I had never thought of it that way. I couldn't just stop hanging out with my best friend, though. Suddenly, it became very clear to me that Bryan was just trying to protect me, only I didn't know how to help the situation. I stared at him helplessly. "I really shouldn't have said anything. He's gonna find out."

"How?"

"The same way I found out he was spreading dirt about us," I suggested.

"Well, I'm not gonna tell him I know, so you don't have to worry." I sighed at him, pressing my back against the couch again. Just thinking about it stressed me out. "Also, I wouldn't necessarily call that 'dirt'."

"What would you call it then?" I asked.

"The future." He shrugged. "And that's not to pressure you. It's just that we've been going out for a few weeks and we're both eighteen, so it's—it's foreseeable, don't you think?"

"Well, now, that's an interesting way to put it."

It got me thinking: I've always wondered what it'd be like. Would I like it so much I'd fold over like a towel you tried to stand on its side? Would I fall asleep halfway through and potentially ruin my entire relationship? Would both of these things happen simultaneously, leaving me single *and* humiliated? There were many possible outcomes to take into consideration.

"Have you ever tried it by yourself?" he asked. Awkward question, I know, but he didn't sound pervy in the least bit.

"What? No!" I scrunched my nose up at the thought. I knew my face had rouged even though I couldn't see myself.

"It's not dirty." He laughed. "Look, I'm not here to judge you. I'd just like to know if you can handle it, you know? For future reference."

I chuckled. "I'll keep you posted."

Using the arm that was up on the back of the couch, he propped his head up on his hand and released what sounded like a content sigh. I could sympathize fully with his fulfillment because I had really started to enjoy how close we were despite my previous apprehensions.

When seven o'clock hit, Bryan and I had both gotten hungry. His dad came in through the front door as we walked up the stairs together, and he stopped us on the foyer to say, "You've got mail!" in the automated AOL voice.

Bryan flashed an intrigued look at me and proceeded to open the card-shaped envelope, revealing a solemn piece of cardstock with a marble pattern and gold lettering on it. He began to relay the message aloud, "In loving memory of Caroline B. Empfert ... shit."

Instead of finishing reading, he held the card against his chest so I couldn't see it anymore and stopped talking altogether. I looked up at his face to find that he had bitten his bottom lip and screwed his eyes shut, clearly enduring some self-inflicted chastisement. "You okay if I read this?" he asked softly, cracking his eyes open a sliver.

"I'm fine. Keep reading." He nodded at me and swallowed, though he read the rest of it in his head this time. I wondered if I had an invitation waiting for me at home, but I knew my mental state would prevent me from going to the memorial service. Bryan set it aside and led me the rest of the way upstairs so that we could forage for snacks.

"Hey guys," Jade said, briefly alarming me. She was sitting cross-legged on the floor in the living room with her right hand stuck under a UV light and the TV turned on, though I'd never seen the program that was playing before. There were numerous sample-sized bottles of nail polish sprawled out on the floor around Jade. "Missy should be here with pizza soon. Aleida too."

"Missy's my aunt," Bryan clarified for me. "She and my mom were fraternal twins." It suddenly made more sense why she lived with them.

"It must be nice seeing the resemblance in her all the time," I said, but Bryan shook his head at me.

"It's like living with a zombie. Mom's *gone*, but at the same time she's coming home with pizza as we speak. And from what I remember, their personalities are way different."

"Oh." I frowned. I'd never realized that could be a negative thing. If my father hadn't been an only child, I think I would have smothered his siblings to death. I decided to lighten the mood a bit. "Sam doesn't look like my dad at all—actually, he looks like my mom. But I still don't like him."

"Yeah?" We walked into his room. "How's it going with him?"

"Horrible. He's such a bottom." I huffed. Bryan raised his eyebrows and laughed at my affront, but I chose to expand on my point. "He just stands in the corner whenever I'm in the room, and when he does talk to me, it's all quiet and wary. I don't think he'd be a great patriarch."

"You think maybe you alpha'd him?" Bryan suggested. "I wouldn't be surprised."

"What's that supposed to mean?" I asked, plopping myself

down on Bryan's red comforter while he sat in his revolving office chair directly across from me.

"Some men can't handle strong-willed women." He smirked.

"You think I'm strong-willed?" I asked teasingly.

He spun from side to side in that chair but never disconnected his gaze from mine. "I do," he said. "But I think I can manage."

He stood up and joined me on his mattress, adjourning the use of words but insinuating a feeling with those finch-brown eyes of his. I let my smile fade in accordance and leaned backwards a little bit. Bryan followed, so I continued until my back touched the cherry-red comforter. Now poised on his side, he used one arm to keep his head up, placed the other hand on the side of my stomach, and hovered his face over mine to kiss me. I cupped my hands around his jaw for lack of anything more dexterous to do with them.

His skin was so warm in comparison to mine. It wasn't very soft on account of his light stubble, yet still pleasant to the touch. He smelled like black tea with a hint of flora, just like that night we'd spent at Cemetery Drive. Aromatherapy. And his hair felt almost cold because of how sleek and clean those locks were. I found myself raising my head up off the bed as if that made the sensation any more profound—but I'd never French-kissed anyone before, so all I could manage for now was to wait until *he* decided to advance. I wasn't offended by the idea.

I recoiled when his fingers started to travel down below my waist, and, like a gentleman, he retired his hand immediately. But I pulled it right back down; it had only been a brief discomfiture. Humming in satisfaction, he slowly but firmly grasped the space on my thigh below the hip, simultaneously pulling me toward his toned person.

He must have analyzed his new bout of confidence as a perfect opportunity to push his tongue into my mouth, so that he did, running it first over my bottom lip and then encroaching. It was warm and glacé, kind of like a Maraschino cherry on top of a sundae, if you will: sweet, sultry, desirable.

A ruined pair of hazel eyes entered my mind, and my heart skipped a beat. They were hooded and raw from weeping— they were Leo's.

By some God-awful instinct of mine, I shoved Bryan back by the shoulder with incomparable force and sat bolt upright, staring in horror at the floor where my legs hung off the edge of the bed. He didn't say anything at first but sat up with me and licked his lips, probably wondering just as much as I was what the hell had just happened.

"Uh, sorry if that was too much," he finally said, clasping his hands together awkwardly in his lap.

"No," I shook my head, turning to read his face, "*I'm* sorry. I-I didn't mean to push you. I really don't know what came over me 'cause I was enjoying … that."

"Well," he sighed, "are you okay?"

"I'm fine." I swallowed down a pellet of embarrassment, waiting for Leo's glare to dissipate from my imagination. What was he doing up there?

There came three all too quick raps at his bedroom door and a woman barged in; I was thankful I'd had that little paroxysm then because surely the humiliation of having a stranger see us make out would have stimulated a cataplexy attack if continuing to expand that kiss hadn't.

The woman in the doorway was young and energetic like an intern, as her knocking pattern had already proposed. She wore her thin hair straight down her back and bolded her blue doe eyes with black eyeliner wings. Chic. She had a deep dimple on the left side and a square jaw. I could see Jade in her, but with Bryan it was a bit harder. I knew this had to be the infamous Aunt Missy.

"Pizza's here," she said to Bryan, grinning in a way that

suggested she was incapable of frowning. She gave me a little scrunch of the nose and a wave of the hand, like she desperately wanted to say something embarrassing about Bryan but stifled it because she could put two and two together that we were preoccupied.

"We'll be there in a minute," Bryan said. "This is Jamie."

"Hi." I smiled at her, pumping my legs up and down as if the bed frame were a swing set.

"Pleased to meet you! Missy!" She waved once again and left us alone after that.

I turned to Bryan. "Now I'm kinda glad that happened." He chuckled, nodding his head.

"That woman does *not* wait long enough after knocking." He stood up and held his hand out for me so that we could go get some food, but before I joined him, I had something to say.

"Bryan?" He raised his brows in response. "Don't be discouraged. I'd like to do that again."

He smiled at me and helped me up. "Me, too," he said.

I fell asleep in the middle of eating and woke up with Bryan's whole family standing around me at the table. It made for a very interesting introduction—I'll just leave it at that.

Hush Money

I HADN'T GONE out to eat in a very long time. When I did, it was weird being around so many people I'd never seen before; I was too used to the same swarms of paranoid teenagers talking about who they willed all their Yeezys to for whenever they'd be murdered. I liked being around Bryan and Tommy and now even Jade, but I really needed a change of atmosphere every once in a while.

That's the only reason I wasn't completely pissed off about having to get an early dinner with Sam and only Sam. Mom suggested it as a bonding period and, although I was against it, I was also hungry enough to accept. Besides, I liked Panera.

We sat at a table by the glass wall looking out into the parking lot, where nature was recovering from a rainstorm. Sam said he was relieved I had agreed to go out with him when I could be spending time with Bryan or "Timmy." Then he told me a little about himself. I found out his last name was

Fredericks, he had a son named Matt, he was the president of a family-run HVAC company, and he had met my mother in a bar while I was out somewhere. He was indeed pretty funny, as Tommy had told me a week or two prior, but his general diffidence had kept me from learning that any sooner.

I told him Bryan and I had only been going out for a short time and that we skipped a lot of the icebreaker steps that usually take place when building relationships, hence our closeness. I also told him Bryan had lost his mom when he was little and that although he missed her, he had moved on by now; by saying that, I hoped to convey that I was okay with Sam dating my mom, for the most part. Of course, I still preferred to think of him as my mom's *friend*, not *boy*friend, but we made definite progress that day. It wasn't even five-thirty when we wrapped up, and since then, the clouds had fully parted. The humidity made my skin stick to the leather seats in his car.

"Your mom's gonna be really happy when I tell her about this," Sam said, glancing at me and then back at the road. "Or we could both tell her if you want. I think she'd appreciate that."

"Sure." I shrugged, resting my elbow against the window.

He said something else, but I don't remember exactly what it was and wound up dozing off. My little nap turned out to be quite lengthy—when I'm not disturbed, I can go into full bear-in-winter mode. Before long, though, I was disturbed awake by the doorbell's obnoxious ring. I was lying on my bed when Mom opened the front door, and she talked indistinctly for a minute or two before my ears perked at the words "restraining order."

"Oh, was there a problem with it?" her muffled voice asked the guest. "I've never really had to get a restraining order before, so … well, why don't you come on in?"

"I'm actually here to speak with your daughter," the guest corrected her. It was a woman's voice, and her Jersey accent was thick. "My brother has asked me to relay some information to her, but he knows she won't take it from him."

"And who are you exactly?" asked my mother. I could hear her words frosting over like morning dew in October.

"My name is Sofia Capodi," she said. "I'm Leo's older sister."

I went into the hallway as their exchange grew louder because I was afraid that if I kept hiding, my mom would send Sofia directly to my bedroom. I stole a glance at her in the living room, where she was sitting patiently on the couch with her back straight and her hands between her knees. Her face was round and zaftig, and her golden-brown hair was incredibly curly. Lioness. She donned a charcoal-colored pencil skirt and a matching blazer, so I knew she was a professional at *something*. If not, Leo had probably styled her with a "fake it till you make it" approach at getting to me. Either way, her getup was a wise choice. She was the most beautiful woman I'd ever seen, hence the name Capodi.

When I announced my presence at last, she stood up, buttoned her blazer, and extended her right hand out to me. I shook it, finding that it was clammy but strong. Her voice read like a doctor's in a pill commercial. "Hi, Jamie. I'm Sofia Capodi."

"Hi," I said timidly, glancing at my mother to see what she thought. She was standing behind the couch and shrugged at me. "Can I help you?"

"I'm here to ask a favor of you," she began, her pale eyes pleading with me as she tilted her head to the side. "I understand the kind of anguish Banshee is dealing with regarding the recent murders. Believe me, there are police officers coming in and out of my house every night, and my sister Tess and I are beyond stressed … yet I still firmly believe my little brother is innocent. Whether you agree or disagree isn't why I came here, however.

"Speaking as his big sister, it pains me to see Leo losing

sleep and regurgitating every meal he eats. Word of your situation against him got out, so now I'm *begging* you to cancel the restraining order. I'm a paralegal; I can reimburse you for any fees you've already paid, and I'll add interest. Just please consider this. He already feels less than human."

I remained silent.

A second later, an exclamation point appeared above Sofia's mane of mousse, and she reached casually into her blazer pocket, extracting a triple-folded piece of notebook paper. Black pen ink bled through; it looked amateur. "Leo wrote you this apology, and he wanted you to see the photo inside it. He didn't tell me why, but he said it was 'proof' and that you'll understand when you see it."

I accepted it cautiously, the photograph spilling out of it as soon as I touched the brittle paper. The back of the photo was dated to February twenty-eighth and said something in cursive that I couldn't quite make out, but it was the actual image that startled me upon looking at it for the first time. There, formed into a little semicircle in a dolled-up living room, sat seven people with their arms around each other: Nichole, Leo, Wes Martin, Teach, Sistine, Reba, and another guy in our grade named Joey Ramadhan. There was a picture of Mother Teresa suspended behind this ensemble and a Christian cross made out of wood hanging next to it. Everyone in the photo was wearing quartz beads around his or her neck, all variants of the rosary I'd seen Leo whip out of his pocket multiple times.

Bible study.

I can't remember much of the discussion I had with Sofia after looking at such a game-changing picture, but I do know my mother and I agreed to her terms. She left us with the letter, the photograph, and a blank check, none of which I could take my mind off of for the rest of the evening. I was too afraid to read the letter right away, but when I finally did, I was in shock.

Dear Jamie,

I am so greatful that your reading this. I know I been skating on thin ice lately, but I truly mean well. I wanted to say I'm sorry because your the first person that needs to hear it from me, out of everybody at Bridgewood. I would say it in person but you know. I didn't mean for you to fall over the first time I tried giving you this letter, so I rewrote it to be more deep. And when Bryan told me to f-ck off after that, I realized he only said that because he knows your afraid of me. Because why else would he say that to me, I'm his friend? Or <u>was</u> his friend. I don't really know. People don't talk to me no more minus Nichole and Sistine but I hate them, just like you, and they hate me too. I been praying for some strenth to confront them, no luck yet.

Your the most simpothetic person I know. When I came to your house, which I am also sorry for because I know I crossed a line there, you looked at me like you were starting to understand. I needed that. I know why you kicked me out though and I totally get it, but that really spoke to me.

So maybe you will hear me when I say I'm dying here. Literally. My hair is falling out. I don't eat no more, just drink water and coffee and sometimes yogurt cuz I think that's all my stomach can handle for now. I was kicked off the Messiers and can't go back to the rink no more, or the store or leave the state or drink or smoke or anything. I have to piss in cups. I just want a joint. Probetion really sucks, J. Can I still call you that?

They gave me 2 PO's, not 1. Dunno why. And their not even doing surprise visits, their almost always with me, till 9:00 pm in the evening when I basically go on house arrest. They said that has never happened to nobody before but me. So I really was not lying when I said I got cops up my ass. I am begging for your simpothy so that I can show my face, take a shower or do ANYTHING ever again without all the unesessary scrutiny. I'm so humiliated every time I walk into class. The teachers are scared of me and will not help me with HW. Even my teamates can't look at me no more. I'm on tender hooks here.

I'm waiting for the evidence to be analyzed already so this all gets over with. You can tell Banshee never dealt with this kind of thing before, or else I would be free by now cuz we'd be on a priorty list or something. I feel like this is a trial of Hell and God wants me to endure it, but I just can't do it alone.

That's another thing I been telling the truth about- Teach was hosting secret bible studys after school & on evenings on the weekend because she ain't allowed to teach creation in bio. Whoops, wasn't*. I miss her a lot. She was a rightious woman. Just look at the pic for proof. You can even ask Joey R. if it's true because he never lies. Please believe me, I was just learning about God and the beginnings of earth and humans cuz my family ain't really religous. Hahaha, I guess we don't fit the stereo type. That's the only reason I asked if you saw Nichole or Teach that 1 day a few months ago- I wasn't sure if we were still on for that night. (I know somebody told the police about that but IDK who).

Truth is, I really like you. I didn't always felt this way but ever since you got mad at me that one time, all I have wanted to do was make you forgive me some way or another and now I have a crush. And I know your with Bry now but that doesn't change how I feel about you at all. It would really help me out if you consider what I am saying. At least SOMEBODY deserves to take the high road.

You never have to talk to me again or look at me and I will 100% understand, but if you do except this letter, maybe even reply to it, I will know you have pardoned me and blessed me with your favor. "He that covereth his transgressions shall not prosper; but whoso confesseth and forsaketh them shall obtain mercy." I'll write my number at the bottom of the page. Use if you want. Thanks again.
Yours truly,
Leo
(908) 555-0159

Through the paper, which was slowly but surely becoming transparent, I could see two careworn lips moving, producing the words scribbled out before me on the crackly paper. Everything it said, I saw. And heard. I couldn't tell you whose voice it was. Eyes and a nose appeared slowly above the ever-moving mouth. And as he serenaded me, the man's hair glittered and rippled as though it were a moving pot of caramel; the smell, it was like a ballad. Strong, rustic. Eyes of hazel that appeared sleepy. But everything I visualized quickly dulled.

At the time, I couldn't put a name to this physiognomy I was seeing, yet he was achingly familiar. I reached my fingers up to stroke his ashen cheek only to find that it effloresced at my touch. The mirage began to dissipate, and again I was in a room by myself. He was permanently gone. *Who are you?*

Agent, I know my life has been woeful for as long as I've lived it. Narcolepsy with cataplexy; my father's death; the drama with Nichole, Sistine, and Reba. … All of it was pure, cyclical hell, and I wouldn't wish it on anyone. It definitely became worse the day Mrs. Tomlin was killed because that was when my idea of a daily routine, or, in other words, dealing with everyone's problems including my own, was flipped wayward. I had a crush who became violent and twisted, or so I thought. My best friend and I faced our own issues. I got a boyfriend. That last part isn't so bad, of course, and it was actually very therapeutic having another major figure in my life who was in no way connected to the madness. But survival became oh, *so* much harder when I read that letter. I was no longer the target; Leo was. He was a scapegoat, if you will, for all of the hell that *I* was living because he had been forced to deal with *my* heavy load when he somehow became known as the Banshee Murderer.

Something was off. I realized it when the mirage disappeared.

Hamlet

I HAD SOME trouble staying awake the following day. I'm one of those people who can't drink coffee to hype themselves up; some narcoleptics can, but if it contains caffeine, it makes my heart race and my stomach hurt. I'm much better off drinking ice cold water and dozing off every two hours, though it is an enormous nuisance.

It really didn't help that I had a completely new opinion of Leo *again* and that that was all I could focus on during classes. Without the facts, it was hard to say whether he was innocent or not, but my heart was leaning toward the latter. Perhaps he really *was* the Renaissance Man, a victim of society. *Perhaps.*

When I read his letter, the guilt and pity that it inculcated in me caused a cataplexy attack. I wasn't sure how I'd react when seeing him in person. Thankfully, I'd gotten myself used to the negativity surrounding him by then, so I could stand to look at him without feeling woozy or downcast.

I stopped him before I had to go to Calc because that was the first time I'd see him all day. He trudged past my locker, hair falling over his eyes, and flinched when I appeared beside him. His two officers followed us from a distance of about three yards, though they looked distracted. At this point, they were just there for show.

He stopped walking when he noticed me. "Shit," he uttered. "So, you got the letter? I put my number on it."

"I know," I said, "and I'll use it. But I thought I'd sound more sincere in person."

He nodded, gesturing at the wall so we could get out of people's way. "Is it okay for me to ... to talk to you? I dunno if you can do that or not."

"Is that a probation rule or something?" I asked. Then I realized he was only asking because he didn't want me to collapse on him again, so I held up my hand to stop him from explaining himself. "Look. Thank you for the letter. It made me feel a lot better."

"Yeah, no prob," he said, gripping his backpack strap tightly. His fingernails were bitten short and uneven, and the skin around them was red.

"But I can't really help you about the other thing you mentioned," I grimaced, referencing his crush on me. He made a face as if that went without saying, so I felt a little bad. "It's gonna take some time for this to feel normal again, so if I don't want to talk, please don't take it personally. Well ... you know what I mean."

"Course." He nodded.

"And I know you weren't lying." His stiff shoulders relaxed after he heard those words.

"Thank you so much," he said quietly. And then, in his normal, collected volume, he added, "I don't expect you to talk to the police or nothin' and try changin' their opinion. I'm just glad you know the truth. It's real hard bein' the only one to believe somethin' that big."

"Must be," I mumbled.

We were quiet for a moment, and then the late bell rang. Leo looked nervously over my head at the officers; it probably made him look even worse to be late to class. I started to lift my arms up, aiming to give him a half-hug, but I paused; he looked intrigued, refreshed. It was almost cute. Any render of emotion was a good look on him because his face had been blank for weeks.

"Will you get in trouble?" I asked.

"No." He chuckled, opening his arms back at me. We dropped our backpacks on the floor, and I stood on my toes and hugged him, though it was wholeheartedly, not half like I'd intended. He put his chin on my shoulder and touched my hair. When I let him go, I manifested a tight-lipped, slightly uncomfortable smile, grabbed my belongings off the floor, and proceeded to walk around him before I could glimpse any other emotion that played out on his face. I feared how that might make me feel.

Bryan happened to be leaning against the threshold at the mouth of the hall, his eyes alone bearing the most disappointed look I'd ever seen on him. He didn't look sad or jealous, just annoyed.

"You're still standing," he said to me when I was within earshot.

I hadn't told him about the letter. I figured I'd get around to it eventually, just like I had with my Tommy issue. That time it seemed to work out fine.

"I am." I looked straight ahead of me as we started toward the math wing. His eyes were glued on mine, and I could see in my periphery that he was not going to let this go anytime soon.

"Well?" he demanded, stopping. His voice practically echoed in the desolate hallway. "What the hell was that?"

I could feel my cheeks flaming up. I was already dead tired,

so this conversation was really difficult for me to have. In a re-
stricted voice, I confessed that Leo said he liked me. Better to
rip the bandage off than suffer for longer. I could feel a sleep
attack coming on very soon.

Bryan laughed. "You're kidding, right?"

"No, I'm not." My voice was monotonous.

"Jesus fucking Christ," he spat, startling me. He slapped his
hands down to his sides in resignation. "When are you gonna
realize you can't treat people like this?"

"Like what?" I scoffed. I looked over my shoulder to find
that Leo and the cops were gone, which was probably a good
thing. For Leo's sake.

"Exactly, you don't even realize it. You continue to get
Tommy's hopes up *every time* you hang out with him. Now
you're making yourself late to class to get friendly with only
the most dangerous *thing* in the *state*. And don't act like you
don't toy with me, either—every other day I see you flirting
with some guy I'll never be. Chris, Leo, whoever the hell cross-
es your path. You think it's okay with me 'cause you're not used
to the attention, but it's not."

"Excuse me?" I said loudly. "When did you get so insecure?
There's a reason I hugged him just now."

"So, he's not just one of your hundred-and-eight suitors, is
he, Penelope?"

I realized that if I escalated this conversation any further,
there'd be consequences, so I walked away from him with
steam pouring out of my ears. He was mature enough to know
that by evading confrontation, I was only protecting myself,
but he hollered something foul at me as I left, and if it's all
right with you, I'd rather not repeat it. It's not important to
the case. I collapsed to my knees in the middle of the hallway,
and he hurried to break my fall, but no words were exchanged
after that.

I fell asleep for all of Calc and missed an important lesson that my class was later tested on. Next was lunch period, which I realize I've never taken you through—but that's wholly because lunch was even more boring than the three study halls I had on either end of my schedule. I never sat in the cafeteria with the rest of my class but instead brought a trayful of cardboard "heart healthy" food to what used to be Ms. Stratford's classroom. Temp was still filling in, but she allowed Tommy and me exclusive access into the room for lunch because we were "diligent students."

Boy, did I have a story to tell him.

"*Heeeeey*," he sang upon seeing me in the back of the room, where we both sat for class. Sometimes, we met up in the hall on the way to lunch, but other times we got caught up in the cafeteria line and came at different intervals. This was one of those days.

"Hey," I droned back, resting my cheek on my fist as I scooped potato chips into my mouth.

"Yo, what's the matter?"

"Bryan." I sulked. I didn't really want to talk about what had happened with Leo, so I had some difficulty phrasing my exact problem. "He's … I … I messed up."

"How so?" Tommy furthered, slapping a carton of juice down onto my tray. He hated the school juice but bought it for me because I didn't.

"Let's just say you were right about me being selfish." I shook my head slowly in self-disgust; the longer I thought about it, the more defeated I felt. *Ha. This is everything a selfish person would say.*

He chuckled a little. "You gonna have to elaborate on that one, J. And for the record, I was talkin' outta my ass when I said all that."

"Well, I hugged a guy in the hallway," I started, "and Bryan saw it, and now he thinks I'm a manipulative bitch because apparently that's a common thing for me to do. God, why do I have to be like this?"

"He said that?" Tommy gawked, but I gave him a look with my eyes that told him I was exaggerating. "Hey, it's okay, J. I know he ain't a bad guy. Maybe he's havin' a morning."

"He called me Penelope," I whined, slamming my hand down on the tabletop. It frustrated me that he was defending Bryan and not me, but in retrospect, I know that was the right call.

"Who?" Tommy, just barely clinging onto his Honor Roll claim, asked.

"Never mind."

I ate the rest of my crummy meal in silence so that I could listen to him for the remainder of the period. Tommy was always so cheerful and always had something to say, so his words comforted me when little else could. Afterwards, I had Physics and then would return for English, so my day was pretty back and forth, aside from Tommy's unpredictable anecdotes. My undulating schedule didn't help me feel any more energized. Excessive daytime sleepiness can be a major pain.

The next time I saw Bryan was in English. He contributed his normal amount to the discussion, though the way he argued with Temp was weirdly affectionate, as were her responses to whatever whimsical thing he happened to say. It reminded me of his banter with Stratford, only this time around, I actually cared about him enough to read into it. Eventually, I nodded off, though it only lasted for a minute or two because there was a noisy controversy going on about a scene in *Hamlet*. I'm not even sure if it was real.

"Ophelia's just *copying* Laertes," declared Emily Hoke, one of the girls who sat off to my right with Aleida and formerly Caroline. "She's just trying to tell him that his advice was stupid. It doesn't make her any deeper as a person."

"But it does," Bryan argued, spinning around in his backless stool to look Emily in the eye; she groaned right away, hinting that her input hadn't been an invitation for further discussion. He never once looked at me, but somehow, I still felt attacked. "She's using his words to remind him that hypocrisy is a sin and that if he wants to take the high road, he should heed his own warning when he goes to Paris. The fact that she came up with that on the spot makes her, by definition, *deep*."

"Very nice, Lukin." Temp nodded slowly. "Because Ophelia makes these quick remarks, it inspires pity in the audience when she loses her mind. You're meant to sit back and think to yourself, 'What a shame!' when reflecting over this scene after reading *Hamlet* in its entirety."

I never liked *Hamlet* much, so this entire discussion felt like a hallucination to me. Twisted and ambiguous.

"If I may," Bryan added, raising his hand—something I'd never seen him do in all of four years. Temp gave him an encouraging nod, resting her elbow on her desktop and leaning toward him as if she were slowly watching him come upon a realization that she had already known. His body was still facing Emily, but his eyes were on the instructor for a long moment, and then he slowly dragged them across the room like it were a panorama and landed on me with sluggish intention: "It really is a shame Ophelia spiraled out because Hamlet *loved* her. Yet she was told from the get-go that it was wrong and believed it herself, and I think that's a major theme some of us tend to overlook."

Silence followed. The class was convinced.

I sat upright and brought my eyes down to my lap, trying hard not to let his words get to me. But they did. Tommy glared at him and put his hand on my back as soon as the class advanced to another debate-worthy *Hamlet* topic. Tears burned the corners of my eyes, but nothing happened after that; I could not pass out in front of Bryan during a time like this, not again. I needed to be strong. It took everything in my power to think of something happier.

Using all that power then led me to fall asleep again in my final study hall before riding home with Tommy and Reba.

"Don't Look Back in Anger"

AFTER SCHOOL THAT day, I was in a major downswing. I sat in the shower for an hour, wasting the hot water away and soaking in its steam. In the meantime, I toggled between the ways I could try to contact Bryan regarding the English class incident.

I could text him, but I didn't want to seem pathetic and too scared to talk about it in person, even though I was. So, I ruled that out for the moment.

Then there was the option to call him, but the problem with calling was that I had no clue what to say. My ego was so inflated, I simply couldn't tell him he was right; in fact, if I did that, it could translate as "you're right" *and* "I'm just using you." That was not what I wanted to tell him at all. Besides, Tommy had convinced me he *wasn't* right. That he was just being irrational due to unexplained and unrelated stipulations.

I went back to the option of texting him and sent a simple

Hey. Its solemn end punctuation would certainly gather Bryan's attention. I had yet to plan out my defense, but when he read the message and ignored it, I had nothing better to do than call him and get it over with. Indecision is an ass, and I was at a loss no matter which road I took. Luckily, he picked up after a couple of rings.

Without saying the usual "Hello?" greeting, he skipped right to the chase. "Jamie, I don't feel like talking." His deep voice startled me, and his cursory words were no more assuring. "I don't either," I empathized. "Look, you already made your point. I just want to make mine."

After a brief, breathy pause, he agreed, "All right."

"You weren't wrong about me not being used to the attention," I said, squeezing my eyes shut and pinching the bridge of my nose. It was actually *hard* producing those words, double-negative and all. *How embarrassing.* "When Leo first started talking to me on a regular basis, I'll admit, I was into him. *At the time.* But all of his problems brought me this horrible amount of stress, which you've seen yourself. He recently gave me a letter explaining what went wrong and where, and he mentioned that he liked me and that was why he chose to write to me of all people. I really didn't mean to make you upset by hugging him today, I just … I felt for him. I'm seeing him with different eyes now."

"What about the restraining order? You just change your mind or something?"

"Yes," I sighed, "after reading the letter. Bryan, he had his *sister* come to my house and deliver it to me. I'll let you read it, too, if you want. He was just desperate."

"I see," he mumbled, still unconvinced.

"What you said about how I act around Tommy was probably true, too. But you have to understand that I haven't suddenly started hitting on him, or rubbing you in his face, or acting any different. We've had this same dynamic since we were kids, and I can't just up and change that. If I did, he'd know some-thing was wrong. He'd wanna go back to the way things are now. You have to trust me."

"And as for me?" So, he'd been waiting for this three-pronged apology after all.

"I am *so* sorry for jeopardizing our relationship like this," I told him. My voice broke as I apologized; there were no tears, but still I was very uncomfortable. I had to sit down on my bed to avoid concussing myself if I should go limp and fall. "I'm working on being less selfish, I really am. I don't know what to do to fix this though. I guess I could avoid Leo for some time … no, that's stupid. I dunno. But I'll fix it. I—"

"Hey. Hey," Bryan intervened as I started to spit out words that didn't make sense together. For that, I was thankful. His voice was already much lighter and more forgiving.

"What?"

"About the 'major theme' you missed in English today," he began. It didn't seem relevant, but there was an inkling of hope in his voice all of a sudden that made me curious.

"I was kinda hoping talking about it would solve that issue?"

"Well, hold on," he insisted. "The point was that, in a way, Ophelia was trained to look at her romance like it's forbid-den because of … certain aspects of her life. But you start to wonder whether she loved him half as much as he loved her, and maybe some of her external affairs—such as hugging a suspected serial killer—are what caused the confusion in the first place."

I was certainly not anticipating that. The message was crys-tal clear, but I still wanted to be wary. I wondered if his little speech meant he forgave me or just that he was all the more hurt because of the profundity of his feelings for me—but either way, I found myself relieved. I shut my eyes as the con-solation crashed over me in waves. I felt like I'd finally snapped out of my trance and could see clearly now that I wasn't so tense. My third eye had been crusted shut until that moment.

"Bryan?" I asked, the word sounding like a breath of air.

"I know why Tommy, Leo, and I all like you, Jamie. You're an oasis."

"I—"

When I tried to move my jaw, my mouth remained open. My phone slipped out of my fingers and descended into the narrow space between my headboard and the wall; I found my world tipping sideways as I fell onto my pillows, and my eyes welled up with tears. Had I any control of my face I would surely have been smiling even bigger, but I didn't, so I couldn't. The "up" volume button on my phone must have been pressed when I dropped it; I could hear perfectly as Bryan asked me repeatedly if I was okay, if I'd gotten weak, whether he should hang up or not, and more.

What really delighted me though, was that he *didn't* hang up. All ninety seconds of waiting for me, he uttered out little worried phrases until I showed any sign of understanding. That had been an unusually long time for me to remain immobile, but alas I picked up my phone from the dusty depth, finding a new crack in the bottom left corner of the screen, though that was the least of my concerns. I was planning to ask Bryan if he could come over as soon as I regained mobility, though I discovered he was already driving when I lifted the device to my ear and heard the mellow hum of tires on asphalt. What a coincidence.

He arrived at my house in a matter of seconds. I zipped past Mom and Sam in the living room and went straight out the front door, only to be cut short once again: Bryan was already standing there. Our synchronization that night was unmatched.

I didn't say anything to him, just grinned and put my arms around his neck. We both knew what we were feeling, and there was no need to spoil the moment by speaking. I often find that words are just obstacles when trying to express my

truest, deepest emotions—the common man will find this ap-
palling, as words are his only platform. Before that moment, I
had never thought that that degree of cheesiness was realistic,
but I learned that it definitely is. I'd had my *Notebook* moment,
and there was no going back from that. We were cemented.

Bryan's eyes twinkled as he let out an alleviated chuckle.
"Thank God for *Hamlet.*"

I laughed at him, feeling lighter in weight. Because of the
fight we'd had, I had been so scared that I'd ruined things that
this encounter felt like heaven.

"That's never happened to me before," I said.

"What?"

"I've never had a cataplexy attack for any *good* feeling." In
retrospect, that may have been an accidental lie, but any other
time that *could* have happened was long bereft of me.

Judging by his silence, I could tell he didn't know what to
say. Then his gaze shifted over my head for a brief moment.
"We've got company."

I spun around slowly, leaving one arm looped around his
waist while we both peered through the open threshold. There
Mom was, waving awkwardly as she began to close the front
door. She reminded me a bit of Bryan's aunt Missy in that she
hadn't exactly been invited, only my mother was much demur-
er than Missy had ever been.

"Hi, Mrs. Hessen." Bryan waved to her, a big smile on his
face. I remembered him saying my mom reminded him of his
own, and that made me happy in turn.

"Hi, sweet pea." She smiled back, excusing herself: "I was
just shutting the door. Be back by nine, okay, Jamie?"

I shrugged up at Bryan. "I guess we're going somewhere."
He nodded in the direction of his car, guiding me to it with
the hand he kept on my shoulder. He didn't tell me where we
were headed, but then we wound up on Cemetery Drive. How
sweet.

"We were just here about a month ago," he remarked as he parked beside that wondrous cliff. "Crazy how time goes by."

"Look at you, being all poetic." I chuckled.

To anyone else, he wouldn't seem like the type of person to be so seduced by a good piece of literature, but I'd gotten to know him well enough to acknowledge that that was a major part of his personality. English was the one class he seemed to care about, whether he was good at it or not, and football was a decent escape from the other boring subjects he had to endure. Those were his brand: literature and athleticism.

I know I told you Tommy thought Bryan was shallow and audacious. In fact, most of Bridgewood thought that about him, but that's not the point. Now that he had developed a rapport with Temp similar to the one he'd had with the late Ms. Stratford, Bryan's Parnassian nature would soon be writ large in Tommy's eyes, and whatever jealousy might have existed in my friend would evaporate. He would finally see the acumen that I so admired in Bryan.

And even though I had already detoxed enough that day simply by professing my love for Bryan to myself, I *still* felt much better when I acknowledged Tommy's indifference. I wouldn't have to bicker with him anymore because he was starting to see that I was right and that I had taste. I suppose that's not important now, but back then that was something I held in high significance.

Bryan and I sat down on the ground with our backs against the side of his car like it was April all over again, only warmer this time around. He had some of his music playing at a medium volume from inside the vehicle; the playlist consisted of all variations of nineties rock, ranging from Oasis to Nirvana to Semisonic. They were interesting choices coming from him, though I thought his music taste made his affinity for literature all the more exciting. Maybe he looked at lyrics the same way he looked at classic novels.

"I was having a really hard day today," I told him, "but now I completely forget why."

"Good."

We went home long before nine o'clock. Visiting Cemetery Drive wasn't supposed to be this huge milestone but rather just a reminder that things were okay between us, and that they would probably remain that way for a while. Seeing as everything around us *wasn't* okay, that visit was much needed. Cathartic, almost. Like we'd been baptized.

All of this is irrelevant to what was going on in Banshee, though, because while I was still awake that night at three in the morning, a sickening realization came upon me:

If Leo was innocent, which I truly believed he was at this point, then the killer was still out there.

Roaming.

Reba Hicks

I KNOW I'VE been talking a lot about my relationship and its seemingly minor details, but I believe they're pertinent to your understanding of why I started regaining my trust for Leo when I did. I had been going to Bridgewood School District with him for my entire life, and given that there weren't even five hundred high-school-age people in the county, it's safe to say that his life was an open book. Fear had stood in the way of the truth, even for me.

Everyone knew he had been an athlete since he was in diapers, hockey being his strong suit.

Everyone knew his mother, who worked for Armani online, had inspired his unparalleled fashion sense.

Everyone knew he went to Mount Crew Barber, run by Aleida Brown's grandfather.

Everyone knew he had gotten a 1000 on the SAT and that school was just an obstacle for him; he was waiting to get drafted by the NHL.

Everyone knew he was nowhere near intelligent enough to be a scheming murderer—or at least *I* knew that. Other people believed what they wanted to believe. I knew he couldn't have faked his anguish regarding the four deaths, nor could he have pretended to be alarmingly thin. His entire act looked authentic because it wasn't actually an act.

These thoughts coursed through me for hours, days, and eventually weeks on end, but I'm not at that point yet. Every time I looked at the back of his head in English and saw him slouching in between Officers Petty and Hart, I felt crushed. There was a crop circle around him; no other students dared to sit within a two-chair radius of him. I could breathe just fine, and my muscles still had full control over themselves, of course, but my soul? It had been severely marred.

Injustice is one of the hardest things to behold and not have the power to change. It truly scars you.

So, after English period one Friday afternoon, I told Tommy not to wait for me for study hall while I lingered in the back of the room after class was over. Bryan said his dramatic farewell to Temp and me and left. Sistine and Nichole followed him out, skipping while giggling about the fact that the former had received six more hours of detention in that period alone. Reba piled her belongings into her backpack at an amazingly slow pace. Leo finished typing something up on his phone, the POs standing impatiently behind him; it had become regular for him to be the last person in and out of the classroom. Everyone was in their own little world until I interrupted them.

"Excuse me," I said to neither officer specifically. The female one, Hart, turned around and raised her stenciled eyebrows at me ever so slightly in response. "May I speak to you about a concern I have?"

"I'm not your guidance counselor."

"No, I know ..." I started, my face heating up in seconds,

"it's about Leo."

At that, three heads snapped up in spirit of inquiry: Leo's, Officer Petty's, and Reba's, even though she was excluded from the conversation. I gulped deeply, afraid that I was doing the wrong thing. It certainly was weird having all eyes on me for once.

"Whatcha doin', J?" Leo asked me quietly, lowering his head as if it made his question any more secretive. He looked bewildered that I'd spoken out.

"We all know it," I whined, glancing from him to the police and back. "There's still a murderer out there. I don't feel any safer just because *you* have two policemen on you."

"Should we consider this a tip, young lady?" asked Petty. I opened my mouth to speak as he grabbed a notepad from off of his utility belt, but I ended up shaking my head, and so he put it back, tutting in disappointment. I was embarrassed.

"I trust your methods completely, but I don't feel that you're focusing on the right person," I explained to them timidly. I might have contradicted myself with that one, but I was nervous.

Reba loomed out of my periphery and appeared on my left. "I agree with Jamie. We need a bigger task force at the very least. We don't feel safe here, and it's not because of Leo."

Petty and Hart shifted uncomfortably, but Leo stood back a little ways, his eyebrows slanted upwards with gratitude for our adventitious intervention. He looked at me, teary-eyed, like I was proposing marriage to him. I was surprised Reba was on my side, but I didn't have time to question it or look as flummoxed as I felt—doing so would only weaken our stance anyway.

"Look, ladies, there's nothing we can do," Hart said apologetically. "You can call the police station and maybe speak to the lead detective about the issue in your own time, but we have a specific duty to fulfill here, and it isn't messin' with the case. Sorry."

"Best be going, Capodi," Petty added with a dramatic sweep of his arm toward the door; he had completely lost focus of Reba and me. The two officers shepherded Leo out of the classroom, and they were gone in seconds. I looked around and saw that Temp had been eavesdropping.

"Ladies," she said as soon as we were alone, beckoning us over to her desk. "You said you feel unsafe on school premises? If so, you need to report that."

"It ain't just here, it's everywhere I go," Reba complained. Her voice sounded strained yet fierce, like this was a topic she had disclosed many times unto deaf ears. I could hear pieces of Tommy in her pleading tone.

I took a second to look at her after registering what she had said. So, it seemed she was feeling *personally* targeted. Was that the reason she ran away from home?

"Those cops ain't doing jack shit," she added. Temp made a face of disapproval at the profanity, but she let Reba continue. "My best friends think I'm crazy, but I-I've been getting death threats."

Temp was suddenly at a loss for words as she fumbled around her desktop for the landline, though it didn't look like she knew who to call, so her fingers remained on the phone for a couple of seconds. Her eyes never left Reba's. "Death threats? From whom?"

"Uh … anonymous."

"And what are they saying?"

"A lot of things." She shrugged. "'Be careful.' 'Don't go to sleep.' The like." The way she rattled them off, it sounded like she had had some time to get used to those warnings.

I took some deep breaths as she listed the threats to Temp. After hearing them, it made even less sense to me that she hadn't gone to the police first and filed an actual report. When we were dismissed, both carrying late passes despite my not needing one, Reba and I walked in silence, hanging our heads. There had been *something* left unsaid back there. I didn't know what it was, but I knew she hadn't given the whole truth. And it made me uneasy.

"I had no idea," I said to Reba suddenly. We both stopped walking.

"Well how could you? We don't talk or nothing."

"I know," I said. "Look, you're not crazy. You can't believe when people tell you that, especially when it's Sistine and Nichole. Everyone should be as on-edge as you are."

"But ain't you biased?" Reba asked. "Sis, sure, she's a little excited. But Nicky's real smart. Nobody knows me as good as her."

I didn't know what to say. Reba obviously knew them better than I did, and that was valid, but I stood my case that Sistine and Nichole alike were in over their heads—both were too apathetic about other people to care about the crimes going on and had surmised that Reba was "crazy" for thinking otherwise. A small part of me missed Reba. If we were still best friends, who knows whether she would have received those threats? Or if there'd be any murderer to fear at all?

The more I thought about the transactions of my childhood, the more they seemed to affect the present day.

"I know you're just trying to help, but I'm still alive, so I think I can do this."

"Wait," I demanded, putting my hand on her gaunt shoulder. "They called you crazy 'cause you're being *threatened*. Doesn't that raise a red flag?"

She hesitated before admitting that it did.

"You did the right thing just now," I reassured her. "We can keep contacting the police. They have to hear us eventually."

The longer she stood there silently, the more anxious I grew. I finally took my hand off her shoulder as her lips began to twitch and her pinkish eyes glossed over with tears.

"Sis and Nicky can't know about this, okay?" she cried, gesturing from me to her with her pointer finger. I nodded my head nonstop. "They find out about everything, but they *can't* know about this. They found me when I ran away—makes me wonder if anyone else could."

"They won't figure this one out," I promised. She lunged forward and wrapped me in a frantic embrace, her skeletal form trembling against mine. I wondered if she had lost weight for the same reason Leo had, or if she was naturally that skinny—I had never paid special attention to her appearance until that day. She was actually rather pretty.

I offered Reba my phone number in case she wanted to talk about her situation more, and she accepted it reluctantly. Was Nichole so controlling that she looked through her friends' phones? I told her to text me whenever she needed to and then I headed straight for study hall, where Tommy's mind was about to be blown.

Sadly, in reality, he wasn't convinced the armistice between Reba and me had actually happened. But I could tell there was some skepticism lying underneath his denial.

Initially, I didn't think it was a big deal that Tommy thought I was deceiving him, but then I thought about it, too, and realized it might have made Reba's situation much worse. If Tommy wouldn't believe she simply *spoke* to me, who would believe she was being threatened? Especially if her best friends wouldn't?

Thus, another reason injustice stings worse than anything.

Helter Skelter

CAROLINE'S MEMORIAL SERVICE, which I had indeed been invited to, fell on a Sunday in the end of May. I had been preparing myself for it specifically so that my attendance could help commemorate the beautiful human being that had been Caroline Empfert, and with some light persuasion, my mom agreed to let me go. Bryan and I carpooled together.

The day was warm and sunny, though slightly tainted by the events that were sure to occur. The Empferts had reserved the local park for the afternoon and set up a table under the pavilion to be covered in photos, jewelry, artwork, and more of Caroline's memorabilia. It was like having a second wake for the lost daughter. Looking around at all of her school friends and seeing how torn they were was difficult, but it became even harder when I noticed Sistine and Nichole there, too, sulking in the opposite corner of the pavilion from Bryan and me.

I tugged on his sleeve as soon as I laid eyes on them. "Hey."

"Hmm?" he answered, leaning down a bit so as to keep the conversation between us; we didn't want to disturb the quietude of the memorial.

"I didn't think they'd be here," I said, nodding at my enemies. They were just sitting there, really, Nichole in a Regina-George-type outfit and Sistine in "Complicated"-era Avril Lavigne attire. Neither was dressed for the occasion, which is probably why I noticed them from in between large swarms of people.

"They were her friends," Bryan told me, putting his hand on my shoulder. He was my voice of reason that day. "Bitchy or not, they deserve to be here."

I took a deep breath and nodded in acceptance. We found Tommy and Reba, who suddenly seemed *light years* closer to one another, as soon as they arrived at the service.

"Hey," I greeted them. Tommy hugged Bryan and me while Reba nodded at us civilly, glancing at her friends in the corner.

"I feel bad for them Empferts." Tommy clicked his tongue and shook his head at the matter.

"Hey, Jamie?" Reba said, tilting her head to the side so I'd come and speak with her privately. When we separated from Bryan and Tommy, who were chatting like they'd been friends forever, she said to me, "I was thinkin' one of us could call the police station tonight and talk to the detective like that cop said."

I nodded. "Sure. We don't really have any evidence, though."

"If you don't got any evidence, why'd you even bother sayin' something?"

I paused, embarrassed. In reality there was the letter, the photo, the gut feeling ... but it all seemed phony when I envisioned myself telling *you* about it, and that was why I denied its status as evidence at first.

"Well, I guess I have *something*."

Reba nodded, content with my words, and tapped Tommy

on the shoulder so that they could find a seat together. Bryan and I split away, too, and ended up standing behind one of the many tables to listen to the Empferts speak.

Soon after everyone had arrived and paid their respects to the family, Mrs. Empfert called our attention. With her husband's arm around her back and her hand clutching her son's, she said a few words of gratitude that we were all gathered there. Then Mr. Empfert read some biblical passages that were probably also read at the funeral weeks before, and he opened the floor for anyone who had anecdotes to tell of Caroline.

The first taker was Jordan, her younger brother. He recited some original lyrical poetry that had been written for her at an earlier time, apparently even before she passed. The melancholic words fit perfectly for the nostalgia and sorrow that hung over us all on that too-bright day. I was surprised at his depth, seeing as he was only in seventh grade. *Way to go, Jordan.*

A few students from school, including Peter O'Quinn, followed shortly after Jordan with their own forms of release. I forced myself not to cry, especially during the happy stories that were told. In fact, I was enjoying the light atmosphere, relatively speaking.

After everyone who wanted to had spoken, I went to use the porta potty located about thirty yards behind the pavilion. It was in plain sight, yet also completely hidden from the event. It had been occupied until I got there, for then the door swung open and foul odors wafted out. The person inside had been Sistine, who was using her shirt as a mask from the smell.

She plucked the fabric off of her nose when she saw me and slammed the door shut—it would have stayed open if not slammed, for the grass was so tall and unkempt that it blocked the latch seal. Her gray eyes softened a bit from their naturally hard glare, but only for a moment. I was genuinely confused by that look she gave me.

"Could I talk to you for a sec?" she asked. The wind carried her ponytail from side to side and rustled her shapeless T-shirt.

"Uh, I guess, yeah." Weird.

She beckoned me around back of the toilet, stuffing her hands in her deep cargo pockets as I joined her in the privacy of a warped porta-potty-shaped shadow. She sighed heavily upon escaping the sunlight. Her eyes still remained savage, though now they were cloaked in shade.

"I just wanna say sorry." She sighed, her lips pinched tightly as if she were suppressing a smile. Was this a prank? She continued on, "I know me harassin' you ain't been making all these killings much easier to handle." *I could care less, actually.*

"Thanks." I nodded even though I was bothered. Her grammar was worse than Leo's (who, if you must take note, didn't show his face at the service), and I practically needed a translator for what she said. I still wasn't convinced she was being genuine, especially because of that twitch in her lips—but I couldn't just *say* that to her.

"We know you was talking to Reebs, too," Sistine added. I furrowed my brow. *They really do find out about everything.* "So, I figured it wouldn't look so weird if me and you was talkin'."

I shifted my weight. "Then why are we hiding behind a porta potty?"

She finally gave in to the muscular dictation of her face and grinned at me, drawing her right hand out of her pocket very slowly as if she were working with a landmine. A pocketmine, maybe. She stepped back with one foot as if to take aim and pointed a finger-gun at me, pretending to shoot me in various places with the imaginary firearm. I was too bewildered to second-guess her reaction to my question.

The pattern in which her hand moved was extraordinary: it was sluggish and poised and looked almost like she were trying to gesture the sign of the Cross onto me, for she'd aimed the pistol at my forehead, my chest, my left shoulder, and lastly my right. Unmirrored. Like she wanted me to do it myself, but

I wasn't cooperating. I remembered seeing her crooked smile in that photo of the bible study session, and that was initially when my heart began pounding out of rhythm, but I kept my ground and waited for her to speak. Suddenly, I didn't have to pee anymore.

"Just so crazy how all these people keep dyin' and all." She giggled. What the hell was so funny? "Just hopin' you ain't gonna be one of 'em 'cause this is rough stuff. Hopin' *I* ain't gonna be one of 'em neither, or Nicky."

She didn't say anything about Reba. No wonder the poor girl felt so alienated by, arguably, her only friends.

I can't explain why exactly my chest hurt after hearing that, but it did, and I had some difficulty taking full breaths. There was this pressure fizzing up in my lungs that only made my anxiety harder to manage. Nobody could see me except for Sistine, a notably disturbed person who was currently *laughing* about the murders even though she seemed nervous about them herself, so my fear was pretty justified. I tried to take a step away from her but only backed myself into the porta potty. I was officially cornered. I wanted Bryan.

Sistine started to lift her other hand out of her pocket as well—innocent enough—and thumbed her belt loop tauntingly. Something about the simple motion, slow as it was, spread a fire in me. I gasped and fell straight forward, my cheek unfortunately crashing into her stomach during my plunge; she cursed at me in disgust, freeing her hands from her pockets, and violently shoved me off of her. There was grass in my mouth for a solid minute before I could move again, and my face was turned away from the direction of the pavilion. The weeds were so tall I was practically buried in green and brown.

When I finally stood up and walked around the porta potty, Sistine had returned to the service and was standing in a triangle with Reba and Nichole, like old times. There were fewer people present. I brushed some dirt off of my knees and dress and walked back, frustrated.

Bryan saw me on my return to the pavilion and met me halfway. He suggested we leave, and I couldn't agree more. I was freaked out. But in the car on the way back home, Bryan noticed something: "You got dirt on your face."

"Oh," I said, flipping the mirror open so I could brush it off, but he reached over and did it for me. "Yeah, I … I passed out by the porta potty."

"What, and nobody saw you? What happened?"

"*You* didn't see me either," I said, and he frowned. "I'm not upset. I just fell asleep."

I wish I hadn't lied to him.

I was video chatting with Bryan at around seven o'clock that evening. I wanted to hang out in person, but I had just woken up from a long sleep attack and wasn't quite awake yet, an important detail.

"I just feel bad for talking to you when you sound so sleepy." Bryan smiled at me, flustered. He was laying down on the couch in his living room with his head on the arm rest and his phone suspended inches over his face; he looked bashful and cute. Generally happy.

"Oh, don't worry, I'm gonna be up all night anyways."

"See? That makes me feel worse!" he exclaimed. "I wish I could give you advice, but …" He shrugged helplessly, or tried to at least, for the arm rest was in the way.

"I know," I said, smiling at his humility. "I always wonder if sleeping alone is part of the problem. You know, I used to be able to fall asleep anywhere, but like, on *command*. As long as I was nice and warm, and my mom was close by."

He winked. "We could test that theory if you want. Missy has guys over all the time, so she won't mind. And my dad doesn't have any authority over me." An interesting point to bring up, I thought.

"Well, there are less people we could potentially wake up at my house," I presented, and he waggled his eyebrows in consideration. "Plus, I can roam the halls guilt-free if I'm still awake."

"Wanna try it?"

The thought made me practically glow; I could see it on my own phone screen. "I'm down!"

It was a Sunday, as you know, but we arranged for him to come and spend the night at my house anyway. We both had unimportant classes first period, so it didn't matter if we were late. This new plan excited me, but in the middle of speaking, I received a text from an unknown phone number that said:

it's reba -- can we talk? there's something up with leo

Just a minute

Seeing as I was distracted by FaceTime and was too muggy in the mind to really care, I waited much longer than a minute to answer her. When my phone dinged a second time, I thought Reba had double-texted, but it turned out to be someone else—I ignored this other message simply because I was busy. Understandable, I think. I could always write back later. It's logical.

"What's that buzzing?" Bryan asked me.

"I keep getting texts," I said. "Don't worry about it." *Worry about it,* my mind argued.

Minutes later, Jade said something in the background that caught Bryan's attention, and he sat up from the couch cushion and craned his neck, appearing to look out the bay window that looked onto the front yard. Then I heard a knock through his end of the phone, so I knew it must have been the front door.

"Not it!" Jade yelled. Her voice was lagging due to poor

connection.

"Dammit." Bryan huffed, looking back into his camera. "I ... answer that. See you ... night?"

"See you tonight," I repeated, hoping he could hear me better than I could him. He kissed his camera in response and hung up. After that, I decided to take a shower to kill some time.

There came a loud banging at my bedroom door while I was getting dressed into pajamas afterwards, my hair still sopping wet. "What?" I shouted, a hint of annoyance in my tone.

"Jamie?" Mom cried out, knocking again. "Jamie, you need to come out here *now*."

God, I remember it so clearly.

"Jamie? Come on out."

She never said my name incessantly like that.

I opened my door and followed my frenetic mother out to the living room, where Channel 8 News was on pause. It took me a minute to notice, but there had been tears in my mother's black-brown eyes, and her hands were shaking ever so slightly. She rewound the report, and I watched Max Figuerra announce that after being spotted conducting a local shooting, Leo Capodi's due parting was upon us.

"What?" I gasped, sitting down on the couch. "What does that mean?!"

"He's dead, honey. He was the killer."

I was still processing when a knock came to our front door—a popular occurrence that night—so Mom went to answer it, leaving me alone on the couch, battling my nervous system's whims. In hindsight, we were fortunate that the visitor was only Jade Lukin, but we couldn't have known how dangerous opening that door was until it was too late. I'll say it again: we were *incredibly* lucky.

She and Mom discussed something in a conflicted tone for only a few seconds before I stood up from the couch and approached them slowly. Mom's gracile figure blocked Jade's face for the time being, so I didn't know what I was walking into. The news about Leo had hit me hard, but, for whatever reason, I was still numb to it.

Mom moved aside and disappeared into a different room with her hand over her mouth, sniffling as she shuffled past me. When I saw Jade's little body standing there in the doorway, my heart dropped immediately. She was wearing workout leggings and a much too large hoodie that had makeup stains all over its chest and sleeves, and dripping down her cheeks were blackish tears. Her mouth was open, and her teeth were bared, lips chapped in the middle as she let out a loud wail. I grabbed the doorknob for stability as my mind traversed into dark places; I knew that wail all too well. I knew it well enough to know it wasn't Leo she was sobbing about, even before she spoke.

"It's Bryan," she wept, stepping forward an inch or so. "H-he might not make it."

The blood drained from my face. My knees softened and hit the ground hard as my whole body went limp. I hadn't had enough time to deal with the information to even cry, but it didn't matter—Jade's agony vouched for both of us. She knelt down with me and screamed for my mother, who instantly went scrambling for a wheelchair because we obviously weren't going to stay at the house to wait it out. All I could see from my crumpled position was the dust on the floor and soon Jade's knees as well as she had come close enough to drape her arms around me. There were droplets of water collecting on the floorboards between us.

I remained unmoving for over two minutes this time, which rarely happens. It truly felt as though I had died, but my soul hadn't been granted closure yet; it was still trapped in that motionless vessel. Too much had happened at once.

When I was finally coherent, Jade told me what had

happened. Upon opening the door to the knocker, Bryan had been shot in the lung with a ten-millimeter bullet fit with a silencer to facilitate the shooter's quick flight from the scene. He was having emergency surgery as we spoke. It didn't take me long to piece together that Leo had committed suicide using the same type of firearm; his half of the story was already pasted all over the news.

I broke down even more when I realized what this meant.

To think I had trusted such a devilish human being and compromised my relationship, my boyfriend's life, *my* life, over him, well, that was crushing. To know that I had hugged him because he was conniving enough to invoke pity in me, that I had formed an alliance with Reba, my longest standing enemy, because we both felt that his crime was badly mistaken, made my heart shrivel up and blacken like charcoal. With these dreadful thoughts in mind, I became paralytic around ten times in a row that evening, just *waiting* to feel stable enough to go to the hospital with Jade.

When I wasn't paralyzed, I was retching and crying. And who knew whether I'd be okay in a hospital setting, where I might pass out even more, or start to seize, starting the process over and over again until I was completely senseless?

Hospital

MOM, JADE, BRYAN'S dad, Missy, and I camped out in the hospital waiting room for hours.

It was expansive and never boring to look at. Much of the art deco architecture was targeted toward children, based on the geometric structures and primary color usage, and so that was probably part of the reason I kept awake while waiting for a surgeon to bring us news. I had it in my mind that I had to remain focused and calm for whatever I might hear, so I'd been meditating.

"I can't sit here anymore," said Bryan's dad, who was also a Bryan, but I'll just refer to him as Mr. Lukin. That was around nine o'clock. "Anybody want Starbucks?"

"Why don't I go with you?" Mom suggested, rising out of her chair and grabbing her purse. She and Mr. Lukin looked at Missy, Jade, and me for orders, but only Jade gave one. I couldn't stomach it.

When they were gone, Missy stretched her arms a little and came to sit next to me. "How you holding up, Jamie?"

"I'm okay." I had been focusing on a bright red triangle cut into one of the pillars practically the whole time we were there, and that was what was keeping me sane. I didn't let myself think thoughts of death even though the odds that the bullet would take him from us were very high. I sucked in a deep breath and looked from Missy to Jade, reading in their eyes a sense of enormous fear despite their outer serenity. Everyone in that waiting room had the same countenance.

"Leo's dead," Jade mumbled to no one in particular, entranced by that night's many stimulating events. The reminder didn't shake me as hard as the first revelation of that information did. Her eyes were red, unfocused, and no longer made up in shimmery eyeshadow. When she looked at mine, a chill traced down my spine; it was like watching a statue move. "He deserved it."

I couldn't say anything in return.

It was ten o'clock when a nurse, out of breath and shining on the forehead, jogged into the waiting room looking for Mr. Lukin. We all stood up and stared as she spoke with the man. From their distance, none of us could make out positive or negative body language, not even at the very end of their dialogue. Mr. Lukin turned around slowly, holding his forehead in his hands, and stripped his face of any emotion until he was back in our earshot. Mom put her arm around my shoulders, anticipating the worst.

"He was dead for three minutes," he finally told us. His mouth cracked open, and his jaw was set as emotions threatened to pour out. He stood there, weeping, while all of us were in a combined state of shock.

Mom and I looked at each other. Either Bryan had been dead for several minutes and now was the only time the nurse could tell us, or some sort of medical miracle had occurred.

I sat back down on my chair, staring at the floor in horror at the extremity of those options; Mr. Lukin had been moved to tears, so either could be correct.

Missy and Jade approached him slowly, both obviously unsure how to feel. As Mom told me that whatever happened would end up okay, the other two pried for more information. I had some difficulty believing my mother though, and my hands started to shake as I woke up from my meditative calm.

Suddenly, there came giddy laughter from Jade and Missy, whose faces were immediately radiating with joy. Mom and I stood up lightning fast and joined the merriment; as traumatic as it had been, that was the happiest moment of my life. It still is. I realized there really was such a thing as a miracle after all.

"Oh my God," I cried out as four different arms reached out for me, keeping me on my feet. All of us were in high spirits, practically *levitating* after the weight of that burden was gone. I remember warm tears trickling down my face and my body going limp in the waiting room, my smile frozen onto my face. We probably provided a little spark of joy—or envy—for the other citizens of the waiting room.

We weren't allowed to see Bryan right away because he was susceptible to stress and pneumonia and other respiratory illnesses; there was still a tube in his chest and one in his throat as well. I tried to understand for his sake, but to me, it just felt like they were keeping us apart on purpose.

Three days later, after I'd just about moved into the Lukin residence, Missy, Jade, and I went to the hospital again because the doctor said it was safe for him to have multiple visitors at that point. Mr. Lukin had gone earlier that morning apparently, right as Bryan had his chest tube removed, and had given us all an update on his well-being via group chat. I was bubbling inside, still dizzy with a mix of relief and anticipation. I wanted to see him so badly, hold his hand, touch his skin …

"Why don't we go in separately?" Missy suggested, huddling

us outside Bryan's semi-private room that Wednesday morning. We had all skipped work and school for the occasion. "I don't want him to be overwhelmed or anything. The doctor says he's going to have some PTSD, but he's processing right now."

"If you don't mind, I'd like to go last," I said. I needed to be able to have a moment with him that wouldn't feel rushed.

Missy and Jade were very understanding and wound up going in together even though that went against Missy's suggestion. Looking through the window while I waited, I saw a woman in a full-body cast with her arms and legs suspended. There was a blue polka-dotted curtain separating her from what lay in the other half of the room though I could see the shadows of Missy and Jade standing beside a monolithic figure.

An older woman stopped me and asked if I was lost. I realized that to a foreign eye, I was just this small girl peering into an occupied room, which was fairly embarrassing on my part. I told her I was fine, and she continued elsewhere. About twenty minutes later, Missy and Jade exited the room, both glowing and talkative.

"Knock yourself out," Missy encouraged me, squeezing my arm before starting off down the hallway. She stopped and asked, "Oh—should we wait for you, or?" I just shook my head and waved them off.

I was starting to feel nervous about going to see Bryan. Would he look deathly ill? Did he have a gaping hole in his chest that I would see into? Was his memory impaired? The questions kept running through my head.

I let myself in, making horribly exaggerated eye contact with the gauzed-up woman. It felt dirty to be standing, *bragging* about my working legs in front of her, so I stayed still for a moment and recalibrated my breathing, trying hard to look calm for Bryan.

"Ma'am?" said a voice from the corner of the room. I jumped at it as the door swung shut, revealing a nurse who was sorting through a drawer like they have in doctor's offices. Her scrubs were the same color as the wallpaper.

"*I'mgonnapassout*," I said, my chest heaving. She rushed over to me and put her hands on my arms for support. "White Coat Syndrome?" she presumed. "You're okay, you probably just need to sit down. Are you here for Miss Walter?"

"Lukin," I gasped out, looking in the direction of the curtain I had yet to see past. "I-I have narcolepsy with cata—"

"Okay, let's go sit down. You're gonna be fine." She took me to a chair in that corner she'd been hiding in when I first entered the room and fetched me a Dixie cup full of tepid water. I couldn't explain what was happening to me; maybe all the meditating I'd done for three days straight had helped me stay mobile during this little panic attack, but I was fine in another few seconds. The vapid body-cast woman was staring at us.

When I grew the nerve to flaunt my ability to walk in front of that poor woman and finally crossed the room, I was startled upon seeing Bryan. His purple lips were closed around the plastic mouthpiece of a respirator, and he looked spaced out of consciousness. He blinked for a long second as if registering that I was there, his dull eyes fixated on me.

The nurse beside me pulled the chair that was against the far wall and brought it to the right side of Bryan's roller bed for me. She asked if I would be okay by myself from there on out, and I nodded at her graciously. As soon as she was gone, Bryan blinked again, his fingers twitching. He looked so ... caged.

"It's so good to see you," I whispered, my voice breaking. I didn't want to disturb my own moment by speaking too loud, and the room was only semi-private to begin with. Miss Walter was *definitely* eavesdropping.

Bryan lifted his forearm completely, and as I listened to his labored breaths, he lowered his middle and ring fingers to produce the "I love you" signal. It made my chest heat up like a blaze, and I felt the smile on my face as relief overcame me.

"I love you," I said back, grabbing his hand with both of mine. It felt so good to say what I was feeling, to touch him after so long despite the sheen of sweat that coated his palm. I still missed the way my hand fit in his. "I'm so proud of you. You're gonna get through this."

His fingers tightened around mine. I yearned to kiss him and sleep with his arms around me, but I had to wait at least another 48 hours until I could do so, and that pained me to think about. His life had dangled before my eyes only days before, yet here he was, breathing, intact. He was going to be okay. I could wait as long as he needed.

Zombie

"MRS. JUNE RETIRED. She finally had enough of us."

Bryan's doped-up smile grew bigger and bigger. "Finally," he said, sounding sleepy. "Old ass."

He grabbed my hand and interlaced his fingers with mine; it had become a regular practice of his, but I couldn't blame him. We both wanted that physical contact. It was only a matter of time before the PTSD presented itself, making the simplest of knocks a shock-inducing reminder of his trauma, so I resolved to enjoy the little things until that point came.

"These look cute," he said, eyes on my nail polish. It was three simple coats of red gel—Jade had painted them for me while I was crashing at her house. "You do this yourself?"

"Actually, it was your sister," I said cheekily. "She's pretty good."

"Are you guys besties now?" he asked.

"More like brand new sisters," I explained. "But don't worry, that doesn't make you my brother."

"Well, thank God."

I'd been lying on his roller bed with him basically every chance I could. It was Saturday now, almost a week since the incident, and Bryan was due for discharge from the hospital in just a few hours. He had been avoiding kissing me because his throat tasted like blood and he "didn't want it to transfer" though I was craving his affection at this point. I missed car rides with him and evening trips to Cemetery Drive. He just wasn't the same when he was forced to limit himself. Under *any* other circumstance, I might have said I'd kill the bastard who did this to him.

Which reminds me, it didn't seem to faze Bryan one bit when his father told him Leo had died. I, on the other hand, had a minor breakdown after I returned from the hospital the previous Sunday, terrified of the tragedies that were going on in Banshee, yet also immensely relieved that they were over now because the culprit was finally out of my life. It seemed too good to be true, yet not a second of it was worth it.

When Bryan was finally sent home that afternoon, still somewhat sedated for the pain of the chest tube removal and stitches that underlined his right pec, he was immediately contacted by the football coach with whom he'd had that four-hour dinner conference. I was there when the phone call took place, and I'll never forget the way he looked as he heard the coach's words.

We regret to inform you that your full-ride has been revoked, Bryan. You won't be in shape in time for the season, but we hope you feel better, Bryan. It's for the best, Bryan.

My heart shattered when I saw him cry for the first time; not only was he in constant excruciating pain after being *shot*, for God's sake, but now his dreams were crushed, too. Leo's death just wasn't enough justice for the aftermath he'd left for Bryan. His life was literally ruined.

Pretty soon the lack of justice became unsatisfying for me on a much deeper level. I wanted something to go right for the first time in months. It hurt me to see Bryan so distraught, to know that after having his scholarship withdrawn, he was out of chances. Having that on his conscience brought on the PTSD effects much sooner than we had anticipated, given how fast his initial recovery rate was. The grace period was up.

Mr. Lukin, Missy, and Jade established a plan to drive Bryan to therapy four days a week using an alternating schedule. I would have joined, but as you know, I can't drive. Narcolepsy. And because of my condition, I was having my own difficulties. Entirely sleepless nights ensued, I was having multiple cataplexy attacks each day for various reasons, and I don't even know where to begin counting the hours I would sleep during the day. I had a seizure for the second time in my life and wound up in the emergency room for a few hours. I even upped my medication, thinking it would help, but those first weeks after the surgery were too taxing on my mental health.

Tommy was driving me to and from school again, only we started skipping first and last periods' study halls so that I could find time to be with Bryan. Tommy was a real sport during that hell period—I never had to tell him if something was the matter because he just *knew* there was. In some ways, he was to me as I was to Bryan: a much-needed caretaker.

As for Reba, she and I had stopped talking completely. She resumed riding home from school with her witch friends. After all, we had only been affiliated for that short time because of Leo, but now the problem was solved. Both of us had been wrong about him and were through with putting our faith in the wrong hands, so it was healthy for the two of us to return to our actual friends and forget what had happened. Reba, Sistine, and Nichole went practically radio silent for a week, but I didn't know that at the time because I simply cut ties. It was good—maybe the only good thing to come out of this ordeal.

And then, in the beginning of June, about three weeks before the end of school, Bryan hit me with some news. It didn't affect me in any way aside from the fact that it irked him.

"Missy's pregnant," he told me, his grip around my hand loosening while we sat in his bed after school. His eyes were petrified, and when he finally looked at me, he came close to tears. I didn't know if I'd be able to handle seeing him cry again. It reminded me of Jade in the waiting room when she said Leo was dead—utterly chilling.

"What's the matter with that?" I asked softly, bringing my hand to his face. He shut his eyes and appeared to relish the intimacy.

"It's my dad's," he said. His voice was low.

I swallowed hard. So, Missy would be his aunt *and* his stepmom now.

"How did I not see this coming?" he cursed, reaching up to touch my fingers. "They're fucking *twins*. Of course, he's in love with both of them."

"Hey, you couldn't have expected this," I reminded him. "Try and look at the bright side. Your family could use some light after all this."

"Light?" Bryan scoffed, evidently disgusted. I dropped my hand. "Do you know how shitty it's gonna be hearing a crying baby at three a.m. when I already can't sleep for shit?"

"Why don't you call me next time you're awake that late," I said calmly, "and I'll talk you through it?"

It took a lot of strength out of me, but I never allowed myself to be offended by his anger. He deserved to have an outlet, and I was practically wearing a neon sign saying, "Use me!" by being around him all the time. There were a couple of moments when I wanted out, but I owed it to Bryan to stay with him; after all, if I had taken those two texts seriously the night he was shot, things would have probably been different. I felt it in my gut. *I owed it to him.*

As it turns out, the second message I received that night had been from Leo, asking me for help about a "serious matter." I didn't realize how serious the matter was until it was too late. You cannot incriminate me for that.

"Jamie, I can't do this anymore," Bryan said after he told me Missy's news, minutes after he came out of his rage spell. He said things like that quite often, actually, and each time, I had to read a mental script given to me by his father. The list of phrases that should allay him comprises: I want you to be here, you have so much to live for, you're getting stronger by the day … you get the picture. It hurt so bad to see someone so close to me chip away. It was like watching my mother mourn over my father all over again. Like the sky had fallen, and all that remained was ice-cold space.

Here's another way to imagine it: your best friend is threatening to jump off a building, only you two have been growing distant for some time now, and so you're afraid your coaxing words will go unheard. Your heart begins to ache as he steps further away from you, but you won't know if he's actually committed to doing it until it's too late.

Eventually Bryan's PTSD medication started doing its job. He was still beyond furious, believe me—not even therapy could fix that—but he could sleep much easier, he stopped cussing me out for the most part, and he kept his suicidal pleas between him and Dr. Manta. It was a long road, but he finally started feeling like himself again and, eventually, exercising again. Things still weren't completely normal, just slightly easier to swallow than before.

I'm sorry if this update seems all over the place. It's hard to remember the exact events that happened between the day he was shot and June tenth, but I'm working on being as concise as possible for you. This was a particularly hard time for me, one that, to this day, I'm still trying to move past so that Bryan and I can both recover from it completely. There were, however, a few memorable nights that I'd be glad to tell you about.

Every Friday since he'd been discharged from the hospital, I packed my bags and stayed at his house the entire weekend, or sometimes vice versa. Remember how I said I didn't sleep during the night anymore? I think I could have passed for nocturnal. It was an incredibly peaceful time of day for me despite the circumstances: I could think, I could scroll through Instagram, I could play music in my earbuds, and I didn't have to worry about homework because it was a weekend. I could completely de-stress, contented in the presence of my boyfriend, whether he was conscious or not. Even though I was more exhausted than I'd ever been in my life, I savored those post-midnight moments.

Once when Bryan and I were spending the night at my house, something extraordinary happened. The clock hadn't even struck two yet, but Bryan appeared to wake from a nightmare. It was like when you see a dog sleeping and his paws pad against the floor because he's dreaming of digging up a bone. For a couple of seconds, I found Bryan's activity endearing, but then I noticed something was wrong.

For about a month after the surgery, he had to sleep upright, and he also started sleeping with shirts on because of the stitches. So, as I was laying on my back, phone in hand, I noticed right away when his chest started heaving and he threw his arms in front of his face in a panicked state, tugging at his T-shirt like it were on fire.

"Bryan?" I asked, sitting up fast.

"Go!" he shouted. I jumped at the extreme volume; hopefully, my mother didn't wake.

"What?" I said, debating whether his eyes were open or closed. "Hey, calm down!"

"Get away from the door!" "Jamie, no!" "*No!*" Those were only a fraction of the many exclamations he made, quieter and quieter each time, like he'd been defeated by some kind of dream force.

I was in disbelief, wondering if maybe *I* was the one asleep and dreaming. But when Bryan grabbed me and leapt from the edge of the bed with me in his arms, shaking, incanting, I knew it was real. Undoubtedly, I made his nightmare even worse by going limp, but I couldn't help it; I was terrified beyond motion. He started crying, cradling me like an infant. I think he thought I was dead because I wouldn't and couldn't move.

That was the first "interactive" nightmare he'd had, at least with me in close proximity. When I could move again, I put my arms around Bryan and prayed that the version of me he was dreaming about had been resurrected. He was still trembling uncontrollably, but he seemed convinced that everything was okay after a few moments. The next morning when I asked him about it, he told me he didn't know what I was talking about and that I was delusional, but I think he was just embarrassed.

These nightmares persisted through the rest of the school year, happening two or three times a week according to Jade, not including the nights I was with him. Sometimes, I had to sit on his lap while he was dreaming and hold him tight so that he had something living, breathing, to reassure him that neither of us was dead nor dying. It was deeply disturbing on my end, but I could only fall further in love with him after realizing that he was trying to protect me.

I could safely assume this would be his reaction if I were to die in real life. Maybe it's just my selfish roots speaking, but I loved that idea. In all other senses, though, his nightmares were disheartening not only because I had to witness them, but also the progress he had been making gradually deteriorated as the nightmares grew worse. It was a cycle; he would start to do better, then a nightmare would hit, and he'd regress.

In the wise words of Leo Capodi, it felt like this was a trial of hell, and God wanted me to endure.

You

IT'S WEIRD WHEN all of a sudden you look at someone who makes you realize your time is running out, but not in the conventional way that humans naturally think of first. I wasn't aging—rather, I was on a hit list. Most likely, anyway.

Mr. Edwards' wrinkled, gray face looked dull behind the glass pane that separated his headshot from the cursed air at Bridgewood. Cursed, I believe, because he was the sixth casualty already in what we all devised was a copycat killing. Dr. Oakhurst had the audacity to tell people he'd died of natural causes, thinking the poor janitor's archaism would be explanatory, but the truth had been splattered all over the news the day before—just like his blood in that press-released picture. It had been a bullet to the back of the head. The only thing we students weren't positive about was who'd be next. Me? Tommy? Oakhurst? Another beloved teacher, perhaps?

Yet the superintendent refused to cancel any more days of

school for us. When it was Mrs. Tomlin's sanctity in question, everything was shut down, but now that it was some antiquated steward, Bridgewood could care less. Really shows where white men of rank hold their priorities; thank God this is your case to solve, Agent.

Tommy, Bryan, and I walked away from the old, smiling photograph, hanging our heads low with respect for our late custodian. Deep down I knew this had something to do with Leo, despite his being dead, too, but I had to reserve my opinion in the presence of Bryan, who was still triggered by talk of Leo. I was surprised he could even handle the news of Mr. Edwards without panicking.

We were headed to English. In all this time, Temp had actually taken the official position as Stratford's replacement, but no one called her Miss Camper like her new name plaque suggested we should. "Temp" had a nice ring to it—kind of like "Teach."

Class took place in the courtyard that day, the weather being so amicable. Our ongoing assignment was to read a book of choice that we would eventually have to write a research paper on, but thankfully, Bryan and I had been exempted from the essay portion because we missed around two weeks' worth of research in total due to personal complications. I really appreciated Temp for her empathy when it came to Bryan's health, and mine too—she was nothing like Ms. Ross, the wretched substitute who had tainted Stratford's class for a week. Temp actually understood that Bryan wasn't the only one suffering here and that I needed some slack as well. So, the rest of the year (a whopping seven school days) wasn't going to be *that* bad, aside from Mr. Edwards' homicide weighing heavily on our consciences.

Bryan and I chose to read *All the Light We Cannot See* by Anthony Doerr together. It was only a few years old and could pass as an eleventh-grade novel, which was partly why we chose it, being as stressed out as we were. The chapters were concise and insanely deep, too, which was another factor that appealed to both of us. Lying spread-eagle in the courtyard under a blond sun with Bryan's head in my lap, reading together about a genuine love for education during a time where that was forbidden—it was beyond serendipitous when, for four harrowing months, nothing else in our lives was.

Every day in English, I felt at peace once again. But every day before or after that class, I was threaded through and through with thoughts like, *I'm next*. Seeing Mr. Edwards go just like *that* was a major factor in this hysteria from which I suffered. I hadn't needed more than the occasional therapy session since the incident, but you might say I was dealing with PTSD at that point, too.

My doctors put me on new anxiety and depression meds as well as an even higher dose of Modafinil. That helped mostly with taming those cataplexy attacks I would have during the day. Bryan, however, was taking more pills than he ever had, understandably, and somehow it didn't seem to dampen his mood one bit, at least not after all the chemicals balanced out inside him. Sure, he was fatigued all the time and never hungry, but still as charming and motivated in class as he was before. He was back. That also helped a little, arguably more than my pills.

After school, the day we saw Mr. Edwards' photo, Tommy, Bryan, and I all went to my house. It was one of those weekends that Bryan would be staying over, and since the whole ordeal had brought him closer to me, he had also bonded with Tommy. It only made sense. I liked seeing my boys hanging out together.

Mom had Sam over and was outside sitting on the deck with him when we arrived. "Yo, I haven't been here in so long," Tommy noted as we walked into the living room. He looked around as if we had remodeled the place.

"Yeah," I acknowledged. "Frankie's been asking about you."

"Awww."

"Frankie? I thought it was Fran," Bryan said, sitting down on the arm of the couch. Tommy toyed with the TV remote.

"Either or," he hummed, eyes glued on the screen as an episode of *The Simpsons* aired though it was muted.

"Her name's Francesca, but no one says that," I elaborated. "My dad called her Frankie, but when Sam showed up, she was Fran all of a sudden."

"That's why you hated him for so long?" Bryan concluded, half joking, and grabbed for my hand while I sat down on the cushion beside him.

"I dunno," I said, considering the possibility. "Could be."

"That's so petty." He laughed. I chuckled right back, noticing the shadows in the room shifting as Mom and Sam approached the sliding glass doors. She waved at us but proceeded further into the backyard until she was out of sight.

"What's her maiden name, J?" Tommy asked, sitting down on the edge of the coffee table with his back to the TV.

"Spencer," I said. "She has a sister named Cathy. We don't see her much."

"Why's that?"

"Apparently, she lives in Wyoming."

"Now hold up! I call bullshit," Tommy said, making an incredulous face. "Nobody lives in Wyoming. That shit ain't real."

Bryan snorted. "You're one of those?"

I shrugged. "We haven't heard from her the whole time she's been there. It's a void."

"Wait, you're *both* one of those?" Bryan laughed, his burnished eyes lighting up with amusement. Tommy and I grinned at each other. "You know, I have some family up there."

"Or so you *think*," Tommy argued, raising his eyebrows as if to push his opinion onto Bryan. "Cathy Spencer was sucked into the void, and now she thinks she's from there. I bet the same wack shit happened to y'all Lukins."

"Lemme guess—the world as we know it is a government simulation?" Bryan asked, clapping his hands as he bellowed out laughter. Tommy hesitated, probably because he claims to be the lead conspirator on that subject.

I swore I heard a couple knocks at the front door while Bryan was laughing, and so my face froze. Luckily, he was looking at Tommy and didn't seem to hear it, but a couple of seconds went by, and nothing happened. I passed it off as an auditory hallucination.

"Yo, there's someone at the door," Tommy said suddenly, nodding his head at the dark figures now standing behind the clouded glass. Bryan and I couldn't see from where we were seated unless we craned our necks. "Why they just standin' there waitin' on us?"

"Maybe it's for me," Bryan suggested quietly, knowing anyone who'd come to see him wouldn't have knocked. But none of us believed that; I had heard the knock. "Jamie, I better go somewhere else."

"Yeah, why don't you two go to my room?" I said, hurrying them with my hands. I was amazed that the guests were so patient. We all stood up off the furniture, and like a shepherd, I pushed Tommy and Bryan into the mouth of the hall, praying with all of my might that these visitors wouldn't make another sound.

But when the guys were halfway to my room, and I was still standing in the foyer, anxiously debating whether I should open that door or not, it seemed to burst open by itself, following a loud bang and the words, "Federal agents!"

I must have jumped out of my skin the first time I saw you, Agent, with a handgun positioned right before me. My legs were growing weaker by the millisecond. Tommy and Bryan shouted some things that I couldn't make out because I was so disoriented, and then everything went black as a long body swan-dove right into me from my left side, knocking me over with immense force. The two of us crashed into the ground in seconds, our forearms breaking the fall for our heads. I could barely see what was happening because of how my face was turned, but needless to say, I became paralyzed with fear. It seemed like slow-motion.

I can't describe how destructive that moment was for Bryan's healing process. From the end of the hallway, he must have seen the tip of your pistol and thought his nightmares about my demise were coming true. Once he felt I was out of harm's way, his body curled up around mine and would not move—it was like he was suffering from his own kind of cataplexy. I don't know where Tommy scrambled off to, but soon he, Mom, and Sam were all in the room with us, crowding around Bryan and me on the hardwood floor as we lay there in shock. I couldn't see you anymore from my vantage point, but to be honest, I didn't even try looking for you. And whoever you were with, well, he wasn't exactly my problem, except that he had broken our front door with his enormous boot.

"What happened?!" Mom cried out, looking down at the scene in horror. "Who the hell are you? Tommy, my God—what happened here?" Her words were all jumbled and panicked, which probably didn't make the tribulation any easier.

"I'm Agent Andre Luzhkov," you said; a rustling noise followed, so I assumed you flipped your badge open for my mom. "I'm leading the Capodi case."

"What Capodi case?! The boy is *dead!*" Sam shouted, sounding flustered. Mom knelt down, seeing that I was frozen and that Bryan was in his own little forcefield. She avoided touching us but so clearly wanted to.

"Tommy, sweetie, go call Jade for me," she whispered as Sam argued with you and your companion. "I-I don't know what to do. Sir, could you point that thing *anywhere* else, for God's sake?"

"Are you Francesca Hessen?" you asked. "I'm afraid your daughter's a prime suspect in a serial homicide case. She could be dangerous."

"*LOOK AT HER!*" Mom, Sam, and Tommy all hollered. I could see some of them gesturing down at me with anger. I think that was when you sheathed your gun, finally.

"She has narcolepsy. A-and the boy, he has PTSD after being … shot … in the lung." Mom had mouthed the word "shot" lest we be reminded, but that was futile. The damage had already been done.

"What?" you asked. "Her eyes are open."

"Ever heard of cataplexy?" Mom sighed. "She's paralyzed every time she feels strong emotion. It might take a while."

"I'm very sorry for causing your family any added distress," you apologized, sighing loudly. "How long is this going to take? I'd like to bring Jamie in for questioning."

"How could you assume she's part of this? She's obviously a victim," Mom argued pleadingly.

"Relax. She's not under arrest yet." *Yet?*

The thought of going to jail frightened me, but not nearly as much as your presence. I twitched my index finger, and then my hand, and then my arm. When I could swallow again, I turned my head to the right, where I could only see the crown of Bryan's head due to his fetal position. I hadn't noticed earlier, but his arm was laying heavily across my stomach like a paperweight, only it was shaking like a leaf; his whole body was. I could hear his breaths slowing down by the second, and I put my hand on the side of his face, letting him know I was okay. He'd tackled me like this was football, but I'd had the advantage of not feeling a thing.

"Hey, Luzh," huffed the man who'd kicked the door in, interrupting the icebreaker conversation between you and Mom. He gestured at Bryan and me on the floor as soon as he noticed we were moving. Or that I was.

"Hi there," you said. "I'm Agent Luzhkov." Mom groaned at your ignorance; everything she'd taught you had dissolved.

"She's been conscious the whole time." I don't blame you for knowing virtually nothing about narcolepsy at the time, but I think your reaction was important to note. Everyone has to learn *somehow*.

"I need a minute," I mumbled. I remember distinctly how surprised you looked that I had the nerve to say that to you—yes, I know I can be mouthy sometimes, but I had a weeping boyfriend to take care of. He just wouldn't calm down if it was Mom, Sam, or Tommy trying to console him, and had it been you or your buddy, Bryan's reaction might have been so severe he'd need to be hospitalized. So, thank you for letting me have a private moment with him. I really appreciate you doing that.

When the room cleared, Bryan finally sat up, his T-shirt dripping with blood. By crashing into the floor so hard, he had reopened his incision. It was bad.

You (pt. 2)

"WHAT CAN YOU tell me about this photograph?"

You slid a piece of laminated paper across that cold, metal table, eyeing me intently. Your black gaze never left my face, and you probably felt satisfied when I teared up and fell limp at the sight of the picture.

It was the selfie Caroline and I took on May first, minutes before we went into the thrift store; I had completely forgotten about it seeing as we'd taken it on her phone and she had never posted it to any internet platforms. Even in a motionless snapshot she looked lively and beautiful, like a princess whose pleasure it was to take *me* out shopping with her—*me* of all people. Why?

The ligaments in my neck creaked as my head fell to one side, and I started involuntarily sliding out of my chair. It was cold and metallic, just like the table, and I could practically hear my tears dripping onto it due to your profound silence. The lights were uncomfortably bright.

"Jamie, you're making this real hard for me." You chuckled lightly though it was obvious you were annoyed with me. You gestured at Amy, the woman from my interview with Officer Jahr, who was there for the sole purpose of keeping me upright. She straightened me out so I could see you as you pressed me further. I don't think this was what she signed up for when she took the job, so I felt just as bad as anyone else whenever I became paralyzed or fell asleep in that unaired interrogation room.

"We went shopping," I uttered at last.

"The picture is dated May first. Do you know what happened on May first?"

"We went shopping," I repeated, "and then she was killed." You took a deep sigh. "I saw it on the news, and I had a cataplexy attack after hearing about it."

"Like you did just now?"

I nodded.

"You're the last person to have seen Miss Empfert alive," you told me, your stern voice insinuating that I was lying to you. "Her parents say she didn't come inside after she parked outside her house."

"It's not like she's my neighbor," I said pleadingly. "I couldn't have walked home fast enough to—to *shoot* her and get away with it. She dropped me off at my house and then left."

"Then tell me this," you said. "Could you not have driven yourself home? Or had an accomplice—say, Thomas Hicks?"

"No," I insisted. "I can't drive. And Tommy would *never* have agreed to that."

You glanced down at one of the manilla folders laid out before you and opened the third one, which *somehow* had a document involving Tommy in it. "But he *would* have agreed to that," you taunted, "and we both know why." You didn't take out the specific document and show it to me, but I inferred anyway that it was a statement from Tommy. When did you have the time to talk to him?

I paused. "Because he's ... in love with me?"

"See? You're thinking straight now." Why the hell had he felt the need to tell you that?!

"Sir," I said, sitting forward and putting my hands on the tabletop. You just shifted in your seat, looking smug as always. "You don't understand. Tommy and I are both scared for our lives. If he thought I was killing these people—"

"Which you have reason to do," you interrupted. "The record shows that you 'had beef' with one Laurie Tomlin. Who's to say you didn't feel the same about, say ... Fiorella Stratford, Debra Blane, or Caroline Empfert?"

You must have gotten that from my interview with Officer Jahr.

"We already established that Leo killed them," I said, clenching my jaw in frustration. That probably didn't help my case. I slumped before saying, "I just don't have it in me. I cower at the sight of a gun."

You smirked at me, leaning back in your chair—which, for the record, looked much more comfortable than mine—and I could've sworn you were about to applaud me. "You're one smart cookie."

"So, what, you're just testing me or something?"

"One could say that about the interrogation process, yes," you practically teased, "but I'm impressed, nevertheless. Using your first impression on me to build your case."

My lungs deflated, and I held my head in my hands, muttering under my breath: "How?"

You shook your head. "I know you didn't kill those teachers. I even know you didn't shoot your boyfriend. But I've gathered enough evidence suggesting you harbored Leo in your house several times when he sought asylum, and maybe some of his choice weapons are hidden there as well. And the janitor,

Edwards …" you snickered, "he was your most recent prey. All the signs point to you."

"Signs?"

"Like when you approached Leo's probation officers and tried convincing them he wasn't guilty," you proposed, shrugging in a way that belittled me. "*Not* a wise move, sugarplum. Neither was embracing him in the hallway. Now why would you do that unless you were on his side? Oh, and this, too. Look."

You slid another photograph toward me, this time one of my house. The lights were on, and Leo's car was parked in the driveway. "What you're telling me is that someone took a picture of my house *knowing* Leo was there? Does that not raise a red flag?"

"If you're confessing to intentionally harboring a murderer in your place of living, I need you to say it directly. You've got papers to sign."

"I wasn't harboring *anyone*. Ever. I even had a restraining order filed against him."

"We have no record of that, Jamie. I would have seen it."

Suddenly, I regretted ever listening to Sofia. She hadn't been reimbursing us; that was just hush money.

I sighed in defeat, and a long pause ensued. Then you mentioned Mr. Edwards one more time, but whatever you said about him went in one ear and out the other because I was still examining that picture of my house. It had obviously been taken from the inside of a moving vehicle, for its passenger side window was rolled down two-thirds of the way, and the grass was slightly motion-blurred. You could read Leo's license plate with ease.

It looked staged.

Looking at the lower half of the image, the foreground, I caught sight of a reflection in the sliver of window that hadn't been retracted yet. There was a red or pink phone case in it—that was probably the phone that took the picture. I spotted a very particular sticker in the bottom corner of it that I had *definitely* seen before, meaning someone I knew had been driving past my house when they saw Leo's car parked outside it and figured it was picture-worthy. It just didn't add up.

"Leo came to my house on May third," I said, almost to myself because it caught you so off guard, "after Caroline passed. He was only there for, like, ten minutes. I kicked him out because he wasn't invited over in the first place. I-I was scared of him. I just don't understand. Someone had to have followed him in order to take this."

After a moment's hesitation, you smirked at the tabletop and looked me devilishly in the eyes: "Are you interested in detective work yourself, Jamie?"

"What?" I asked, nonplussed. "No, I-I want to be an English lit professor." Then, to take some of the pressure off of myself, I asked something that had been nagging at my subconscious for the whole of the interview: "Are you really not interested in what I said about Sistine to Officer Jahr?"

"Let's discuss that at another time," you insisted. "Banshee is small enough that anyone could have driven by for any reason at all. Everyone knows Leo was involved somehow, so whoever took this was simply looking out for the owners of the house."

If I could find out whose phone case that was, the case might turn around.

"I'm going to ask one more thing of you, Jamie," you said definitively, forking through those other bulging manilla folders. You picked out one last photograph—the one that would never, ever allow me peace, even months after I saw it—and it glided over the table toward me. It took me a second to register what I was looking at.

There Leo was, the inside of his head exposed from where he had shot himself, with a message scrawled in green ink on the shower wall:

HICKS
&
HESSON

When I realized what it said, combined with the sight of a human brain and skull in fragments, a sound escaped me. I'm sure you remember it. I wasn't quite crying, but I was definitely shocked, and after I slapped my palm against my mouth, my forehead slammed down onto the edge of the table, and I lost myself completely. I even threw up onto my lap. That time, I fell out of the chair, and Amy regrettably helped me up. I think you had to help her lift me, but I can't quite remember that much; I do know she placed me in my chair at an angle so I wouldn't choke on my vomit.

I'd thrown up for obvious reasons, which might have clued you in on my honesty, my non-criminal status. But seeing my name—spelled incorrectly, I might add—as well as Hicks made my head spin. I thought I was going to get sick again, but thankfully, I kept it inside the second time. For some reason, it never occurred to me that the Hicks twins could be targeted; my mind immediately went to Reba, who had complained about receiving death threats. Now that Reba and I had been spotted talking about these threats and the controversy of Leo's innocence plea, someone was out for us. That was my guess.

"I take it you had no prior knowledge of this then," you said quietly. I stared at you, hoping my blank eyes alone could convince you I was innocent.

The door burst open all of a sudden, and a police officer rushed in, panting. "There's been another shooting." Way to keep it private.

"Who the *hell* are you working with?!" you demanded

angrily, though it didn't look like you were addressing me specifically. You stood up and slammed your huge fist onto the table, which only made me feel worse, heavier. Amy had her hands under my armpits like I were a baby whose diaper she was sniffing. I felt like chattel.

"Sir," said my pro bono caretaker. I could see her face in the mirror behind your back, and her eyes were begging for you to be more sensitive. I'm glad you received her telepathic advice and sat back down.

We were all quiet for another thirty seconds or so before I eased out of Amy's grip, signifying that I was ready to talk again. You looked me up and down—well, my top half—and suggested I conduct the rest of the interrogation because your way was *obviously* faulty. You're about as brash as I am.

"Do you know Sistine Moore?" I asked, planning on addressing the hunch I had formulated moments earlier.

You nodded fondly. "Yes, she visits me often." At the time, I didn't realize that that was because her dad was one of your agents, but I chose to ignore it in the moment anyway, finding it perfectly rational that she had been in trouble with the FBI before.

"Maybe she took the picture," I proposed. "Maybe she's the accomplice you're looking for." The only thing I could say to support this was that she had approached me behind the porta potty at Caroline's memorial, and when I did, you didn't seem completely persuaded.

"The only mention of Sistine in this entire file is that she 'gets detention a lot,'" you stated. "Is it in any way possible that you hallucinated that interaction?" My heart dropped into my stomach, and my face froze because I didn't realize you would suggest anything so demeaning as that. "You do have hallucinations, correct? I did some research on narcolepsy prior to this conversation."

"Rarely."

"But you still *can*, yes?"

"... Yes. But I *didn't*."

"Well, is there a witness to your encounter with Sistine?"

I remembered telling Bryan I had simply fallen asleep behind the porta potty and that was why he spotted some dirt on my face. Once again, I was at a major loss, and just shook my head at you. You stared for a long while before finally releasing me, no charges.

I cried for hours that night. Bryan couldn't believe that I was a suspect, but I'm glad for that because it meant he didn't feel any uneasiness around me, and so he still wanted to stay the night. He had completely recovered from that little episode he had when you first showed up at my house. Mom, Sam, and Tommy were all on my side, too, of course, and were actually more offended by the events of the day than I was.

I don't know why, but I truly expected everyone to forsake me as soon as they heard I was involved in the case. Like what happened to Leo.

A Milestone

I WAS AWAKE all of Friday night but ended up sleeping until twelve o'clock on Saturday, ridden with thoughts of you. I was scared that Bryan would have another night terror, but he had been relatively peaceful throughout the night. He started sleeping on his back again so that may have helped.

"Afternoon," Bryan said to me when I finally woke up. He was dressed and showered but still laying down next to me, phone in hand, as if he hadn't moved since the night before.

I hummed, stretching my arms out. I felt pretty well-rested, though that was new. Any sense of routine that my sleep schedule might have picked up was almost immediately trashed. "How long have you been up?"

"Bout an hour or two." He shrugged. "Don't worry though. I like watching you sleep."

"You're in luck! I have narcolepsy." With a smile on his face, he handed me my weekly pill dispenser and my water bottle.

"Having a good day?"

"Mhmm." He nodded. "It's good to be able to get back up after something major happens." That was sweet.

Sweet but also ironic because I later realized Bryan was just *barely* coping with the events of the day before, and putting on a happy face with phrases to match it was just part of the process. After all, everyone thought you had a bullet with my name on it, including you yourself. So, kudos to Bryan—personally, I've never been good at hiding my emotions. In fact, I'm way better at causing scenes because of my emotions. It's in my DNA. But Bryan remained chipper at least until dinnertime, when he started spacing out and generally losing his focus

I was nervous because I knew exactly what was going on as soon as it started.

When the sun began to set, he told me he needed a shower, not his first by the way, and that was when I decided to intervene. It was difficult watching him crumble slowly.

"Bryan," I said calmly as he dug through his duffel bag for a change of clothes. He didn't look up at me when I addressed him but kept rummaging.

"Hmm."

"I'm okay," I told him. He finally stopped and looked me square in the eye, his bottom lip quivering but no words following. "Let's just think short term for now and not focus on what happened yesterday."

"I don't know what you mean." He continued making a mess out of his belongings, shaking his head at himself as he found the shorts he'd been looking for at last. "I'll only be a minute."

"You already took a shower today," I noted, "and you look stressed out. I'm just worried."

"Well, don't be," he urged, a little snap in his voice. I stood there in silence, waiting for him to turn around and head for the bathroom because clearly I'd failed, but he dropped his clothes back into his bag. His next words impaled me. "Jamie, this is fucking humiliating."

"I was just looking out for you."

"No," he shook his head, voice cracking. "Crying in front of you so many goddamn times over a false alarm. *That's* what's humiliating." His face reddened up a bit as he avoided making eye contact with me; I sensed he was past the point of return. His tears caught the light seeping in through my bedroom window.

"It wasn't a false alarm," I reminded him.

"But it wasn't a real threat," Bryan argued. He was standing on the opposite side of the bed from me and suddenly sank down to the floor, his back pressed against the wall. I walked around to his side and crouched beside him, knees touching the hardwood. "The same shit happens when I have nightmares. I just get so worked up." So, I was right. That's why he had called me delusional; he didn't want me to know he was remembering the nightmares.

"It's okay," I murmured, caressing his hair. He wasn't looking at me and didn't seem to want to, so I brought my fingers down to his chest and rested my chin on his left shoulder, feeling his swollen muscles tighten under my touch. "Look at that. You're still so strong."

"What?" He sounded surprised.

"Did you know you pick me up in your sleep sometimes when you want to protect me?" I added. I was improvising.

"More like concuss you."

I touched his bicep with my right hand and moved my other under the hem of his shirt. "No. What happened to you, that didn't make you any weaker. You're the most resilient person I know, and your heart's in a good place. And look at me. I'm *fine.*"

His abs seemed to grow only more tense when my fingers glided over top of them, and when I grazed over his surgery scar, he finally looked me in the eye, his chest moving up and down faster than before. Anxiety.

"In college football, they're gonna see this scar and think how badass it is," I continued with a smile, strategically assuring him he'd get that scholarship back. "This one, too." My fingertips then brushed over his gunshot wound, and his eyelids fluttered shut at the memory. He reached up and stopped my hand from moving, the fabric of his shirt creating a barrier between our skin. "No one thinks any less of you," I whispered as tears rained down from his closed eyes.

"Shit," he whispered back, resting his head against the wall as he squeezed his eyes shut tighter. He straightened out his legs and patted his lap invitingly. Once I was seated, he wrapped his arms around me, kissing the side of my head. "Thank you."

"Anytime you need to hear this, you call me, okay?" I instructed him. He nodded a couple of times in reply.

I pulled my head back from his shoulder and looked him in the eye. They were much less worry-ridden now, and to prove his higher spirits, he kissed me. Our lips remained apart a moment or two before either of us committed to it, and when we did, it was like fire.

He seemed to have torn down a wall inside him when I first felt his scars, and so I went for it again, though I kept my fingers outside of his shirt this time. He deeply inhaled when I did that and paused for a long second, breathing harder this time. I thought maybe I'd made the wrong move, but then he leaned away and took his T-shirt clean off, giving me a million different ideas. I smiled, knowing he was starting to own those cicatrices on his chest.

"Jamie," he whispered ruggedly. I didn't even realize how impassioned our congress had been because my mind was concentrating more on his impressive self-actualization than his racy teenager thoughts. Foreheads together, I looked him in the eye, but then he brought his lips to my ear and said to me,

"I can't go much further than this." He wasn't even cleared to run a lap around the block yet.

I nodded, beginning to step off, but he anchored me down and gave me a look. The little flicker of disappointment I felt had been snuffed out by his lusting grip on me. "What?"

"What if I did something for you?" he panted. I paused a moment to think about what he meant by that, and it made me bubble up inside.

"Okay," I consented.

I won't go into details. You obviously know what went down after I gave him the greenlight—well, probably. Didn't mean to assume. But it was a whirlwind of anxiety, insecurity, pain … and then it became serendipity. I didn't think I was capable of feeling such divine emotions all at once, much less without losing control over myself, but I did it, and it was beautiful. Seeing the satisfaction on Bryan's gentle face was a reward in itself, and to answer your burning question, no, I did *not* fall asleep or become paralyzed.

Phone Case

MONDAY, WE WERE in better moods. It was only three days after the terrifying interaction with you, Agent, but what happened between Bryan and me on Saturday was still on my mind. I can't explain why I was obsessing over it, other than that it was chemical. Pheromones or something.

"So, how was your weekend?" Tommy asked on the way to English, using a singsong voice. I was practically skipping in the halls, so I couldn't blame him for questioning my reason.

"It was fine," I stated simply.

"That's great!" he said. "Now tell me how it *really* was." Temp's room was just around the corner, and so I was quiet but remained beaming until we got there.

"All right, all right," I said at last and proceeded to whisper my secret to him. He didn't believe me, at least not based on the face he made after I said it, but I told him to watch Bryan during class and see if he could pick up any "vibes."

We were back in the classroom that day because it was thunderstorming, but we kept the lights out for immersion and read some throwback Edgar Allan Poe works to take a break from the research project. As usual, Tommy and I were sitting at our lab table repurposed into a desk. The girls in the cluster on my right were whispering instead of following along with the text, and Bryan was turned around in his stool to face me. He had his elbows up on his table and wasn't reading either, but he told me he'd practically memorized everything Poe in the first three years of high school, so he wasn't missing out on anything.

"Miss Moore, Miss Tomlin—I'd like you to put your phones away now, please. You're interrupting."

Hearing those words in the midst of our gothic storytelling was equivalent to flicking the lights on and damaging thirty corneas in a split second. Leave it to Sistine and Nichole to break the ambience.

"It's my daddy," Sistine said as she showed Temp her phone screen, causing some laughter around the room for immature reasons. "He's on the SWAT team. It's important, Isla."

"To you, that's Miss Camper." An even bigger joke to the class. Bryan looked over at me, waggling his eyebrows. I nudged Tommy so he'd take notice.

"What's your excuse, Tomlin? Pray tell."

"Oh, it's my mom," she stammered sarcastically. "Reading all these ghost stories just makes me feel closer to her, you know?"

"That's enough," Temp said with a bored look on her face. "I'll take your phones on my desk then. Bryan, turn around so we can continue."

"Don't worry about me," he said to her, eyes glued on me.

"Oh, I'm not worried. Don't make a fool of yourself, Lukin."

"'I have great faith in fools … self-confidence my friends will call it.'"

"What's he doin', callin' himself dumb for?" Sistine laughed though no one entertained her remark. That in itself was funny.

Temp paused, chuckling and shaking her head at Bryan as though Sistine hadn't said a word. I didn't know it at the time, but that was a quote from Poe that my boyfriend had rattled off. In retrospect, it's not so surprising. "Very nice. Miss Moore, why don't you pick up in the next paragraph for us since you're so hell-bent on using that mouth of yours?"

Sistine rolled her eyes melodramatically but obliged. "*Shaking off from my spirit what must have been a dream, I scanned more narrowly the real aspect of the building. Its principal feature seemed to be that of an excessive...ant...tick...wide...ee.*" It amazes me that she wasn't placed into the general English class.

"Objection, Your Honor," called Bryan, whirling around in his seat to look at Temp at last. "You've called an analphabetic ignoramus to the stand."

"What? *Stand?*" Sistine scoffed, grimacing at his word choice.

"He's callin' you a simp," Tommy interjected, at which everybody—even Nichole and the ever-quiet Reba—giggled.

"Mr. Lukin, I'd like your phone till the end of the period as well," Temp demanded though it was clear she found the situation risible just like the rest of us. Bryan looked back at me and released a loud laugh, throwing his head back in satisfaction despite his consequence. I glanced at Tommy, who lifted his eyebrows back at me, showing he believed me now.

Bryan swaggered his way across the room—not to Temp's desk but to Sistine and Nichole's, offering to take their phones up for them. His smug expression was the laughingstock of the class. The girls ended up thrusting their phones toward him in an angry manner, and when I caught a glimpse of them in Bryan's hand, an abyss opened in me.

One of the phones wore a hot pink case with a pastel sticker on its bottom corner. I couldn't tell who had given it to Bryan since the two devices were stacked, but I knew I could figure it out soon anyway. My heart rate increased as I thought about how to approach them with a question.

"You good, J?" Tommy whispered to me. I blinked in response, staring blankly ahead of me as Bryan returned to his seat. "Hey. Talk to me."

All I could say to him was, "Nothing," and then I fell asleep. I was on the floor when I woke up seconds later from impact.

At the end of the period, when thunder was still cracking and the class was leaving, I watched from the back of the room as Sistine and Nichole went to retrieve their iPhones. Sistine happened to grab both of them, which didn't really help me figure out who had taken that picture of my house—I knew they had to have been together, and if I couldn't determine whose phone was whose, then that wouldn't really be an issue, but I *yearned* to know—maybe for my own sanity.

Those questions you asked me, the pictures you made me look at ... they disturbed me. So, seeing that phone case in real life and assigning a name to it was justice for me if not for all those other victims.

"What's this one's problem?" Nichole asked rather loudly from the front of the room, leaning into Sistine and pointing at me. Bryan saw this interaction right away and joined Tommy and me in the back. Temp was talking to another student privately, hence why this confrontation wasn't shut down as soon as it started.

"I don't think she's the one with the problem," Tommy said. He looked at Reba, who was standing at her table like a deer in headlights, or maybe a baby in the center of a wrestling ring. She was deciding on whose side to stand. Odd.

"Maybe she's jealous of us, Nicky," Sistine grinned, obnoxiously putting her arms around Nichole's cinched waist. "Ain't no other explanation."

"Jealous of what, exactly?" I asked, tilting my head to the

side. "Your flaming imbecility or your lack of social regard?"

"J, *what* are you doing?" Tommy whispered to me.

"You and Bryan was both talkin' outta your asses today," Sistine shook her head, making a critical face at us. I had to laugh.

I bit my lip in frustration and paused, getting ahead of myself by thinking too many thoughts at a time. Without giving context, I found myself asking them, "Why did you take that picture?"

"'Scuse me?"

"You know what I'm talking about," I insisted. "You took a picture of my house when Leo was there. Why would you do that?" I was so heated, I didn't even notice Bryan flinching at the name Leo.

Nichole's eyes widened with amusement, and Sistine just shook her head devilishly slow, smiling as though I'd cracked some cryptic code of hers. Meanwhile, Reba's whole body seemed to buckle, and she said something inaudible to Sistine and Nichole. I didn't register that something might be going on with her until Tommy rushed to her side, and Bryan put his hand on my lower back protectively, knowing *something* was bound to transpire. Something beyond our understanding.

Suddenly Reba screamed, and although I couldn't see her face due to Tommy blocking my view, I was positive she was crying. "*Fuck you, Nichole!*"

"What's going on?" Temp suddenly shouted as she and the student realized there was a scene. "Tommy?"

"I dunno!" he said back in panic, and Sistine and Nichole made a run for it. Bryan and I creeped closer to Tommy and his sister, hoping not to be scarred by what we saw.

Reba was in a ball on the floor; seeing her like that reminded me of Bryan when you entered my home abruptly, and so I told him it would probably be best if we let Tommy deal with her on his own. He agreed and walked with me out to the parking lot, a grim look on his face.

"You okay?" I asked, shoving my bag into the back of Bryan's car. He turned the ignition and took a deep sigh, nodding eventually as if he had to think about his answer. I nodded back to be sure.

"Can't help but feel bad for her," he sighed, waiting for a car to pass before we could leave. "It must suck ass to be so hurt by your best friends."

I looked down. "It does. I wonder what went wrong."

Bryan glanced at me, raising his eyebrows. "Think it might have to do with you?"

"What?"

"Like when you and her got close for a couple days." He shrugged. We were on the road now. "They might have viewed that as treason. They're dramatic like that."

"You're telling me." I couldn't help but chuckle. "I dunno, that might be it. But she looked really messed up back there."

"Yeah."

Later that evening, Tommy came to my house while Mom and Sam were making dinner. He had tears in his eyes, and he looked deeply shaken, so I brought him out back to sit on the deck, hoping it would help him feel better. This was before he told me what happened, of course.

"Everything okay?" I asked at last, sitting on the edge of a plastic rocking chair with my elbows on my knees. Tommy was staring out at the bamboo forest at the end of my yard and wouldn't look directly at me. It was warm out; I could see his upper lip perspiring in the peach-toned light.

"My parents just admitted Reba to Summit Oaks," he droned, lips hardly moving.

"What's that?"

"A psychiatric hospital."

I grew tense at the word "psychiatric." I was silent for a moment, unaware of a way to lighten the mood. Tommy finally looked at me, his black eyes especially puffy, and told me, "She been acting up at home for weeks, but we never seen it coming."

"What's she been doing?" I asked.

"She cries till three a.m., and we can all hear her," he said, counting on his fingers. "Thin ass walls. And she throws shit at us when she's angry. She's a complete baby."

"You sound annoyed."

Suddenly, he raised his voice. "Yeah, 'cause that ain't even the worst of it! She been calling the cops on every little thing my mom does to her, she ain't eating, she won't listen to no one. ... She ain't even sneaking out to be with her bitchass friends anymore. Says she got a secret she can't tell us. She's crazy, man. Nothing to it."

"I'm so sorry," I said, feeling defeated. Tommy was more of a soldier than I'd imagined. "I had no idea."

"She talks about you sometimes," he added, shaking his head spitefully. "I know you didn't do nothing, but she thinks you helped bring this on."

"I'm sorry," I repeated in a quieter voice. I considered whether this might have been because of Leo dying and the murders continuing; we were both so sure of his innocence and then were proven wrong, only to be given a false stretch of relief.

As a person receiving death threats, Reba's newfound paranoia didn't surprise me as much as it did Tommy. Sure, he'd spared me most of the details, but he looked stunned beyond comparison.

"Man, I looked it up, and Summit Oaks ain't even a good facility," Tommy cried, holding his head in his hands. "Bad reviews all around. She gon' die in there, J."

"Hey," I said, planting my hand on his arm. "She'll be all

right. You just need to continue supporting her, and she'll come back."

"How do you have so much faith?" Tommy asked me, putting his hand on top of mine and squeezing it. "S'almost like you never hated her guts."

"Recent events have changed my opinion of her." I shrugged. He pressed his lips together and trained his gaze on the wood planks below our feet.

"Mine, too," he said quietly.

"Why don't you and I go visit her sometime?" I suggested. "Maybe I don't have to go in the room with her if she thinks I did something, but I don't want you to feel so alone."

"We could do that," he nodded, "thanks."

I leaned out of my chair and put my arms around his shoulders, stroking his back a couple of times before sitting back down. "It'll be okay."

"There's another thing I wanted to tell you," he said rather cautiously. "Seeing you with Bryan all the time ... it's like conversion therapy, man."

"Taboo in today's standards?"

"No." He chuckled. "A'ight, maybe that was bad wording. But I'm completely over it now. You're like my white sister."

I laughed at that, sighing in relief. "Well good. That's good. I'm glad."

"Don't sound *too* upset about it," Tommy scoffed, holding his hand over his heart for theatrics.

I invited him to stay over for dinner, but he explained that he needed to be with his parents that night, and I understood his reasoning. I went inside and told Mom and Sam everything that was going on with Tommy and Reba—they both deserved to know ahead of time in case you or your subordinates should barge into my house again searching for answers.

Mom and Sam felt sorry for Reba and were equally as curious as to what was eating her up, but that I couldn't help them with—although I had a pretty good idea what it was.

Roller Coaster

ON THE LAST day of school, I was supposed to take finals for Calc and Physics, but Mrs. Pitt and Mr. Handy told me apologetically that I would have to make them up later in the summer due to "prior engagements" of mine that had been arranged unbeknownst to me. Mr. Handy, whose exam I would ideally take after Pitt's, sent me to the office where I discovered I had more business to roll out with the police.

Hearing this news nearly gave me a heart attack. I didn't want to see your face ever again, and I *definitely* didn't want you to have to employ poor Amy to be my keeper every time you showed me a gruesome photo. I texted Bryan that I wouldn't be riding home with him. Instead, I was to be escorted to the police station by officers Grantley and Stevens, waiting for one Agent Andre Luzhkov to grill me once more, something I chose to omit from my text to Bryan.

I'm sure it won't shock you to know that I fell asleep on the car ride to the station. Officer Stevens was craning his neck to look at me as Grantley drove in harsh silence, and when I woke up, Stevens' bulging blue eyes startled me.

"This isn't nap time," he said though he was grinning. He looked too young to be an officer.

"I have narcolepsy," I informed him. Hopefully, this case has spread awareness of narcolepsy in legal settings, where authorities tend to be ignorant. It's accountable for many of the things I do and those that happen to me.

"What's that?"

Grantley, in a private, soft voice, whispered to Stevens that his nephew knew a girl who had narcolepsy, and it was a "disease" that "makes you faint." I quickly remembered Grantley's nephew was Tommy and realized he probably wasn't the one who passed this WebMD description along to him.

"Well, hey," Stevens said to me after Grantley's half-assed explanation, "you got nothing to worry about. The feds aren't that scary."

When we arrived, I made it as far as the lobby before paralysis hit me; I didn't have my mother with me, and I was worried about my consistency during the last interrogation, and about Bryan. All were valid reasons to panic, only I didn't realize today's "interrogation" would be in a much lighter air or that I truly didn't have anything to worry about, like Officer Stevens promised. You had obviously learned something from Amy's lesson in compassion for other human beings. Also, as I came to learn, I was no longer being accused of three felonies, so you had three less reasons to be furious with me.

"Afternoon, Miss Hessen," you greeted me when we entered the bright white room. It was still just a cage for fear and sweat to live in, but I felt much better about being in there when I sensed how lax you were. Your navy-blue suit created a nice balance of color between your pale dress shirt and sepia skin. "Sorry to take you out of school like that. It was urgent."

"Mind telling me why?" I asked.

"Circumstances have changed, and we've determined there is no reason to doubt your story," you said, though you looked a little disappointed. "I'm afraid I have some bad news for you, though. It's about that message that was written on the wall in Leo's shower."

You reached for the manilla folder the picture was in, but I held up my hand to stop you. "Please. I can't look at it again."

You nodded. "Very well. Even though your name was spelled incorrectly, this officially endangers you and this Hicks figure. Now, I'm not from around here, so I need you to tell me as much as you can about Hicks." The name must have tasted foreign in your mouth, the way you emphasized it. But you knew "Hicks," so this felt oddly redundant.

"There are only two people Hicks could refer to," I said, "and they're equally valid."

"How do you figure?"

"Reba Hicks," I started. "She's just been admitted to Summit Oaks. She told our English teacher she was receiving anonymous threats, and I think that might have something to do with it." You appeared to take mental note of this and waved your hand for me to continue. "And her twin brother Tommy, whom you already know. He's my best friend."

"So, you think he could be at risk due to association with you?" you clarified, and I nodded, thankful that you understood me before I could finish my thought. It didn't scare me much at all because deep down, I *knew* the message was intended for Reba and me. Tommy was a friend to everyone; he couldn't possibly be a victim here, unless this were a hate crime, though the other victims' races had established that it wasn't. "Thanks, Jamie. This helps narrow it down. Did you know there are fifteen Hickses in Banshee?"

"They're a big family," I affirmed. "Officer Grantley is their uncle."

"They're multiplying," you joked. I smiled a bit and then looked down at my lap; it felt wrong to laugh in that room. "Well listen up, Jamie. I'm going to hold off on hiring a task force for you and the Hicks twins for now because we all know what that did to Mr. Capodi. But this leaves you with a major responsibility to speak up if you feel unsafe or if you see *anything* related to the case. Capisce?"

At that, I remembered all the times Leo said "Capisce?" to me and grimaced, but I agreed to the conditions.

"One more thing," I said. You tilted your head with intrigue. "Last time I was here, someone came in saying there was another shooting."

"Unfortunately, yes, there was," you nodded at the shameful statement. "He was another janitor at your school, uhhh … does the name Jason Heather ring any bells? It happened after hours, so he may not have been as present as Mr. Edwards. There hasn't been as much press coverage this late in the game."

I shook my head in reply, though that didn't make me any less upset about his loss. I don't know what pushed me to say it, but I added, "My boyfriend has PTSD from all of this."

You looked down at your lap and nodded slowly. "That's right. I have to apologize for holding my weapon in your faces for so long. That was pretty ignorant of me. It's a miracle he survived a bullet wound like that, but he seems to be doing really well for someone in his shoes. Never let him forget that, okay?"

"I won't," I promised. "Thank you."

"Anytime. We'll find whoever's continuing the dirty work for Leo, no matter what it takes. You won't be late for your graduation ceremony tonight, will you?"

"No."

You dismissed me after that and I rode home with Grantley and Stevens, the latter of whom was blatantly hitting on me the entire time. I'm sure his neck started to hurt from staring back at me for so long, but I decided to let it happen because he deserved to feel pain for every misogynistic microaggression that came out of his mouth.

During my time at the police station, Bryan had been at physical therapy because he didn't have finals and told me he was up and running like usual. He still expressed pain and stiffness in his chest every once in a while, but that was no major hindrance anymore. We had made plans earlier that day to meet up at his house after graduation, an event that wasn't anything spectacular in relation to the case, so I'm skipping it for now. I had Sam drive me while Bryan was in the shower.

It was breezy inside his house because all the windows were open; in fact, I felt kind of cold despite the outside's temperature being tropical. Jade, who let me in, had Aleida over and welcomed me into their little discussion as soon as I arrived. They were sitting opposite each other on the floor with a bunch of White Claw cans in between them in the formation of a triangle.

"Want one?" Jade offered, extending me one that had a metallic pink sash across it. I just shook my head at her. Alcohol.

"Hey," said Aleida, sipping on an orange-colored one. "Where were you for the Calc final?"

I shrugged. "Something came up. I'm gonna have to make it up later this summer."

"At least we're done after this, right?" She grinned, nudging me in the arm. I nodded at her, a little shy. She was much closer with Jade than me.

"You guys are lucky." Jade groaned. "I'm gonna be stuck at Bridgewood *without* you."

"At least you won't have to deal with Bryan in the halls anymore," I teased, and she laughed at me.

"Speaking of Bryan," Jade said, "*how* does he take such long showers? I feel bad for you, girl."

"I know, right? And get this: he tried taking *two* the other day," I complained, though I will admit I was just trying my best to contribute to the conversation. It didn't really bother me how long he took in the shower. Hell, I took longer, especially when I fell asleep in the midst. Still, I told the girls, "Sometimes I think he's trying to get away from me in there."

Jade scoffed. "Ha! No way. He thinks you're a saint."

"It's true," Aleida chimed in. "Even I know that, and I'm not here as much as you."

"You're too kind." I giggled. Jade's phone buzzed, and when she looked at the text she received, she gave Aleida a disgusted look.

"Pete?" she asked, and Jade nodded.

"Wait, aren't you still dating?" I asked, pointing at Jade for clarification. She slouched over and shook her head at me.

"He wishes," she complained. "I'm bored of him, you know? I got other things to worry about."

"He's totally too clingy," Aleida added, gazing down at her overgrown acrylic nails. "Hey, you think you could take these off for me?"

"Sure," Jade agreed. She was very interested in cosmetology, nail art specifically. It showed.

"Wait a minute," I interrupted. "You wouldn't happen to have any other guys in mind, would you?"

She looked up at me from her phone and waggled her trimmed eyebrows at me, clearly intrigued. Then, suspiciously, she asked, "Why?"

"Tommy's not talking to anyone," I said suggestively, knowing he was emotionally available now. She exchanged frenzied eye contact with Aleida and then back at me, her dimples getting deeper as she grinned.

"Ohmygod, Jamie!" she exclaimed. "Could you set us up or something?"

"Of course! I'm on it!" I was proud of myself for doing that, and Jade seemed to respect me even more after the fact.

Seeing as I was facing the long hallway to which the bathroom was appended, I could see when Bryan got out of the shower and went into his room. He must not have known I was there yet, or maybe he couldn't see me through the cloud of steam that followed him into the hall.

"I was gonna cut Aleida's hair tonight," Jade said to me, unaware that Bryan was almost ready. "You in?"

"Oh, I don't know." I chuckled, instinctively grabbing the ends of my hair. It barely fell past my shoulders, but I was hoping to let it grow.

"Well, why don't you wait till she's done with me and see if you trust her?" Aleida offered, clearly hoping I'd oblige. I humored them with a "maybe" and then explained that I'd better get going because Bryan was *finally* out of the shower.

His bedroom door now sported a plaque that read "DO NOT KNOCK" in unmissable letters, kind of like a road sign. I stood outside with my hand on the doorknob and called out his name, but instead of answering, he opened the door for me a couple of seconds later. The rate at which he could get dressed compensated for his long showers.

"Hey," he smiled, bending down to kiss me, "you been waiting long?"

I shook my head. "Aleida and Jade are good company."

"For some." He snorted, sitting down on the edge of his bed. I sat in the office chair.

"I'm setting Jade up with Tommy now that she's single," I added, a smug smile on my face, but Bryan only looked confused about it.

"You think he'd appreciate that?"

"Oh, he's over me," I assured him. He gave me a look that suggested otherwise, and just like that, my confidence crumbled. "He told me so!"

"Jamie, Jamie, Jamie." Bryan sighed, shaking his head and clicking his tongue. I narrowed my eyes. "You don't actually believe that, do you?"

"Of course, I do," I said. "He wouldn't have said anything unless …"

"Unless he wanted to take some weight off your shoulders," Bryan proposed. I exhaled in deep disappointment, holding my head in my hands. I believed him because that sounded like something Tommy would do out of generosity.

"But I just promised Jade I'd set her up with him," I whined. Bryan pulled me closer to his bed by my ankles and put his arms around me when I was within his reach.

"It's okay," he said though he sounded amused. "It's sweet how innocent you are."

"It's a curse!" I protested, my voice muffled by his shirt. I noticed then that his hair was still dry and made a point to ruffle it; he must have been taller than the showerhead. "What am I gonna do? She looked so happy."

"Try it out," Bryan suggested. I pushed away from him so I could look into his eyes. "Tommy could use a girlfriend. I think it'd make things easier for me."

"You don't think there's competition, do you?"

"Not necessarily *romantic* competition," he shrugged, "but … there's a bond between you two that's different from this one."

"And it's a damn good thing it's different from this one," I reminded him. "Ever seen *White Christmas?*"

"Yeah …?"

"'Lord help the sister who comes between me and my man,'" I quoted from the iconic film. Then I whispered for clarification, "Tommy's my sister."

Bryan laughed. "Good to know." I cheekily smiled at him.

The longer I looked at his dry hair, the longer I wondered what really went on in that shower of his. I began to worry that he used the time to let his emotions out and that was why he seemed so easygoing in the moment, but he'd just come from physical therapy a few hours prior, and usually exercise kept his mind out of the bad place. When Bryan caught me staring, he asked me, "Penny for your thoughts?"

"What took you so long in the shower?" I asked.

Clearly, he was taken aback. "I'm sorry?"

"I have reason to be concerned," I added, toying with his hair. It was sleek as usual, slightly damp, presumably from the steam. "I just have to make sure everything's okay, you know?"

"Well, in that case," he sighed, "... no, I can't tell you."

"Oh, come on." He just laughed at me, beckoning me closer with a shake of his finger.

"I've been practicing my breathing for you," he whispered, stowing one hand on my thigh and sliding it up fast in a way that enraptured me. A quick little gasp escaped my lungs, and I drew my head back so he could see my face. He looked proud of himself. That, Agent, is the power of implication.

"Really?"

"Oh yeah." He nodded, smirking. I didn't quite know what to say, but I could tell my face was red just by how hot I felt after that, and Bryan laughed at my modest reaction. "Are you sorry you asked?"

"No," I chuckled, "but I'm proud of you. This should make physical therapy go faster, right?"

"Right." He nodded. "I ran a mile today. The doctor says I'm on the healthier end of the spectrum, so I shouldn't have any problems with PT. Might even get a new scholarship."

"That's great!" I grinned. I pushed his hair back and kissed his forehead, proud that he was doing so well.

The door swung open quickly, revealing Missy. She didn't give any verbal warning like I did when I first came to the room, and I thought maybe that was the reason Bryan looked so annoyed at her. He lifted his hand off my thigh and looked at her expectantly without so much as asking what her business here was.

"Hey, Jamie." She smiled at me, her upbeat expression faltering when she looked at Bryan. "Hey, Bry, I was just letting you know, I'm going in for a checkup. I'll be back in a few hours."

"Bye."

I was shocked by his spiteful tone and was almost offended by it myself, especially when I saw Missy frown as she turned to leave the room. She shut the door behind her and shuffled away in her flip flops without another word; I waited until I couldn't hear her anymore to say something.

"What the hell?" I gawked. He gave me a look that suggested he had been expecting me to be on his side.

"She can't walk around here pretending she's my new mommy," he said defensively. My face fell. I completely forgot she was pregnant; it was still early on, and she wasn't showing yet. Besides, Bryan rarely talked about it. "Don't even get me started on my dad."

"What's wrong with him?" I asked.

"He's doing jack shit for the baby, that's what's wrong with him," he grumbled, pulling his legs up onto his bed and turning to face the headboard. This was one of those times where I just *couldn't* take his rage personally, or else maybe we'd start to have deeper problems. "He won't listen to me and Jade, and he's started day-drinking as if that aborts the damn thing."

"Hey, be sensitive," I scowled, heaving off of that office chair and sitting down on his comforter in front of him. "Why'd you hide this from me for a month?"

"'Cause I don't wanna fucking think about it, that's why," he huffed. He wasn't looking me in the eye, which gave me hope that he wasn't becoming upset with me on a personal level. "Dad and Missy ... pfft, it makes me laugh just to think about it. That baby is gonna have a world of problems."

"You gotta be more positive about this," I told him, reaching for his hand. He shut his eyes as if separating me from his angry thoughts. "And listen to me, you *cannot* treat Missy like that if she isn't getting support from your dad either. You don't know how hard being pregnant is."

"You don't either."

"*No*, but my conception of it is much better than yours, and we both know it."

He finally looked me in the eye, shaking his head at himself, and snatched his hand out of my grip. I moved away until my back touched the headboard and waited for his little storm to pass, staring awkwardly at my lap while he brooded by himself at the foot of the bed. That wasn't the first time this had happened.

"Jade's been drinking Missy's White Claws now that *she* can't," Bryan told me. "She's gotten drunk more times in the past month than I have in years."

"I had no idea you guys were struggling this much," I commented, keeping my eyes low and my hands together.

"I had bigger things to worry about than to tell you," he muttered. "Like, did you know they gave me a manual that teaches me how to *stab* myself in case my lung collapses again? I don't think I have the energy to yell at my dad anymore, and I am *not* being this kid's father."

I cringed at the graphic image. "I didn't know that. And no one said you have to be the father."

"But?"

"*But* maybe you could have a civil intervention for your dad's drinking," I suggested. "Get everyone involved. He's more likely to listen if there are more of you."

"And what exactly am I supposed to do then? Remind him that his being drunk when I was a kid made me the asshole I am today?"

"Wait, what? No one said you were an asshole."

"*I* said it," Bryan snapped. He finally stood up and walked over to one of his windows, leaning against it with his elbows up on the sill. I couldn't see his face directly, but the reflection in the glass wasn't pleasant. "He's the reason my mom's gone. He's the reason Jade's a fucking junior alcoholic. He's the reason I'm as depressed as I am, and how obnoxious everybody *thinks* I am."

Tears stung the corners of my eyes. I hated hearing him talk like that. Naturally, this brought on a cataplexy attack, but Bryan didn't acknowledge me until it was almost over. He turned around with a certain energy about him that highlighted how furious he was, but he softened completely when he saw that I wasn't moving.

"Shit, I'm so sorry," he said, flustered. He rushed over to the bed and sat down, supporting my heavy head with his hands. "I didn't realize this was bothering you." He cursed at himself and held onto me, making sure I looked comfortable even though I couldn't move or even feel my body. I dozed off as soon as I *could* move though, and Bryan let me sleep in peace. I suppose that was nice of him.

He wasn't in the room anymore when I came to. I found the thought of walking through his house alone discomforting, but I did it anyway, and the first person I ran into was Jade in the middle of the hallway. She was carrying a can of White Claw under her arm as she was holding multiple curling wands in her hands. It saddened me.

"What time is it?" I asked her, my eyes still adjusting to the light.

"Seven forty-five," she said. So, I'd been asleep for about an hour and a half. Odd.

"Where's Bryan?"

"Thought he was with you." Then she walked away.

I went further down the hall, through the kitchen, into the living room. ... He was nowhere. Halfway down the stairs, I started to hear some rather unsettling noises. It sounded like sniffling, or hyperventilating, or both. Whatever it was made my heart sink and my palms sweat to the point that holding onto the railing was useless. I continued down the stairs cautiously; I didn't want to startle whoever was down there.

"Bryan?" I called out in a gentle, easy voice. No response.

Yet there he was, sitting on the floor with his back against the bottom edge of the couch, holding his head in his hands. He was visibly shaking and had a half-empty water bottle and two pills on the floor beside him; the image was truly heartbreaking. Before he noticed me standing there, however, he downed the two pills and drank a quarter of the water.

"Hey," I said softly. He opened his eyes, revealing that they were bloodshot. The natural light pouring in from the sliding glass doors on my right made him look sickly, maybe even cancerous. "Are you okay?"

"I'm fine," he said, wiping his nose with his shirt collar. I sat down beside him and put my arm over his shoulder—it was a stretch, given our size difference, but I could manage it—and he leaned his head against mine. It felt intimate.

"What's the matter?"

"I just fucked up a lot today," he said. I was glad he was being real with me, but it hurt to hear him say those words, especially when they were wrong. "I was doing so well."

"Everything's okay," I whispered, pressing my lips against his temple a couple of times. "Did you talk to Missy or your dad?"

"Just Missy," he answered. "I said I was sorry, and I'd try to get Dad to change his mind."

"See? There you go," I encouraged him. "I'm sure she really appreciated that. You should be proud of yourself."

"I still feel so bad," he cried. I could feel his tears soaking into my shirt. "What I did to you—"

"Hey," I said, "you didn't do anything to me. I was just fed up, okay? You're doing fine."

"Okay."

"What was that pill you just took?" I asked. "And how many?" I wasn't sure how many there had been before I came down the stairs; they were uncoated, and I could see a fair amount of powder residue on the floor where the little pile had been.

"Five or six," he said. I stiffened up and nudged him until he sat upright. He looked me in the eye, obviously worried. "What? I'm huge."

"I-I don't know if that's a safe dosage," I stammered. "What kind of pill was it?"

"Zoloft," he said. "Twenty-five times six…" He was counting the milligrams, and that only made things worse.

"Bryan," I whimpered, resting my head against the couch. He cursed himself again, promised me he'd be right back, and ran upstairs. I wasn't sure if he had gone to look for an adult, his phone, or the toilet. I was in such a worried state that I couldn't move for about two minutes after that, and even when I could technically move again, I remained where I was, frozen with fear. I couldn't lose Bryan again. I wanted to be upstairs with him, no matter which path he took, but I just couldn't watch something bad happen to him.

Jade came down to my level in twenty minutes' time and checked on me, Aleida tailing her like a puppy. I was physically fine by then but was still too afraid to go up those steps and see what was going on.

"Hey," she waved to me, "Bryan wants you. Something happen?"

I just shook my head at her and followed them up the stairs, where she pointed me to the end of the hall. The two of them disappeared into the dark kitchen as I entered Bryan's room without a sound except for the door shutting behind me.

He was seated on the edge of his bed with a pillow held tight against his chest and his eyes trained on the floor. I sat down next to him, unsure of what to do except put my arms around him and wait for him to do the same; he didn't.

String of Texts

THE EVENTS IN my last update were extremely hard to write but even worse to actually live through. Bryan and I promised each other we wouldn't tell anyone what happened. I was straightforward with him and said I was worried he actually *wanted* to overdose, but he assured me I was wrong and that he was out of that awful phase where he needed therapy eight days a week. It was an honest mistake, he claimed, and he was trying hard to feel better for the good of everybody.

Anyhow, I spent the night at his place and watched over him in his sleep like some sort of guardian angel. I had gotten an extra three hours that evening due to multiple sleep attacks but wasn't feeling very refreshed at all, though I still couldn't sleep. I felt like I was dreaming ... or nightmare-ing. That's insomnia for you.

Somehow, I skated by with an all-nighter and some ice-cold water in the morning that should have helped me feel perky, but every time a thought about the Lukins or future Carter-Lukins crossed my mind, I started to wilt. Their family had more issues than I could fathom. While it was relieving that I no longer had to worry about school, it was still hard to manage my time and energy after something so traumatizing had happened the night before. Somehow, I felt personally responsible for cleaning up the mess that was the Carter-Lukin residence.

Missy was up early, and I could hear her gabbing on the phone to some of her colleagues at the Sephora she managed in the mall. I interrupted her briefly to ask whether I could take a shower. Bryan was probably going to be asleep for a few more hours, and I had about a lifetime of sorrow to wash off of me. Afterwards, I could only really get dressed into the clothes I'd worn the day before, *or* I could borrow a sweatshirt from Bryan in an attempt to be hygienic. I decided to go that route. He stirred awake a minute or two after I finished changing, presumably from the noise.

"Good morning," I said, wringing my hair out in my towel. He smiled a bit and inhaled slowly, putting one hand on his chest where the surgery scar was. It must have been sore.

"Morning," he hummed back, his voice raw. His cheeks were a little puffy from crying so much the day before, but I decided not to say anything in case it brought back that tornado of emotions. "C'mere."

I went to his bed and lay down on top of the covers, scanning his face for any lingering remorse, but he seemed to have wiped his entire slate clean. I waited for him to say something; for a while, though, he just stroked my side and stared into me like I was a mirror.

"Thanks for staying with me last night," he said softly. I nodded in return, bringing my finger to the bottom of his chin. The same stubble as always was there, and I loved the feel of it.

"Of course," I whispered. He edged closer and touched our foreheads together, shutting his eyes for a moment.

"I would've stayed dead the first time if I didn't have you to live for."

I didn't say anything to his dark confession, but he still pulled me closer to his body and held me tight. I reveled in the intimacy; it felt nice being so close to him without either one of us crying or about to cry. So much had happened.

Back at home, Mom was watching the news, but she turned it off as soon as she heard me come in. I had a couple of guesses as to why.

She told me the answer before I could even question it: "There's been another murder. Mrs. Gomez from your school."

"I don't know her," I admitted, but I was still upset.

"Says she worked the night shift as a janitor," Mom told me, frowning. "They had a press conference all the way out in Newark about it. We're getting famous."

"Great," I said. "Whoever's doing it has already killed three people. What are we supposed to do, let it slide?"

"Don't get too freaked out about it, honey," she advised me warmly. "The latest victims have all been janitors, and school's not even in session anymore."

"Leo broke the female teacher pattern," I reminded her. "He shot Caroline and Bryan and himself after the first three teachers. There have been three janitors. You follow?"

Mom groaned. "See, now you're just overthinking it. Maybe we shouldn't watch the news anymore."

"And not stay informed? Funny."

She scoffed at me, knowing she couldn't do a thing to make me think sensibly. There was *another* wack job on the loose, so I wasn't the one in the wrong here, was I? Mom just shook her head in frustration and walked off in the direction of her bedroom, which was across the hall from mine. Our relationship had been pretty unhealthy over the past three years, and this was a prime example of why. Miscommunications galore.

I went outside and sat on the deck, meditating in the eighty-degree weather. I stayed out there for hours, only going inside to pour myself some lemonade and to grab my earbuds from off of my nightstand. In all those sleepless nights, I'd compiled a playlist of soothing songs that made life more bearable, and when I played it with the sunlight drenching me, I felt at ease. I'd had the night of all nights just twelve hours prior. Bryan's capricious temperament paired with my general instability made for one wild adventure, and I just thought I deserved a little break. Nature was a haven.

In the middle of "Operator" by Jim Croce, a song my father used to play on his guitar all the time, my phone vibrated in my lap and agitated me. But it was a text message from Bryan, so I forgave him for disturbing the peace. It said:

My dad wouldn't listen to me.

And so, I responded,

What exactly did you say to him?

Allow me to transcribe the rest of the conversation for you.

I didn't know how to be "sensitive" so it got heated pretty fast.

Well what happened?

. . .

We turned on Jade instead and poured out all the vodka and White Claws. Those seem to be her beverages of choice.

Bryannnnn

Don't get mad at me. We have one less problem to solve now, right?

Yeah whatever
You need to make sure your dad does the right thing for Missy tho :(

I had a question about that actually.
What if your mom spoke to him?

And said what exactly

What I clearly can't...?
I'm running out of ideas.

You think he'd listen to her? They're only friends because they met in the hospital

Well Jamie, anything's worth a shot. I really need this.

I hear ya

And then I shut off my phone, hoping I could talk to my mom some other time about confronting Mr. Lukin because she and I were now having a silent standoff.

Fourth of July

INDEPENDENCE DAY WAS actually one of the few happy times I've had since my senior year first went downhill. Because my family was so small, Mom talked with Mr. Lukin, Missy, and the Hicks family, and planned a barbecue where all of us could celebrate. For once, it felt like a normal day.

We went to the park, the same one where Caroline's memorial service had been, and gathered for the whole afternoon, since there'd be a public firework show in the evening. Bryan and I were planning to steer away from that event for obvious reasons. Summit Oaks wasn't going to release Reba for the holiday but still claimed visitation hours were much more lenient that day, so I promised Tommy we'd visit her after the festivities.

Tommy groaned. "Man, it's hot as balls out here." We were sitting on a swing set in a line: Jade, then Tommy, then me, then Bryan, then some thirteen-year-old Hicks cousins who weren't part of our conversation. All the swings were taken up by the six of us.

"Oh, quit complaining," I scolded him, giving him a look that urged him to pay more attention to Jade. I was trying really hard to make him like her, but things didn't look hopeful.

"You uh ... you want a soda, Jade?" Tommy asked. I laughed a little; he glared at me like he'd been harshly punished. Bryan and I remained on our swings as the two of them got up and headed straight for the pavilion, where there were about a million red, white, and blue coolers set up in wall formation.

"He'll start to like her," I promised Bryan, watching the two walk away slowly. "She's lovable."

Bryan cringed. "If you say so. Poor Pete's still her number one 'best friend' on Snapchat. You know how I know? 'Cause she won't stop talking about it."

"Poor you." I pouted, pretending to wipe tears from my eyes. "She's, like, the prettiest girl I know. He's all over that." She could pass for a Capodi.

"Explains why he likes you," Bryan teased, reaching his hand out for me to hold. I liked when he did that; it reminded me of our first date, when we were at Subway a tad too late at night.

"Ha ha, hilarious."

When we ate lunch, Missy and Mr. Lukin formally met Tommy's parents, aunts, and uncles, as well as Sam and his son Matt (who even I had yet to meet). Wedged between Sam and Bryan on one of the pavilion benches, I was almost to the point of overheating; the area was loud with friendly chatter and hot with the fire of a grill, plus the fact that it was July. The sun was beating down on the ground, deeming puddles too bright to look at. It was seriously a New Jersey summer if I've ever seen one—but still I loved the atmosphere.

Mom suddenly stood up from the table during a rich gossip session with Mrs. Hicks. Seeing as my back was turned to the street, I couldn't tell what she was so excited about, but she plucked Sam and me out of our seats on her way around the table. I grabbed Bryan along the way.

As we walked, I followed her gaze to a very particular pink Cadillac in the church parking lot across the street from the park. The plate was from Wyoming, meaning only one thing: Aunt Cathy was here. I wasn't told ahead of time that she'd be coming, but it was a pleasant surprise because it had been so long. Sam, Bryan, and I tagged along at Mom's heel.

"Frankie!" Cathy shouted as she exited her flashy car. Bryan and I looked at each other, hanging behind as Mom and Sam rushed ahead of us to greet my long-lost aunt.

She looked just like my mother, only a bit older and more sophisticated in the way she presented herself. Her skin was darker, firmer. Her hair was in ringlets and her wrists were practically weighed down to the ground by stacks of bangles. Last time I saw her was multiple Christmases ago, and she was an ER nurse then; what a 180 her life had made.

"Hey, Jamie!" she exclaimed after she was done swarming Mom and Sam in hugs. How she already knew him, I didn't know—maybe they'd been planning this for a while. "How has my favorite niece been?"

"Good," I said, stepping forward to hug her. When I let go, she squeezed Bryan as well. She was certainly not shy and reminded me very much of someone.

"You must be the boyfriend!" Cathy gleamed.

"I guess you've heard about me." He laughed. "Nice to meet you. I'm Bryan."

"You picked a good one," she whispered to me, shaking his hand despite the overzealous embrace from seconds before. The five of us walked back together in a line, but Bryan and I didn't sit back down in our old spots. We agreed that it was a little crowded and would prefer to find someplace where the sun wouldn't burn so much.

We sat under a pink tree next to the pavilion, our backs facing the party to add to our privacy. We had a nice view there: a couple of houses stood in the distance where people were hosting cookouts of their own, and the smells wafted into the park grounds. The background noises of cars and people talking were so humanizing, I thought, because I spent most of my time holed up in a house and had only recently started using the deck for quietude. School made me take everything for granted, the outdoor world being at the top of the list.

"I don't know what I'm gonna do this summer," Bryan sighed, coaxing individual blades of grass out of the earth with his fingers. "We were gonna go to England in a few weeks, but I can't fly yet."

I frowned. "That's too bad."

"I think Missy's gonna go anyway," he said, but he didn't look upset about the fact. Even though his opinion of her was bittersweet, the apathy in his face wasn't because he didn't care about her whereabouts—no, it was more like he thought she deserved this trip, and so he wasn't the least bit jealous that he couldn't go along. That was some definite improvement.

"My mom and I usually drive down to Atlantic City every summer," I said. "You should come with us this time."

"Sure," he smiled, "thanks."

"Don't thank me yet," I warned. "Wait till you've been locked in a car with Frankie for two hours."

"Oh, I'm *so* pumped!"

I fell asleep on Bryan halfway through that conversation. When I woke up, we had the pleasurable company of Tommy and Jade, who were apparently fed up with the adults by that point in time. There were other kids in the pavilion still, but none of us were close with any of them. Bryan had probably invited Tommy and Jade over out of boredom.

"*A daughter was born, and they called her Aurora. Yes, they named her after the dawn, for she filled their lives with sunshine,*" Tommy monologued, for he was the first to acknowledge that my eyes were open.

I was quiet for a second before saying, "It's amazing how many Disney movies you can quote."

Jade and Bryan both punched him in the biceps until he jumped to his defense: "I got a twin sister and a girl best friend, a'ight?"

With my voice sounding hazy to my own ears and my cheek still leaning on Bryan's chest, I looked over at Jade and told her, "Ask him why he likes Belle the best."

"I said it a million times, and I'll say it again, *ain't nothing wrong with a French chick*," he emphasized, making large hand gestures. Jade laughed pretty hard, and I thought I saw Tommy smile as a result, but maybe I was hallucinating. "Plus, you know, she likes ugly dudes."

"Belle *is* pretty hot," Bryan piped in. I made a face at him, and he started feebly correcting himself. "Hot for a ... a tramp ...?"

I rolled my eyes, surprised that he and Tommy seemed so into princesses. Aside from my longstanding knowledge that Tommy had an expansive Disney inventory in his brain, I never would have pictured the two bonding over it.

"You know," Jade added, "Bryan and I are French."

Her brother shook his head at her awful attempt at flirting, and I watched his chest heave with laughter. It was nice to see his progress. "Jade, Jade, Jade."

"What?"

Bryan held out both hands like a scale and said, "Carter ... and Lukin. Where does French come in?"

"Are you telling me *Ancestry.com* is a liar?"

"No," he said, "I'm saying we're *obviously* Belarusian."

Tommy smiled. "Belarus, huh?"

The rest of the day played out something like that. I did end up talking to Matt, Sam's son, who was going to be a freshman at Bridgewood the following school year. He claimed he was TikTok famous and actually proved to be quite funny, just like his dad; it was weird to think of him potentially becoming my step-brother, but seeing as I had only seen him once in all the time Sam and Mom were dating, I knew it wouldn't become an issue.

Tommy, Bryan, Jade, and I all went to Summit Oaks together in the evening. The original plan was just for Tommy and me to go, but the four of us had really connected that day as a friend group and we didn't want the fun to end at the park. Obviously, visiting a psychiatric hospital was going to dampen our moods, but it was better to do it together than not. It was an hour drive—plenty of time to play car games and cajole secrets out of one another.

It wasn't until evening struck that I began feeling nervous pangs inside me. Seeing the hospital in the flesh made me realize that it was real and that there were unfortunate souls in there who couldn't get out because they needed help. Plus, Tommy had mentioned earlier that Reba thought I had done something to her, and whether that idea remained in her mind, I wasn't positive. I was also on edge about seeing so many people with mental health conditions at once, and worried they'd try to talk to me or my friends, seeing as I wasn't prepared to handle anyone's grievances *except* Reba's. But I kept it together for Tommy, who was even more nervous than I was, based on the way he bounced his knee up and down in the lobby of the visitation center. It looked just like a doctor's office, only no one handed out face masks and no squalling children were present. Jade was probably the youngest person there.

You could hear shrieks echoing from deep within the building if you tuned out the buzz of conversation; they were awful, blood-curdling screams that only ceased when sedatives were administered. Poor patients.

I know I said the Fourth of July was a happy day for me,

and that's still true—it was. But "happy" is merely subjective, and for me it means "at peace." When I finally saw Reba that day it felt like I'd been lustrated.

She *hugged* me.

Ch-Ch-Ch-Ch-Changes

PRETTY SOON MY house became everybody's house. You know, public property? Take what you want and don't feel bad about it? That kind of thing.

Two days after the Fourth of July, Mom told me Cathy would be staying in one of our basement rooms for a few weeks because she was "going through another major lifestyle change." As a woman who had spent *years* consistently studying medical procedure, it amazed me how whimsical she was; she was like the Missy of my family. *That's* who she reminded me of.

In fact, the two of them quickly became friends due to their similar personalities. They were practically carbon copies of each other. Missy was over at my house all the time, and whenever I went to Bryan's to escape the loud laughter and constant "I miss wine" jokes now that Cathy had pledged to abstain from alcohol in support of Missy's pregnancy, they followed me. Hearing all of their noise was especially hard when I was trying to study for my Calc and Physics finals. I thought going someplace else would help, but it really didn't. I even thought about crashing at Tommy's but ruled that out since his family was struggling with enough at the moment.

Having *another* Aunt Missy to deal with was stressful for Bryan. I felt bad that I couldn't even warn him about her because she had never been present in my childhood and I was learning her eccentricities at the same time as he was. As a result, he took his frustrations out on me. I had to mentally prepare for the yelling and hostility each time I saw him; to put it simply, it was like the week after his surgery was happening all over again, only neither of us was physically hurt.

So, almost as quickly as Mom broke the news of Cathy's move to me, the chaos began.

We were planning to have dinner as a family when my mother and her sister stopped to chat in the middle of cooking and burned all of the food. That emitted some lovely fumes. Then Sam had an emergency to handle with his ex-wife as *soon* as they slapped something edible down on our plates, and his leave ruined the togetherness we were striving for, if you will. It was then that Cathy announced she would be dabbling with entrepreneurship during her stay and that she needed money from us. When Sam returned, he and Mom declared that he'd be moving in as well, and that I'd have to get my things out of the basement to make room for Matt when Sam had custody of him on the weekends.

Oh. My. GOD. Talk about a nightmare.

Needless to say, this brought on a couple of cataplexy attacks, and I dealt with them in the privacy of either my bedroom, the shower, or the deck, where I often went to escape the hoi polloi swarming my home. You really can't blame me for being dramatic; I was *just* getting used to living with only one other person, and now there were three, plus Missy, Matt, Tommy, and Bryan on some occasions. That made seven.

I called Tommy on the phone to deliver the news that he was never going to see my house again because I couldn't deal with another human being clogging it like sentient cholesterol.

"I don't know how to tell Bryan I probably won't want to hang out as much," I admitted, knowing this was yet another problem these new developments had posed.

"Then don't," Tommy suggested, nonchalant. "He'll get it. He's chill."

"No, you don't understand," I groaned, slapping my palm against my forehead. The sun hung low in the sky, melting into a slop of orange as I spoke, but the glare was a lot less prominent with my hand in my face. "If I don't say anything, he'll think I want to break up. Also, you know how I told you Bryan's aunt Missy and my aunt Cathy are, like, besties now? Well Bryan thinks that's just *sublime* and whenever he gets pissed off about it, he goes all Bruce Banner and takes it out on me. *Me.* I mean, don't get me wrong, I love the guy, but with all these new people in my house twenty-four-seven, I don't think I can deal with one who actually has something to say to me. Something bad, anyway. Does that make me a bad person? Avoiding him when he's stressed?"

"Damn, J," Tommy said somewhat quietly, chuckling at my ranting. "I'm not even gonna ask how you know who Bruce Banner is, but lemme just say, you got a right to be so upset. You're just claustrophobic. Where you at now?"

"Out back," I told him. "I'm afraid I've taken the deck for granted up until this point. Tomorrow, it'll be recolonized."

Tommy laughed at me. "Yo, relax. You'll be a'ight. Go for a walk. Swing by my place. Man, it's like a ghost town up in here."

"Really? Why?"

"No Reba? No Sistine and Nichole," he explained. That made sense. "I ain't heard from those two in a *looong* time. Bless up, right?"

"Truly." I laughed. "I haven't heard from them either. Maybe it's just 'cause school let out."

"They don't live too far from us though. Thought we'd see 'em in public by now, but I guess not. It's like they're hiding."

Interesting.

"I've been so wrapped up in my own issues that I didn't even notice they were gone," I admitted. "I hope I'm not, like, ignoring you or something."

"No, you good, J."

"Good." I turned my phone's speaker away from my mouth and sipped on my Starbucks iced tea, which Sam had gotten for me on his way back from his ex-wife's. He was sympathetic. "Anything new with Jade?"

"I dunno." He sighed. His tone implied he didn't feel like delving into the subject. "She's real nice and all but—"

"Hey," I interrupted. "Stick it out, okay? Please? She's more than 'nice'."

"Since when do you care?"

I screwed up my face, hoping desperately that I wouldn't spill Bryan's assumption that Tommy still liked me. "Well ... she's going through a lot at home and all. I would know."

"Right. It's just so awkward 'cause she's a sophomore," Tommy whined. "I dunno how I feel about that yet."

"Oh, please. She's more mature than you," I pointed out.

"Yeah, but she's *fifteen*," he added. "What if I wanna ... you know?"

"Well, that's very sweet of you to consider, but I don't think that'll be a relevant problem for at least a couple more months given the rate you're at. She'll be sixteen by then."

"What if I told you I like older girls?" Tommy asked. He was seventeen, and I was eighteen, so this comment made Bryan's theory all the more accurate. "A brother could always go after a cougar and feel like a winner."

"Oh, shut your face."

Late that evening, I finally found some peace. It was short-lived, but I liked it anyway. From my bedroom, the house was dead quiet, and I wrongly assumed it was because Mom had fallen asleep and Cathy had gone to Missy's; as it turns out, the three of them were actually having margaritas, virgin for some, out on the deck. I could hear their loud, jocular chatter when I left my room to get some water and the pit in my stomach expanded when I realized the fun wasn't over.

It must have been eleven-thirty, which is late for my mom. Missy seemed like the nighttime socialite if you ask me, so her energy wasn't surprising; Cathy, well, I can't speak for her. But the two of them, amazingly sober, certainly brought a beast out of my mother that would not go to sleep until the wee hours of the morning.

In the meantime, the three of them stampeded into the house. Mom was obviously inebriated, and Missy and Cathy likely were probably living vicariously through her; together they made enough noise to wake up all of Banshee. I was a little concerned when they went out the front door and piled into Cathy's pink Cadillac, which I could see through my bedroom window of course, and headed in the direction of Bryan's home.

Shortly thereafter, I received a complaint text from my poor boyfriend, expressing wrath in a series of cuss words. When he called me on the phone, I was admittedly a little scared to answer.

"Hello?"

"Hey," Bryan said, though he sounded terse. "What the hell."

"Look, I didn't send them over," I said, preparing for a war. "They left without saying a word to me."

"Doesn't look like you tried to stop them either!" he yelled. "Jade and I are trying to sleep, and now everyone's yelling at my dad. Has Missy been drinking?"

"Of course not!" I cried. "I think you're forgetting that I have to *live* with this now."

"I think *you're* forgetting that *I* have to live with it, too," he huffed. "The hell are we supposed to do? Move out?"

"God, I wish." We both seemed to settle down after that. I told him I was worried about the sanctity of my old life being destroyed, but that really applied to the both of us. "What are they saying to your dad?"

"Your mom keeps yelling the word 'crib'." He sighed. "I think they're finally intervening."

Funny, I had completely forgotten to talk to my mom about that like Bryan had asked me to. I bet he didn't expect her to do it completely hammered, but, you know, that's a judgment call.

I frowned. "I don't know how serious he'll take it if one of them is wasted."

"Two of them, actually," Bryan said. "Dad's had a long night."

Even though I could hear some shouting through Bryan's line, there was something so hollow about his voice right then that made me want to bawl my eyes out, but I held it together.

"I'm sorry," I mumbled.

I imagined Bryan shaking his head in understanding of my apology. "Look, it's fine. You let things get messy, but it'll be over tomorrow. It's fine." Ouch. When I didn't say anything in return, he asked, "Hello?"

"I'm still here," I said, hurt. "I didn't 'let things get messy.' I don't babysit thirty-year-olds."

"What, you don't think tonight would've been a good day to start?" Bryan asked. "I mean, do you *hear* this?"

"Yes, I hear it," I snapped. "If you think I had any say in how crazy things got tonight, then why don't you go do something about it? If they'll listen to me, they'll listen to you, huh?"

"Oh, for fuck's sake." Bryan groaned. "You know why this is your problem? 'Cause they were at *your* house. Not my fault they started a party and brought it with them."

"That doesn't make it my fault either! I was hiding out in my room because they were being too loud!"

"I don't even wanna hear it, Jamie."

"Well, fuck you! Is that what you wanna hear?" I hung up on him right as my legs grew weak. I didn't go completely limp like usual, just fell on the floor and had some trouble standing back up.

I sat down on my bed and stared at the wall, hoping something good could come out of this argument. The longer I gazed, the people in my posters started to dance and the words became three-dimensional, so I looked away because I didn't want to focus on anything right now except how wrong Bryan was. Healthy, right?

Sistine Moore

"SHE WASN'T EVEN *sweating.*"

After Bryan and I had the argument about our irresponsible family members, we didn't speak at all overnight. The next day, however, something extraordinary happened to Bryan while he was at the gym, and he said he needed to fill me in on it. I only decided to listen to him because he mentioned Sistine, who had been amazingly quiet ever since summer break started, and I was naturally curious about what he had to say. My phone was on low battery, so I was forced to hear the details in person.

Sitting in his office chair, facing the bed where I sat, he told me his story. He had been trying to bench press when she approached him, seemingly by happenstance. This would have been believable had she been wearing workout clothes rather than her usual baggy skater attire. Of course, her mere presence at a gym and the fact that she wasn't there with Nichole were additional red flags. At first, Bryan feared she would ask if he needed a spot, but instead she just knelt beside him and talked about the latest news report.

"She said it was Dr. Oakhurst this time," Bryan told me, his eyes on the hardwood floor. "I hate to be *that* person, but I'm not even surprised anymore."

"No one is."

Bryan flicked his eyes up at me, not entirely surprised that I'd offered input despite being mad at him, but clearly, he was affected by the undertow of my comment. I felt kind of bad after seeing that look on his face, but I didn't do anything about it for the sake of staying on topic.

"Anyway, uh," he started, straightening his back and touching his scar through his shirt by a force of habit. Maybe just talking about another murder reminded him he could have been killed when Leo shot him. It reminded me, at least. "She started going on about how Reba was so upset about the deaths that she was put in a rubber room, and that Dr. Oakhurst wouldn't be the last by the looks of it. She's probably right.

"And then I asked her what she wanted, and she grinned at me like I'd said a keyword or something," he continued. "Then she stuck her hands in her pockets and just walked away. I dunno, it felt like she was seeking me out. I thought you should know."

"Why exactly?" I asked, tilting my head to the side. I wasn't *actually* curious if that helps clarify my bitter mood for you. "She's harmless. She's just like that."

Again, his puppy eyes scrutinized me, moving up and down my face like a scanner as he found the words to confront me. "I'm not digging this passive aggressive thing you got going on."

"Well, suck it up. I don't wanna be here."

"Jamie," he said pleadingly. "I know you're mad at me, but you gotta understand I'm a guy, and I don't get sensitive about the same things you do. I just want to have a civilized conversation."

"I'm gonna choose to ignore how sexist that was so we can focus on the *first* mistake you made," I scoffed. "And what was that?" he asked. "Does it have anything to do with the fact that I'm angry 'cause I was shot in the lung two months ago?"

"Yes!" I exclaimed. "I get why you're struggling, and I'm normally fine with being your outlet, but sometimes you take things *way* too far, and I don't like it! Remember last time? And now this? You actually had the audacity to blame me for two adults getting drunk and yelling at each other, about an issue that *needed* to be talked about, if I might add."

Bryan looked at me like he was going to say something, but instead he chuckled at himself, bringing his gaze to the wall on his right instead of staying on me. His open mouth formed a smirk, and he began shaking his head. In all honesty, I didn't know what that meant, so I was terrified at the idea of him screaming at me again and turning this into a much bigger problem than it needed to be. But he didn't say a word for another few seconds, and while my heart rate climbed, his temper plummeted.

"Can't believe I'm saying this, but I'm just now realizing how ridiculous I am," he mumbled, refusing eye contact at this point. I could see his cheeks turning pink. I let out a sharp exhale, somehow finding relief in his pitiful expression. "Sorry."

It couldn't be clearer how humiliated he was.

"Thank you," I said, reaching forward to place my hand on top of his.

"Yeah."

"I don't know if this helps," I tried, "but Sistine came up to me one time and did some freaky stuff, so I don't think she went looking for you specifically. I think she's just weirdly outgoing."

He grabbed my hand back and finally looked at me. "What'd

she do?"

"She, like, signed the Cross on me or something." I shrugged. It was discomforting to make light of that scenario, but it was necessary in the moment. "Which I don't think you're supposed to do on other people, at least not if you're Sistine Moore." That made him laugh. Good for me.

"You know what bothered me the most though?" he asked, bearing a pensive look on his face. "She doesn't seem to care about Reba at all anymore. It was like she's the reason she's in the hospital in the first place. Don't you think? Something didn't feel right about how she talked about her best friend like that."

This might be another thing for you to consider, Agent. I know I did.

You know, something I find inconceivable is that back in March and April, I thought I was so inured—I think "numb" was the word I used—to those three teachers dying, but now that a ninth person had passed away, the news felt like a simple weather report to me. Yes, I was stung and mourned for each of the victims thus far, but the panic attacks and existential crises dwindled down to practically none after Bryan survived.

In no way do I mean any disrespect for the deceased; they are all severely missed, by me and many others, but no longer was I feeling personally targeted by these homicides. And I think I meant it this time.

Later in the evening, Bryan's family and I were watching the news together—that was risky for people like us, but somehow it seemed to be the only watchable item on TV lately. Everything else was too cheerful with its Hollywood cribs and false senses of reality. Max Figuerra didn't sugarcoat things for us.

It surprised me to see you on that big screen. Or maybe it

surprised me that I hadn't seen you on it until that point, five months after the first shooting. Either way, everyone sat forward as soon as they saw your stark face, and I could've sworn I heard our collective heartbeat thrumming louder and louder by the second.

A familiar yet all too blurry picture appeared in the top right corner of the screen while you spoke about a potential new suspect who was a "flight risk" that had indeed fled. When you finally said the name Wesley Martin, my lungs deflated. I knew for a fact that he was on his way to Cuba at that moment, and he wasn't going there to seek asylum.

"The suspect is an eighteen-year-old male whose relationship to Capodi is potentially romantic," you said. "He has regular access to weapons, which we discovered in accordance with the various bullet sizes found in the victims." Mr. Lukin shut the TV off after that, so we didn't get to hear the rest of the report, but frankly we didn't need to. I looked at Bryan, whose eyes were wide.

"I told you he was bi," Bryan murmured, but he looked shaken up. I couldn't tell whether his disturbed state would escalate or not, so I took him by the hand and dragged him to the privacy of his bedroom. He was always relatively embarrassed or sometimes even disgusted with himself after breaking down—I was doing him a favor by taking him out of other people's sight.

"I should be over it," he said to me, sitting down on his bed and cradling his own head in his arms.

"No one else is over it yet," I reminded him. "You're doing great, Bryan. How do you feel?"

"I don't know," he hummed. I put my hand on his back and sat down at his side, unsure of how to handle the situation because it was alarmingly mild. "I just can't believe Wes would do something like this."

"Well, who's to say he actually did?" I asked. "I was a suspect for a while, but look at me. I'm no criminal."

He finally sat up straight and nodded at me, collapsing me in a bear hug. I kissed his cheek and continued stroking his back in a circular pattern, still wrapping my head around how calm he was. At the time, I was more confused than proud, but now I'm just proud. Very much so.

Cathy Spencer

MOM AND SAM left me alone to babysit Matt and Cathy on the following Saturday.

I say "babysit" because, well, neither my mother nor I knew Matt's level of maturity very well, but both of us knew Cathy's. While she could be serious when it was absolutely imperative, like in the hospital where she used to work, other times she was flaky and quaint.

Bryan was unavailable to keep me company because he had therapy, and Tommy was at Summit Oaks. At first, I was annoyed at the fact that I had to go at this alone, but I got used to Matt and Cathy pretty fast. We all kind of went our own ways; Matt was already familiar with the house for some reason, as was Cathy, who had taken up cooking since her arrival less than a week prior. I spent less time supervising and more time lazing around on the couch.

She made us some Monte Cristos for lunch. That was when

I really started to get to know Matt, who, by the way, would not take his eyes off of Cathy the entire time we talked. Is it incest if it's his nonlegal step-aunt?

"So, you two go to the same school, right?" Cathy asked us.

"Would," I corrected her in the midst of chewing. "I graduated."

"And I don't technically go there yet," Matt added. "Hey, what's up with the principal?"

"What's *up* with him?" I asked, almost choking on my food. "He passed away three days ago."

"Yeah, but wasn't it on the news or something?" Matt asked. "I don't pay much attention to it, but my mom won't turn Channel 8 off for the life of me."

"And it's a damn good thing," I told him, glancing at Cathy for approval before realizing she had only been here about as long as Matt had. "You guys don't know, do you?"

"I'm gonna go with 'no'," Cathy chimed in, winking at Matt. "I do know that poor kid," she paused, gesturing a line on her neck that indicated suicide, "himself."

"He wasn't a *poor* kid," I said. "He shot five people and then himself."

"Holy shit!" Matt exclaimed, laughing at my statement. I gave him a stern look, and he quieted down promptly. I don't know why he found that impressive. "Who were they?"

"Three were teachers, and two were students," I listed. I pushed my plate away from me and looked down at my lap, suddenly feeling too full to eat. In a soft voice, I told them, "He shot Bryan."

"That your boyfriend?"

"Mhmm."

"Well, I'm glad he's doing better," Cathy commented. "He is, isn't he?" I just nodded.

"Wait, if the killer is dead, who killed the principal?" Matt asked. "Maybe it's a ghost."

"Police think there's a copycat killer now." I sighed, thinking about how you suspected *I* was the one fulfilling Leo's duties. "There were three other victims before the principal that the new guy killed. If he follows the same pattern as Leo, he'll get to one other person and then ... and then kill himself. I hope it ends there."

"That's heavy," Cathy mumbled, sipping from her ice water.

"How do you know so much about it?" Matt asked me.

I really didn't want to tell them I'd been questioned as a suspect and accused of three felonies, so I said my mother was like Matt's in that she never turned off the news—plus, I knew each of the victims personally, so it was hard not to pick up a pattern.

Matt's mouth fell open. "Wait, so do you know Wesley Martin? I think I heard that name somewhere."

"I do," I said, "and he's *not* a fugitive." Yet.

"How do you figure?" Cathy asked.

"He's in Cuba," I said, chuckling at the simplicity of it. "He goes every year to see his grandparents. He's not hiding from anyone."

"But ... wasn't he, like, in love with the murderer? Is that what that FBI guy said?" Matt asked, squinting out of confusion. "I don't get it."

"There's nothing to 'get,'" I demanded, my hands losing most of their strength. "He's innocent!"

The two of them shrugged at me, and Matt concluded, "You would know."

When I could lift my plate, I threw my quarter-of-a-sandwich in the trash and excused myself, knowing at this point that Matt and Cathy were civil enough that I didn't need to micromanage them.

Talking about the deaths wasn't as sweet of a release as I thought it would be. Instead, it reminded me of my time in the interrogation room, and in Leo's car, and in the hospital with

Bryan. All bad memories. But worst of all, it reminded me of the message scrawled on Leo's shower wall: "Hicks & Hesson." Misspelled, whatever—it was still my name. Just about half the Bridgewood population was illiterate anyways, so that wasn't a clue of any kind.

The names didn't make any sense to me. Like I said, there would supposedly be one more victim before the copycat killer offed himself, and the fact that there were two names made me uneasy. Maybe the kills weren't intended to be an exact copy of Leo's—maybe the list was going to expand this time and continue in a lethal cycle, adding by one each round until Banshee contained no one but the perpetrator.

Only for a moment, I wondered if the copycat killer had been Reba Hicks, for it was her name listed on top of mine. She could have chosen me and then planned to kill herself. But Dr. Oakhurst had died while she was still under Summit Oaks' security, and she of all people would know how to spell my last name, so she would have told Leo the correct spelling. And so would Tommy, but I never for a *second* believed he would have the capacity to shoot five people and then himself.

I fell asleep for a couple of hours in the bathroom while I was washing my hands. I only woke up because the sink had overflowed, and water was dripping onto me. There was some periodic knocking at the door that I *thought* was part of my dream.

"Jamie?" called Cathy's voice. "Hello? Everything okay in there?"

"I'm fine," I called out, opening the door as I wrung my hair out lest she knock again. She glanced at me, noting tile impressions on my face, and then at the running faucet, which I was in no rush to turn off. I was still feeling a little hazy.

"What happened?" she asked. "Matt's trying to take a shower."

"I fell asleep," I said. She made an awful face at me, like

that had been some horrible excuse for taking so long in the bathroom. "What?"

"That's hysterical!"

"Excuse me?" I snorted. "You *do* know I have narcolepsy?"

She drew her neck back and relaxed her facial muscles as she realized she didn't actually know that about me. Either that, or she had forgotten completely because she had lived in Wyoming for practically my whole life. My heart dropped to the floor at her lack of consideration. She stammered out, "I-I gotta go find Frankie," and then hauled herself out of the threshold. I spotted Matt a little ways down the hall, holding a bath towel in his arm. He raised his eyebrows at the embarrassing encounter.

I locked myself in my room after that.

Family Pedigree

WESLEY MARTIN WAS arrested on July seventeenth, directly after he returned home from Cuba, directly after Willam McGuire was shot and placed in the ICU. The bullet *just* missed his brain, according to Max Figuerra. But he had already lost an eye no matter what his fate was.

What made things a thousand times worse was that Willam had supposedly been attacked from behind, based on the details of his injury, so he couldn't see who the perpetrator was. I think that's one of several reasons the names Martin and McGuire spread like a disease in the town. I remember Willam's oblivion being a major setback for you, but if this copycat exercised precision, we only had one more event to watch for now: a suicide.

Amazingly, that fact put Bryan's mind at ease, but for a short time, I was about as stressed as when I had found out Caroline was dead. I could barely walk after hearing the news about

Willam, even when I *wasn't* in the midst of a cataplexy attack. I just had this unrelenting image in my head of unwrapping Willam's bandages eerily slow, but when I came upon the last layer of gauze, the thing I saw in replacement of his eye socket was bloody and throbbing and deep and large enough to bury my entire fist in.

I think the main reason I was panicking were the questions I couldn't seem to answer. Was I wrong again about who the killer could, or couldn't be? Had I put my faith in the hands of a rotten murderer for the second time in just two months? What did that mean for me? Was there something criminal in everyone *else* I trusted? Or in me?

Bryan spent the night at my house after we found out Wes was apprehended. The whole evening, he reassured me the nightmare was almost over and that we just had to wait for the "grand finale." Looking back, I see that had been a pretty sick way to put it. I understood why he wanted the terrorist to die, but I wanted the killings to stop in general. Copycat suicide included. I'd have felt more secure if he were caught and sentenced to life in prison. Killing himself, however, would leave an even darker stain on my conscience, a lack of justice so harrowing that nothing could repair it. Whose problem would suicide even solve? Leo's? Because last time I checked, it was a little too late for Leo to still have a problem with the citizens of Banshee.

"Something's bothering you," Bryan said after a short quiet period. I opened my mouth to spout out something sarcastic, but he held up his hand in protest. "Something *else*."

Nervously twiddling my phone in my hands, I looked over at the wall and back to Bryan. "Cathy."

"What's up with her?" he asked. I could tell the subject piqued his interest.

"Remember how I told you she didn't know I had narcolepsy?" I asked to refresh his memory. "Ever since then, she and Mom have been arguing, and it's just so awkward having her here."

"What do they argue about?"

"Nonsense," I said. "Whether we should have the news on, whether Cathy should be making so much food, whether her whole business approach is a good idea ... oh, and why Cathy randomly showed up after so many years of exile. You know what came out of *that* argument? That she's legally bankrupt and didn't wanna tell us. She's a leech, Bryan. A literal leech."

"Jesus," he remarked. "I had no idea. She seemed likable."

"No, she did not," I scoffed incredulously, rolling my eyes. "Don't even pretend you don't hate her guts. It's okay, a lot of people do."

"A lot?" Bryan asked.

"Think about it. The only person she gets along with is Missy," I told him. "Just listen. You can hear them laughing from here." I held up my finger to ensure he listened, and it was true. She and Missy were in the jacuzzi out back, and we could hear them shouting and splashing.

Bryan sighed, pinching the bridge of his nose at our problematic family members. "What are you guys planning on doing about it? I mean if you've considered doing anything at all."

"We need to make sure she gets a job first," I determined. "Mom sent her resume to four restaurants, the hospital, a clothing store, and Sephora. I think she was trying to cover all the gray areas of her interests."

Bryan groaned. "God, I hope she gets the Sephora job. That way she'll be so tired of Missy by the end of the day they won't want to hang out."

I laughed despite our cruel subject matter. "Hear, hear. Have Missy put in a good word for her."

"Oh, I will. Sometimes, I swear they're involved," Bryan said, shaking his head at the thought.

"Maybe they are." I shrugged. "Cathy's single."

"Wait. That'd be so complicated 'cause Missy's having a baby with my dad," Bryan said, his words slowing down toward the end of the sentence as he registered what he was saying. "If Missy is my aunt *and* potential stepmom, and she winds up marrying your aunt, does that make Cathy my aunt and stepmom, too? Will I have three parents? Does that make us related? Are we gonna be cousins?"

I laughed some more at the twisted thought and wondered aloud, "What about Missy's kid? What's its relation to us?" Something about the fact that this revolting conversation had nothing to do with murder was very heartening.

Bryan hummed, gazing at the ceiling in ponderation. "If Missy is my aunt and stepmom, and my dad is the father, the kid is my cousin and half-sibling. Since marriage would make Missy your aunt, the kid would be your cousin, and I'd be your cousin's half-brother. So ... half-cousin?"

"God, I hope not." Already this offbeat talk was making me feel better about Willam and Cathy. "And hey, if they don't turn out to be lesbians and get hitched, then I don't have to worry about all that. Only you do."

"Oh, well sign me up!" Bryan teased. "You didn't happen to write down that whole pedigree, did you?"

"Unfortunately, no."

Then we delved into the subject of Tommy and Jade getting married, and whose titles that would alter. That reminded me that I wanted to video call Tommy at some point that night, and Bryan was on board with the idea. Anything to keep us distracted.

Tommy answered my call within a couple of rings. He was sitting in his car but not driving anywhere. "Yo."

"Hey," I said, and Bryan waved.

"What's good, Bry?"

"We were just talking about the possibility of becoming cousins," Bryan summarized, and Tommy's reaction caused me to burst out laughing. "'Cause our aunts might be lesbians and all."

"Whoa, what?" Tommy asked. "Time out, time out."

"It's just a theory," I explained. "They're the only people that can stand each other, and they're together twenty-four-seven, so it makes sense. We wouldn't be surprised if they were romantically affiliated."

There was a soft voice coming from Tommy's line, and then he revealed that Jade was in the passenger seat. What a surprise for Bryan and me. He grinned when he saw his sister on the screen, probably because he hadn't expected Tommy to start actually going out with her in public.

"Cathy and Missy are *lesbians*?" she repeated, her mouth agape.

"Well, not exactly," Bryan corrected her. "They're just way too close for a couple of thirty-year-old women who're next to broke, don't you think?"

Jade rolled her eyes. "I don't think that makes people gay, Bryan."

"Oh, it doesn't," I added. "You had to hear the full conversation for this theory to make sense."

Tommy laughed. "Whatever you say. Whatcha up to?"

"We just told you," I said. "What about you guys? Why're you in the car?"

"Well, uh ..." He sighed, adjusting in his seat. He turned his phone sideways so that Jade fit in the frame and set us down somewhere on his dashboard. "Is it okay if I talk about Wes?"

Bryan nodded. "Sure."

"We just left Reba's," Tommy said. "She ain't takin' the news too well. She's convinced he didn't do nothin' wrong."

"Why's that?" Bryan asked. Maybe this would be difficult to talk about after all since each of us seemed to have different opinions.

"Well, Willam didn't see who it was, so he can't confirm,"

Tommy said, lifting a finger as if to count the reasons. "Reba put on a real convincing show, too. She act like she *knows* it ain't Wes." Two fingers now.

"Yeah, she kept saying she knew who it *actually* was," Jade piped in, screwing up her face at the puzzling fact. Tommy lifted another finger. "But then again, she wouldn't tell us. And, you know, she's ... she's in there for a reason. They made us leave early 'cause she was so riled up."

"There's that, too." Tommy nodded in agreement. "I dunno what to think of it."

"Do you believe her at all?" I asked.

He shrugged. "I believe *she* believes it. Y'know, she also thinks someone's out to get her."

I swallowed hard. After you told me there would be no task force protecting me and the Hicks twins, I'm almost positive neither of them got the message that they were potential prey like me. That's flawed, especially since Reba had figured it out on her own.

"Well, sure," I said, my voice too airy to sound natural. "Everybody thinks someone's after them. Desperate times."

"Nah," Tommy shook his head, "it's more than that. She actually was gettin' death threats before she went to the hospital, so she might be right. But doc says it could be schizophrenia."

"Right." I frowned. I looked at Bryan with worry in my eye, so he grabbed my free hand and squeezed it gently.

"She told me Nichole came to visit her, but it didn't go well, probably for the same reason," Tommy said, sighing shamefully. "And Willam probably won't ever see again. Was it both eyes, or?"

"I heard it was just his left," Bryan contributed. "He's already legally blind though, so this didn't do him any favors. I know because he didn't get cleared for hockey."

"He's in the ICU, isn't he?" Jade asked. Tommy nodded at her. "He'll be okay, right?"

I started to nod, too. "Other than the pain—"

"And a lifetime of therapy, yes." Bryan did the honors of bringing reality to our speculations.

"Shit," Tommy muttered. "Y'all sure this is okay to talk about?"

Bryan and I glanced at each other and then back at the screen. "I could stand to change the subject," I said, deducing from the look in Bryan's eyes. And then it was like we'd never said a thing. Tommy started driving home and Jade held his phone, the two of them keeping us entertained with horrible radio duets until Tommy's mom called, and we had to hang up.

"He's sweet," I said to Bryan. "Taking her to go see Reba and all."

"Does that mean anything?" Bryan asked. "I mean, the four of us went together."

"It's just nice." I shrugged. "Clearly, he trusts her to visit his unstable sister."

"I see."

I sighed heavily. "Reba's so different now."

"I know," he said. "I used to hate her guts. Now I feel bad."

"I wonder what she knows," I said, leaning my face against his chest. "Or *thinks* she knows. Maybe it's the reason she stopped talking to Sistine and Nichole. Well, maybe just Sistine now—who can say."

Bryan chuckled. "I just wanna know what she could have possibly done to lose their trust. They were, like, sisters before all this shit happened."

"Well, girls are nasty to each other," I said. "It's that simple."

"Even the ones they like?"

"Sometimes, yes."

"What about guys they like?"

"Only if they deserve it. And trust me, you'd know if you deserved it."

Bryan and I went to bed a little bit after that. I had trouble falling asleep—nothing new there—because I couldn't stop thinking of poor Willam, and whether Wes really had become a crazed murderer. Bryan had a nightmare that night that involved me dying, though it was milder than the previous ones. It both warmed my heart and broke it to know he would cry at the thought of losing me and that the thought was always floating around in his subconscious. Other than at night, he was thriving—it's always the darkness that brings people to their lowest.

The same goes for me. That night I saw a figure standing in my room with a rifle in its arms and I couldn't, for the life of me, take cover from it.

Godrick

MISSY HAD A baby appointment the following day. Her abs were starting to protrude a little bit, but that was the extent of it—no one in their right mind could call that an official baby bump, not even an Ob/Gyn. She was supposedly at a milestone and would come back bearing news, and that she did. But not before Bryan received a life-changing letter in the mail.

We were sitting on the patio in the back of his house, basking in the eighty-degree weather that day; it was clearly about to storm, but the breeze and lack of sun made for a pleasant setting to sit and talk in, whereas the rest of the week had been hot and bright. I could see Tommy's house from Bryan's backyard.

Our conversation wasn't anything special until suddenly Mr. Lukin came outside, leaving the sliding glass doors open a smidge. "You've got mail," he said to Bryan before sending a thick envelope paper-airplane style toward his son's chest. He caught it between two fingers and rolled his eyes.

"Thanks, AOL," Bryan said, squinting to read the small print. "Rutgers Admissions ..."

My eyes grew wide as he paused and stood up, clearly taken aback. Mr. Lukin and I glanced at each other, hoping to see magic before our eyes, and then ... voilà. Bryan chuckled at me and tore open that red and gold letter, shaking his head in shock despite not knowing what it said yet. It was safe to assume he'd received good news because after his full-ride was nullified back in May, the contents of that letter literally couldn't be any worse.

"With excitement, we offer you a gleaming second-chance ...." His eyes skipped down to the middle of the paragraph, "...ten thousand dollars to put towards your future as a Scarlet Knights quarterback!"

The way Bryan looked at his dad after he read the letter is something I'll never forget. His smile opened up like a canyon, and his eyes glossed over. Glazed, pigmented—like the inside of a peach. I, sitting across from this magnificent sight, laughed out of pure joy and engulfed Bryan in a humongous embrace. He lifted me and spun me around happily. I might have cried as well, but because I wasn't paralyzed, I can't quite remember if I was moved to tears. I was moved, all right, and my grip around Bryan grew weak and pathetic, but I was still on my feet, bubbling with triumph. It was one of those amazing moments in life when you want to give a person *everything* you own: your blood, your oxygen, your thoughts, your heartbeat. That's what it feels like to want the best for someone other than yourself. I didn't get to feel that kind of pride very often.

"Your physical therapist told me she talked to the football coach at Rutgers," Mr. Lukin said, placing his hand on Bryan's arm supportively. "He knows you're in good shape now."

"Oh my God," Bryan said, brushing his palm against his forehead as he tried finding the right words to express his gratitude. "I-I gotta thank her. I can't believe this."

"Hey, you deserve it." I grinned. "I told you this would happen!"

"That's right," Bryan recalled. "You did."

Mr. Lukin winked at me and touched my shoulder before heading back inside, leaving the two of us teeming with high spirits. Bryan must have had a little *Eureka!* moment because he yelled at the top of his lungs until his voice echoed against the barrier of evergreens at the bottom of the hill. He seemed so relieved, almost like every disappointment he'd ever had was gone from the face of the earth, and he could finally just *live*. It showed in the way his ash-colored skin became saturated for the first time in months and the way his smile didn't falter. When it started to rain at last, he praised the sky, then he beamed at me before carrying me inside like a bride on her wedding day. Jouissance if I've ever seen it.

"I'm so proud of you," I told him once my feet hit the floor in the downstairs room. I sat on the edge of the couch and tugged him down by his hand, and when he sat, he pulled me onto his lap. It was just one of those I-need-to-touch-you moments.

"Today's a good day," he whispered, rubbing my sides gently with his thumbs. I was glad he'd said so because it was often hard to tell with him. Even though his face gave it away that time, the happiness he felt *needed* to be acknowledged lest it fade away all too quickly.

I rested my forehead against his and shut my eyes, savoring the feeling. Whereas earlier I'd been wallowing in the weather, now it was the pure joy that radiated out of Bryan. It practically warmed me up just being in his presence, and that was how I wanted it to be. He kissed me until the door leading to the garage opened up and Missy paraded in, glowing as well. It didn't feel like an interruption, but more of an extension to the glee that pulsated around that room.

"Hey!" Missy waved, holding a venti Starbucks coffee in one hand and a full drink carton in the other. She kicked the door shut with one of her cork wedge sandals. "I didn't know if you'd be here, Jamie, but I got you something anyway."

"Thanks." I smiled, swiveling my legs over the couch cushion so I could get off Bryan's lap and accept the drink she'd bought for me. "What is it?" I could tell it was coffee, and that made me nervous, so I wanted to know what kind.

"Iced vanilla decaf," she shrugged, "is that okay?"

I nodded graciously and handed Bryan a similar-looking beverage, which he accepted like a toddler receiving candy. Missy started to head up the stairs, but then she stopped and grinned at us with a chaotic fire in her eye, claiming she had something to tell us and that we should come upstairs to find out.

"Oh, God," Bryan cursed under his breath as we followed behind her, "why can't you tell us now?"

"Because that ruins the surprise," Missy explained. All of a sudden, she stopped in the middle of the foyer. Bryan bumped into me from behind, and she gave us a look of concern. "Wait. No one told you anything yet, right?"

"Unless it has to do with college, I'm gonna go with 'no,'" Bryan said. We were terribly confused. We continued up the stairs, finding Jade and Mr. Lukin sitting at opposite ends of the dining room table.

"You ready?" Mr. Lukin, hidden behind a bulky laptop, asked Missy when we made ourselves present. "Did you tell them?"

She grinned. "Nope." I started to perceive that this had something to do with the sex of the baby, and it turned out I was right. After distributing the remaining Starbucks drinks, Missy stood against the wall where everyone could see her and waited for Mr. Lukin to finish whatever it was he was doing.

Finally, he shut the lid of his laptop and rubbed his hands

together to up our anticipation. "So today, your aunt and I found out—"

"It's a girl!"

Lots of cheering ensued. We each took turns hugging Missy and congratulating the peculiar couple, and Missy told everyone—yes, me included—that she was taking name suggestions, and that she and Mr. Lukin both wanted something out of the ordinary. You could just tell he was giving her most of the say in this child's name, presumably because, to put it simply, he knocked her up, and she deserved this opportunity.

"Define 'out of the ordinary'," Jade said pensively, sipping on her coffee.

"Mmm ... something no one's ever heard of," she explained. "I was *gonna* go with Cleo, but that's ... risky."

"How 'bout Bryan?" my boyfriend teased, not without first tensing up at the name Missy had just dropped.

"My goodness."

"Okay, for real this time—are you looking for an obsolete male middle name kind of deal?" he asked.

"I'm not sure how many obsolete male middle names I can think of," Jade said, her expression resembling cowardice. "In fact, the only one I can think of is David, but that's the opposite of obsolete." Bryan and his father smirked at each other.

"We might *have* to go with Bryan then," Mr. Lukin said.

"Yeah, we're gonna have to think about that," Missy added, giggly. "Is there a Subreddit on this kind of thing, or—"

Bryan nodded. "Probably. Now, if you don't mind ..." He placed his hand on the small of my back and started turning me around, but Missy insisted we stay and help brainstorm. I wasn't completely opposed, but I felt a bit unwelcome because this was obviously a family matter.

"I'm just confused," Jade said, tilting her head at Missy. "Are you looking for something you'd see on a headstone, or not quite that old?"

Missy held up both of her index fingers and met eyes with all of us. "Hey, no one said *old*."

The curious banter carried on for a couple of seconds while Bryan and I stood in silence, enjoying the unique names Jade listed with maximal effort. Mr. Lukin stared helplessly into his coffee cup, snorting occasionally at the quirky suggestions. Then, all of a sudden, Bryan lifted a hand in the air and said, "Godrick."

Everyone's expressions changed, including mine. Do you remember when I mentioned my father's name, Larry G. Hessen? Guess his middle name.

As Missy's mouth opened up like a flower at dawn, Mr. Lukin groaned in protest and hid his face behind his beverage. He looked so unenthused, but she gave him puppy eyes and begged relentlessly: "Please, Bryan, please, please, please! Think you owe me this, dude. At least consider it." She pointed to her stomach.

"Maybe we should instate a veto rule," Mr. Lukin suggested, setting his coffee down gently on the tabletop.

"Or maybe we should instate a maternal executive order rule," Missy remarked, giving him a cheeky grin. Now she had two cards to pull when she wanted something from someone: prenatal *and* presidential. You could see her single dimple clearly along with her smirk. "All in favor, say I?"

"I," Bryan—*my* Bryan—said.

"I," Jade said.

It felt wrong for me to have a say in the name of someone else's child, but everyone was staring at me as if they wanted me to, so I voted at last. "I."

Mr. Lukin shook his head at me in mock dismay, causing laughter to erupt out of each of us.

"Godrick," Missy repeated admiringly like it were an engagement ring she'd recently been given. "Where'd you hear that one, kid?"

Bryan looked down at me and grinned, urging me to tell her. Assuming she didn't know off the top of her head that my father was dead, I made it a point to use past tense while explaining that it had been my dad's middle name. To be honest, I'm not even sure how Bryan found it out—it was probably one of those Jamie's-asleep-so-can-I-hang-with-you-Mrs.-Hessen? conversation topics.

"I love it." Missy grinned. "Lemme go call Cathy!"

Though I never would have thought to assign it to a girl in the twenty-first century, I loved it, too.

From Bryan's bedroom, we could hear Missy gushing to Cathy on the phone about the new name idea, but she was still taking suggestions in case she changed her mind, which was very plausible. The sound of her excitement was, for once in my life, heartwarming. But I quickly began to overthink the name she was so bubbly about. *My* father was going to be that little girl's namesake.

At this point, I was thinking out loud: "What if this is a mistake?"

"Huh?"

Bryan stopped what he was doing, which was spinning in his office chair, and blinked the dizziness out of his eyes so he could read me. I realized then that I should have given him some context so that the best day of his life didn't suddenly sound like the worst, following the assumption that I was breaking up with him.

"The name," I clarified, "Godrick. What if that's not such a good idea?"

He was visibly relieved; I could tell by his sigh and the way his shoulders loosened. "Jesus, Jamie. But hey, as long as Missy likes it."

"No, of course," I shook my head, "but what if we're not

together anymore by the time she's born? Then she'll be named after her half-brother's ex-girlfriend's dead dad. It would just make her feel bad to know who she was named after."

"Are you trying to tell me something?" Bryan asked, leaning forward in his chair. Again, a little context goes a long way.

"No!" I assured him. "I'm just worried for your half-sister is all. Seriously, aren't you?"

Bryan smirked. "I see what's going on here."

"Nothing is 'going on here.'"

"You're afraid of commitment."

I began to protest, but I changed my mind and asked, "Why does that prospect make you so happy?" How impudent.

"Because this is a classic role reversal." He laughed. "It's healthy, Jamie. Don't worry."

"But I am worrying!" I whined, cradling my head in my hands. "Something feels wrong about naming her Godrick. I just don't want to see this turn to shit, you know?"

"Well, I don't know about you, but *I* know what I want out of this," he said, raising his eyebrows at me. He stood up off the chair and bent down in front of me, fists denting the mattress at either of my sides. His face was inches from mine. In a husky voice, he whispered, "Does that scare you?"

"Stop it," I laughed, clapping my hands against either side of his face. He pushed me backwards with almost zero pressure and kissed me on the neck. It took me back to our first passionate kiss, only this time, it was … well, it was elevated. A lot.

Frankie Hessen

THINGS TURNED SOUR once again shortly after the Godrick situation. Of course.

I decided that day that I was going to stay at Bryan's house overnight; we were having such a good time, it felt *necessary* to be there. The agreement between our parents was that while we both still had issues to sort out regarding Bryan's PTSD and my narcolepsy, we could sleep together occasionally. I figured I could convince my mother this had been a bad day and that I needed to be there for emotional support.

I simply texted her to notify her of my plan, seeing as I already had some of my toiletries scattered around Bryan's bedroom and wouldn't need to stop home for more.

I'm staying at Bryan's

Her immediate response alarmed me:

You need to come home right now.

So, I gave Bryan a worried look and proceeded to call her on the phone. "Is everything all right?" I asked her, skipping the hello.

"Everything is *not* all right, Jamie! Do you know what my sister just said to me?!" she snapped. Her voice was shrill enough that I recoiled at the volume, and Bryan could definitely hear her loud and clear. When he sensed the tone she was using, he put his hand on my back as if to protect me from whatever I was about to hear.

"No, what?" I asked nervously, squeezing my eyes shut in anticipation.

"She said Missy is naming her daughter Godrick! *Godrick?!* Are you fucking kidding me, Jamie Elizabeth?"

I turned my volume down almost all the way so Bryan wouldn't feel bad. "What the hell, Mom!"

"How else could she have heard that name if it weren't for you?"

"You know," I said, standing up and pacing around the room as I grew heated, "maybe I suggested it because Bryan is my *actual* family and I'd be *honored* for my dad to be his sister's namesake. You have a boyfriend, Mom. You shouldn't be so hung up on it." Bryan looked down as soon as he realized I'd taken the blame, and also that I'd trodden into a touchy area.

Mom was quiet for a second or two before she insisted, "I want you home right now, Jamie." She was crying when she ended the call.

Despite how scared I was, I would have gone home as soon as possible if I hadn't fallen weak for so long. Bryan had to call her back on the phone and explain with an embarrassingly smarmy tone what had happened to me, and that he was going to drive me back as soon as I could hold my own head up.

In the car, it amazed me that he didn't try to defend himself for suggesting the name or even mention the thing I'd said about him being my real family. He walked me to the door and wished me luck without saying much else.

Inside, Cathy and Sam were seated on the couch with awkward, tense expressions on their faces. So, Mom had lashed out on everybody, not just me. Matt was nowhere to be seen though, despite it being a Sunday. That made things easier.

"There you are," Mom said, storming toward me as soon as she noticed I was present. Cathy and Sam both stood up, relieved that I had arrived. They stood behind Mom and flashed terrified looks at me, practically blinking an S.O.S. message while charading her anger in various melodramatic poses. "I don't want you sleeping with him anymore, Jamie. You're too close."

I laughed. "You're joking, right?"

"Do I look like I'm joking?!" she seethed. Her brown eyes were bulging and vibrant, just like her cheeks and the veins in her neck. Sam stepped forward and placed his hand on her shoulder warily, giving me a quick little nod to signify that it was okay to carry on. Like he would know.

"I don't understand," I said.

"Don't act so innocent," she spat at me. "I know what you do with him at night. You're not making that much noise 'cause you're *sad.*"

"Christ, Mom! In front of everybody?"

"I don't care!" she wailed, her voice breaking off halfway through. "You're done. This isn't happening."

"What?" I asked, my own blood beginning to boil. "What isn't happening?"

"You need to break up with him *now.*"

"Frankie, that's enough!" Cathy shouted, her own tears flowing freely now. She glanced at me apologetically and walked around Mom to stand at my side. "You can't control who she dates. Besides, last night you were telling me how much you like him."

"She's gonna get hurt." Mom continued to sob, her face contorting into the purest form of defeat I've ever seen. She was looking right at me through a sheen of tears, but the way she spoke made it seem like she didn't realize I truly was there, in the flesh, hearing her words and entertaining them with my temper.

"What do you mean?" Cathy asked, softer now. Sam looked down at the floor and took his hand off of Mom's shoulder, realizing before anyone else what this breakdown was about. He put his hands in the air in surrender and walked away. Cathy took hold of Mom's shoulders and forced her to explain; she still wouldn't take her eyes off of me though.

"She's already lost him once," Mom babbled out, her voice high and painful.

To make things clearer for you, Agent, she was comparing my relationship with Bryan to hers with my dad. I guess hearing his middle name brought back a tsunami of feelings she'd chained away in her heart, right next to her mother-daughter relationship with me. And to hear his name in the context of *my* boyfriend was her absolute breaking point. Although I was saddened by the memory, I started to pity Sam for choosing a woman who wasn't over her ex yet.

"I'm not you," I said, and then I turned around and walked back through the front door. Bryan's car was gone.

A Nightmare on Elm Street

A COUPLE DAYS after I told Tommy what happened with my mother, he started offering me his couch to sleep on, but I politely declined. She was still working things out with her delusional relationship problems, but that wouldn't stop me from staying at Bryan's place from time to time. In fact, I recall spending at least seven consecutive nights away from home after that.

"I think she and Sam might be over," I said to Tommy in the middle of the week, two days after the incident. I sipped from the glass of water he'd given me, then nearly dropped it due to the intense condensation. It was scorching outside. Spotlight sun.

"Why you say that?" he asked, squinting as a white SUV rolled by, blasting bass-boosted rap music.

"She had a full-on breakdown about her dead husband in front of him," I recapped, "and she turned to her sister for help, not him."

"Well, does he still live there? 'Cause if he still lives there, I think they good. It's just a little setback, J. Maybe you should go back tonight and check. If not, you know I'm here."

I wasn't listening. "And she thinks Bryan's gonna disappear or die again." I frowned, shutting my eyes against the sunlight and resting my elbows on my knees. The thought was painstaking, but even I knew the chances of him getting fatally hurt a second time were scarce.

"Why?" Tommy asked.

"Because my dad died and ruined her life," I shrugged, "I don't know."

"A'ight, man." He seemed sorry he had asked, but I shook my head in dismissal, ashamed that this was my life right now. It was pathetic. "How's Bry dealing with it?"

"I haven't talked to him about it yet," I admitted. "I'm afraid he's gonna feel bad for himself when he shouldn't. It's my mom's problem, not his."

Just then, Mrs. Hicks frantically pushed the screen door open, and when we turned around to see what the problem was, she beckoned us in, glancing left and right down the street. Her dark cheeks had some pinkish color to them, and her eyebrows were strung together with worry. "Why don't you kids come on inside, all right?"

"What's up?" Tommy asked, picking up our water glasses.

"Joey Ramadhan's just been found dead," she told us, very clearly troubled by the news. "He was such a sweet boy. Well, y'all get in here."

Tommy and I looked at each other; the world suddenly shrunk around us until it was reduced to outer space. I was able to carry myself inside, but I sat down on the steps immediately, feeling my knees, and hips, and thighs tingle like I was falling from a cliff in a very bad dream. That's all this was, a very bad dream. My hands grew spastic.

"How'd it happen?" Tommy asked as his mother shut the door behind us.

She slowly shook her head, folding her arms. "I don't know yet, but I don't want you two out on the streets where there's a murderer on the loose. Joey lives right on our block, too."

I let out a shaky breath, squeezing my eyes shut despite the room being considerably dimmer than outside. It was hard to focus on pleasant things, but the strength I scrapped together kept me from turning completely flaccid.

"You okay, sweet pea?" Mrs. Hicks asked me, sitting down beside me on the wide wood panel. Tommy knelt on the foyer in front of us, using the bottom step to keep his balance. "I know this is hard to swallow."

"It's horrible," I mumbled, staring down at my fingers as they shuddered violently.

"Ma, can I go run down to their place?" Tommy asked. "Say somethin' to Anisa and their mom?"

Anisa was Joey's older sister, who had just completed her first year of college. Poor, poor Anisa. Poor Mrs. Ramadhan.

Mrs. Hicks gave him permission to go as long as he was extra careful, though careful of what I didn't know because no human could dodge a bullet. She put her arms around me, telling me this was just a part of life. That you and your subordinates would find the guy who did it and slam justice in his face eventually. That Joey would be happier in paradise. She must not have known he was the only Catholic in his otherwise Muslim family, which makes sense because the bible study sessions he attended had been under wraps.

I didn't want to believe her one bit; it was too painful. But, you see, she was right—this *was* just a part of life now. A murder on every corner. A new victim of a heinous crime, whose original motive we didn't even know yet, surfaced almost every week, all concentrated in the small town of Banshee. Population decreasing. He was one of the good ones.

***

Tommy returned home promptly. He told his mom and me that he couldn't speak to the family because the whole street was blocked by news vans, police vehicles, and an ambulance that was in no particular hurry because the corpse was unsalvageable. He said he saw a couple of classmates including Sistine and Nichole there, standing across the street on the sidewalk, and when they saw him, they walked away. It was uncomfortable for reasons other than the death that rued the day.

"I can't even believe it happened," Tommy said, dumbfounded. At this point, his mom and dad were on their way to Summit Oaks to check in with Reba, so it was just him and me. "Yo, you wanna call Bryan, see if he's okay?"

"Yeah," I nodded, "soon as I can type again."

"Shit," Tommy cursed, plucking his phone from his back pocket and proceeding to call Jade. I found that thoughtful for two reasons: one, I was a major advocate for his relationship with Jade, and two, he didn't *have* to contact either of the Lukin siblings for me. I sat quietly while he and Jade spoke for a minute, and then he told her to check up on Bryan for me because I was "indisposed."

The update I received was that Bryan had heard the news and wasn't handling it very well. That was a little surprising, given his reaction to Dr. Oakhurst's and Willam's reports, so I had Tommy drive me to his house so I could find out what the issue was myself. I could control my limbs just fine by that point and brought Tommy inside with me. I knew he'd want to see Jade, and I no longer needed to ring the doorbell to announce my presence. I found Bryan curled up on his bed with his back turned to the door, hugging a pillow against his chest. It broke my heart to see him like that after he had made *so* much progress.

"Bryan?" I asked in a soft voice, approaching his bed slowly and quietly. "Are you okay?"

He turned his head slightly to acknowledge me and sat up at last, keeping the pillow tucked under his chin and his petrified eyes on the floor. "I don't know why this time's any different," he mumbled monotonously. I sat down beside him and put my hand between his shoulder blades, tracing the outline of his T-shirt tag. Embarrassingly, I didn't have any words for him, so I stayed quiet for a moment.

"He was such a good guy," Bryan mourned, shaking his head pitifully. A little wall of tears rimmed each of his lower lids, threatening to fall as he spoke to the floorboards. "I don't know what's going wrong with all these *good* people." *Huh?*

"What do you mean?"

"First, it was Leo," he said. I was concerned that he brought up Leo on his own and wondered how Leo was relevant to Joey. "He was my friend. Then he fucking *shot* me."

"Bryan?" I asked, utterly confused at this point. I had no clue what Leo's damage had to do with Joey's death; as far as I was concerned, he was just another victim.

"What?" he returned, finally looking at me. "Didn't you hear?"

"Hear what?"

"Joey killed *himself*," Bryan spat. "Means he shot Willam and Dr. Oakhurst and all those janitors, too. ... God is corrupting all the good people, Jamie. Why else would Joey be dead?"

"I didn't know that," I whispered in horror.

Suddenly, it made sense why he was so torn. He wanted this death to be a relief, but he was too close to the one who had done it. Again, the words I wanted to say stumbled soundlessly out of me; I could do nothing to console Bryan except swallow this gigantic pill brought forth by Joey's suicide. Of course, our fear was based on a *theory* Bryan and I had concocted, that if the killer were to mimic the Banshee Murderer's crimes down to the last detail, he had to martyrize himself at the end, too. Since the conditions were indeed the same as Leo's, the realism of Joey's wayward sacrifice fell down on us like rain. It was enough to ruin my clothes. My hair. My mood. My entire day—no, my week. Maybe even my year. And everyone else's, too.

"I'm terrified," Bryan cried to me, the tide in his bay-colored eyes finally cascading down his face. "I don't want you to go through what I went through."

"I won't. It's over now," I reminded him, sneaking my free arm under the pillow so I could hug him properly. He put it back onto his bed and swaddled me up in his arms, one hand cradling my head. He adjusted so that he was sitting cross-legged on his bed and could face me directly, so I did the same. "It's over," I repeated soothingly. "We'll be okay."

"How are you so calm?" he asked me. I pried my face away from his chest and cupped his stubbly jaw, nodding to make sure he was paying attention. He nodded back and allowed me to wipe his tears before I spoke.

"I'm not calm," I told him. "Anyone who is doesn't realize what just happened. But I need to make sure you're okay before *I* get to overthinking." It's weird to me how honest that was of me.

"I'm so pathetic." He chuckled, resting his warm hands on my wrists. "I've never cried so much in my life. Not until May."

"That doesn't make you pathetic at all," I said. "And you have a reason. You've had a tough few months."

"And what about you?"

"Well, my life's tough, too, but I try not to cry 'cause I like being able to move." He smiled when I said that.

"Shit, am I flexing my mobility on you?" he teased. I chuckled at him and gave his hair an affectionate ruffle. He was back.

That night while Bryan was asleep, I contacted you via email and asked if you were able to update me on how the case was coming along. At this point, it was important for my sanity. I wanted to know whether you had released Wes Martin from your custody, whether you had seized Joey's family for questioning, whether you conducted a thorough search through his house and found a horde of different handguns. Whether there was another green message written anywhere in the house or the yard where Joey died. That's how the post-suicide process played out with Leo's case, so I could only assume you would take the same precautions.

And you sternly said no, it wasn't "okay" for me to be in the know just because I was a suspect for a couple of days. That frustrated me because I wanted answers, not only for my sake but for Bryan's, too. I wanted to be able to tell him he could rest assured that this case was over now, that there were no more spins and twists, but I simply couldn't live with myself if I were to give him false hope. And even if I did tell him those things, the alternative to giving him false hope was him having an angry spat that I couldn't physically or mentally afford to tackle. I just wanted answers. So, I'm sorry for pestering you and clogging your inbox with novel-length updates on a civilian's side of the case; I thought it was helping, but I know now that the only thing I can do for the masses is finish this soliloquy before the trial.

With bitterness, I do hope the trial is postponed another few week, but only so that I have time to collect myself and prepare Bryan for giving testimony. You would understand.

Church

THERE IS SOMETHING intrinsically poetic about sitting in the pews of a church. Stained glass casting colorful apparitions over the dark wood floor, a stoup for holy water to cleanse with and *really* feel its purity, and church adherents whose intentions are genuinely good. Even though I'm not particularly religious, just influenced by those around me who are, I find solace in the eloquence and spirituality that course through St. Joseph's. It's the only church I've stepped foot into, and it's within walking distance from Bryan's house. I went there to seek guidance the Sunday after Joey Ramadhan passed.

I entered the building after the sermon was over, when only a few people remained. I didn't want to speak to anyone, really, though maybe my presence there suggested I did. Truth is, I didn't know if I was interfering with a post-service activity just by being there, so I sat in the farthest pew from the front and shut my eyes, silently hoping no one would disturb me. I needed some peace to gain closure.

Who am I supposed to talk to? I thought. *God? A saint? Maybe Saint Vitus, patron of oversleepers; Mother Teresa, who cared for the destitute; Joseph, Mary, and Jesus ... who else is there? Can you hear me? I'm helpless.*

When I opened my eyes, there was no one standing in the vast hall before me. It was darker than when I entered, afloat with orange light, and more temperate. I could see that I was physically alone at this point, but it felt as though there were people surrounding me, filling up the remainder of that pew. Like heavenly chills, intense warmth filled me from the bottom up when I looked to the left.

On the far end of the pew sat Tommy. He was trying to communicate something to me with a side-glance but, out of respect, faced forward. He was translucent; his dark skin blended with the wall.

One seat closer to me, on Tommy's right, was Reba, who had her back to the chancel. She bore the posture of a problem child on a school bus, rocking slowly to and fro.

Nichole was beside Reba, and her eyes were squeezed tightly shut, keeping the external forces out. She had lines on her face from straining but was otherwise proper.

I could see the silhouette of your chiseled face and shoulders creating a barrier between the first three people and the remaining six. You were wearing a gray suit that had dark, non-specific splotches on every article that wasn't white.

Soon Miss Camper, or Temp as you know her, fluttered into place from somewhere that emanated divine light. She was glowing even after the portal closed.

My mother soon blocked my view of Temp, and she was nagging at me to face forward. She had nothing fruitful to say.

Beside her was Jade Lukin in the form of a petite little girl wearing pigtails and viscous lip gloss. Innocence. But it was definitely Jade.

Then someone whose name was on the tip of my tongue appeared. He had sleek, voluminous hair that rippled under the rays cast down on us by the stained-glass window. His stance was almost posed, like a king in an oil painting. A stallion. I fixated on his mouth, his mauve, careworn lips.

But I could no longer see this familiar figure when Bryan Lukin materialized on my left side, the shadow of his hand casually darkening my thigh. He didn't seem as present as I was; he, too, translucent.

The air felt heavier, thicker than normal, like I was a part of it now and didn't truly understand its resistance until then. I could only move in what felt like slow motion. I shared its density.

At last, I looked at the aisle flooring. Empty except for a single churchgoer's dirty shoe print. I didn't want to look directly at the row of lost, foreboding souls sitting in the corresponding pew in case the sight of them overpowered me, though something rooted deep in me said that the closest one was that of Leo Capodi. I could feel his sunken eyes on me despite not returning the stare.

I blinked, and I was alone again. It had been an hour.

"Are you all right, dear?" asked the preacher.

Mommy Issues

"MAYBE YOU SHOULD just go see how she's doing."

The preacher had to call Bryan to pick me up after he found me lying in an otherwise empty pew, and Bryan was clearly having some trouble understanding what my issue was. I had a pounding headache and wasn't feeling talkative.

From my position on the couch in Bryan's downstairs den, I side-eyed him, still hazy from my church encounter. I was like a figurine made of glass: dense, transparent, breakable. I just wanted to be perched upon my shelf and not communicate with the living world for a little while, *especially* with my mom.

"Hey," Bryan said defensively after the intent of my glare registered with him. "How many times have you made me talk to Missy and my dad when I didn't want to? I love you and everything, but I *know* you're not a hypocrite."

"You don't get it," I grumbled, rubbing my eyes with the heels of my palms. There was a low thunder rolling in my cerebrum, slowly devolving from a migraine. I flipped myself onto my side so that I was facing the back of the couch, away from Bryan.

"What don't I get?" he asked. I felt the cushion depress as he sat down behind me.

"*I* don't even get it." He sighed audibly after that and put his hand on my side. "What would I say?"

"Well," Bryan considered, "you could apologize for hiding from her."

"And then?"

"Tell her you're okay," he added. "Doesn't help her much to know someone just died and her daughter won't show her face."

That was a good point. But I was almost positive Frankie was using Cathy and Missy as liaisons to spy on me, as they were both chatty by nature and had probably been coerced by my mother. Also, at the time, I honestly didn't know if Sam had been too offended by her breakdown to stay, and I sort of hoped he did so that he could help us get past this rough patch. Truth is, it was very painful seeing my mother cry again; it had been three years since I last had to see that type of mental collapse. If Sam was good for anything, it was making sure my mother was okay when I couldn't.

"Will you go with me?" I asked, rolling onto my other side to look Bryan in the eye. His face was dark because of the light seeping in from the sliding glass doors behind him.

He nodded at me. "Sure."

We left promptly. I was nervous, but also felt my anger slowly building at the thought of seeing Frankie; I expected the carbonation within me to eventually explode that day. The ride to my house felt prolonged, almost like Bryan was reluctant to go and had taken a scenic route so he could gather his thoughts. He had an honest reason to be reluctant though; the whole Godrick situation was probably humiliating, and I prayed it wouldn't come up. To my surprise, it didn't.

The front door was unlocked, so I dragged Bryan inside with me and gripped his warm hand tightly, startled by just being in the house. I could hear forks scraping against plates and some light chatter; the dining room lights were on but none else. When Bryan and I left the mouth of the house, we saw who the noises were sourced from.

It was Mom and Sam, casually eating dinner, unsurprised that there were two visitors in their house now. Sam glanced at us and put his silverware down. That was when my mother finally looked at us, swallowing her bite and tilting her head to the side trivially. The way her skin glowed under the ceiling light, she could almost have passed for amused. It was like she didn't want us to see how deteriorated she had really become.

"Whose clothes are those?" she asked upon noticing me. *Really, Mom?*

"Jade's," I answered, glancing down at the Adidas leggings and sweatshirt Bryan's sister had lent me the past week. Mom and I looked at each other for a long moment before she returned to her plate and started eating again; it looked like something Cathy might have made, though she wasn't in the room at the time, and she wasn't at Bryan's place hanging out with Missy before we left either. It was probably a good thing that she was out.

I was offended that Mom didn't have anything else to say to me. I know I can be passive aggressive from time to time, but that doesn't mean it doesn't piss me off when other people are.

I scoffed heavily until she and Sam looked up again. "This isn't just some breakup, Mom—you don't get to act like you're *over* me. I'm your *daughter*."

Surprise, surprise. That one got her going:

"If that's so true, then you need to quit acting like a middle schooler and own up to your shit," she snapped, standing up from the table at last. Sam followed her, looking sideways at

Bryan, presumably for some guidance. Though it wasn't like Bryan had any experience in subduing my mother or me when we were having a fight, so both of the men stayed silent. "You know how quiet it's been around here? You left for a week, Jamie. A *week*."

"Yeah," I nodded, "after you went all helicopter-mom on me and treated me like chattel. I was standing *right there*, Mom."

"What are you even talking about?"

"I'm eighteen! You don't get to act like you still have any control over me!" I shouted, beginning to feel woozy. I found it ironic that I didn't even have full control over myself, yet I was punishing my mother. I fell hard onto my knees, but I was still able to speak for the time being. Bryan crouched down and held me up so I wouldn't hit my head on the floor. "Don't you remember what you said to me? About Bryan? And Dad?"

Even though I couldn't move anymore, I was still raging inside. Mom looked at Bryan and then down at the table, reaching for a napkin that was crumpled up next to her plate. She balled it into her hand and shook her head several times. "I don't want to talk about that."

"Child," I managed to say before going completely limp. Mom was obviously troubled by now, for she whispered something to Sam and started to visibly hold back tears. Her shiny lips were pinched together. I could only see her peripherally once my head fell backwards, Bryan's bicep serving as a neck rest.

I could tell Mom was exhausted from the conversation by the way she threw her hands up in surrender, saying, "Just say sorry and we'll be done with this." There was now a bitter smile on her face, taunting me as I slowly regained mobility.

I hesitated until my lips could move again. "Well, I guess we still have a predicament because I'm not gonna take the plea deal for this one."

When I could, I stood back up and folded my arms across

my chest, feeling some intense stares on me from Bryan, Sam, and Mom. But none of that mattered; I truly wasn't sorry, and I wasn't going to act it.

"Jamie—" Sam started, but Mom told him to stand down and he looked at the floor; she knew it'd be useless for a person so removed from my life to try and "mansplain" what the issue was. He flashed her a confused look, probably embarrassed that he'd been excluded from this family matter; Bryan was smart for getting through this so quietly.

"You're a lot stronger than I am," she mumbled, her voice so soft I had to strain to hear. She sniffled, wiped her nose with the balled-up tissue in her hand, and chuckled. "I wasn't independent when I was eighteen. You are, and you've got it much worse than me."

I paused for a moment. Gasp! Was that regret I heard in her voice?

"We're not that different," I said, the anger in me ebbing away like a tide. It'd be back, but it had subsided for now.

I didn't feel like being in her presence any longer, so I trudged down the hall and went into my room. It was almost eerie how nothing in it had changed, like looking into an old photograph; the space was chilly and organized like I left it. I was a little surprised that Bryan didn't follow me right away, but when he finally arrived, he shut the door softly behind him and leaned against it, peering at me with an indecipherable expression on his face. I sat down while I waited for him to say something, anything.

"You're ballsy," he finally mumbled. I chuckled at first, but the longer I stared at him, the worse I felt, and suddenly my smile morphed into tears. That argument had taken *everything* out of me, and it didn't feel resolved yet. He sat down next to me on the bed and put his hand on my back, rubbing in slow circles. It was like a tangible lullaby; in fact, I wound up napping next to him for around half an hour.

When I woke up, he had his eyes shut but didn't seem to be sleeping. He proved me correct when he opened one eye and inhaled deeply, tightening his arms around me.

"Hey," he said. His voice suggested he had indeed slept for a little bit, but not as long as I had.

"Hey," I said, yawning. I rested my palm in between his pecs, feeling with my thumb a little dent where his gunshot scar was, and closed my eyes for a brief moment. Bryan snaked his hand up to my face and stroked my temple lovingly, my hair slipping through his fingers.

"I apologized to your mom," he said suddenly, which surprised me to say the least. I looked him in the eye, perplexed. "Not because of you. But I don't think she likes me anymore."

"Please," I scoffed. "She loves you."

"How can you be so sure?" he asked, his eyes flitting down to the floor beside my bed. He looked disappointed in himself. "She gave me an ultimatum."

"She *what?*" I asked, sitting up straight and hooking my finger under his chin to turn his face toward mine. He shut his eyes, sitting up as well.

"I handled it," he assured me, grabbing my wrist and pulling it down from his face. "In fact, I made her a deal. Just to make things right, you know?"

"What was it?" I asked quietly, suddenly terrified that he'd sold himself out of the relationship.

He smiled slightly, looking down at his lap. Why was he shy all of a sudden? I slumped my shoulders, knowing at this point he wasn't going to tell me. "Just trust me," he said. "It's helping all of us."

"I deserve to know—"

"And you will." Bryan leaned down and pressed his lips into the top of my head. "I just gotta work on gaining her trust again, and then everything'll be all right."

"Me, too," I said, practically melting at his gentle tone.

I forgot all about that deal for a while. Months.

Bryan and I stayed cooped up in my bedroom all evening, talking about things that had happened to us lately like we were on a date. It did sort of remind me of our first date, the hockey game and Subway. Until then, it hadn't occurred to me that love and dating were real parts of life, but now they were my *whole* life. Aside from the murders, of course, every moment of every day was graced by thoughts of Bryan. His angelic laugh, his stubble, his bergamot scent, his choice of athletic wear, which was all he wore, and everything in between.

You can call me naive, but my relationship is a valid reason for my not knowing who this new Banshee Murderer was when others were starting to open their eyes. I was in a trance if you will. Completely blind.

Laurie Tomlin

I WAS OVER at Bryan's the next day, per usual, watching a Netflix show in his room. We'd never done that before, mostly because he understood movies and shows were difficult for me to get through, but summer was only getting more and more boring. As a graduate, I didn't have any more high school to look forward to come September. I didn't even have a bucket list, and Bryan was still in physical therapy, so there wasn't much we *could* do besides live vicariously through actors and fictional plots. It was quite sad, really.

Since I'd somehow gotten through a multiplicity of crime shows with minimal cataplexy attacks, he thought I would like *Shameless*. "It's risky," he had said, "but it's the same kind of humor. And if anything, I'll be here. I've got plenty of dark dramedy shows for you."

After he spent five minutes selling me on the idea, I agreed to watch it with him, but we didn't get as far as ten minutes into the first episode before some shouting from the next room over triggered us. Jade's room.

"Tommy!" she cried out, following the sound of a door opening quickly. Bryan and I looked at each other, worried by her shrill voice. We practically flew to the door, and I whipped it open, watching as Tommy stalked down the hall while Jade stood alone in her wide door frame.

"What happened?" Bryan asked her as I followed Tommy at his heel. I didn't get to hear what Jade said before planting my hand on Tommy's broad shoulder and scanning his face for emotion; there was nothing. He just looked startled that I'd touched him.

"I don't get it," I said, taking a step back. "You look fine."

"Cause I am," he answered, short and simple.

"Why are you ditching Jade then?" I pried, nudging him further into the living room and sitting on the couch. He sat down beside me, using awkwardly slow movements and staring at the wall ahead of him. "Hello? Earth to Tommy?"

"She kissed me," he mumbled. Finally, he drew his eyes away from the wall, reaching up to scratch his head. "I'm sorry, J. Just tryna go home."

"What?" I asked. "Don't apologize to *me*, apologize to *her*."

"I can't," he stressed, visibly cringing even though I couldn't see his face at his point. "Just ... sorry, man. I gotta get outta here."

"What the hell," I whispered to myself as he stood up and turned toward the stairs. Bryan and Jade came down the hall with angry and confused looks on their faces; Bryan had his hand on her shoulder as he glared at Tommy, so I guess Jade hadn't spared him any details.

Tommy reached for the door handle, and Bryan shouted, "Bye!" as if this were English class, where he regularly pestered people like Tommy. His eyes were wide in reaction to the ridiculous walkout. All of us were a bit dumbfounded.

"See y'all later," Tommy said, raising one hand in farewell as he yanked the door open. But he didn't step outside. He just stood there, hand still in the air, and stared at the front yard. It was like he'd been ... well, never mind. I won't go there.

I decided to follow Tommy down the stairs and see for myself what the problem—the *second* problem—was, and I froze when I saw you and your jacked-up guard sauntering up the driveway. Subconsciously, I pushed Tommy out of the way to make room for myself out on the porch. I figured things would go smoother if you saw me first.

I may not have looked it, but I was scared out of my wits to see you in the flesh again. Maybe it was the context: we were at Bryan's house, and everyone who was there I held in my heart, so I didn't want there to be any damning evidence against them. To think of any of my friends being in trouble was like a stab wound to the chest.

When you saw me standing there, bewildered, you exchanged a few words with your buddy and lifted your hand so that he would stand back.

"Jamie," you called out, extending me your hand to shake once you were within an arm's reach of me. You looked dapper in your suit, but I knew it was just to make the interrogation process all the more intimidating for whomever else you needed to speak with that day. The rest of us, we were wearing lazy summer clothes.

As I shook your hand, Tommy asked me in a low voice how I knew you. He must have just forgotten what you looked like or something, or else he would have been more respectful. I heard Bryan rush down the stairs to see what was going on.

"Jamie," he said through his teeth while hooking his paw onto my shoulder from behind.

"It's okay," I told him. "Hi, Agent." It felt weird addressing you by a title instead of a name, but then again, I probably didn't have much of a say.

"We just made a visit down the road a little ways," you told me, weirdly conversational given the reason you sought us out. Why would it matter to me where you were?

"Sir?" Tommy asked, as you'd pointed in the direction of his house. Oh.

"I'd like to have a word with you down at the station, if that's all right, Tommy," you said. Bryan pulled me closer to him while Tommy squeezed past us, following you down the steps. I felt like a dog on a leash, wistfully watching you leave the premises.

"Bryan," I whispered, searching for an explanation for his protectiveness, and he cocked his head toward the man patrolling behind you and Tommy. He was holding a large gun of some kind, which I thought unnecessary, especially when approaching Bryan's house. You didn't think *you* were a target, did you?

Bryan was obviously anxious. "That's a fucking submachine gun."

"All right, we'll go back inside." I turned myself around and waited for him to go into the house.

"Don't sound so annoyed."

"Why, 'cause only one of us can be annoyed at a time?"

It escalated so quickly, but it came down just as fast. Bryan, after gesturing me into the house before him, swallowed hard and put his arms around me. That mood swing nearly gave me whiplash.

"I'm worked up, okay? I don't like that guy," he explained, speaking in a private tone as Jade was still at the top of the steps. Then, for her sake, he added aloud, "Tommy's a dick."

"Yeah," she huffed, strutting away like this was no longer her business.

"She tell you what happened?" I asked, taking Bryan's hand and leading him up the stairs. We sat down in the living room this time.

"Yeah." He nodded, raising his brow at me scornfully. "What'd I tell you, Jamie?"

I halted for a second. I didn't want to say it, but I did. "He still likes me."

Bryan shook his head. "'Like' is an understatement. Should've known he was just dating her for you."

"This is my fault, you know," I said. "I never should've told Jade he was available, especially in front of her best friend. I feel like a royal ass."

"Hey."

"It's nice that you're so protective of her though," I added. "I wish I had a brother."

"You have Matt," he offered. "Sort of."

"Matt plays Xbox. Plus, he's fourteen."

Bryan chuckled at the fact, playing with my fingers for a quiet moment. We heard Jade in the kitchen for a second or two. She must have been on FaceTime with Aleida because she said something remarkably along the lines of, "*Never* date an older guy!" before retreating to her bedroom once again. It only made me feel worse for her; I'd have to talk to Tommy about respecting women for the thousandth time whenever he came back from the police station.

Just thinking about him being at the station made me nervous. My mind started to drift from thought of Tommy to thought of Leo to thought of you, and why the three of you were related, I had yet to consider. What did you need to know from Tommy, and why? Was he a suspect now, too? Tommy tends to get loquacious when he's nervous, so I prayed that you would think twice before accusing him of three-plus felonies. It wasn't realistic, this next part, but the longer I thought about it, the clearer the picture in my head became: there was Tommy in that interrogation room, upper body slackened, poor Amy propping him up by the armpits while you slammed your fist on the metal table and glared. Saliva flung out of your angry mouth in strands, and Tommy was in a persistent vegetative state. Like me, but worse.

"Jamie?" Bryan asked me, noticing I was definitely awake and mobile but somehow locked in place. Locked inside my conscience, rather. He gently touched me on the shoulder and repeated my name.

I finally hummed in response, blinking the trance away. My eyes were unfocused.

"Pizza?"

Tommy didn't come back to Bryan's house after you questioned him, which was understandable, but he did text me saying he needed to speak to me about something important. Bryan and I were in the middle of the second episode of *Shameless* when I got the message. I brushed it off at first, but then it occurred to me that the last time I disregarded someone's text, Bryan wound up hurt. Hell, he had died because of it.

"Pause this," I said, nudging him on the arm. My eyes were glued to my phone screen all of a sudden.

"Why?"

"Tommy says it's important," I said. Bryan sat patiently while I responded to the text. Here's what we discussed:

Yo I need to tell u smth. Its important

Hit me

Luschkov or whateva thinks Teach still alive

He what?

Ya man. He thinks shes the one doin the killing. Got a anonymous tip or smth

He brought Nichole and Sistine in for questioning too cuz we were all outside Joey's house the day he shot his self

But like who wouldntve been there

Omg…

What did Nichole have to say about that

Idk, mans wouldnt say

But ill tell u what. Somethin's fcked up here J

Very

"He thinks Teach is still alive?" Bryan asked, and I nodded in horror. "But there were pictures. And a funeral."

"Closed casket," I said, sitting up straight to consider what this meant. I chuckled. "If it's true, then I'm *definitely* next. You don't think it's true, do you?" My smile faded, and I gulped down a ball of fear.

"Course not," Bryan scoffed, though there was something hesitant about his general demeanor at that moment, something that suggested he was as apprehensive as I was. He brought his brown eyes down to his lap and cursed to himself. "You know, that FBI guy has been wrong at least three times now."

"But he has to figure it out at some point," I argued, slumping my shoulders. "I really don't see this one going cold. There's too many people dead for that to be realistic."

"True," he considered. "Have they even talked about any evidence on the news?"

"Nothing other than the guns found in their houses." I shook my head. "Just the suspects. Oh my God, they didn't put *me* on the news, did they?"

"No," Bryan told me. "Trust me, you'd know if they did. Wes Martin's family went back to Cuba to get away from the press. They're like ... wasps."

"Jesus. And they live down there now?"

Bryan nodded slowly. I wondered how I had missed that information. I was taking special care to monitor my breathing and keep my emotions stabilized. Bryan asked if I was okay, and I just nodded at him to avoid speaking for a couple of seconds. He had shown me some of his breathing exercises because they always helped him come down from panic attacks, hyperventilation, the like—and we found that they helped me, too. Thanks, Dr. Manta.

Mr. Lukin came into Bryan's room without warning, his solemn expression saying it all. We waited for him to speak, but it took him a minute to find the words.

Alas: "Either of you know Giovanna Moore?"

I looked back at Bryan; his eyes were wide with sympathy. "Isn't that Sistine's mom?"

Trip to England

THERE WASN'T EVEN a funeral.

That's how I knew things were way, way worse than I had ever anticipated. Maybe I'd been so distracted by Bryan's healing process that I couldn't comprehend the severity of the crimes going on in Banshee, but when the SWAT team arrived at Teach's alleged hideout location, Giovanna Moore—*not* Teach—was shot in the shoulder and then the neck for "attempting to evade arrest." The agent who did it had been the weapons caddy who followed you around everywhere and kicked my door down.

All of the puzzle pieces just fell further and further apart. Each piece was a magnet, and they all had the same polarity. Maybe we'd lost a magnet or two in the midst of scattering them; who could tell anymore? Everything I thought I knew, I didn't, and it was so frustrating.

As far as I could tell, Sistine wasn't even mourning over

her mother. Why she lamented the death of her best friend's mother and not her own was beyond me. Then again, she didn't seem to care when Cousin Leo kicked it either—she'd practically rejoiced at the sight of his face on the news. She did fall under the radar, but only for a few days, so the fact still stands that Sistine had her priorities backwards.

Something I didn't know, however, was that your little body-guard, the one who wouldn't stop parading his personal weapons armory, was Agent Patrick Moore, Sistine's notoriously unfeeling father. Rumor had it this was the reason her parents were divorced. I knew she preferred him to her mom, but I don't think I'm wrong in saying *anyone* would be traumatized if their father had committed matricide. What made Sistine the outlier, besides every teenager's parental skirmishes?

The whole SWAT team had mistaken Moore's ex-wife for Laurie Tomlin. According to Max Figuerra, the physical description was a match, for Giovanna had dyed her hair blonde since the last time Patrick had seen her. That little detail was what turned things fatal.

Agent Moore had his weapons confiscated for a couple of weeks. It didn't seem like much of a penalty, though. I don't mean to assume anything that's false, but the FBI must have covered his ass when they turned over that warm corpse and found an innocent woman's face attached to it. Right? Anyhow, his suspension ameliorated Bryan's uneasiness and also Tommy's because he had told me with anger that "that Navy dude wouldn't stop starin'" at him during his interrogation while you asked nerve-wracking questions.

I had an uneasiness about the whole thing, questions that remained unanswered. Like, who told the police Teach was still alive? And how did you settle on Sistine's mom's address specifically?

Back at my house, the cold war between Frankie and me had simmered, and now things were becoming civil again.

Mom seemed especially interested in Giovanna's death, seeing as it could pass as an act of police brutality and not a heinous Capodian murder. The drama behind it read like a soap opera to her, so she sat Cathy down to re-re-recap all of the horrible events that had taken place here over the last five or six months. She had a good time doing it, at least until she went into detail about Bryan's injury. Then she talked noticeably quieter, as if I couldn't hear her voice once she turned it down a notch.

I was eavesdropping from the kitchen where I had poured myself a bowl of cereal for lunch. Cathy remarked, "That's *awful*. I mean, I knew he was shot, but I didn't know it was that bad. There's so much backstory I missed."

"Yeah," Mom sighed, "did you know he died for three whole minutes? I think that's a record."

"The one case of Lazarus syndrome I witnessed at my hospital in Wyoming lasted around that long. ... I can't remember for sure," Cathy said.

Lazarus syndrome. Haven't heard that one yet, I thought, my curiosity piqued.

"Goddamn," Mom commented, shaking her head slowly at the matter. "Well, after Bryan, the shooter killed himself. And then the whole thing repeated, starting with the three janitors down at Bridgewood."

"That's her high school, right?"

"Right. And then they got the principal, and then that poor kid ... William? Or was it Wes? Jamie, what was his name?"

I dropped my spoon into my Frosted Flakes and looked at the two of them. They were sitting together on the couch, arms over the back as they stared at me expectantly.

"Willam McGuire," I said. "Only one 'l'."

"Willam, that's right." Mom nodded. "Hey, you ever hear if he was okay?"

I paused to think for a moment. "Well, Bryan goes to see him sometimes," I said. "It's therapeutic or whatever. He told me they keep bringing dogs into the room with him to keep Willam from having a nervous breakdown."

Cathy groaned. "Poor kid. He was the one shot in the eye?"

"Yeah." I looked down at my cereal. It felt wrong talking so casually about something so atrocious, but it felt even worse that I was physically okay with it. If Bryan were there, I might have told my mother to shut up, but he wasn't, so I didn't. It was better that way. I'd been awfully mouthy with her lately.

Sam came home from work relatively early that day with a horror story to tell. His brother Garth had overdosed on oxy again and needed to be hospitalized, yada yada yada. Garth is in court-ordered rehab now and is probably not thriving, but the only reason I didn't care at the time was that my mind was foggy because I'd been forced to think about Bryan and Willam being nearly gunned to death.

After a brief, sporadic nap, I walked myself over to Bryan's house to hang out with Jade because I didn't feel like being home anymore, and he told me he was outside running. His mile times were getting shorter and shorter every week, so I knew I wouldn't need to wait long for him to come back.

Unfortunately, when I got there, I found that Jade was still upset about Tommy, but at least she wasn't blaming me for it. I had honestly expected her to move on from him because of how quickly she'd gotten over Peter Windward, but I suppose Tommy was different to her. She had invested her feelings in him.

She and I sat down on her bed and talked about it for a little while, and I did my best not to say anything bad about him or myself in case she decided to hold a grudge. She seemed like the type to do that, so I had to be cautious.

"And now I have all these texts with him that were for nothing," Jade complained, thrusting her phone in my face to show me the long conversations she and Tommy had held. "I don't wanna delete them."

"It'd be better if you did," I advised her. "Looking at them will just make you sad."

"Yeah, but I miss him," she said. "Can I even say that? I don't even know if we were dating. I was probably just another chore to him."

"Hey," I frowned, "I know he liked you at least a *little* bit! Maybe things were just moving too fast for his liking."

"Too fast? We were going out for, like, almost a month, and *I* had to kiss *him* first!"

"Well listen," I said, "Tommy's going through a rough time with his family and ... other stuff. This might be for the best."

"What 'other stuff' is there?" she asked, but then her glossy lips separated and formed the shape of an O in surprise: "Wait, does it have to do with him being arrested?"

"What?! No!" I exclaimed. "Tommy was never arrested. That's not what that was."

"Then who was that guy?" she asked. "Oh, was it his dad? Is he a cop?"

"No," I shook my head, embarrassed at how little he had told her about his home life, "his dad's a pharmacist. That was the head agent working on Leo's case. He just needed to ask a few questions."

Jade looked down at her lap, then at her long nails, and ran her thumbs along the tips of each of them. Two of them were jagged and broken and another had a Band-Aid wrapped around it. "I want a drink," she murmured.

It felt like a cloud of black was condensing inside me when she said that. "Why? Is everything okay?"

"No," she said louder, her blue eyes suddenly surrounded by pink. There were small streams building in her inner corners that she didn't seem to want to release. "I can't stop doing my nails and curling my hair. It doesn't even help to talk to Aleida anymore. Everything about me is just dead and broken." Her hair did look rather dry now that she mentioned it.

"I'm sorry."

"Missy said she's putting the crib in my room," she scoffed, dabbing her eyes with a single knuckle so as to preserve her mascara and eyeliner. "And when you're not here, Bryan freaking *screams* at night. Do you have any idea how hard it is hearing that? Wait, what am I saying? Of course, you do. I don't even have Tommy to rant to anymore. I just … I want something to drink."

"You may feel that way, but it's so much better now that you can't," I said, but when Jade glared at me afterwards, I realized that might not have been the most helpful thing to say. "Have you considered going to therapy?"

"No," she said.

"Well, are you against it?"

She hesitated. "No."

I nodded encouragingly. "Talk to your dad about it, and maybe he'll set you up. Believe me, this kind of thing *needs* to be talked about. Also, thank you for confiding in me. I know I hate talking about stuff like this to other people."

"Sure," she nodded, blinking the tears out of her false lashes. "You're my sister."

At that, I smiled at her and opened up my arms to hug her. I heard the front door open and some heavy footsteps, so I assumed it was Bryan returning from his run. Jade held on though, even when he stepped into her room.

"Hey," he said, breathing hard. "I'm gonna hop in the shower."

"Okay," I said, my jaw hitting his sister's shoulder as I spoke. She let go of me at that point and looked at Bryan, who was still there, awkwardly awaiting an explanation. "We're fine," I told him tersely. That was satisfactory enough, for he headed back in the direction of the bathroom.

"Maybe this week'll be easier anyways," Jade sniffled, "what with Missy and Cathy leaving."

"Wait, what?"

"They're going to England," Jade informed me. "It's all they talk about. I can't believe you didn't hear."

"Me neither." I chuckled.

"It was supposed to be the whole family, but Bryan and I don't really want to go anymore."

"I thought it was because he couldn't fly," I said.

Jade shook her head. "He's been cleared for three weeks now."

I looked away, swallowing nervously. Bryan never told me that, and something deep in me made me believe it was because he was either too scared to leave or too depressed to even *want* to go. Either option was unfortunate, and the thought only fed that dark cloud inside me.

"Can you tell me something?" I asked quietly. Jade nodded, prompting me to continue. "How often does he go to therapy? Like, psychiatric therapy?"

"Uh ... maybe once every two weeks." She shrugged. "Don't worry, he's still taking his meds."

"This whole time, I thought he was going every week," I said. "Maybe even twice a week."

"Do you think he's avoiding you? Or avoiding therapy?" she asked me, her voice softer now. I didn't like my options.

"Sounds like maybe both."

Bryan took an hour in the shower and invited me to his room after he'd gotten dressed. Before leaving her room, I gave Jade a look that promised I'd confront him.

"How's my girl?" he asked me, bearing a big smile as he sat down on his office chair. I felt bad that I'd be going out of my way to say something less happy and potentially bring on an argument.

"Just fine," I said, smiling down at the floor. I bet my

face looked ruddy. "I actually wanted to talk to you about something."

"Hit me," he said.

"So, Missy and Cathy are going to England," I started, to which he only nodded, wearing a look of interest on his face. "And ... and ... I was just wondering if you wanted to stay over at my place while they're gone."

I couldn't do it. There were too many times I thought I'd lose that smile of his, and I wasn't going to lose it again if I could help it.

He chuckled. "Always!"

Reconciliation

AS PROMISED, BRYAN and I spent a few nights at my house while Missy and Cathy were gone. It was very quiet despite Mom, Sam, and Matt all being there, and that was something I'd missed. I was so accustomed to the noise that I forgot what the silence felt like.

On the first night, which was actually the day after I found out about the trip, Bryan brought some extra clothes over to my house. I had lied to him and said I didn't have anything of his because I wanted to keep them, and he completely fell for it.

It was relatively late, maybe ten or eleven o'clock, when Tommy invited himself over. That was odd for multiple reasons—I'm sure I don't have to clarify them for you.

Mom was the one who let him inside, and so after that he stood outside my bedroom door and said my name, knowing it was unsafe to knock. I just glanced at Bryan with confusion and called out, "Yeah?" because neither of us were expecting company, much less his.

"Y'all decent?" he asked. The doorknob tilted slightly under the weight of his hand, but he didn't open it. He must've known he was on thin ice; otherwise, he wouldn't have been so hesitant.

"Yes." I rolled my eyes. Tommy opened the door and then shut it behind him, not daring to move closer to us.

"What's your business?" Bryan asked, leaning back on one of his hands. He was closer to Tommy based on the orientation of my bedroom, so I couldn't see his face—I didn't have to though. I knew it was bittersweet for him, seeing Tommy, a friend, after what he'd done to Jade.

"Look, man, I know I been a pain in the ass, but I got some bigger stuff to worry about for now," he said to Bryan, gesturing with his hands as he spoke. "S'actually why I'm here. It's uh … it's Reba."

"What about her?" I asked. Suddenly, I was interested, so I furrowed my brow in question and waited for him to talk. There must have been a filter in his throat or something because it took him a solid minute to gather his thoughts. There was some redness in his eyes.

"Somehow, she found out about Sistine's mom," he started, his voice trembling. Despite the raw emotion in his words, his face remained blank. "And she tried to kill herself."

"Shit," Bryan gasped, turning his face away from Tommy's.

"Oh my God," I said at the same time, bewildered. "Is she okay? Did she—"

"They put her on a suicide watch," Tommy narrated. The way his gaze was fixed on the floor it was almost like there was a teleprompter hidden down there, but that's just something Tommy does: when he's fighting the urge to cry, he avoids eye contact. Something about a person's eyes just breaks you.

It was relieving to hear that Reba was still alive, but the

circumstances made my heart ache and apparently Bryan's, too. He never liked Reba, and I never liked her either, but both of us had become more sympathetic of her situation once we realized the toll it was taking on her mental health. In retrospect, this probably had a lot to do with that God complex she had during elementary school. Everything in her world slowly came crashing down under her reign, and so she was bound to feel alone. No friends, no family, just white walls.

"My ma ain't coming home for a while," Tommy added. "Doc says Reba won't stop screamin' for her, so she can't be this far away from her. Got a motel for the week."

"It's just you and your dad?" I asked, standing up off my side of the bed and walking around so I could hug Tommy. When I did, he buried his face in my neck without saying anything. I could feel his staggered breaths condensing against my skin. He smelled very faintly of weed as if he'd gotten high in the afternoon; that was unusual, but I didn't comment on it because I wasn't a demon from hell and understood that he was going through something.

"It's just us," he finally bleated out. He sniffled and let go of me, immediately hiding his face behind his palms.

Bryan stood up from the bed and put one arm around my back, one around Tommy's, and said, "We're good, okay? You were right—you have bigger stuff to worry about." I felt proud that he said that without my directive. "I hope Reba gets the help she needs."

"Thanks," Tommy said. "Sorry to interrupt. I'ma get outta here."

I nodded and asked him, "Will you be okay?"

He didn't know.

Bryan and I sat back down after he'd left, astonished by what had happened. Although it had happened at least twice in the community already, the idea of Reba committing suicide was extremely heavy for me to think about. Maybe that was because the context of it was different than Leo's or Joey's, and Reba was someone I could actually afford to feel for. After all, she was my best friend's twin sister. It was hard enough seeing them apart for so long, but a lifetime without her would be much, much worse. I kind of missed seeing them lock horns in the halls because even then, Tommy called her "Reebs" out of love, and she still had input that was sound. Now, though …

"Why are our lives so fucked up?" Bryan muttered, shaking his head. "The three of us. I mean, is that why we're so close? Did someone plan all this shit to happen to us?"

For someone who'd completely lost faith in God, Bryan sounded awfully Calvinist just then. And that's not a bad thing—I was just amazed that he thought a deity had anything to do with this. It's just life, Bryan, *life*.

"I dunno, but none of us deserves it," I said. "I don't know what I'd do if I lost either of you to suicide."

"Well, I can't speak for Tommy," he told me, "but I would never do that to someone I love as much as you."

"I know." Bryan kissed me on the forehead, his warm scent lingering even after he leaned away. I thought out loud, "Sometimes, I can't believe Reba of all people is taking this the hardest."

"There's gotta be a reason," he mumbled in response. "I don't think she's *crazy* crazy."

"Me neither," I said in agreement. "This kind of thing doesn't just *happen* to you. Something causes it."

"Well, the thing that got her admitted was something about a picture of your house, wasn't it?" Bryan asked. "She had a fit in English or something?"

"Right." I nodded slowly. "But that doesn't add up. She wasn't there."

"You think maybe she knows *why* they took the picture?" Bryan suggested, raising his brows at the idea. I tilted my head in consideration—it seemed viable.

"Either way, I don't think she'd tell anyone."

"Oh, definitely not."

Chris Arden

ON THE THIRD day of Missy and Cathy's vacation, my mom and I had a surprise visit around noon.

Sam was at work, Bryan was visiting Willam, and it wasn't a weekend, so we didn't have Matt with us—thank God for that. Even Tommy was away in New York City for the day with his dad, trying to distract himself from Reba's troubles. That meant Mom and I were completely alone, just like old times. It was almost eerie.

We'd been watching the news together over lunch. There were no related reports today, just the weather and a story about a drug ring across town, but I was still on edge the entire time, nervous that the next thing Max Figuerra would announce was the death of another one of my friends. I had good reason to be so apprehensive, but he didn't say anything that affected me.

However, my heart nearly leapt out of my chest when three loud, daring knocks sounded through the door. Mom and I both bounded off the couch; she was worried that I'd been triggered, and I was worried that Bryan might have heard it even though he wasn't even present. Just goes to show what my life had been reduced to.

"You okay?" she asked me frantically, searching my face for emotions and my form for paralysis. But I was still standing. Still moving. "I swear I put a sign out there, sweetie. Maybe the doorbell doesn't work."

"We'll get it fixed," I said in a startled tone, steadily coming down from my adrenaline rush. We stood there in silence for a moment or two before the knocker struck again; before then, it didn't occur to us that knocking was the universal signal to come answer a door—it had been so long since either of us had heard a knock anyway. What the hell was so urgent?

"God! I'll get it," Mom grumbled, annoyed at us for waiting too long and at our guest for being so impatient. I hovered in the living room while she shuffled toward the front door, mumbling to herself.

"Can I help you?" she asked, quieter now because of her distance.

"... looking for Jamie."

I walked toward the entryway a little so I could try and see who it was. The last time someone came "looking" for me, it was to trick me into making Leo look more innocent when the cops got involved. *Damn you, Sofia.*

But to my surprise, when Mom moved to the side, she revealed a very skinny-looking Chris Arden. He was wearing a black hoodie and generally heavy clothes for summer, which wasn't his style at all based on the few times I'd seen him around school. He swallowed hard and looked over his shoulder at the vehicle he arrived in: a white SUV with mud stains. I'd seen it before.

All the blood had drained from his face. When he looked me in the eye, I knew something was wrong.

"Get out of here," he whispered, appearing terrified of something. "Please. This is your last chance."

"Chris?" I asked, stepping away as he lifted the hem of his hoodie, showing us a pistol tucked into his pants. "Oh my God!"

"Jamie, go!" Mom shouted, beginning to slam the door shut, but Chris, who was muscular because of hockey, stopped it with his palm. Mom jumped away from the door and stood in front of me, though that was useless; she must not have noticed when I crashed into the floor, frozen from hysteria. I couldn't see anything except her from down there, but my heartbeat alone said it all.

"I'm not gonna do it," Chris wailed, his voice exhibiting pure horror. "I can't do it! I can't!"

"I'm calling the police!" Mom threatened him, rummaging through her pants pockets for her cell phone. Her fingers were shaking too much for her to get a proper grip on anything though.

"No, please. You gotta help me!"

"Get away from here!"

Chris stayed quiet for a moment. I still couldn't see his face, like I said—but his bottom half entered the foyer, and he left the door wide open behind him, the sunlight bleeding in like ink behind his silhouette. Mom stepped backwards, tripped over me, and fell onto the floor, her legs draped over my abdomen.

What I saw next, I really don't want to get into a second time. But I will because it's crucial to you.

Chris was staring down at us when he suddenly crouched to his knees and removed the gun from his waistband, his movements controlled and graceful as if he were on ice. His face was shining with tears all over, his lips were chapped and ashen, and he had extremely dark eye circles; *everything* about him was off. I would have screamed if my lungs allowed me, but I couldn't even move my eyes away from him.

"I'm sorry," he bleated, cocking the gun and pointing it at the floor for the time being. I'd never been more terrified in my life. "I'm sorry, Sistine."

I couldn't breathe anymore. *Sistine* Moore? *Jesus, Jamie, what other Sistine is there?!*

There were all these questions racing around in my head, but then he raised the gun and buried a bullet in his own throat. There's no other way to word it, and I won't even *try* making it sound pretty. I just can't.

Drops of his blood splattered everywhere, landing on both me and my mother, both of us too stunned and violently quaking to move. There was a dead sixteen-year-old in our house. He was so pale—paler than I'd ever seen him. Lips almost blue now that I could see them up close. His corpse stared at me while I lay leaden on the wood floor; that eye contact we shared might have been the worst part about it. It was like he'd positioned himself in front of me for the sole purpose of haunting me forever.

While my mother screamed at the 9-1-1 dispatcher, my stomach contents crawled out of me like bugs.

You asked me to describe the weapon he used, and I thought that was ridiculous. It's just a pistol, I said. That's not the important part; besides, one of your men looted it.

You asked me what type of sound it made. I said barely any, Agent. Then again, your voice sounded a bit quiet that day, too. My ears were ringing.

You asked me about his mannerisms. He was crying and sick, I said. All kinds of sick.

You asked me to remember his appearance. He was alone, I said, and he was wearing baggy clothing. That was weird for him because he wears Sperrys. *Wore.* Sorry.

You asked what happened to his car after he died. It disappeared, I said, but I thought it was towed after the ambulance came.

No, you said, it wasn't there when the ambulance came.

And that was when I remembered. *Sistine*.

"Oh my God," I whimpered, causing all the heads in the room to turn toward me and the eyes to go narrow in scrutiny. Although I was already sitting, I completely collapsed on that armchair you had me perched on, and my head rolled back and hit the wall with a loud thump. Someone, a random officer, I don't remember who, placed a cold single-use water bottle under my neck to hold it up. Innovative.

That was in the lobby of the police station. News reporters from Channel 8 were presently clustering around my house, so thankfully they hadn't followed me to the station. Surrounding me now was a group of junior officer interns who looked as though they'd dropped out of the police academy and were taking the alternative route. Half of the unit's police officers stood in an arc around me along with the juniors, as well as Agent Moore and you yourself. The number of onlookers was very inconvenient for privacy purposes, and I had more trouble jogging my memory than ever because of them.

"What is it, Jamie?" you asked, snapping your fingers at some of the junior officers so they'd write faster. "Can you speak?"

"Sistine," I uttered.

I was looking at Agent Moore in particular. In the corner of the lobby, he had his arms behind his back for lack of a firearm to prop up, and his Adam's apple bobbed prominently when I pronounced his daughter's name. Like I'd made him nervous. You and everybody else slowly rotated to look at him.

"What about her?" Moore grunted at me, visibly uncomfortable.

"She made him do it," I breathed out.

It felt as though my lungs deflated and my eyeballs were frying under the LED lights. My skin in particular felt heavy and swollen after my fall, still a bit sticky from the blood that had bespattered it just minutes earlier. The note-takers turned away from me and directed their attention to Agent Moore, and you stood up straight, clicking your tongue in disgust. You two must have been buddies.

I fell asleep for a minute or two after the interview was over, perhaps as a coping mechanism. In all of that time I just desperately wanted to see Bryan, to tell him I was physically okay, to ask if *he* was okay, if my mom was okay. She wasn't in the lobby because another herd of curious officers was asking her the same questions; I was thankful you'd elected to talk to me instead of some random official, but despite your familiarity I was melting in a puddle of vomit and tears and emotional trauma the entire time we spoke. Thanks for your patience with me that day; not everybody reacts to narcolepsy the same way you do after you learned about it. Thank you as well for agreeing to let me type out this account instead of delivering it in a press conference. You've spared me many cataplexy attacks.

I woke up almost as fast as I fell asleep because there was so much commotion amongst the people in the room that, even in my deep sleep stage, I could not ignore. Through the many glass walls, I could see right away when Bryan's car arrived in the parking lot outside. He burst through the doors and searched for a face he knew in the small crowd surrounding me. Perfect timing, huh?

"Jamie!" he finally shouted, plowing straight through the barricade that had formed around me. The image I have of him in my mind right now is like a mirage because I still struggle with a fuzzy memory.

I do know this: seeing Bryan wasn't as satisfying as I thought it would be; he was just so distressed that I *couldn't* enjoy it. His tear-stained face only made things harder, so even though I had been regaining mobility, I lost it yet again. I was positive at that point that he'd had a breakdown, though it amazed me that he found the energy to run into the police station like that, especially after visiting a fellow survivor. He looked heartbroken, exactly like when he would tell me to take cover in the middle of the night during a bad dream—only this time the threat was real, and I *felt* dead. It's a shame we were both conscious enough to live through it.

"She's all right," you assured Bryan, aware that I couldn't speak anymore. But he didn't acknowledge you aside from touching your arm, and then he crouched in front of me.

"Jamie," he whispered, putting his hands on my face. Feeling his skin against mine only reminded me that there was probably still some puke on my chin and hair; the intern who cleaned me up after throwing up a second time was very disgusted to have to do so. "I'm so sorry I wasn't there."

"Ladies, gents, let's give them the room," you insisted, scanning the people around us. They all dispersed at your command. "Thank you for your cooperation, Jamie. You're free to go whenever your mom finishes up."

Bryan didn't falter at all as you or your subordinates spoke. His bloodshot eyes were locked on mine the entire time, and I thought for a moment that I might have hallucinated his presence there because he was frozen and quiet for so long. Almost as long as I was. I could practically see through him.

But he really was there. I could feel an earthly warmth radiate from his fingertips and his terracotta eyes as they gazed at me in what appeared to be a combination of fear, remorse, and shock. The way he couldn't focus on anything but me—and vice versa—was like gravity.

Suddenly, he blinked, a couple of tears rolling down his cheeks. "I-I almost lost you," he stammered, peeling my damp torso off the armchair and leaning me against his chest like a newborn. It felt nice being so close to him, my safe space, after something so horrendous had happened. I still couldn't move my limbs no matter how medicinal his presence was. For a moment, I was afraid there might be a pistol under his belt, too; but that was irrational, even for me. And besides, I couldn't feel one.

"Now I know how you felt," Bryan cried, spreading his fingers out on my back and breathing hard against my neck. "And Chris."

I was almost finished getting Chris off of my mind.

"I-I don't know what to think. I'm so glad you're safe, Jamie."

I kept on crying, maybe for hours. I couldn't move or keep track of time or breathe steadily the entire time I was paralyzed. Bryan drove Mom and me home in a deafening silence, and he didn't let go of my hand once during the entire ride.

Thankfully, the foyer had been cleared and sterilized while we were away. It felt like a century had passed, but I know now that it was probably only around forty-five minutes in total, from the second the bullet left the barrel to our arrival back at home.

Mom called Cathy and told her everything that had happened. Sam arrived home when we did, so he got to hear the story through that phone call. I was so shaken up by what I had seen that I thought everything I looked at resembled those two cold, dead eyes and the pool of red that had expanded under Chris' anemic face. Bryan was able to snap me back into reality whenever he saw me slipping away, and for that, I will always be indebted to him. He still helps me out with that problem seeing as it's only been a month since the events I've recounted here. We're symbiotic.

PTSD is a nightmare, Agent. I cannot express its profundity in words.

The Truth

I REMEMBER EXACTLY what happened to me when I learned how Leo had died. How he had *really* died, I mean.

It was two weeks after I'd gone home from the police station the day Chris killed himself. I was engulfed in my own thoughts and analyses, horrified at what I'd come to know.

What followed was a full-body takeover: my eyes began to sting, my knees grew weak, my skin itched all over in the process of losing feeling, and my heartbeat hastened. It felt as though I'd fallen asleep in an iron maiden and, on top of that, had a vise pinched around my lungs. Knees colliding with the floor, I remained mobile for the time being. This wasn't like any cataplexy attack I'd ever experienced, but at the same time, it was *so* much worse. All I felt was pure, blue sorrow. Down I went. I couldn't move my mouth out of its tense open position, and I must have bloodied my throat by retching so much by the time my sobs finally became audible. Alas, I was paralyzed, though that was the one step I'd seen coming.

It hurt to picture Leo with a gun in his hand, terrified of his instruction to kill Bryan, then at his failure to do so, for that meant his own life was next. I was finally aware of the pain Leo, Joey, and Chris had gone through, the damage that had been done by their reluctant red hands, and how deranged my worldview was up until this point. It made so much sense to me why those boys had chosen to take their own lives over Bryan's or Willam's or mine. I knew everything now; I was omniscient.

It also hurt to be aware of such things. It hurt to be alive. I felt like the monster now, falling down, down, down to the floor.

When I went to you for confirmation, I must have blacked out for hours after hearing the words come out of your mouth in what *should* have been a justified explanation for the murders. But there's no excuse great enough to recompense the ruins. The whole time you explained this to me, I dreamed of being in Leo's shoes because now I actually knew what that meant: I wasn't just some crazed killer. No, I had been *handed* an FBI-grade firearm by my psychotic malefactor of a cousin, and then I followed her order to shoot a civilian despite my lack of gunmanship. If I were to disobey, my family would be dead meat, and those I loved would be harmed. I couldn't consult the police, her father, about it; who would believe me? You might say I failed the mission on purpose. Just to find peace. Just to end the hell.

The truth came upon us after Chris' suicide in my foyer. You had apprehended Sistine by then and fired Agent Moore for being responsible for the weapons to which his daughter had access. In a vain attempt at humoring me, you said she was practically wrapped in a tobacco leaf and high as a kite during her interrogation, which made her ready and willing to answer all of your questions. Legally, this might be a red flag, something about her "state of mind." Why you told me all of this extra information, I don't know; you must have known at this point that I was mentally unstable and that my therapist *would* hear every detail, so maybe it was to distract me from the part I *should* have been focusing on. The part the public couldn't know just yet.

But, aside from seeing my life flash before my eyes and Chris', too, what really shelled me was what you told me about Sistine's behavior.

Allow me to recap: yes, she was high, but you couldn't do anything about that. This stupefaction made her seem *eager* to answer your questions, almost like she believed the monstrosity she'd committed wasn't something she would ever be penalized for. After all, she'd made it months with no roadblocks. Personally, I don't think her being high made her lips any looser; she was non compos mentis and probably prospered from the attention she was receiving.

Her folly isn't the surprising part of her behavior though. As I've stressed before, she is a headcase and has been her whole life. Somewhere along the line, however, she had implied that she was acting as someone's lackey, as you determined during the interview. Some latter-day Charles Manson was pulling the strings, and Sistine was simply obeying, but she cheated a little in that she forced Leo and Joey and Chris to pull the trigger for her. It wasn't like anything you or your department had ever seen before. Not in Banshee at least.

I remember the interview transcript you let me read that day; it's ingrained in my mind:

Subject #23 - Moore, Sistine Emilia

Primary Information
Subject Name: Moore, Sistine Emilia
Record Type: Person

Bio: 18 yr. old, White, Female
Birth Date: 07/17/2003
Place of Birth City: Quantico
Place of Birth State: Virginia

Luzhkov: It is presently 1632 hours on August 15th. Speaking is Agent Andre Luzhkov, currently at Banshee Police Department, Banshee, New Jersey to interview Sistine Moore on the allegations of murder and conspiracy to murder.

Sistine: Well said.

Luzhkov: (laughs) All right, Sistine. You're a senior at Bridgewood High School, correct?

Sistine: Yeah.

Luzhkov: And your parents are split up? I know your mother just passed away in a police firing. My condolences.

Sistine: Please, she ain't my mama no more.

Luzhkov: She's not? Who is she, then?

Sistine: But of course, a corpse!

Luzhkov: (silence) Right. For the purposes of this interview, we'll call her your mother. It doesn't look like you're mourning, Sistine. Why is that?

Sistine: 'Cause I wanted her dead. I planned for her

to be dead.

Luzhkov: How so?

Sistine: Get my daddy to kill her. It was a big risk, but we was willing to take it, and hey! We won.

Luzhkov: You keep saying "we."

Sistine: Yeah. It was a big win for us, gettin' Mama dead

Luzhkov: Who's "we?"

Sistine: I ain't tellin' you that yet, mister.

Luzhkov: Not yet, I see. Well, I suppose you'll tell me when you're ready. But keep in mind, I'm sure you have better things to do than sit here and answer my questions; I know I do.

Sistine: These ain't hardly even questions, really. How you gonna solve any crimes if you keep on askin' people if their parents divorced?

Luzhkov: (silence) If you'd like me to be straightforward, I'll be straightforward. You're the frontman on this mission, so how many people have you yourself killed?

Sistine: (laughs) Here we go. I taken eight lives. Teach, Ms. Stratford, Mrs. Blane, Caroline Empfert, Mr. Edwards, another janitor, that Spanish lady, and Oakhurst.

Luzhkov: Who are the janitor and the Spanish lady? Mr. Heather and Mrs. Gomez?

Sistine: Yeah, they the ones.

Luzhkov: Where did you get the weapons to kill these people, and where did you store the weapons afterwards?

Sistine: I got 'em from my daddy's big closet and put them in my cousin's house after. My cousin Leo Capodi's house. I mighta moved some to Joey Ramadhan's place but I don't remember that good.

Luzhkov: Why did you plant the weapons there, Sistine? You made Leo miserable.

Sistine: (laughs) He deserved it. Scum of the earth. And what better way to get away with murder? He wouldn't do it, so.

Luzhkov: (silence) You and your partner really thought this through, huh?

Sistine: Partner? No, she's way above me. Worship her. I work for her, not with. Worship her.

Luzhkov: Are you ready to tell me her name, Sistine? Who's the master of puppets?

Sistine: (silence) Nicky.

And I'll sever it right there.

No wonder Sistine always followed her in the halls and not vice versa. No wonder Reba detached herself from them. Poor Reba. No wonder she degenerated, like Ophelia.

Reba must have known all along that Leo was being not only framed but pressured into killing Bryan. She tried her best to get Officers Petty and Hart to listen to us, but hers was a fruitless attempt. Had she proclaimed his innocence any louder, Reba certainly would have been added to the hit list. These days, I can't help but wonder who Sistine would have sent out to get her.

That brings me to the final point I'd like to make before skipping to present-day: the highlighter-green "Hicks & Hesson" scratched into Leo's shower wall.

Even though CSI found the marker and only Leo's prints were on it, it had been a setup. As it turns out, I was wrong about whom the message was directed at. Partially, anyway. Hesson, no doubt, was still about me, and I knew that because of the transcript, in the end of which Sistine confessed her intention to waste me on the day of Caroline Empfert's memorial service. But Hicks wasn't about Reba. And it wasn't about Tommy, either. It was about their sweet, oblivious mother. As it turns out, the three twisted sisters had planned a triple matricide. Just as Teach had died under Nichole's command, it was expected that Giovanna would be next, but a little change of plan catalyzed Sistine's rampage, which Nichole not only permitted but apparently endorsed. She and Sistine wound up steamrolling their way through a small-town high school community of innocent teachers and students and janitors, one after the other, in search of the opportunity to terminate Giovanna Moore and Kerry Hicks—that is, until Reba backed out and brought those plans to naught. We have her mental health crisis to thank for Mrs. Hicks' survival.

Sistine and Nichole were arrested alongside Agent Moore in the culminating conclusion of what has been the most sustained nefarious killing spree in United States' history. It hasn't quite sunken in yet that I survived it by a nose.

Life As We Know It

I WENT TO the cemetery by myself a few weeks after learning the truth. For a long time now, I'd owed someone an apology, and that someone was Leo.

His headstone was charcoal gray and shined under the August sun; it looked almost glazed, but I don't mean to make a painting out of it when the actual art lay in a sarcophagus six feet below it.

LEONARDO ALPHONSO CAPODI

Even his name was elegiac.

I crouched down on the ground, facing the stone with my knees poking into the earth. Grass had grown over his burial site by now and remained thick and healthy for months, but everything was still so drab in my eyes. The sky was cloudless—in fact, it had been particularly striking that afternoon—but to me it was just a blank shield separating me from the stars. Color bore no meaning that day.

But there was so much activity tumbleweeding around in that cemetery that kept me from saying what I wanted to say. There were dandelions sprouting up around tombstones, and week-old grass clippings. A can of Monster that had been crushed by funeral attendees days prior, almost unrecognizable aside from its flaming green font. And there was a single black crow.

The way it ducked its glimmering head and prodded the earth with its beak, it almost looked affectionate, like a cat nudging you for more neck-to-tail strokes. Had I not realized it was indeed a bird and not a house pet, I would have extended my fingers to its nostrils and offered it an introductory sniff. That should give you an idea of how lonely I was feeling at heart, despite all the foliage and afterenergy encircling me like a hawk. Or a crow if you will. A single black crow.

I looked back down. There was a scuffed-up hockey puck leaning against Leo's stone, and beside it stood some plastic flowers in a vase that had been driven into the soil like a screw, lest it tip over or ride the wind elsewhere. It saddened me that no one was keeping his grave for him whereas the rest of the cemetery looked so sharp. He deserved living flowers, ones that needed to be watered regularly, so that people were obligated to come every week. Hell, I would do it myself. I petted the blanket of grass and wiped a smudge of dirt off the bottom edge of the stone; it looked like the corner of a boot print, and that only made my inward storm brew stronger.

This stone isn't just some drink can you can kick around and squash with your heel.

I held myself together because I had things to say, closure to reach.

"I miss you," I whispered to the stone. It seemed to be listening. It had no ears, of course, but I could tell my words resonated. The hushed cemetery was too serene for me to want to disturb it, so I kept my tone soft, but I was close enough where Leo could probably hear me from down there if he strained. Or up there, whatever you choose to believe.

"You were right," I said to the stone, my eyes focused on the "LEO" engraved in it. "I *did* like you. Heh, I was in love with you for almost a decade." The thought made me giggle, but I quickly shushed myself in accordance with my surroundings. "A small part of me knew you were innocent. And I'm so sorry for changing my mind so fast. Twice, I guess. And I want you to know that I forgive you for everything, and Bryan will, too. I hope you'll forgive *us*. It's … it's important to me that you know that."

A single tear slipped across my downward-angled face and brought on what turned out to be a reservoir hiding in my eyes. I was already on the ground, so there was nowhere I could fall should I need to, and no one to catch me either. I remained in my little ball and sobbed somewhat loudly until my body weakened and my forehead touched the top edge of the stone. It burned my skin due to its sunlight exposure.

There was no one else present, though it seemed like there was. I think, if anything, the sensations I perceived so vividly were Leo telling me everything was okay. Maybe that's what he had been trying to tell me in the church, back when I wasn't ready to accept that any of this was true.

"I love you," I wept, pressing my palm into the turf with all of my might and clenching my teeth hard. I wanted so badly to be silent, to give these people the rest they deserved—but there was an icy hand resting gently on my shoulder that stood as a constant reminder that Leo was *right there*. Right underneath me. And if I were any sicker in the head, I might have tried to join him in that box of his.

I just couldn't shake the feeling that he was with me, even long after I left Cemetery Drive. For a while, I imagined I was his vessel, and I'd carried a part of him home with me.

Yesterday, US Daily, a more generalized news station than Channel 8, featured a very particular line of guest speakers: the Capodis—or what's left of them.

Standing before the Tidal Basin in Washington, D.C., Anton looked trim in a navy-blue Armani suit, his collar unbuttoned and his hair slicked back; however, despite his dapper mien, his eyes had been reduced to two gaping black holes since the last time I saw him, and the skin on his face looked papery and tight like a cigar wrapper. It became sickeningly clear that his son and sister weren't the only things bereft of him.

He rested his paw on the shoulder of his youngest daughter, Teresa. She was emaciated and petite compared to the others, her long hair lackluster on camera. She wouldn't take her eyes off of the ground for anything. *I know that feeling, Tess.*

Sofia and her mother, Lucia, stood beside Anton and Tess with pitiful expressions on their faces; they all looked undead, and I'm sure the bleak weather didn't help with that.

It didn't surprise me one bit that Sofia was to do the talking. Her voice was bold and steady despite her rocky appearance; it burrowed into me like a shovel through hard earth, and I felt chills roll down my spine in waves as she delivered those inconsolable words about her family members' deaths. She wore the same look in her eye as when she begged me to forget the restraining order, and that was how I knew her speech would help bring justice to the Capodi ménage and many others like it.

In all, I had made accurate assumptions about Leo three times over: the first was immediately before he'd been arrested in front of everybody, the second when I found him innocent out of the blue, and the third when I learned he was the one who had tried doing away with my boyfriend. Now I felt so wrong for having such a fickle opinion of him all those times when I should have listened to his plea. Truth is, I had held a grudge against him for shooting Bryan, but I see now that he didn't have any alternative options. It's going to be hard for Bryan to see through the face behind that gun, but I know he has it in him—just let me handle that.

Thank you for putting an end to this six-month struggle. I owe you everything, Agent.

With a heavy heart, I bid the following people a final farewell:

Mrs. Laurie Tomlin

Ms. Fiorella Stratford

Mrs. Debra Blane

Caroline Empfert

Leo Capodi

Mr. Amos Edwards

Mr. Jason Heather

Mrs. Maria Gomez

Dr. Sean Oakhurst

Joey Ramadhan

Mrs. Giovanna Moore

Chris Arden

and my deepest regards to those remaining:

Bryan Lukin Jr.

Willam McGuire

and Reba Hicks.

Sincerely,
Jamie Hessen

About the Author

EMMA TIBBETT WAS born in Maryland and raised in Pennsylvania. She has been spinning webs of fiction ever since the sixth grade, back when her subject matter mainly revolved around her idols. Now that she has her own cache of characters, plots, and backstories, Emma is well on her way to becoming a YA mystery-romance novelist. She spends the majority of her free time writing, watching sitcoms, and listening to rock music, which inspires some of her heaviest scenes.

CPSIA information can be obtained
at www.ICGtesting.com
Printed in the USA
LVHW090349250621
691123LV00003B/542

9 781954 175068